A Year of Trials for E.G. Rawlings

The Second Book in the E.G. Rawlings Trilogy

by Jane McCulloch

Published by JJ Moffs Independent Book Publisher 2021

JJ Moffs Independent Book Publisher Ltd
Grove House Farm, Grovewood Road,
Misterton, Nottinghamshire DN10 4EF

ISBN 978-1-8383697-7-4

Printed and bound in Great Britain by Clays Ltd, Elcograf S.p.A
Typeset by Anna Richards
Cover by Jeremy Hopes
Proof read by James Bacon

For Jane Moffett

Also by Jane McCulloch

Novels
The Strange Year of E.G. Rawlings
The Brini Boy
Parallel Lines
Triangles in Squares
Full Circle

Verse
Saint or Monster
Between Sanity and Madness

Children's Books
Diggory Loppet
Sir Edward and Nimrod
Do's it Have a Hamster?

Prologue

For those who have not read the first book of the Rawlings Trilogy, a short account might prove useful before embarking on the second.

The Strange Year of E G Rawlings begins in January 2017. E G Rawlings, a noted war correspondent, has been forced into early retirement after a serious injury in the field. Looking for a vacant mooring for his houseboat, he arrives at one which, to his surprise, belongs to an old friend from Afghanistan, Isobel Mallinson, the widow of a British diplomat. On hearing that Rawlings is writing an account of his war experiences, Isobel lets him settle on her mooring while completing his memoir.

During the months that follow, Rawlings, suffering from PTSD and in terrible emotional and physical pain, gains solace from the peaceful life on the river and the small, close-knit community. Although a loner by nature, he becomes very attached to Marnie, a middle-aged and mildly eccentric art teacher who lives in a boathouse nearby. During their many evenings spent together, she persuades him to tell her about his life. He explains the unexpected events that have resulted in what he calls 'turning points', taking him in new and surprising directions.

For six months, Rawlings enjoys this calm existence, until in June, come news that shatters them all. His estranged son and daughter-in-law are killed in a car accident, leaving behind their son, Felix, aged ten, a child that Rawlings hasn't seen since he was a baby. Being the nearest relative and also guardian, Rawlings sets out to collect the boy from his prep school and bring him back to Isobel's house, where she has prepared a room for him.

Over the next few weeks, Felix seems to settle happily into his new surroundings. He quickly forms a great bond with Isobel who resumes the role of surrogate grandmother, looking on the boy as the grandson she never had.

Rawlings also unexpectedly finds this grandson fills a void in his heart, a hole that has been left by the death of his great love Mia, killed in the same explosion in which he suffered his own terrible injuries in Afghanistan.

With the funeral over, Felix starts to enjoy his life on the river, making many new friends. On a happy day in August, they celebrate his birthday, and Isobel announces she has found a new school for him nearby. All progresses well until Rawlings receives unexpected and shattering news. The family solicitor informs him that Felix's aunt, Sarah, and his only other living relative being the sister of his mother, has requested that her nephew lives with them in Australia. It seems an obvious decision. She has children of his age and he could enjoy a normal family life. Rawlings and Isobel are devastated by this news. They know Felix is happy and settled with them, but on paper, Sarah's request looks sensible. She is also the child's other official guardian, so they find it difficult to produce arguments against her proposal.

Rawlings is forced to bow to the inevitable, and although he has great misgivings about sending the boy so far away, he breaks the news to Felix. The boy becomes hysterical and angry when told of this plan, but finally, when he can see the adults have made up their minds, he reluctantly gives in and departs for a new life in Australia.

Rawlings is heartbroken. Missing the boy, in pain and drinking, he sinks into a deep depression. On New Year's Eve, he invites Marnie over for supper. After a great deal of champagne, they end up in bed for a night of passion. Marnie, already in love with Rawlings, feels this is the start of a long relationship. Rawlings, on the other hand, knows it would be a disaster. Abruptly breaking it off with a letter, he informs Isobel he is departing for a new life in London, leaving the boat for Marnie to use.

The second book sees Rawlings regretting certain decisions, navigating yet another turning point in his life and taking a new direction.

Chapter 1

February 2018

The panic in his voice echoed round the room. 'Don't shoot! I'm unarmed! Unarmed! There's no need to shoot…'

The nurse quickly moved across to his bed and regarded Rawlings in some alarm.

'I'm unarmed' he repeated and then gave a low moan.

She shook his shoulder with some force until with a sudden movement that made her jump back, he sat bolt upright staring straight ahead.

Was he awake? She couldn't be sure. He was a strange one…

'You must wake up now Rawlings' she said firmly. 'You have a visitor, and we need to get you looking a bit more respectable.'

She bustled about, tactfully waiting for him to fully shake off whatever it was he'd been dreaming about and fetched him his dressing gown and the one slipper. Rawlings slowly and gingerly moved himself sideways off the bed. His right leg still in plaster, felt heavy and cumbersome. Thank God, the bloody thing was coming off at the end of the week and not a moment too soon.

The nurse handed him his crutches and still feeling distinctly unsettled, he took them from her. At the same time, he gave her a reassuring smile having noted her worried expression. His PTSD nightmares were evidently outside her experience and it was quite possible he had been shouting. Even so, it was unusual for him to have a bad dream during an afternoon nap. He looked at her. This nurse had only been around a short while, one of the few he'd immediately taken to; partly because she was pretty with a charming Irish accent, and partly because her badge revealed her name to be Esme. He informed her he'd had a houseboat called Esme Jane and she'd laughed, making her look even prettier.

She now attempted to run a comb through his hair, but he pushed her away saying crossly, 'I'll do that.' He pulled himself up on his crutches adding, 'What do you mean I have a visitor? Nobody knows I'm here.'

She sighed. He certainly wasn't the easiest of her patients but there was something about him she found intriguing. For a start, why did he insist on being called by his surname and why did he suffer from these strange nightmares? This was the second time she had come in on him in this state. It wasn't usual after a leg operation.

'You not only have a visitor Rawlings, but Sister says her name is Lady Mallinson. What do you think of that?'

This news didn't seem to please him at all. 'Isobel? For God's sake, how on earth did she find me?'

Nurse Esme regarded him thoughtfully. Her other patients welcomed their visitors. Not this one. He seemed genuinely cross about it. She eased him into his dressing gown and her accent became more pronounced as she said, 'Well, I certainly wouldn't be knowing how she found you. But as the good lady has taken the time and trouble to come and see you, try and behave. And don't be growling at the poor woman the way you do me.'

Rawlings made a face, but meekly made his way towards the bathroom before sending Nurse Esme his Parthian shot. 'As you think this visitor is so bloody posh, you might bring us in some tea and those biscuits I like.'

Moments later he was sitting in one of the two armchairs with Isobel opposite him, regarding him with some amusement.

'They've certainly made you comfortable here Rawlings. This is more like a hotel room than a hospital.'

'Fortunately,' he said in acid tones, 'I'm still on private medical insurance left over from the original accident and I hope to God this is the last time I will have to use it.'

Isobel knew Rawlings too well to be put off by his surliness. 'How's the leg? I gather from Sister your surgeon is pleased with the operation. She also told me you weren't the easiest patient, which I'm afraid didn't surprise me in the least.'

Rawlings gave a shrug. 'I find being confined and fussed over very irksome.' He tapped his plaster. 'This comes off at the end of the week and then I'll know if it's been a success. They've explained it will be the last chance they get to work on it so if I'm still in pain after all their efforts, I'll have the bloody thing taken off.' He looked across at Isobel, elegant and beautiful as ever, and reflected there was nobody in his life that he loved or admired more. 'How did you know I was here? I deliberately told no-one where I'd be.'

Isobel sighed. 'My dear Rawlings you're not that difficult to trace. If you remember, you left me the name of your solicitor and I rang him.'

'Graham told you I was here?' Rawlings almost choked on his biscuit. 'I'll fire the bloody man.'

Isobel gave him a reproving look. 'Do stop swearing Rawlings. Someone had to know where you were. You have responsibilities. Supposing your grandson in Australia needed you.'

'I'm in touch with Felix on Skype all the time,' he said, but added a trifle grudgingly, 'you're right I suppose. Although if something dire did happen, I presume gloomy Graham would let everyone know.' He was silent for a moment and then smiled charmingly at her. 'I am actually pleased to see you Isobel and it's good of you to visit, especially in view of the inclement weather. Even in this prison I can see the swirling blizzards outside my window. The sky has been depressingly dark all day.'

'I think the worst of the so-called "Beast from the East" appears to be over. London is almost back to normal now.' She regarded him thoughtfully. 'I'm relieved you've made such good progress since your operation,' adding wryly, 'and it's reassuring to see your time in hospital hasn't changed you in any other way.'

He acknowledged her mild reproof in silence as she inquired what his immediate plans were.

Rawlings gave a sigh. 'Well as you may have gathered, my operation was postponed from early January to the end of February, something to do with my blood pressure. However, this may have been just as well in the circumstances. My new flat needed considerable alteration, some of it structural and this will now take to the beginning of April...'

Isobel interrupted him. 'Then you must certainly come down to stay with me while you recuperate. With Felix gone there is plenty of room and you'd be most welcome.'

Her offer took him back to the long months of

recuperation that he'd spent in the Embassy in Kabul, when Isobel and her late husband Peter had taken him in after the explosion that had damaged him so badly, both physically and mentally. But now the circumstances were different.

'Much as I'm tempted Isobel, I think I must turn down your kind offer.' He looked at her and continued pointedly, 'There's the complication of Marnie for a start. It wouldn't be fair to be in such close proximity, so soon after rejecting her. I still have some guilt at causing her unhappiness and wouldn't want to do anything that might further exacerbate the situation.'

Isobel spoke briskly. 'You need have no fears about that. Your rejection of Marnie, although upsetting at the time, appears to have been the making of her. She's considerably changed and in the throes of becoming a successful businesswoman.'

Rawlings looked astonished. 'Good God! It's not four months since I left. Marnie? A businesswoman? How on earth has that happened?'

Isobel poured him another cup of tea. 'I agree it sounds improbable. Even I've been taken aback by the swift change in her.' She handed him his tea along with the plate of biscuits. 'You remember her project?'

Rawlings took another biscuit. Of course he remembered her project. He'd made a financial contribution towards it. 'As I recall, the gist of it was to work with people who suffered with dementia, giving them art classes as a kind of therapy.'

Isobel gave a nod. 'The moment you left she threw herself into it and developed the idea into a definite plan. As she explained it to me, the patients were to be presented with a picture of some object from their past. This would then trigger a memory – a vintage car, a seaside poster, an old photograph – that sort of thing. Then they'd be encouraged to draw that object, day after day. Apparently, the repetition helps dementia patients. It sounds simple enough, but evidently it works. Tried out on a few patients the results have been remarkable, and the idea is now being developed into a business.'

Rawlings felt bewildered. 'A business?'

Isobel was amused to see the effect this was having on him. 'It was a stroke of luck really. The husband-and-wife team who run the care home where she has been working, have taken it upon themselves to promote her venture, obviously seeing its potential. It makes sense. After all, dementia patients are a growing problem in every part of the world. The husband runs the business side of the partnership and he's helped Marnie turn her project into a viable business. She now has a website under the name Marnie Peters. You should look it up. It's impressive and dare I say, rather slick and American. The upshot is that she's off to the States for a two-month promotional tour. After that there are plans to take the project to Australia and New Zealand.' She smiled at him. 'In view of her new career Rawlings, you really don't have to worry about Marnie because she won't be in the boathouse.'

'Why does she have to go abroad? Why not try it out in this country first?'

'I think that must be for financial reasons. There isn't the money for that sort of scheme here,' Isobel said briskly.

Rawlings grunted. 'No surprise there. The poor old NHS. I feel guilty being in here, which as you pointed out is extremely comfortable.' He drank his tea in silence and then said, 'Well you've astonished me. Difficult to get my head round it. Marnie never struck me as a businesswoman, far from it.'

Isobel smiled at his discomfiture. After all, Rawlings had left the poor lovesick woman in the worst possible way and although she understood he'd genuinely thought it the best course of action, his abrupt exit was devastating for Marnie at the time, so it was rather satisfactory that his ego might be slightly dented at the news of her quick recovery. She gave a laugh. 'I think you'd find it hard to recognise her as well. She's slimmed down and changed her wardrobe. All the smocks and kaftans have gone. Now it's tailored suits. Even her hair looks different, the curls have been straightened and worn in a stylish bob. No greys either, just a beautiful shade of red.'

Rawlings regarded Isobel a trifle crossly. He could see she was relishing this as an apt punishment for his behaviour. Even so, he shook his head in disbelief. 'I don't like the sound of it at all. I'm sure I'd far prefer the old Marnie.' He paused for a moment and then said, 'Although Marnie is no longer a problem Isobel, I won't be taking up your kind invitation to stay. The fact is, the friend from whom I bought the London flat and who owns the rest of the house, has invited me to stay with him until my place is ready. Max has plenty of room and this arrangement has the advantage of my being able to keep an eye on how the work is progressing downstairs. Max also has a sister, who goes by the rather exotic name of Arabella Lambton Smythe, and she just happens to be an interior decorator. So naturally I hired her.'

Isobel laughed, 'You have an uncanny knack of falling on your feet Rawlings.'

He wasn't sure this was true. At this particular moment the direction of his life seemed both uncertain and chaotic, but he merely said 'I will of course keep in touch Isobel and the moment I can drive, I'll invite myself down to see you. In any case you have my number.' A thought struck him. 'Why on earth didn't you ring and tell me you were coming today, rather than go through Graham?'

Isobel stood up. 'Because my dear boy if I had, you would have told me not to come.' (Dear boy? He was edging towards seventy.) 'Now don't haul yourself up on those crutches. I'm going to leave you in peace. How long before they let you out?'

'Once the plaster is off, I think it'll be about two weeks. I'm to be presented with a boot and physiotherapy. If all goes well, my hope is to get to Max by the end of the month.'

'Then I will see you soon after that. Do try and be a good patient Rawlings.'

She kissed him on both cheeks and left.

Nurse Esme came in and collected the tea things, while Rawlings made his way to the bed and lay back thinking about Isobel's visit. He wasn't entirely sure why, but it had somehow unsettled him. It wasn't only the news of Marnie's transformation, it now struck him as odd that Isobel hadn't talked about Felix. Should this concern him? He chided himself for failing to ask. Isobel had been so close to the boy, he needed to know if she also had worries about him. Just lately he'd had the impression that all was not well. Nothing he could put his finger on exactly, but the last Skype left him distinctly worried. Felix seemed oddly distant, the conversation difficult and his answers monosyllabic. It was very different to when he'd first arrived in Australia. Then he'd been bubbly and excited at being part of a family. Now there was no mention of his cousins, or any of the outside activities he'd been so enthusiastic about. It was as if the boy had become withdrawn in some way.

Rawlings turned restlessly, finding it hard to get comfortable. He made a mental note to ring Isobel in the morning. He would thank her for coming to see him and then ask her about Felix. Maybe it was just that the boy's life in England had become a distant memory and the Skypes from his grandfather were now an irritant. Could that be true? Surely it was a little too soon for that to happen. But something told him the honeymoon period was over and Felix wasn't finding his life in Australia quite as he'd expected. He asked himself again the question that permanently haunted him. Had they been right in sending the boy so far away? It seemed the right decision at the time. After all, when his parents died in that car crash, Felix was left without any family. In England there'd only been him, a grandfather he didn't really know, and Isobel who, although like a doting grandmother, was no direct relation. It seemed a natural decision to send him to be with his aunt's family, who had children of the same age. But this was Australia. If only they'd lived somewhere in England and not the other side of the world. Lying in his hospital bed he'd become increasingly angry at the blow dealt to him personally. Both he and Isobel loved that child and Felix had been contented and happy living with them. He'd liked Isobel's house, the river and his houseboat and was desperate not to leave, pleading with them to let him stay. It had been heart-breaking. If the boy now wasn't happy out there, what the hell had their sacrifice been for?

Rawlings felt tempted to make a trip to the bathroom for a calming fag but resisted, as another thought struck him. When Felix did return for the summer holidays, what would he make of all the changes, especially the fact that his grandfather no longer lived on the houseboat? This made him sit up and exclaim loudly, 'Damn!'. The boat was another subject he should have tackled with Isobel. He'd given Esme Jane to Marnie, but if she was now working abroad, what would happen to it? Would she want to sell it? Felix would be really upset if he found the boat had gone. And another thing, he'd promised to visit Felix in early May. That would now have to be postponed because of the delay in his operation. It seemed unlikely he would get out to Australia before June. Would the boy feel he was being let down yet again? Probably, but the circumstances were out of his control. He gave a groan of exasperation just as Nurse Esme came back into the room with a trolley of drugs.

'Are you in pain Rawlings?' she asked anxiously. 'Would you like something for it?'

'No, I would not' he replied crossly. 'As I keep telling everyone who offers them, those bloody painkillers have terrible side effects, so I refuse to take them.'

The nurse once more reflected how different he was to everyone else, all of whom continually demanded painkillers. She said patiently, 'You could have paracetamol. They don't have any side effects.'

'They don't do any bloody good either!' He managed to look contrite and gave her a disarming smile. 'Don't worry I wasn't sighing with pain, just with life. I'm all right. At least, nothing that a large whisky won't cure.'

Nurse Esme laughed. 'Don't I know that. But you won't be getting that wish granted until you leave here. And I know you've been smoking in the bathroom again. If this goes on, I will be confiscating your cigarettes.'

'You wouldn't be so cruel.'

'Yes, I would.' She walked to the door. 'If the weather is better tomorrow, I'll take you into the garden and you can have a smoke then. It's only just thawed so it'll be a short visit, just to give you time for the one.'

And with that she departed, leaving Rawlings alone again with his thoughts. These now returned to the subject of Marnie. Much as he hated to criticise Isobel, who always seemed to him a paragon of virtue, he couldn't help feeling she'd over-relished informing him of Marnie's quick recovery. Yes, he'd left both the woman and the boat with indecent haste and yes, Isobel had been somewhat critical of his actions in spite of him assuring her his motives were honourable. Honourable? Maybe that wasn't the best choice of word, but he was still convinced it had been the right decision. After their one night of passion – which they'd both enjoyed – there were only two options left to him. One was to stay, which would have meant moving into a permanent relationship, and the other was to make a clean break of it. Well, he hadn't wanted the former, so he'd taken the latter, knowing it might upset her for a while. This was something he regretted but it had seemed the only solution. He'd loved Marnie, 'in his fashion', but not enough to commit to living with her, and his instincts also told him she was in danger of making him an obsession. During those last weeks on the boat, she'd become jealous and possessive, never a good sign. He frowned. In view of this apparent obsession, her recovery from a broken heart had been indecently quick and to his annoyance it was amusing Isobel.

Leaning over the bed he scooped up his laptop and Googled the 'Marnie Peters' website, then stared in shock.

It was certainly glossy, and Isobel was right, it was slick and American. The bold heading Marnie Peters – Art Therapy Sessions, was above a large photograph of her. Except it wasn't Marnie. What glared out at him was a person he didn't recognise. The features were the same but somehow, she had metamorphosed into something out of Hollywood, glossy and packaged. He quickly glanced through the blurb about the success of the sessions, the forthcoming tour of the States and how to apply for the details. At the top of the page were several headings, including costs and contacts. He presumed this is where the business manager came into it and the thought crossed his mind that she might be being ripped off. Had it all been drawn up legally? Had she kept her copyright?

He snapped the laptop shut. It was none of his business. Marnie and he were now most definitely in the past. There had been a few occasions when he wondered whether he'd taken the right action, moments when he recalled how she'd wander over to the boat from her boathouse, clad in a cerulean blue kaftan, her red hair wild and untidy, clutching her great carpet bag from which she would produce her latest offerings. He missed the delicious casseroles and their long evenings of wine and conversation, where he had told her more about himself than he'd ever imparted to anyone. Well, that was all definitely over. A loose end tied up, leaving him not with a bruised ego as Isobel imagined, but with a feeling of enormous relief. No need for any further guilt.

The door burst open and his surgeon entered the room, followed by the formidable Sister.

'Good news Rawlings,' he boomed. He was a big built man with large hands to match. Rawlings had always imagined surgeons to have rather delicate fingers with which to perform intricate operations, but orthopaedic men were obviously a race apart, needing strength to hack off limbs. Alastair Manners was one of these. He spoke briskly. 'I've had a look at the latest X-rays, and I think we can remove your plaster tomorrow. You'll be put in a boot for at least two weeks and undergo physiotherapy. If all goes well, you should be able to return home then.'

'That's far better than I expected.' Rawlings was surprised but pleased. 'Do you envisage any further surgery will be needed?'

The surgeon shook his head. 'No, I think there is little likelihood of that. Your leg, to put it in layman's terms, is a damned mess. Those Army chaps in Afghanistan did brilliant work on it and somehow managed to save the limb. Something of a miracle. Since then we have been doing a patching up job but now have no more options. I am hoping you will have less pain, but to be frank that limb will always give you a bit of gyp, and arthritis will likely add to the discomfort eventually. But with a bit of luck you will have improvement that should last you a few years, always presuming you avoid violent sports.' He gave a hearty laugh. Rawlings ignored his attempt at humour and assured him violent sports were off the agenda. 'You'll be moved to another wing once your plaster is off.' The surgeon looked at Rawlings over the top of his glasses. 'Be a good chap and co-operate with the physios. It will help with the recovery.' He turned to the Sister. 'I'll need to see him in clinic in three weeks. Can you make the appointment?' Shaking Rawlings by the hand, he said 'Well done!' rather unexpectedly, then abruptly left the room.

Rawlings lay back on the pillows. This was good news indeed. The last of the operations done. He would ring Max in the morning and warn him of his imminent arrival. Then he'd make further plans. A visit to his sister in Scotland was long overdue, but first he must tell Felix of the delay in his visit until June. He also needed to talk to Isobel about the boat. It would be sensible to make a list.

He closed his eyes, suddenly very tired. These were tasks for the morning. Definitely no more today.

Chapter 2

Two Days Later

'I'm sorry but I won't do it Jolyon! Nothing will induce me to write another bloody book, especially one about Sarajevo. I covered all I wanted to say about that place in War Memoirs.' Rawling's voice was angry and he was aware he was shouting. This visit was unwelcome, and he would never have agreed to it except the wretched man told him it was urgent. Jolyon Jordon-Smith was a good agent and he didn't wish to upset him, but even so...

Jolyon regarded Rawlings thoughtfully and sighed. His many distinguished clients gave him varying amounts of trouble which he'd grown to expect, but he reflected that up until now, Rawlings had been one of the more co-operative ones, and unlike several of his authors had always met his deadlines on time. Maybe it had been unwise to visit him in hospital, but the offer he brought was an exceptional one and extremely lucrative. He could always bring in the other factor if pressure were necessary. Tact was needed now.

'As your agent Rawlings,' he said in soothing tones, 'I am obliged to inform you of the offers and options as they come in. The advance for this book is exceptionally generous and it could be an extremely lucrative project...'

'I don't need the bloody money,' Rawlings interrupted sounding his belligerent best.

Jolyon shifted in his seat. This was an unusual situation. Most of his clients were keen to know about the offer even before they knew what was involved. He bestowed a patient smile on Rawlings. 'The facts are these, dear boy. Your War Memoirs book was well received and, as you must have gathered even if you didn't read them, the reviews were excellent. However, the sales were certainly not overwhelming. The publicity department are confident this will change when the television documentary based on your book comes out early next year. It is expected then that the book will start selling extremely well.' He looked across at Rawlings who was wearing a bored expression, but at least he wasn't interrupting. Jolyon continued. 'The publishers who have made the offer for this book on Sarajevo have obviously taken these factors into account. Which is why they want the next book…'

The inevitable interruption came. 'But I covered Sarajevo in the previous book.'

'Yes, but as a war correspondent, not as a personal account.' Jolyon decided to try another tack. 'How long did you endure the Siege in Sarajevo?'

'Over three years,' Rawlings growled.

'Exactly. You must therefore have plenty of material for a personal account.'

'And that material is private,' Rawlings said firmly.

Jolyon leant back in his seat and closed his eyes. He would have to play his final card. Opening his eyes, he said with a sigh, 'There is another reason for my visiting you today, which I'd hoped I wouldn't have to mention. The fact is, I have to go into hospital next week and I wanted to put this proposition to you myself before then.'

Rawlings was immediately concerned. On closer

examination he could see that Jolyon was looking far from well. There had been definite weight loss, which on first glance he'd presumed was intentional – the man was short in stature and had certainly been on the rotund side, some would even say obese – but now he observed Jolyon more closely, he could see there were dark rings under his eyes and his complexion had a faint tinge of yellow.

'My dear man, I'm so sorry. Is it serious?'

Jolyon sighed. 'Who knows. The doctors tell one so little. I'm to go in for exploratory tests, after which they will decide what to do. Apparently, it's a digestive problem.' Here he gave a wan smile. 'No doubt due to my over-indulgence in all things epicurean.'

There was a brief silence. Rawlings decided to be practical.

'Leave me the paperwork and I promise to study it. I know my first reaction was hostile. The Sarajevo Siege is rather a sensitive topic with me. But I will give it consideration and perhaps we can find some sort of compromise.' Quite honestly, there was little hope of this, but he didn't want to send the poor man into hospital without any encouragement.

Jolyon did indeed look relieved. 'Thank you, dear boy. That is most reasonable of you.' He stood up. 'When do you leave this place?'

'At the end of next week. I'll call you when I'm back in my flat. At the moment, it's undergoing a restoration job. I have an interior decorator by the name of Arabella Lambton Smythe.'

If he'd hoped to impress the man opposite him, he was to be disappointed. Jolyon merely looked amused. 'I've met that lady on several occasions. I believe she's married to Clive Lambton Smythe, owner of an excellent gastro pub down on the river which I often frequent. They do a superb Sunday lunch.' Rawlings might have known Jolyon would know her. He had always collected celebrities and persons of note. 'When you contact the office,' Jolyon continued, 'you'll probably be speaking to my partner Sheila Wilson. I think you've met her?' Rawlings shook his head. 'Well introduce yourself. She's very able.' Here he gave a chuckle, 'though maybe not as indulgent with client's moods and tantrums as I am.'

Rawlings also stood up and in a rare gesture he gave his agent a hug. 'Good luck with the tests, Jolyon. Let me know how you are. I'm sure we'll be having a Garrick lunch together very soon.'

But as he left, Rawlings had a sense of foreboding.

*

Two weeks later, he was sitting in Max's living room in the Putney house, with its large windows looking out towards the river.

'It's a strange thing Max,' he mused, 'that although I am extremely pleased to be still on the river, the Thames here has a completely different character from the Thames that lapped at my houseboat. That was a country river looking out onto a weeping willow tree, the surface only disturbed by the river birds and the occasional pleasure boat.' He smiled at the recollection. 'Those birds you know, had the most wonderful routine. Swans sailed majestically downstream in the morning, the Canada geese paraded upstream in the evening, while the heron took up position on the opposite bank during the day.'

'Very poetical,' murmured Max.

Rawlings stood up and walked to the window. 'This is most definitely an urban river and quite different, even though it's still the Thames. Here I look out onto tall buildings on the opposite bank, a railway bridge with its constant rumblings and there's continual traffic on the water making it a busy thoroughfare.' He sat down again. 'You mustn't think I'm complaining. I'm pleased I still look out on the river.' He thought for a moment. 'Maybe it's also different in character because it is tidal here. That seems to change it somehow. I don't think I'd like to be in a houseboat on the tidal part of the river, although I know a great many people are, but to me there's something very satisfying about the river being at a constant level. Felix had a pet goose who permanently floated by the side of the Esme Jane like a sort of appendage,'

'What happened to it?'

'Harrison? Unfortunately, he died, just before Felix left for Australia. We think it was of old age, although I had my suspicions.'

Max was looking amused. 'If you've quite finished your river musings Rawlings, I need to inform you about this evening. My two sisters will be coming over for supper and they come with a health warning. When my family are together it is inevitably extremely noisy. You've already met Bel.'

Rawlings smiled. 'I have indeed and very formidable she is too.' Arabella Lambton Smythe, or Bel as Max called her, had taken on the conversion of the flat and its re-decoration, and had been amazingly efficient. It was nearing completion and he hoped to move back in a few weeks. No doubt she would tell him more tonight.

'You'll also meet Henrietta, Hetty, the older sister. She's

quite different from Bel in every way, but when they're together the noise levels go up considerably.' He chuckled. 'I just wanted to warn you. They have been known to send some of my friends into shock.'

Rawlings smiled. 'I'm quite sure I'll cope.' He paused. 'Henrietta and Arabella sound straight out of a Restoration play. In which case Max would seem rather out of character?'

'Well spotted sir!' Max gave another chuckle. 'I am actually Charles Maximilian, but I had a cousin called Charles of the same age and so to save any confusion I became Max. And you're right about our names. My mother had a passion for all things Restoration. Our youngest brother is called Rupert. Now if my father had been allowed to choose our names, we'd probably have been called after one of the books of the Apocrypha. I might have been saddled with Esdras, Maccabees or Baruch. So maybe I had a lucky escape.'

'Maccabees Winterton,' Rawlings mused. 'That would have been a name that called out for attention. Your father I presume was a clergyman?' Max nodded. 'And your younger brother. Where is he?'

Max frowned. 'He went native, left these shores years ago and never came back. Last heard of somewhere on the banks of the Amazon making a study of tribal languages and living in a village with a native woman by whom, according to Hetty who gets the occasional postcard, he has three children.' He stood up. 'I must leave you and go shopping. The girls are doing the cooking tonight but have provided me with a list, which I have been instructed to follow to the letter.'

'If only I could get into the boxes downstairs, I have a good selection of wines. You must allow me to contribute in some way Max.'

'I wouldn't hear of it.' Max sounded adamant. 'There'll be time enough for your wines when you're entertaining me.'

He departed and Rawlings limped to the kitchen to refresh his coffee. He had now discarded his heavy boot, but still moved rather gingerly on the repaired leg. The pain hadn't completely gone, but it was certainly an improvement and he was hopeful of it improving further.

Switching on the kettle he thought about his time living with Max. They were an odd couple, but even so, it had worked out better than he'd expected. It wasn't as if he knew Max that well. They'd only recently renewed their acquaintance last December, when they'd spent a drunken evening in the Frontline Club. Good God! That was only four months ago. Hard to believe that so much had changed in such a short time. That particular night they were both drowning their sorrows; he, because he had just put Felix on the plane to Australia, and Max, because he thought he had to sell his beloved Putney house to pay off his gambling debts. Rawlings had heard about Max's reputation as a gambler when they were together for a short while during the second Gulf War. They were both reporters but had worked for different papers, Max for a tabloid, whereas he'd always worked for a broadsheet. Consequently, their journalistic paths were inevitably far apart. He was often asked the difference between the tabloid and the broadsheet. The simplistic answer was to say the former was more serious, the latter slangy and sensational. Max would be the first to admit he'd never been a serious journalist. He still worked for his tabloid, now as a TV critic, which was not a job that made great demands on him, merely requiring him to shut himself away in his study for a day, watch a few hours of film and then send in his copy. For this he received a large remuneration. Rawlings knew little of Max's background but was aware he appeared to be well connected, always helpful when working for a tabloid. He gave an inward smile. The more he knew of Max, the more it became evident he took very little in life seriously. He was something of a maverick, a renaissance man, a 'jack of all trades', but not really a master of any of them. Unlike himself, Max was gregarious, and never happier than when at the centre of a social gathering. He was a wonderful host, a popular guest and in demand at parties and events, where evenings would often end up with him at the piano. He was not a classical pianist, but one of those enviable people who could play almost anything from jazz to musicals, even improvising as well. It was clear he loved performing, his favourite party pieces being Tom Lehrer and Noel Coward. This brought back a memory of his lost love Mia. She had been a pianist too, but classical. Now, he would never hear her play again. That ended the day she was blown up in Afghanistan…

Rawlings poured out his coffee and carried it back into the living room still pondering on his present situation. That drunken evening in the Frontline Club had thrown up solutions ideal for them both and against all the odds it had worked out perfectly and most surprisingly of all, without a hitch. By selling Rawlings the flat, Max was able to pay off all his debts and keep his beloved house, and for him it was a perfect London base with the added bonus of a garden leading down to the river.

He looked out of the window. The tide was low, the faint rays of Spring sunshine were glinting on the water and the daffodils were out in the garden. When his flat was finished this would be his outlook too. Sipping his coffee, he found himself wondering what Hetty, the third sibling, would be like. Bel, tall, angular, with a brittle beauty, bore no resemblance to her brother, who was short, plump and balding. Bel was spiky and sharp in character. Max was charming and amusing. Now that he had recovered from his gambling nightmare he was relaxed once again, with a naturally happy disposition. Would Hetty be somewhere in between? This 'family life' that had been suddenly thrust upon him felt daunting in many ways. He'd never been part of a family and had spent his whole life avoiding it.

Despite this, he was definitely intrigued, and found himself looking forward to the evening, albeit with some feelings of trepidation.

Chapter 3

The Supper Party

Squawks of laughter heralded the arrival of Bel and Hetty.

'You have to be joking. I just don't believe it!' one of them shrieked.

Rawlings, waiting for them by the fireplace, suddenly had an urge to be somewhere else and wished this was an evening he didn't have to face. The two women followed by Max, fell into the room still laughing. They stopped when they saw Rawlings. Max, removing their coats said, 'Rawlings you've met Bel already, but this is my other sister Hetty.'

Hetty moved across the room and embraced him warmly. 'It's wonderful to meet you at last. We've heard so much about you.'

'All good I hope,' Rawlings said rather feebly.

Bel flung herself into a chair. 'Why Rawlings? Isn't it rather affected to call yourself by your surname?'

Rawlings smiled. 'Many do say that. It has become rather boring explaining why I do.' He sat down and looked directly at her. 'In the same way, I find the sudden profusion of double-barrelled names rather an affection.'

Max gave a loud chuckle and said delightedly, 'Touché, touché!'

Hetty also sat down. 'You mustn't mind my sister. She's

rude to everyone. Nevertheless, your name does rather add to your intriguing reputation. I'd love you to explain.'

Rawlings raised his eyebrows at the description of him having an intriguing reputation, but noting Hetty's expectant expression he gave in.

'It's all quite simple. At an early age, I took a dislike to my given names and it seemed simplest to be called either Rawlings or by my initials, EG.'

'Which stood for?' Bel stretched out her long legs in a cat-like gesture.

'Edwin Garrioch,' he said abruptly.

'Edwin Garrioch,' Hetty repeated, bouncing up and down on her chair excitedly. She reminded Rawlings of one of those round Dutch dolls, and it struck him that she most definitely resembled her brother physically, rather than Bel. 'I just love it,' she declared. 'It's the most perfect name, like a character out of Cranford.'

Bel was looking at him curiously. 'I've always felt you could tell a person's background from their names. Perhaps you wanted to keep this hidden?' She threw the challenge at him directly.

Hetty laughed. 'Go on clever clogs. You tell us what you think his background is.'

Bel thought for a moment. 'The name would indicate upper middle class, probably from professional parents, public school and then maybe Oxford or Cambridge.'

Hetty shook her head. 'You're wrong Bel. I think our mysterious Rawlings was probably in the Army, the SAS. What do you say, Max?

Max handed them a glass of champagne. 'I have absolutely no idea. I'm sure Rawlings will enlighten you if he feels thus inclined.'

Hetty picked up the bottle. 'Real champagne Max? How extravagant. All I ever get is the cheapest prosecco on offer.'

'That'll teach you for marrying an impoverished academic darling.' Bel turned to Max. 'Did you get the quails eggs?'

'I did indeed, just as you requested all prepared by the shop along with the celery salt.' He obediently went to the kitchen and returned with a plate of eggs which he placed on the coffee table.

Bel dived in. 'I could live on these things.' She handed the dish to Rawlings who took one as she said severely, 'We're waiting for you to enlighten us.'

Rawlings tried to keep the triumph out of his voice. 'I am delighted to say you couldn't be more wrong. I come from a working-class background and started life in a two up, two down in Dagenham. I went to the local grammar school, left when I was eighteen, and then went straight into journalism, starting as the tea boy.'

There was a moment's silence until it was broken by Hetty laughing gleefully. 'Not one of your more glorious moments, Bel darling.'

Bel shook her head. 'Something's wrong somewhere. Those names just don't fit.'

Rawlings gave a sigh. 'Probably not. My mother was gentile Scottish with a passion for Dickens, hence the name of Edwin. My father was a rough diamond, having served five years on the Russian Convoys in the war. As far as I can gather, they had a whirlwind courtship, married, were cut off by my horrified mother's family and came down south to Dagenham. My father worked at Ford's and my mother in the local library. I had an elder sister Estelle, another Dickensian name but who quickly became Stella. Does that help?'

Hetty leaned forward and persisted, 'But what about Garrioch? That smacks of something more interesting.'

'A family name,' Rawlings explained, 'on my mother's side. 'Mainly to placate two maiden aunts who would occasionally send down sums of much needed money.' He shrugged. 'My father left us when I was ten and we never saw him again. There was no way I could go to university. I had to start earning a living as soon as was possible. My mother and Stella then returned to Scotland and a belated reconciliation with her family.'

There was silence after this, until Hetty broke it. 'Well, I've never seen you lost for words Bel.'

Bel got up. 'I am going to put the supper on. It should take about half an hour.' And with that she abruptly removed herself to the kitchen.

When she'd gone Hetty remarked, 'Bel's in one of her moods. They don't usually last long.'

'Any particular reason?' Max asked, refilling the glasses.

'I think she and Clive had words. He wasn't overjoyed by having to babysit Zach.'

'How old is Zach? Rawlings asked, imagining a toddler.

'He's fifteen. Normally Ben who's eighteen would be with him, but tonight he's out at a football match.'

Max laughed. 'If I know Clive, he'll have taken Zach to a slap-up meal at The Ship.'

Hetty sighed. 'That's precisely what they were arguing about. Bel said Zach needed to stay at home to do his homework.'

Bel came back into the room. 'We're having breast of duck. It should only take half an hour. I can't find the cherry sauce Hetty. Did you bring it in with you?'

Hetty got up. 'It's probably still in the front of the car. I'll get it.' She bustled out.

'I hope to God it hasn't spilled. We'll be sticking to the floor for months if it has.' Bel said returning to the kitchen.

Max was looking amused. 'Do you think you're going to survive the evening, Rawlings?'

'On the strength of champagne and quail's eggs how could I not?' Rawlings said wryly. 'As a matter of fact, I'm finding it fascinating. Having no experience of family life, it's something new for me.'

Max sighed. 'I don't think our family is very typical...'

He got no further as Hetty returned. 'Only a bit spilled. Don't tell Bel, I think I managed to mop up most of it.'

With great efficiency the supper arrived on time. The food was delicious, and the wine flowed. By half way through the meal the mood, particularly that of Bel, had mellowed considerably.

Max said suddenly, 'Bel always likes to fit people in this country neatly into classes. But as I keep telling her, some people just don't fit. I mean, where on earth would you put our family?'

Hetty laughed saying, 'We're too eccentric to fit in anywhere.'

'I think,' Bel said slowly, 'the class system is not nearly as neat as it used to be.'

'Not like that upper, middle, and lower-class sketch, do you remember? I look up to him, but I look down on him,' chimed in Hetty.

'That was a bit facile, but very funny,' Max agreed. 'So where are we now, Bel?'

She gave a rare smile. 'I can see you're all panting for an

argument. Well, here goes. My version of the present class system. One of the great upheavals is the re-distribution of wealth and this has created more divisions. There still is a working class but that's becoming a rare breed, most have moved up into lower-middle class. They used to be solid socialists, but now many will be supporting Brexit and have a longing for the good old "Rule Britannia" days. I only mention Brexit because it has emphasised the class divisions. After the lower-middles, you get to the vast proportion of UK citizens, who fit into the middle classes. This lot have generally done well for themselves, have good incomes, nice houses, take packaged holidays, etc. Many of these will also have voted for Brexit, but for different reasons. Some because their small businesses suffer from European bureaucracy. Others I'm afraid for more bigoted reasons, the "little England" mentality and utter dislike of immigrants of any nationality. This is turning us all into racists and the country into a cruel and dislikeable place in my personal opinion.' She paused and took a gulp of wine. Nobody interrupted her, so she continued. 'We then come to the upper-middle class, which includes the professions – the civil service, doctors, academics, lawyers etc – and one which I suspect we fall into. These are mostly Remainers and pro-Europe. Then there are the straightforward upper classes, those with minor aristocratic credentials, landowners and the like. Finally, the diminishing and inbred aristocracy, who no longer wield power and are finding it increasingly hard to survive.' Bel looked round at the assembled company. 'And there you have it. Bel's potted guide to the present class system.' She finished with a look of triumph and polished off her wine.

Max gave a slow hand clap and re-filled her glass.

Rawlings smiled and said, 'To roughly misquote George Orwell, "England is the most class-ridden country under the sun, a land of snobbery and privilege and largely ruled by the old and silly".

'How apt, and how very erudite of you Rawlings.' Hetty looked impressed.

'I had a great deal of time while sitting out the wars, for reading and mopping up useless knowledge,' he said apologetically,

Max chipped in. 'I remember you were always listening to music too.'

'I presume that was classical and mainly baroque,' Bel said with mild sarcasm in her voice.

Rawlings was by now aware that Bel, for some reason, was determined to provoke him. He was equally determined not to rise. 'On the contrary, I was positively eclectic in my tastes. My girlfriend Mia, an excellent classical pianist, introduced me to a great many composers, but we both enjoyed jazz, and yes, even pop.'

'What pop?' Hetty called out, as she left for the kitchen.

Rawlings thought for a moment. 'We had quite a list; Billy Joel was on it, Janis Ian, Rod Stewart, and then,' he hesitated, 'we both liked Roberta Flack.' He broke off, not wanting to give away a private moment.

Bel looked at him curiously, 'Was that "The First Time Ever I Saw your Face"?' Rawlings nodded as Bel added softly, 'probably the most beautiful song ever written.'

There was a long pause as they looked at each other.

Hetty had been busy bringing in cheeses and missed this moment. She turned to Rawlings. 'Max said you were something of a Don Juan in the past. Would you say that was true?'

Max sounded cross. 'What nonsense you do talk Hetty. I said nothing of the kind, apart from saying you'd find him attractive. Leave the poor man alone!'

Rawlings gave a laugh, determined to diffuse any situation. 'In my younger days I believe I did have something of a reputation. I would only point out I was faithful to one woman for seventeen years and this only ended when she was blown up in Afghanistan.'

There was silence after this, broken by Bel who said, 'It's getting late. We'd better clear up Hetty and get back to my cross husband.'

Max and Rawlings returned to their chairs by the fire. They could hear the clatter and laughter coming from the kitchen.

'How about a brandy Rawlings?'

'Why not?' he said. 'It would nicely top off an evening full of indulgences.'

Hetty burst back into the room. 'Bel was just saying the cherry sauce reminded her of those lollipops we were given as children. They were too delicious, long oblong ones on a stick that sort of went to toffee. Do you remember them, Max?'

Max laughed. 'I do. It probably accounts for the fact we all suffered from bad teeth.'

Bel emerged with another bottle of wine. 'I thought we'd have one for the road.'

'Which one of you is driving?' Max inquired.

'Don't be so pompous Max,' Bel said crossly. 'You've become very censorious since losing your own licence.' She turned to Hetty with a laugh. 'Talking of those lollipops, I'm reminded of that dreadful nanny who gave them to us, the time the three of us had mumps…'

'…that's right. Mother was pregnant with Rupert and not

allowed near us, so Nanny Roberts arrived.' Hetty turned to Max. 'It must have been a summer holiday because you were away at prep school by then and I know you were with us.' Max nodded. 'We had this large room that ran along the top of the house,' she explained to Rawlings. 'It was a fantastic place…'

'…there was a dressing up box,' Bel chimed in, 'and the piano. Max was always at the piano. There was that old volume of English folk songs. We knew them all…'

'…and all the Gilbert and Sullivans,' Hetty added. 'The Gondoliers was Pa's favourite. He used to sing "Take a Pair of Sparkling Eyes" in the bath.'

The three of them were suddenly lost in their childhood memories.

'Do you remember we started writing an opera?' Hetty suddenly said. 'What on earth was it called?'

'Carrantuohill Mountain, Bel replied. 'I only remember that because it was based on a children's book that frightened the life out of me, along with its graphic illustrations. It gave me nightmares for years.'

'I can't recall the actual story.' Hetty was shaking her head.

'I can,' Bell said grimly. 'There was this wicked witch who lived on the mountain and was destroying the livelihoods of all the people in the villages nearby. And then an old man gave this small boy, our hero, three chances to destroy the witch. I can't remember exactly what happened. I think the boy turned her into fire first, but she set the cottages on fire. So, he turned her into water, and she started to flood the place. Finally, he turned her into a piece of bread and then the boy bravely ate her. But she started to choke him and with a cackling laugh told him he would die. At the last minute the old man turned up, fished the bread out of the boy's throat and threw it on the fire and with a terrible scream the witch was destroyed.' Bel shuddered and said crossly, 'I can't think why children's books have to be so utterly gruesome.'

Max was smiling through all this. 'I do remember it. I wrote the music, Hetty did the book and lyrics, and Bel designed the costumes and set.' He went over to the piano and started playing.' He turned back to them. 'This was the opening number,' he said, and then he sang:

'Oh Carrantuohill, dreaming mountain,
Gentle mountain of mist and streams.
Light in the morning, light in the evening
Oh lovely mountain, mountain of our dreams.'

It was a haunting melody and strangely moving. Rawlings watched the three of them, so quickly transported back to their childhood. He felt an outsider, watching something personal and private.

'I wonder if the manuscript still exists,' Hetty mused. 'I saved an old trunk of our childhood stuff. I could look through that.'

Bel, who had managed to drink most of the bottle of wine, was starting to slur her words. 'I expect our precious mother threw it out. She threw out most of our things.' There was anger in her voice.

Max looked at her and stood up.

'I'm calling you an Uber,' he said firmly. 'You can come back and fetch your car in the morning Bel.' She looked mutinous but said nothing. He made a quick call. 'It'll be five minutes. Is your car in the drive?' Hetty nodded. 'Good, then there'll be no problems with parking tickets.'

As they waited for the Uber to arrive, Bel managed to say,

'We can go down to the flat in the morning Rawlings. Things to discuss.'

Their exit was quite a performance. Hetty hanging on to Bel, who lurched across the room. Hysterical laughter started in the hallway and continued down the steps to the waiting car. The front door slammed, and Max returned to the room. 'That poor Uber driver has my sympathies with those two,' he said. Rawlings smiled as Max poured him another brandy. 'I should have kept a closer eye on Bel. She tends to become drunk quite suddenly. It's almost as if she reaches a limit when she is still fine, then one sip more takes her over the edge. The problem is, she doesn't recognise that limit. Bel's a complicated, fragile creature, with a past that throws up problems...'

Before he could say anything else his mobile sounded. He looked at it and made a face before answering.

'Oh, hello Clive... Yes, they should be with you shortly... No, I put them in an Uber... What? No not really, just rather merry, sorry about that. One of those family evenings... Thank you, that's most kind of you. I'll tell him... See you then... Bye.'

He put the mobile down and sighed. 'Not a happy husband. Bel does demand the patience of a saint. Just as well Hetty is with her. She's always been the soothing influence in the family.' He gave Rawlings a funny look. 'Bel has obviously mentioned you to Clive, so he's anxious to meet you. If you feel you can stand more of the family, he's invited you to Sunday lunch at his pub, The Ship. The food is excellent.'

Rawlings smiled. 'So I've heard. Can I let you know about Sunday? I'm not sure of my plans yet.' He looked at Max. 'I really enjoyed this evening,' he said.

Chapter 4

Aftermath

The next morning Rawlings was woken early by the April sun streaming into his room. He looked at his watch. It was only seven. There was no rush to get downstairs, Bel wouldn't be over before ten and Max was having one of his television days so would be closeted away in his study. The admirable cleaner Mrs Bunce who came twice a week, wasn't due to arrive until nine. This would give him plenty of time to take a shower before having a late breakfast, leaving as little time as possible for Mrs B to air her views, which tended to pour from her in a verbal stream.

His thoughts drifted to the previous evening. Unexpectedly he'd enjoyed it, fascinated by the glimpse into the Winterton family life, although it seemed to be full of dangerous corners and there was a permanent feeling of underlying tension, which meant the animated chatter could change in an instant and some chance remark cause instant irritation and even tempers to flare. Last night the undercurrents had mainly been stirred by Bel, and he sighed, reflecting the woman was mercurial and dangerous. In many ways she was like Mia, both physically and in character. She'd put him under attack from the start of the evening, but he recognised this as something sexual, a highly charged game she liked playing. It certainly had not been noticeable in their earlier encounters. Those had been purely business-like. Last night her hostility had been evident until he mentioned the Roberta Flack song. Then her attitude completely changed and there'd been a definite moment between them. Stupidly he'd held her gaze. What on earth possessed him to do that? He should have looked away. It only took a split second to embark on something dangerous. He knew it and he suspected Bel did too.

He sat up and lit a cigarette. Damn! If he hadn't imagined it – which he didn't think he had – then he'd landed himself with a potential problem. It was a situation that had to be nipped in the bud right now. It was absolutely not the time for him to be embarking on another affair, especially with a woman like Bel. Good God! He'd only just extricated himself from Marnie.

He stubbed out his cigarette feeling annoyed with himself. From the little Max had told him, he knew Bel had left a disastrous first marriage, with two small girls that she'd then had to raise on her own. So, she'd had a struggle to put it mildly. But then came her success as an interior decorator, her marriage to Clive and two more children. From that it would appear she had turned her life around. Yet she seemed angry, unhappy, and judging by last night, sexually frustrated. It was likely she gave Clive a pretty difficult time. Was he the problem? Had she fallen out of love with him? Max didn't appear to have a very high opinion of the man. He'd mentioned him being brash, right wing and obsessed by money. Did Bel secretly share Max's view? Was this why she seemed poised for a sexual adventure? Was she some kind of dominatrix? He stubbed out the cigarette.

With a shiver, he chided himself for letting his imagination go out of control. That moment could have meant nothing, but climbing out of bed, he decided that however attractive Bel might be, she was not for him. Quite apart from anything else she was Max's sister, and nothing should be allowed to jeopardize their friendship. It was also his firm rule never to tangle with married women. Pulling on his trousers, he hunted around for a clean shirt. Bel would be dealt with politely but firmly. He had far too many loose ends in his life needing attention to be distracted by an entanglement with Bel, which he imagined would be all consuming. There was his trip to Scotland to see Stella, his forthcoming visit to Felix, and as he walked across the room, he noticed the unopened proposal from Jolyon lying on the desk. Bloody hell! An answer on that was expected as well.

He moved gingerly towards the door, his head decidedly foggy from one brandy too many the night before. A strong cup of black coffee was a necessity if he was to be ready for this ordeal. As he walked down the stairs he tried to think positively. It was quite possible he'd imagined the whole thing and exaggerated the danger he was in.

Bel arrived on time, which was a welcome reprieve, as he'd had to endure a full ten minutes of Mrs Bunce's description of her husband's arthritic problems. She looked pale and wore dark glasses, no doubt also feeling the effects of last night.

'Would you like a coffee before we go downstairs?' Rawlings tactfully inquired.

She nodded and he went to the kitchen to organise it, thankful to find Mrs Bunce had removed herself to clean the upstairs bedrooms. Bel took the coffee from him and gingerly had a sip. He shot her a look. 'I presume you're feeling a little frail?'

She gave him a bleak smile. 'I stupidly overdid it last night and have only myself to blame. Poor Max. I owe him for the Uber.'

'And Hetty? How is she?'

'Oh, Hetty is fine, her usual self, bouncing and hearty at breakfast.'

Rawlings felt some sympathy. Nothing worse than having someone loud and cheerful when you're suffering from a hangover.

'I enjoyed the evening' he said, 'even if we did drink...'

'Bully for you' she cut in acidly. 'Clive compares our family gatherings to the worst excesses of the French Revolution.'

Rawlings gave a wry smile. 'In that case, he must be extremely brave. I believe he's invited me to join you all at The Ship next Sunday for lunch.'

Bel shot him a curious look and then said quickly, 'Hetty will be back in Yorkshire by then, so you'll only have to put up with my family.'

Rawlings stood up. 'This is all new to me. I have absolutely no experience of family life.' Before she could make any further comment, he walked to the door. 'Shall we go down to the flat?'

Bel let him in and then waited for his reaction. Apart from a gasp as they entered, he walked round in silence slowly taking it all in. The change was not only extraordinary but a relief. When he'd initially taken on the flat, it had consisted of several small rooms filled with boxes and Max's junk. Now many of those walls had gone, making the living room one large area. The bleached wood floors added to the feeling of space. The only original feature that remained were the French windows opening onto the garden, and these had been extended the entire width of the wall allowing the light to flood into the room. Halfway down on one side was a period fireplace and the entire wall opposite had been given over to bookshelves. At the street end, an archway led into a galley kitchen. At the other end, a high pine door led into a narrow corridor, off which was his bedroom plus a shower room, and then a small bedroom which would do for Felix. Finally, a door led to a separate bathroom.

Rawlings came back into the main room where Bel was anxiously awaiting his verdict. He took both her hands and said, 'It's a miracle! Exactly what I hoped for. There is so much more space than I'd anticipated.' He released her hands and moved over to the window, looking down towards the river.

'I had a great architect,' she said, 'none of this is really down to me. He just carried out your vision and miraculously came in on budget as well. You could have had a larger bedroom, but you did say you wanted a small room for your grandson.' She moved over to the window and stood beside him. 'It's amazing they finished in three months, considering the amount of work, but it helped that you knew exactly what you wanted. So many clients don't.' Rawlings seemed unable to speak so she added, 'It seems spacious now because there is no furniture yet. We should go through your needs on that.' She hesitated. 'That is if you want me to organise it. It's really where my expertise comes in. My only contribution up to now has been in the supervising and paintwork.'

Rawlings was still silent. For some reason he found himself moved, almost emotional. This was the first place he'd ever actually owned and at the age of sixty-six he found it rather overwhelming. Bel was looking at him patiently waiting for him to speak. Trying to hide his emotions he finally asked casually, 'What's the colour you've used? It seems like white, but it's not clinical, more restful.'

'It's oatmeal white. All the various shades of off-white have become popular. I particularly like this one because it has some warmth. And talking of warmth, there is underfloor heating, and you have the log burner and fireplace as you requested. There's no practical chimney so the fire is electric, but I bought a rather expensive model that looks surprisingly authentic. Put a pile of logs either side and you won't know the difference.'

He smiled at this. 'I actually had a smaller version on my houseboat.'

She hesitated. 'We need to discuss your furniture needs. I've brought some pictures of various bits and pieces with me.'

On impulse Rawlings said, 'It's nearly twelve, why don't you let me take you for an early lunch and we can organise everything then. There's a good Italian just around the corner.'

She accepted his offer and as they walked to the restaurant Rawlings gave a chuckle. 'Poor Max must have suffered, with all the noise and banging below him over the past three months. He's been incredibly good about it.'

Bel gave a mirthless laugh. 'Poor Max wasn't there for most of the time! He removed himself for a month's holiday with his mistress Elsa. Every year they make a trip to the Bahamas in late January.' Rawlings had vaguely heard of this mistress. It was yet another interesting skeleton in the Winterton family cupboard. 'After he returned,' Bel added, 'he went to stay with Hetty and Bernard, so by the time he was back in London, the worst of the noisy work was done.'

They reached the restaurant, and once seated Rawlings suggested a Bloody Mary as the obligatory 'hair of the dog'.

She gave a wan smile. 'I'll be guided by you.'

Two Bloody Marys later and with pasta on the way, Bel looked on the road to recovery.

'Am I wrong?' she asked suddenly.

It was a somewhat enigmatic question, but Rawlings knew exactly what she was referring to.

He paused before giving an answer, saying slowly, 'No, I don't think you're wrong, only maybe in the interpretation. It was a small moment.'

'It was when you mentioned Roberta Flack. I knew at once.' She looked at him intently, and then said, 'Bugger.'

'Precisely.'

The food arrived and they were silent while they ate.

'What happens now?' she finally said.

'Nothing,' he replied firmly.

'What do you mean, "nothing"? We both know the moment happened. We can't just pretend it didn't.'

Rawlings put down his knife and fork. 'We can and we must for many reasons, not least the fact that you're married, and I have just extricated myself from an involvement and certainly do not want to embark on another.' He added with a smile, 'However great the temptation might be.'

'So, you are tempted?'

'Of course, you're a very attractive woman and I have to admit I also felt that illusive something, but on looking back I am inclined to say that for me, it was a brief moment of lust and nothing more serious.'

'Lust would do.'

Rawlings remained silent.

She said crossly, 'This is all too Brief Encounter and so ridiculous.' Looking at him curiously she asked, 'Have you never had a mistress?'

41

'No. I always considered it a rather unsatisfactory relationship, with neither side ending up happy. Too many complications, too much baggage.' He paused, then gave a rueful smile. 'I don't want to give the impression I have always been a paragon of virtue. I haven't. Before I met Mia, I had a great many affairs, but after I met Mia, I didn't.' He was suddenly irritable. 'Quite honestly Bel this is a pointless discussion and will lead us nowhere. I'm going to order coffees and then you can show me the pictures of the furniture you've selected.'

She looked startled at his brutal rejection, then giving him a mutinous look, she obediently dived into her briefcase and brought out some pictures. The first was of a long refectory table. Rawlings peered at it.

'What is that wood? It doesn't look like pine.'

'No, it's elm and a particularly beautiful antique. I can only reserve it for a week, so a quick decision is needed on that one.' She hesitated. 'It's more expensive than some others I could show you, but it would suit the room and could seat at least eight people. I thought I'd look for a church pew for one side and a set of chairs for the other.'

'Great idea,' Rawlings said. 'What next?'

She pulled out a photo of an extremely large, low sofa. 'Again, we're over budget here. You said you wanted a three-seater – this would actually take four people. The covers are in a heavy, slub silk, an Indian material called dupion, which has great texture.' She looked at Rawlings. 'It was the only one I could find in the size you wanted.'

He nodded approvingly. 'And the tawny colour fits in with the neutral colour scheme.'

'Your almost non-existent colour scheme.'

Ignoring this he said, 'Again, I think you should go for it.'

'Right, I'll do that today. I'm leaving you with a couple more pictures of desks, also of coffee tables. Then you can take your time making up your mind. You gave me pictures of your two Indian armchairs, in wood and rattan, that you have in store. They're an interesting shape, but I guess they'd be uncomfortable to sit on as they are. I was going to suggest two kilim cushions for the sofa, and if you agree, I could have kilim seat cushions made up for those armchairs at the same time. It will give a bit of colour and blend well with your Afghan rugs.' She put the photos away. 'That's about it. You wanted me to order your bed, which I think you said will be a five-foot divan. I think you also mentioned a chest of drawers for your room and a low chest for your small television. I presume that will go at the foot of the bed?' He nodded. 'What about the bedroom for Felix, will you be getting the single divan for that?'

'Yes. I'll have time to get his room ready when I get back from visiting him in Australia. He might want bunk beds, so he could have a friend to stay.' He called for the bill.

Bel gathered up her papers. 'I know you said you wanted pine furniture, but there's pine and pine. Antique pine is pale, modern pine is a hideous burnt sienna verging on orange. So, if you don't mind, I'll go for the antique version.' She gave him a curious look. 'You've never once quibbled about the costs. Are you extremely well off?'

He said abruptly, 'I was lucky enough to be left rather large sums of money by my father-in-law and late wife. I am supremely uninterested in money and never touched this legacy until I bought the flat. I have enough left over to buy what I like for it, so you don't have to worry. I can afford what

43

you are doing – and your fees,' he added with a smile.

He could see there were questions she wanted to ask about his past, but he forestalled this by standing up. Bel meekly followed.

As they were leaving, she said, 'Do you have bed linen, kitchen equipment, plates, knives and forks?'

He shook his head. 'No, I left everything like that on the boat. Can you manage that as well, white as far as possible?'

She nodded, then gave a laugh. 'I might go mad with a multi-coloured bedspread.'

'It would probably go straight back.'

They had reached the corner of the road when he suddenly took her in his arms and kissed her long and hard. When she'd got her breath back, she gasped, 'What the hell did you do that for?'

'It was a sort of thank you and goodbye at the same time.'

They continued to walk. 'You bastard,' she said angrily, 'you've just made it worse.'

The rest of the short journey was made in silence. He opened her car door, and she threw herself into the driver's seat without looking at him.

'Thank you', he said. 'You've done a brilliant job with the flat.' Slamming the door shut, she started the engine and drove quickly away.

On looking up he saw Max watching them from the window.

'Was everything all right?' Max asked as Rawlings joined him. He sounded anxious. 'You both looked pretty tense and miserable.'

Rawlings kept it light. 'We're probably both still suffering from hangovers. Bel has done a great job on the flat. It couldn't be better. I took her out to lunch as a reward.'

'Did she drink?' Max asked sharply.

Rawlings decided not to mention the Bloody Marys, which had been his decision. 'We both had water,' he answered quite truthfully.

Max looked relieved and then said abruptly, 'I had a long and difficult conversation with Clive this morning, about Bel's drinking. He's desperately worried. Apparently just lately, it's been getting a great deal worse and she has a hangover almost every morning. I had no idea the situation was so bad. He wants me to talk to her about going to AA.' He sighed. 'Bel's never been good at being told what to do. In any case, Clive says she refuses to admit she has a problem.'

Rawlings paused before saying, 'I think the admittance, is generally considered the major part of the battle.'

'It certainly was with me,' Max agreed. 'I didn't go to Gamblers Anonymous until I was on the verge of losing my house. Well, I would have lost it if it hadn't been for you. I just hope Bel doesn't reach a crisis like that.' He walked to the door. 'Have you any plans for the rest of the day?'

'I've a few phone calls to make and then I thought I'd go down to the flat and make a start on the books. Bel has organised plenty of shelves. I just need to fill them. Don't worry about food. I'll make myself a sandwich and have an early night.'

Max nodded. 'Sounds good to me. I have to finish a turgid television series.'

As Rawlings reached the door he said, 'I'm sorry Max, I find I can't take up Clive's invitation for Sunday. I'd forgotten I'm to see Isobel that day. Various things to sort out before leaving for Scotland next week. Will you thank Clive for his invitation? Maybe we could make it some other time.'

Several hours later Rawlings lay on the bed, having completed most of his tasks. He'd rung Isobel and invited himself down for Sunday lunch. He'd also rung the dragon Sheila to inquire about Jolyon's health. The news was not good. The man had pancreatitis and would be in hospital for some time. Inevitably, Sheila asked if he were any nearer a decision on the Sarajevo book and he had to admit that he wasn't but would let her know soon. Some progress had been made on unpacking his books, but it was a tiring task, and his back was now suffering. No need to panic. He had three more days before seeing Isobel. If he took it slowly, he might have all his books unpacked and on the shelves by Sunday.

His mobile pinged and an email came through from Bel, abrupt and to the point:

The purchase of the table and sofa have been confirmed and will be delivered next week. I found a church pew in antique pine, which would be perfect. Pictures being sent. I will be sending more pictures of the chest for the end of your bed, chairs for the table, and a chest of drawers, when I've found suitable items. I would be grateful if you could make a decision on the pew, desk and coffee table as soon as possible. Do you still want blinds for the windows? I have another major assignment coming up and would like to finish this job by the end of next week. Bel

Rawlings sighed. She was obviously angry and hurt. It was becoming a habit of his, leaving behind him a trail of unhappy and bitter women. Bel really wasn't his fault. He'd behaved sensibly, knocking any potential involvement with her on the head, especially in light of the information just gleaned from Max. But he'd handled it badly. That kiss had been a mistake. He'd meant it as a gesture to end things neatly, but she had responded in a way that showed him she hadn't taken it that way. Damn and blast!

On further reflection, it seemed to him the Winterton family had some serious addiction problems, first with Max and now Bel. Hetty had apparently escaped, but Lord knows what Rupert was involved with on the banks of the Amazon. There had to be a reason for this. Something to do with the parents? Parents were usually blamed. They fuck you up your mum and dad... That Larkin poem had always resonated with him. The guilt was still with him about neglecting his own son. Hugo was dead and there was no way of putting things right. Felix now had to be the priority in his life.

He abruptly left the bed, went over to the table and opened his laptop to examine Bel's efforts. The picture of the pew was impressive. She was right, it would be perfect. Then he studied the photos of the desks and coffee tables, and in both cases, it was an easy decision. He emailed back with his verdict, telling her he would also like blinds but adding he could deal with these himself, if she was short of time. Thanking her again for her excellent choices, he signed himself, R.

Sitting back in the chair, he pondered on Bel's situation now that he knew more about her alcohol problem. Had he made things worse? On balance he thought not. This wasn't a sudden development for Bel. Her alcoholism had probably emerged from something in her past and been aggravated for some reason, by her present situation. He'd known far too many alcoholics, especially PTSD sufferers, not to feel worried about the seriousness of it. The obvious solution was to get her to AA, but that wouldn't be easy. The one contribution he could make was to remove himself from the scene. The flat would be finished in a week or so. He would then be away, first seeing Stella in Scotland and at the end of May he was off to Australia to see Felix. His absence should at least be one less aggravation for her. He allowed himself a wry smile. Just as well his sexual urges were fading. In the old days he would have embarked on an affair without a second thought. His firm action with Bel today had given him a lucky escape from what could have been a messy situation.

Chapter 5

A Visit to Isobel

'I must say you're looking remarkably well Rawlings.' Isobel remarked as she led him through the house adding, 'If it's all right with you, I thought we'd have drinks on the terrace as the weather is so mild.'

Rawlings stood for a moment before sitting on one of Isobel's elegant patio chairs, to look again at the garden, taking in the boathouse and the boat. It was four months since he'd left yet nothing had changed, all as calm and tranquil as ever. Turning back, he sat down and made a study of Isobel. She certainly hadn't changed either, elegant and beautiful as always, although her blonde hair was now a whiter shade of pale.

'Have you reached seventy yet Isobel? You always look so timeless I can never remember your age.'

'What a very strange greeting.' She smiled at him. 'I will reach that landmark in June. I thought we might have a delayed celebration when Felix gets here. You know how he loves birthdays.'

They were both silent as they recalled his last birthday, spent with them. Isobel sighed. 'What a lovely time Felix had. He was so happy that day.'

Rawlings nodded. 'Yes he was, and he'll be with us for his next one as well when he comes over in August. Good heavens, he's going to be twelve…' He broke off. 'Do you think the boy is all right? The last conversation, or rather non-conversation I had with him, left me worried. He seems to have gone inward in some way, finding it hard to communicate. I don't know why, but my instinct tells me something's wrong.'

Isobel paused before answering. 'I have to agree. He certainly isn't as talkative as he used to be. But maybe this was to be expected. When he first went out to Australia, it was an exciting time for him, with a new family and Christmas…'

Rawlings put down his glass and burst out, 'What really worries me Isobel, is that deep down I think we made the decision too hastily. The boy had been through such a traumatic year, what with the death of his parents, coming here, and then the new school. Miraculously he had settled down and was happy.' He added angrily, 'All that importance put on his being part of a family. Bloody nonsense. From what I've seen of family life, it can be absolute hell. We were his family; you, me, Marnie, his friend Sonny Patel, even Jake the gardener, Maria and Paul…'

Isobel took the opportunity to interrupt this outburst. 'Talking of Maria and Paul, I have some news for you.' She paused. 'They're moving into the boathouse in July.'

Rawlings looked surprised. 'Then where is Marnie going?'

'She'll be working abroad for most of the time. Meanwhile, she tells me that she thinks it will be more convenient to rent a flat near her business partner and his wife.'

Rawlings regarded her thoughtfully. Isobel had supported Marnie for a long time, and now it seemed Marnie no longer needed her. 'How do you feel about that?'

Isobel smiled. 'Actually, it has worked out well. With all the talk of Brexit, Paul was threatening to move back to Poland.

Quite selfishly this would have been something of a disaster for me. Maria has not only become my housekeeper, she's also a friend, and as you know, Paul is the most wonderful handyman. Officially he's a plumber, but there seems to be nothing he can't do. When Marnie broke the news to me that she'd be leaving the boathouse I immediately offered it to Maria and Paul, hoping to tempt them away from their decision to leave. Happily, they accepted my offer. I think this was a relief to Maria who in her heart wanted to stay, but if Paul had remained adamant, like a dutiful wife she would have gone with him. She's in the kitchen right now getting our lunch ready.'

Rawlings was relieved to hear this news. He'd had concerns that with him gone and Marnie away so much, Isobel would have been left on her own. There had been no mention of Lydia either, who'd been the carer for Peter when he was dying and had stayed on with Isobel afterwards. 'A great deal seems to have changed in the four months since I left,' he remarked dryly. 'Is Lydia still with you?'

Isobel shook her head, 'No, she moved out a month ago. I am happy to report she has moved in with the woman she's been going on all those cruises with.'

'Is that a relationship?'

'I believe and hope so. It's time Lydia had someone permanent in her life.' She gave a smile. 'You see? I have been deserted on all sides. Even young Jake has gone. He's now at college studying horticulture. Tom, his father, has taken over the garden and Paul helps him out with any heavy work. It works well enough at the moment, but I might need to look for someone else in the summer.'

Maria came out onto the terrace and Rawlings leapt up and hugged her.

She smiled at him shyly her face flushed. 'It is nice to see you again Mr Rawlings. And how is Felix?'

'He's well. I go out to visit him in Australia next month and you'll be seeing him yourself soon. He's due to come over for his summer holidays in August.'

'That is good. I have been missing him.' She turned to Isobel. 'Lunch is ready for you.'

Over the meal Rawlings returned to the topic of Felix, and Isobel did her best to reassure him. 'You will see for yourself Rawlings. It's only a month now till you go. I don't think you can take too much from your Skype conversations. There was bound to be a change in him after the first few weeks. I'm afraid it's inevitable we will become more distant to him now.'

Rawlings wasn't convinced but decided to move onto another topic that had been worrying him. 'If Marnie is leaving the boathouse and away so much of the time, what will happen to the boat?' He now regretted that in a burst of generosity, probably brought on by guilt at leaving her so abruptly, he'd made over the ownership of the Esme Jane to her. It was going to be difficult to explain this to Felix when he returned in the summer.

Isobel smiled. 'I actually have a letter for you from Marnie, about the boat.' She took an envelope out of her pocket and handed it to Rawlings. 'Marnie discussed the decision with me and I agreed with it. Much easier all round.'

Rawlings read the letter quickly. The gist of it was that Marnie had decided to hand the boat back to him. She was very grateful etc., but she wasn't going to be able to make use of it now her circumstances had changed, so Rawlings should send her any papers she had to sign to make this legal. He looked at Isobel. 'That certainly makes sense,' then he paused and sighed. 'More work for gloomy Graham. The man is going to think this frequent change of ownership slightly mad...' he broke off. 'There's actually something else I wanted Graham to deal with Isobel. Would you be willing to become a guardian to Felix?'

Isobel looked startled at this suggestion. 'He already has you and his aunt in Australia. Does he need another one? Nothing would please me more of course. I love the boy as you know, and already look on him as the grandson I never had.'

Rawlings nodded. 'I think it important Felix has two guardians in this country, just in case something should happen to me while he's in England. I'm rather presuming he'll stay in this house with you when he comes back, although I do have room in my flat for him.'

'I think it would be better for him to stay here,' Isobel said firmly. 'How is your flat? Has your smart interior decorator been a success?'

Rawlings made a face. 'My smart interior decorator as you call her, turned out to be something of a problem,' adding hastily, 'not over the flat, she'd done a great job with that. You must come and see it when it's finished.'

Isobel gave him a long shrewd look. 'I am presuming the woman fell in love with you?'

He sighed. Isobel knew him too well.

'There was a moment when it could have become difficult, but you will be pleased to hear I knocked that possibility straight on the head before it had any chance to develop.' He looked at her, 'I also didn't know until a few days ago that Bel apparently has major problems. She's a potential alcoholic and I don't think my rejection made her life any easier.'

'Poor Rawlings,' Isobel said with a smile. 'It seems you're

destined to leave behind you a trail of wailing women.'

'I can't think why,' he said crossly. 'I don't ask them to wail over me. Luckily, I'm going away next week to see my sister in Scotland, and after that I'll be leaving for Australia. So no danger of any more wailing women for the foreseeable future.'

Isobel let the subject drop, but reflected it was the fact Rawlings had no idea why women fell for him that was part of his attraction. It wasn't just that he was obviously handsome, it was this, combined with an easy charm, a strong yet vulnerable quality and always that slight air of mystery. Peter had once remarked at an Embassy reception, observing the women clustered around Rawlings, that it was like wasps around a honey pot.

*

Rawlings drove home encouraged by the way things had gone over lunch, and especially relieved that Marnie had returned the Esme Jane. When he'd given her the boat in that impulsive gesture, it hadn't occurred to him at the time how this would complicate matters with Felix when he returned in the summer. Now the issue was happily resolved. Marnie was cheerfully settled in her new and successful career. Better still, it would appear she bore him no resentment. It was a loose end neatly tied and need bother him no longer. In addition, he was relieved he had also side-stepped the dangerous Bel, an entanglement which could have landed him in definite trouble. The future, like the road ahead, looked clear of any obstacles. His flat would be ready to move into after his return from Scotland. The winter was over, and the weather had turned almost balmy.

Feeling positively cheerful he turned on the car radio and a Bach Brandenburg increased his feeling of contentment.

It was therefore something of a shock when he walked into the house to find the usually placid Max pacing up and down, looking decidedly disturbed and angry.

Before he could inquire as to what was wrong, Max burst out, 'Is this true Rawlings, about you and Bel?'

Rawlings sat down and for a moment felt unable to say anything. At last he spoke in what he hoped were measured tones. 'If you'll enlighten me Max, as to what exactly you mean by that question, I promise to give you an honest answer.'

Max stopped pacing and sat down opposite him. 'I've just had a truly awful lunch with Clive and Bel, made even more ghastly by bloody Bel announcing over coffee that she was in love with you and she was sure you reciprocated her feelings.'

Rawlings felt angry and gave a deep sigh. 'Might I ask if Bel had been drinking?'

Max looked uncomfortable. 'Well yes, and she and Clive were at each other's throats throughout the meal. The boys left as soon as they could, which was when Bel told us about you.'

Rawlings stood up. 'Do you mind if I pour myself a drink?'

Max shook his head. 'I'll join you. I have a feeling I may need it.'

Once more seated Rawlings said, 'I regret this has happened, but I fear Bel is using me for one of her games, and that this is more about her and Clive than anything to do with me.' He paused. 'When I took Bel out to lunch after inspecting the flat, she did make a declaration, saying she'd fallen in love with me. Your sister is an attractive woman, and I wouldn't be human, or honest, if I denied being attracted to her. But I knocked the idea of there being anything between us absolutely on the head. You must believe that. Straight away. She was shocked and angry at this rejection.' He paused again. 'As we left the restaurant, I made the stupid mistake of kissing her. I'd hoped she would see this as a gesture of closure. Unfortunately, it just made her angrier. Which is why as you so rightly observed, neither of us were in the best of moods as I put her into the car. I can honestly say that is all. We've made no arrangement to meet again, there is no need. The flat is finished. Until you delivered your bombshell, I thought this brief complication completely over and done with.' He looked at Max. 'Before your supper party, I had only met Bel twice and we'd talked a few times on the telephone all to do with the flat. I'm extremely sorry this has happened. But I can assure you, the problem is one of Bel's making. If you want me to reassure Clive of course I will.'

Max waved his hand. 'No, no. I totally accept what you've said. I said as much to Clive. I didn't see how there could be anything between you.' He got up to replenish the glasses. Rawlings felt a stab of guilt. If he were honest, there had been that brief temptation and he'd made that stupid mistake of kissing her, but from what he knew of Max, he was somewhat naïve in matters of the heart and wouldn't have understood that moment between him and Bel. Thank God he'd taken the decision to end any involvement with the woman, even if it had been for selfish reasons.

Max sat down again looking abject. 'Rawlings I must apologise. I now remember how Bel attacked you from the outset the other evening and you were extremely patient and polite…' He broke off. 'I think she seems to be in what they call a "bad place", and as I told you all her present actions are fuelled by alcohol. I will of course explain things to Clive. Regrettably, I think another family conference is called for which means I will have to summon poor Hetty down again. She can stay here rather than with Clive and Bel.'

Rawlings really didn't want to continue this conversation about Bel, so he said 'Don't forget I'm leaving for Scotland the day after tomorrow to see my sister. On my return I'll move into the flat.' He looked at Max. 'Bel has done a brilliant job on that. I'll always be grateful for you recommending her, despite what has happened.'

Max gave a sigh. The poor man looked exhausted. 'Well that's a relief. I was beginning to think you'd regret moving in here altogether.'

'Never,' Rawlings said firmly. 'Buying your flat has been one of the best decisions I ever made. In a couple of weeks, you'll be invited down for a house-warming.'

As he let himself into his room, he wondered why life had to be so damnably complicated. It was a comforting thought that on his return from Scotland he would be moving into his own space, and this would make any future problems with Bel easier to avoid.

Chapter 6

Scotland

Two days later Rawlings was on the train north, having left Kings Cross at 10 a.m. and now scheduled to arrive in Dundee at 15:46. Did trains run on time here? He had no idea. This was the first time he'd made a long train journey in this country. It was some relief he was going straight through without having to change, he could just sit back, relax and watch the English countryside speeding by. On the return journey he might do something different, make a break in Edinburgh or York, but that decision could wait until later.

He looked out of the window. They had left the endless ribbon of London suburbs and the view took on a prettier aspect. How green England looked. 'The green and pleasant land' was such a cliché and yet for him, after spending the last twenty years mainly in desert areas, the brilliant verdant colours gave him nothing but pleasure. His thoughts turned to 'the knucklehead' of the North, where he was now bound. He knew nothing of Dundee and although his roots were Scottish, he'd only made a few short visits and those had been to Glasgow. The last time was for his mother's funeral. By then Stella had married a solicitor, a widower called Hamish McNair, who had two children. She'd written to tell him that when Hamish had retired a few years back, they'd moved from Glasgow to Dundee. Since then their communications had been few. When he first returned from Afghanistan, she'd invited him to stay, but he'd turned down this offer. It was a time when he needed to be on his own to recover from his injuries, both mental and physical. Rawlings moved restlessly in his seat again asking himself the question – was he recovered now? Physically, the good medics had done all they could with that last operation. But mentally? That was more difficult to say. In some strange way, the death of Hugo and his wife which brought about the guardianship of Felix, had gone some way to restoring a sense of balance within him. Maybe, for the first time in his life, the arrival of Felix had meant he was compelled to take responsibility for another person. Inevitably this had a sobering effect and put an end to the self-indulgent grieving that he had so wallowed in since Mia's death.

The refreshment trolley came noisily through the carriage. Rawlings glanced at his watch. It was just past twelve, so he ordered a coffee and a whisky. Taking a swift look at the food on offer he decided he was in no need of solids just yet.

His introspective mood continued as he began to think again about his sister Stella. Everything in their lives went back to the 'incident', when his father had lashed out and Stella, trying to protect her mother, stepped in the way and was knocked to the ground hitting her head on the fireplace. Until that moment he remembered her as happy and outgoing. He was only eleven at the time and Stella a year older, but that one moment had changed everything in their lives. For him it was the loss of his father, who did a short spell in prison for GBH and after he came out was never heard of again. For Stella, the direct result of her fall was not only to give her occasional epileptic fits, but also a change of personality. She became inward, moody and sullen. His mother lavished all her time and attention on the damaged child. Looking back, he thought this over-protection of Stella had probably made matters worse for her. Personally, he hadn't minded his mother's neglect having never had much of a relationship with her, only remembering her as strict and joyless. She made it clear to everyone that her marriage had been a mistake and she longed to return to her gentile Glasgow life. Her deep unhappiness pervaded their lives and affected them all. Any sort of fun was looked on as a sin. The realisation came to him that when his father left, there had been an unbearable gap in his life. It was true his father had been a rough diamond and was often the worse for drink, but there were times when he had given Rawlings his attention telling him about his time on the Russian convoys and, in spite of the terrible trauma and horrors he must have suffered, sharing his great love of the sea. Then he was gone, leaving an irreplaceable hole in his life. From the age of eleven until he was eighteen, he'd spent little time at home. Instead he enjoyed the company of his friends more, and surprisingly his years at the local grammar school. The moment he began to earn his living and could support himself, his mother had removed herself and Stella from Dagenham and returned to Scotland. So much for family life. From then on, he only heard fragments of their lives. One of the Scottish aunts paid for Stella to see a specialist and it was found that the original fall had caused a small fragment of broken bone to press on her brain and this was causing the fits. An operation was arranged and the results were impressive, resulting in the fits lessening until they finally stopped altogether. His mother referred to this as a 'miracle from God'. He was more inclined to give credit to the medical profession.

He searched back into the past. What else did he know? Reunions had been few. His mother and Stella had come down for his wedding. This gave him an inward smile. He remembered little about that day. Years later there had been a brief visit to Glasgow after he returned from Sarajevo. Stella by then was working as a secretary in a law firm. Sometime later Stella sent a message to say their mother was gravely ill and an immediate visit was made to see her. She perversely lasted another two years and made it to her eightieth birthday surprising everyone. His last visit to Glasgow was for her funeral just after 9/11. That was eighteen years ago. His impression of Stella then was that she seemed settled with a much happier disposition. Of her husband Hamish, he remembered little. That was all to come, and it struck him there were many gaps to fill. Closing his eyes, he began to doze.

The clatter of the refreshment trolley making a return visit some hours later jerked him awake. This time he ordered some food, a rather soggy roll with an indeterminate filling, made more edible by downing it with another shot of whisky. Glancing out of the window he noticed the landscape had changed and guessed they must be past Newcastle, now hugging the coast with views out across the bleak North Sea. These were the waters his father would have travelled during the war, being one of the few to survive a full five years on the Russian convoys. Rawlings gave a shudder, knowing only too well what the experience of war could do to a man. No wonder his poor man father was damaged and turned to drink, his plight made far worse by his prim and disapproving wife. If ever there had been a mismatch, that was it.

*

Almost exactly on time, the train drew into Dundee and as soon as he stepped onto the platform, he spotted Stella, an upright, handsome woman and taller than he remembered. He waved and then, because his leg had gone to sleep, walked slowly towards her. She embraced him warmly. 'Welcome to Dundee! Your train was remarkably on time, it can sometimes get very delayed. How was the journey?' He noticed with amusement that her voice had a definite Scottish burr. She walked briskly and Rawlings had trouble in keeping up.

'Good' he said, 'except for the refreshments which left much to be desired. It's been something of a novelty for me to see so much of the country. I'd forgotten the many changes of landscape you go through in such a short time.' He was panting now. 'Astonishing really when you think what a small island this is.'

Stella waited for him to catch up and smiled. 'I suppose if you're used to miles of desert it's no wonder it seemed strange.' She looked at him anxiously. 'How's the leg?'

'Better. It's just not good being in one position for a long time.'

They reached the car, Rawlings noting it was large and almost new. His sister was obviously not short of funds.

'We live a few miles from Dundee centre, a wee drive from Broughty Ferry.'

Rawlings smiled and told her that he knew nothing about Dundee and looked forward to exploring the place over the next few days.

Stella laughed. 'Don't worry, Hamish has all the excursions planned. It's an exciting city and there's a good deal to see.

Broughty Ferry where we live is a seaside suburb full of quaint fisherman's cottages. There are plenty of good places to eat, we plan to go to a waterside restaurant tonight if you're not too tired.' Rawlings assured her he would like that as she went on, 'We live in Osprey Place in a new villa just a few minutes away now. Hamish chose it because it would mean he was near an excellent golf course. He's something of a golf fanatic bless him.'

They turned into a landscaped area with trees and paths leading down to a loch.

'And here we are' she said as they reached a wide drive and parked outside the house.

It was larger than he'd expected and at first glance reminded him of a Swiss chalet. Hamish stood on the doorstep waiting to greet them, a small stocky man with a bald head and a rather fierce expression. He smiled as they approached. 'Welcome to Scotland. Stella has been so looking forward to your visit.' He led the way into the house and if Rawlings had thought it big on the outside the interior was even more imposing, large expanses of wood, stonework, and glass. The main room was immaculate, out of an interiors magazine, and he was amused to see plenty of plaid on the chair and sofa cushions, leaving him in no doubt that he back was in Scotland.

'How long have you lived here?' he asked.

Hamish answered him. 'Almost five years. We moved in the moment they finished building.'

Stella sat down beside him on the sofa. 'Hamish used to come to Broughty Ferry when he was a wee boy for his summer holidays and loved the place...'

'After I retired and saw they were building new houses

63

near Kingennie Golf Course, I immediately put our name down for one of them.'

They were now finishing each other's sentences in a way Rawlings had noticed was a habit with many married couples.

Hamish asked, 'Do you play golf at all EG?'

Rawlings shook his head. 'I'm afraid not. Sport of every kind has passed me by.'

'I find it relaxing and it gives Stella a welcome break from my company.'

Stella looked at him and laughed. 'Get away with you, what nonsense you do talk.' She turned to Rawlings. 'We plan to go out for a meal in about an hour. Would you like a drop of whisky before I take you to your room to freshen up?'

It was rather like staying in a luxury hotel but for Rawlings it was almost too pristine, too ordered, to feel any real sense of being lived in. As for Stella and Hamish, what was he to make of them? Throughout the evening meal they continued to finish each other's sentences, always in agreement, their contentment obvious to see, but for some reason it left him uneasy. Did they disagree about anything? Not that he could see, not even about the serious issues. They both disliked the idea of Brexit, but both firmly wanted Scotland to remain part of the UK.

'My son Jamie doesn't agree with this,' Hamish gave a wry smile. 'He's a passionate supporter of an independent Scotland.'

'What about your other son? Is he for independence as well?' Rawlings asked.

Stella laughed. 'Donald never expresses an opinion either way. He's the diplomat in the family.' Hamish nodded once again in agreement.

Was there any need for diplomacy in this family? He found it hard to believe.

By the time they reached the house Rawlings felt exhaustion begin to overtake him, but Hamish insisted he had a last malt.

'This is a fourteen-year-old Tomatin, and you'd be hard pressed to find a better drop anywhere.' He handed him a glass. 'I keep it for special occasions.'

'In that case I feel extremely privileged.' Rawlings took a sip and was surprised by the warm, mellow taste. 'That is good. It tastes almost like a cognac.'

Hamish gave a chuckle. 'You're absolutely right. It has fooled many. For that very reason I sometimes put it in a brandy glass.' He looked at his wife and smiled. 'Stella doesn't like the malts so much. She prefers a plain whisky.' They drank in silence for a moment and then Hamish stood up. 'I am going to bid you goodnight. I think you two will have a few things to talk about before turning in.' He kissed the top of his wife's head, nodded at Rawlings and left the room.

Rawlings looked at her. 'You've done well for yourself Stella. It's easy to see how happy you are with your life.'

Stella gave him a long, shrewd look. 'You're thinking we've had it easy and maybe we're a wee bit complacent?' Rawlings was about to protest but she held up her hand. 'It wasn't always like this. Until we moved here, we had both struggled and suffered a great deal.' She paused before saying, 'I will need to take you back a good way to explain. After I left secretarial college I went to work in Hamish's legal firm, starting at the bottom and working my way up until I became Hamish's PA. Inevitably, we grew to know each other well. All this time I was struggling with Mother who was never easy and had become increasingly demanding. Hamish was also having a tough time, juggling the pressures of his work with an invalid wife and two young boys to bring up. At times it would seem to me he could take no more and was near breaking point. I began to help him out at home. His wife Laura had been diagnosed with MS soon after their youngest son Jamie was born. By the time their boys were teenagers she had kidney failure and was deteriorating fast, a complete invalid, unable to do a great deal for herself.' She paused again and Rawlings once more refrained from saying anything. 'I began to spend as much time as I could at their house helping out, and Mother began to be angry and suspicious. To answer the obvious question, no we weren't having an affair, although it was plain to both of us that we wanted to be together. Even so the younger son Jamie, who'd never had a particularly good relationship with Hamish, now became rude and resentful towards me.' She gave a sigh and poured herself a small measure of whisky. 'He was already a difficult teenager and matters soon took a turn for the worse. Although he loved his mother, he couldn't bear to be with her when she was so ill. He spent his time with the wrong set at school staying out late, the usual hooligan behaviour, you can imagine the sort of thing. Glasgow and Dundee are two cities with dreadful drug problems. It was a terribly stressful time for both of us. Then on my fortieth birthday, Laura suddenly died. Her heart gave out but quite honestly I think she'd just lost the will to live poor woman. Hamish was devastated, guiltily convinced he hadn't done enough for her, but also because of his feelings for me. The year that followed was a terrible one for both of us. We hardly met except in the office. I still worked for him and did what I could, but Mother was taking up all my spare time.' She drained her glass and looked at Rawlings. 'When did you last see her?'

'It must have been just after my fiftieth birthday. You thought she was near the end then.'

'I did,' Stella said grimly, 'but she lived nearly another two years after that, remaining bitter and angry right up until her death. Quite honestly it was depressing and soul-destroying to be with the woman.'

It was now Rawlings who felt guilty. 'I'm sorry Stella, I realise I was no help…'

'Och, how could you be? You were in Iraq, not much you could do from there. And you did send us that monthly allowance.'

'Was it enough? I would willingly have sent more.'

Stella shook her head. 'No, no. Money was never the problem. When the old aunts died, they left their house to Mother. You never saw it, but it was a gloomy old place, so we sold it. We bought a flat with the proceeds, which was spacious and near to my work.' She sighed. 'I was earning enough money to cover all our needs. It was a simple life. While I was in the office Mother remained at home isolated, refusing to take part in any sort of activities and never making any friends. She relied entirely on me for companionship and complained if I ever went out in the evening. Hamish could see how miserable I was. Three years after Laura died, we finally started an affair. The boys were now off his hands, Jamie had gone to study forestry and Donald was at Edinburgh reading law with a view to following his father into the firm.'

'But the elephant in the room was still Mother?'

Stella gave a heavy sigh. 'I suppose that is one way of putting it, but aye, it was. Just before my fiftieth birthday,

I was getting near to a breakdown and Hamish said enough was enough. We'd tried to please everybody and ended up pleasing nobody least of all ourselves. So we decided to get married. But that still left the problem of Mother. The only solution was to have her live with us. Hamish gave her an ultimatum, it was that or a home, and after a great deal of protest, she gave in. By that time, she was pretty much in need of full-time care. We sold the flat which paid for that. Hamish was endlessly kind and patient with her, in spite of the fact she was never pleasant towards him, or grateful. I will never forgive her for that. It wasn't until after her death that Hamish and I finally had time to enjoy our life together. I think maybe because of all we have gone through we appreciate each other more, especially now. This happiness is new to us. I know we are lucky. It's hard not to show our contentment. But I hope we deserve it.'

Rawlings was visibly shaken. Looking at his sister he said, 'You certainly do. I am very happy for you.' Frowning, he blurted out 'I honestly had no idea Mother was such a burden. What was it that made her so bloody miserable? I thought the return to Scotland was what she'd always wanted.'

Stella thought for a while. 'I think some people are just born with a miserable disposition. I know she'd been brought up very strictly. It was probably a joyless childhood and ironically her one rebellion was to make the disastrous marriage to Father, something she never really recovered from. The aunts could not have been kinder and fussed around her making sure she had everything she wanted. She was never grateful even to them. There was always something that was wrong that would niggle away at her, never letting it rest. She seemed unable to find pleasure in anything and quite honestly, she resented it if I ever showed any signs of happiness. While the old aunts were alive, I had enough freedom to make my own friends and my own life and could leave Mother to them. But once they'd gone, it all fell back on me.'

Rawlings suddenly said, 'I have been a bloody selfish being all my life and never had any responsibility for anyone, until Felix arrived last year.' He stood up. 'But the story of that is for another day. I think I'm for bed. It's been a long day.' He kissed Stella on the cheek. 'Thank you for telling me all that.'

He fell asleep almost as soon as his head hit the pillow.

Chapter 7

The Following Day

Rawlings awoke with a start having slept heavily and unusually for him undisturbed by dreams or nightmares. Lying back in the comfortable bed his thoughts returned to the night before. Stella's story had shaken him, and he was annoyed with himself for having been so judgmental about her marriage. It was a bad habit to think you knew and understood people's lives from the outward appearance. In any case, he had such little experience of marriage or family life it was quite wrong of him to be so quick with facile judgements. Things are not just what they seem, skimmed milk masquerades as cream...

What puzzled him was that Stella had never once chided him for his neglect of both her and his mother. She should have been angry, or at least reproachful, but she seemed to accept his excuse that he had been working abroad and therefore couldn't have helped. This was only partly true. He knew deep down his absence from the scene had been sheer selfishness and a fervent wish to remain uninvolved. It had been a similar story with Hugo and to a certain extent Gillian, although his wife had happily settled into another relationship and wasn't damaged by his neglect. But Hugo probably was. Once his son had rejected him early on, he left him to it. Looking back, there had been many times between assignments when he could have visited his son. He just preferred not to, unwilling to have unwanted interruptions in his life. Having admitted to Stella that he'd been selfish all his life, he knew this to be unfortunately true. Maybe it was time he tried to put things right.

Glancing out of the window he could see a layer of mist blocking out the sunlight which was trying to get through. No doubt this was the reason he had overslept, along with the long day and too much whisky. He arrived down at breakfast and apologised for his lateness, but Stella just smiled and told him he was bound to be tired after his long journey. He gave an inward sigh. There she goes again. She's not going to reprove me for anything. Politely refusing the cooked breakfast on offer, he settled for oatcakes, honey and strong coffee.

'I'm afraid our plans have had to change today,' she informed him. 'Hamish had a tour of Dundee organised, but he's unexpectedly been called over to Glasgow. His sister, who suffers from advanced dementia, has disappeared. We had a desperate call from her husband early this morning. Hamish has been urging him to put Flora in a home. The situation has deteriorated badly over the last few months.' Stella sighed. 'Poor woman. She no longer has any idea who she is, or who anybody else is for that matter. She needs to be in a secure situation.' Rawlings was about to make a sympathetic comment, but his sister cut in with some impatience. 'The real problem is that Bruce, her husband, refuses to let Flora go. It's misplaced guilt and does neither of them any good. I hope Hamish will knock some sense into him today, because these disappearances are happening all too often.' She gave him a smile. 'I'm afraid the tour of Dundee is postponed until tomorrow. I thought today we might spend time down at

Broughty Ferry.' This suited Rawlings fine and he told her so.

They parked at the seafront and walked along the seashore.

'We're on the north bank of the Firth of Tay,' she told him. 'This used to be a fishing village with a history of whaling. The cottages are sought after now and very expensive.'

Rawlings stopped to take in the view. The mist had cleared but the May sun was not imparting enough warmth to reduce the chill from the brisk north wind that blew off the water. 'Some of these houses look grander than fishermen's cottages, or was there a great deal of money to be made from the whaling?'

Stella shook her head. 'The larger houses belonged to the jute barons. It was a big industry here a hundred years ago.' She pointed at the two piers and chuckled. 'You will find this hard to believe but every New Year's Day, some brave souls brave the icy waters and swim between those piers.'

'Good God they must be mad!' Rawlings was appalled. 'What happens if there's ice?'

Stella laughed. 'Get away with you. Nothing would stop the Dookers. It's never been cancelled. In 1989 the harbour waters had to be broken with a pickaxe. It's called the "New Year's Dook". There were nearly three hundred swimmers last year.'

After seeing the castle and museum they stopped for lunch, Rawlings relieved to rest his leg. Since the operation he'd been trying to take it slowly and was unused to so much exercise. 'I'd love to bring Felix up here in the summer,' he mused almost to himself, but Stella at once became interested.

'That would be a treat for us,' she said. 'We'd love to meet the boy and have you to stay. You could take him up to the Forest of Atholl where Jamie works. It's the gateway to so many other places. There is the theatre at Pitlochry, they'd be having their summer festival, and then you could go on up north and visit the islands.' She stopped herself and looked apologetically at Rawlings. 'Will you just listen to me. You'll be making your own plans I'm sure.' After a pause she said, 'Will you tell me about the boy?'

It took him the rest of the meal to go through the saga of the previous year; starting with the shock of the parent's death in a car crash, learning he was the guardian, collecting Felix from school, right up to the boy leaving for Australia to live with his aunt's family.

Stella threw him one of her shrewd looks. 'That must have been a wrench for you, losing the boy just as you had grown so close.'

For a moment Rawlings didn't speak and then he nodded. 'You're right. It was heart-breaking.' She took in his anguished expression but made no comment, until he finally burst out, 'I'm not at all sure I did the right thing Stella. I didn't want to send the boy so far away and every instinct told me it was wrong, but on paper it made sense. I was persuaded it would be good for him to be part of a family, especially as they had children of his age. His aunt was his other guardian, so she had every right to claim him, and the family solicitor took the decision as a fait accompli. I went along with it even when I knew the boy wanted to stay here with me. That was the worst part. I lost his trust.'

Stella chose her words carefully. 'It seems to me it's something that could easily be reversed. You can always ask to bring the boy back to England, where you say he had settled so happily.'

'I'm not sure he could take another upheaval.'

Stella heard the sadness in his voice. 'Why don't you assess the situation when you visit him next month? Your fears may be unfounded.' Then deciding to change the subject she said briskly, 'I have some food shopping to do otherwise we won't be having a meal tonight. Why don't you make your own way back to the car? Take your time. There are some interesting shops, including a good bookshop and a rather quaint antiques emporium.'

Walking at a snail-like pace, Rawlings was pleased to have the time to himself. It had been an intense forty-eight hours and many old wounds had been dredged up and examined. He and Stella had seen little of each other over the years, yet he felt surprisingly relaxed and at ease in her company. It had been a good decision to visit, a tidying up of unfinished moments in his life. He stopped and stared out across the Tay towards the North Sea. The watery sun had now given up and the sea looked grey and uninviting. He gave a sudden shiver. His father had sailed these waters for the five years of the war and an extraordinary thought hit him. His father's bones must surely lie somewhere, deep in these waters. Nobody knew what had happened to him but at this moment Rawlings instinctively felt that he must have died at sea. Maybe he should try and find out? He forced himself to walk on. That was for another time, a loose end not yet ready to be tied.

Stopping at the bookshop he bought a book about Broughty Ferry to take out to Felix. After that his next port of call was the antiques emporium which turned out to be an Aladdin's cave of treasure, a jumble of objects of every kind. The idea came to him to buy something for Hamish and Stella, who had been generous with their hospitality not allowing him to contribute to anything, although he had offered. But what on earth would they like? Feeling at a loss he enlisted the help of the man in charge explaining his predicament. Soon he was purchasing a Victorian cairngorm and silver brooch for Stella, and a Georgian noggin glass for Hamish. The latter seemed an extravagance, but he was told it was a rare object, the silver was Edinburgh hallmarked and the glass beautifully engraved, so he hoped it would give pleasure and be useful for his 'wee dram' of an evening.

As he was leaving the shop his mobile gave an annoying ping. It was a message from Hetty which read:

Max says you will be returning from Scotland in three days. Do please break the journey for a night with us. I can collect you from York. Love Hetty.

He thought for a moment and then made the decision. It was just for one night and he was curious to see Hetty in her own environment, so he emailed back saying he would be delighted to accept her invitation and would send her the time of his arrival.

Chapter 8

Yorkshire

Three days later he was once more on the train this time heading south. Looking back over his trip to Scotland Rawlings felt great satisfaction, particularly in his reunion with Stella. The years had simply fallen away which was something he had not expected. It was as if they had been in touch all their lives. He admired the shrewd, clever woman she'd become and was relieved to see that after all that she'd endured, particularly with their mother, she was now settled in such a happy relationship. Maybe her contentment could be partly due to where they lived. He'd felt a great affinity with the place, although this was only his first glimpse of it. Hamish had given him the grand tour of Dundee and it was an impressive city and certainly needed another visit soon. There was going to be a V&A Museum of Design opening later in the year and Felix would enjoy seeing Scott's Antarctic exploration vessel the Discovery. However, it was Broughty Ferry that had really given him pleasure, a place where he could quite happily settle.

The train was stopping. He looked out of the window and saw they had reached Newcastle. Not long now till they arrived in York and his reunion with Hetty. How strange that in all his sixty-six years he'd only known Dagenham, a few parts of London and the small area of the Thames where his houseboat had been moored. The rest of the time had been spent out of the country. Yet here he was hurtling along the entire length of the island, well the East Coast anyway. The West Coast should be tried next. It would be good to take Felix down to Cornwall, or to Wales. This thought produced a pang of irritation. The boy would only be with him a few weeks, little time to fit in all that he wanted to show him.

To his relief they were on the move again. All this sitting did his leg no good at all. He tried to move to a more comfortable position while his thoughts turned again to the Scottish visit. There had been a strange moment during his last evening with Stella. She'd suddenly produced a large scrapbook of press cuttings. To his amazement it appeared to contain everything he'd ever written, carefully cut out and stuck in this book. There was even an account of the journalist award he was given for his coverage of the Siege of Sarajevo. Stella told him, 'Mother was so proud of you and followed everything you did.' It was bewildering. Here was a woman who had rejected him from an early age, and he had certainly despised and neglected her. Yet now he was being told she was proud of him? He'd stammered out his bewilderment to Stella, but with immediate understanding she'd replied, 'Don't forget, her treatment of you when you were a boy. I think she may have felt some guilt about this, but it certainly didn't stop her taking pride in what you were doing and in what you'd achieved.'

He sat back pondering this paradox and then remembered there had been a similar moment when Hugo had told Felix what a successful journalist he was, both clever and brave. This from the son he had always thought disliked and despised him. Yet both the neglected mother and neglected son had apparently been proud of his achievements. It was becoming clear that he lacked any ability to judge people correctly. All his life he had tended to live by the maxim 'If you aren't interested in me, I'm certainly not interested in you.' When he'd wrestled with the subject of his son in the past, he'd always comforted himself with the fact that early on he had made an effort to build a relationship with Hugo, but from a very young age the boy showed no interest in him at all, even expressing animosity. The child already had a doting grandfather and an even more doting mother. Rawlings felt rejected, an outcast. He wasn't needed and consequently removed himself from the scene. Time and again he told himself that the later neglect of his son was mainly due to the fact he'd spent most of his life out of the country, but if he were honest, on the few times he had returned, he'd made no effort to try for a reconciliation. It was only after the arrival of Felix last year that he finally put another human being first. There had been Mia of course, the one long relationship in his life, but that was different. They had been equals, their work being the great bond holding them together, plus the great sex of course. He gave a sigh and couldn't help wondering if Mia had lived after the explosion and he'd been forced to retire because of his injuries, would their relationship have remained as strong? He was inclined to think not. She was too like him, selfish and egocentric. They'd had a grand passion, but that would not have been enough. Mia certainly wouldn't have given up her work to look after him, of that he was certain. He gave a sigh. Life was bloody complicated. A labyrinthian world of complexities.

The train was slowing down. He reached up and pulled

down his suitcase. On to the next experience and quite honestly, he wasn't sure what to expect.

Hetty was on the platform waiting for him, jumping up and down and waving madly to attract his attention. It would have been difficult to miss her. She presented a somewhat eccentric appearance, wearing a long tweed skirt over muddy wellington boots, with an even muddier Barbour, all topped off with a large suffragette hat.

She gave him a bear hug that practically winded him. 'Wonderful you could break your journey Rawlings. How's that leg?' She didn't wait for an answer. 'Transport isn't far. For once I managed to park quite close.'

Transport turned out to be an ancient Volvo also bespattered with mud and as the door opened there was a definite and strong whiff of dog. Rawlings climbed in and she said cheerfully, 'Sorry about the state of the old bus. No point in cleaning it, the dogs soon mess it up again.' After a couple of tries the engine spluttered into life. 'How did you find the train journey?'

'Good.' He gave a chuckle, 'Although rather too much opportunity for introspection.' Before she could make a comment on this, he asked her where they were going. 'I have absolutely no idea where we are, apart from the fact we're in Yorkshire.'

Hetty yanked at the unyielding gears. 'North Yorkshire,' she corrected him. 'We're heading towards Boroughbridge and then onwards to Ripon. We're somewhere in the middle of these two, way out in the sticks . Our nearest village is Skelton on Ure. I'll show you on the map when we get home. It's not far now.'

Rawlings was relieved to hear this. Neither Hetty's driving, nor the ominous smell of burning rubber, gave him any confidence of arriving at all.

'We're coming into Skelton now.' She waved an airy arm. 'On your left is a Georgian windmill. One of the few remaining in the country I believe.' They passed some grand gates. 'That leads to the Newby Hall Estate, which borders onto ours.'

'You have an Estate?'

Hetty laughed. 'A very small and rundown estate, nothing grand I can assure you. Bernard inherited it from his brother. All rather complicated. I'll explain later. Bernard, poor darling, never wanted anything to do with the land. He's an academic and has spent his entire life with his nose in a book. Luckily, his nephew now runs it and lives on one of the farms. We still have the old house and rattle about in it, two old peas in a pod. It's far too large for us of course, and miserably cold in winter. But it suits Bernard, he has peace and quiet for his writing and I have plenty of space for my dogs. I breed border collies. We have four, one dog and three bitches, and batches of puppies about twice a year, which I sell for a good price thank the Lord.'

They had now turned off onto a bumpy track that wound round the hedgerows and except for the latter, would not have been out of place in Afghanistan. Rawlings clung to the side of the seat, fervently hoping this would not be a lengthy drive and greatly relieved when at last there was a sign saying, 'Burwood Manor and Farm'.

'Here we are,' Hetty cried bringing the car to an abrupt halt outside a large, and

what he took to be Georgian, manor house. It was in mellow red brick almost pink with age and one part covered in ivy. It was as far removed as it was possible to be from the pristine and immaculate newbuild he had just visited.

'Leave your luggage,' Hetty commanded. 'Come straight in and we'll have tea.'

She charged on ahead into a large kitchen, complete with a dresser adorned with various china objects and coloured plates, a very old Aga, a huge pine table covered in what Rawlings could only describe as stuff, and several dog baskets dotted around on the floor. 'Sit down and make yourself comfortable,' Hetty said as she pushed some of the clutter away from the top of the table in order to clear space in front of him. 'We'll have tea and then you can tell me all your news. I've even made a cake.'

An hour later, when he'd finished describing his Scottish trip and was about to question Hetty further on their car conversation, the door burst open and a man dressed in old corduroys and a baggy cardigan, who he presumed to be Bernard, came into the room. Without seeming to notice Rawlings he said irritably, 'Hetty I can't find my notes from yesterday. Where on earth did you put them?'

'You had your window open darling, so I put them under the telephone directory on

your desk, to stop them from blowing away.' Bernard gave a nod and turned to leave when Hetty said 'Bernard, this is Rawlings, he's staying the night with us.'

For the first time Bernard looked at Rawlings over the top of his half glasses. 'So you are. Hetty did tell me. I'm a bit forgetful these days. Good to see you. I look forward to making your further acquaintance at supper.' And with that he left the room. Hetty said indulgently, 'Poor old darling. He's up against a deadline bless him. Its these blasted academic books, they always give him trouble. This one's on Elizabethan poets.' She looked out of the window. 'It's still sunny. Shall we go outside? I can show you around the place.'

Rawlings was glad to stretch his legs and get some fresh air. The journey in the car had left him feeling distinctly queasy. Hetty insisted on lending him some wellingtons and as they squelched across the yard, he was greatly relieved she had. Making their way through the muck, they crossed towards some outbuildings, passing a great deal of rusting farm machinery and implements. Finally, they reached one of the larger barns.

'The dog's domain,' she declared as they approached. 'They're only allowed in the house when it's too cold for them out here.' Opening a gate, four black and white collies emerged from inside and rushed towards her across the large yard. She introduced them to Rawlings one by one, giving each a pat and scratch behind the ears. 'This is Dino, the grandson of my very first dog, a wonderful old fellow and a winner of prizes. He's fathered many pups. This is Meg, nearly as old as Dino and an excellent working dog. I lend her to a neighbouring farmer for his sheep. And then there's Molly and the youngest is Maisie, both good breeding bitches. You've just missed Maisie's last batch of puppies. We sold the final one a week ago didn't we girl?' She gave a final affectionate pat. 'Settle back my darlings. I'll feed you later.' They went back out into the yard. 'Have you ever been to any sheep dog trials?' Rawlings shook his head. 'You'd love it,' she told him. 'Maybe on your next visit.'

They left the collies and went back past the house onto a path that led to what he presumed was the garden area, which was as wild and unkempt as the rest of the place. Hetty knocked back the brambles with a stick.

Rawlings' curiosity now got the better of him. 'Tell me, how did Bernard come to inherit the estate?'

They had reached an orchard clearing where there was a wooden seat. It may have had the appearance of Cold Comfort Farm but it was certainly an idyllic spot and the overgrown shabbiness didn't worry him in the least. Hetty suggested they sit down. It was warm in the sun. The fruit trees were in blossom and he could hear the buzzing of bees. Rawlings felt a strange contentment as Hetty began to answer him.

'I met Bernard when he was a penniless bachelor. My father who was a rural dean,

had a parish quite near to this Manor. I knew that Bernard was all set to pursue an academic career, but then one of those family balloons went up. Lance the elder brother suddenly declared he wanted to become an actor, which of course was anathema to his strait-laced parents and worse still, he then told his parents he was gay. It was very brave.' She sighed. 'This was nearly forty years ago and there had been all the publicity about AIDS. Homosexuals were still looked on with suspicion, especially in some quarters. Bernard's father went apoplectic. He was a crabby old man at the best of times and the upshot was he disinherited Lance. So poor old Bernard was landed with the problem, and all the debts. The estate had been run down for a long time and Bernard had no idea about estate management. He struggled for a few years and was about to give up when his nephew Timothy asked if he could come and help. It was a miracle. In no time at all Timothy showed an aptitude for the job and with relief Bernard made over the entire estate to him, just keeping on the manor. My father died soon after this and I was free to

83

marry. We've lived here ever since.'

'What happened to Lance?'

Hetty sighed again. 'Ironically, he died of AIDS.' She gave him a look. 'You never mention your wife. As you have a grandson, I presume there was a Mrs Rawlings?'

'My late wife.' Rawlings took out a cigarette and lit it. 'I married her when I was absurdly young, only twenty two. It was after an extremely brief encounter. Gillian, the only daughter of a wealthy industrialist, announced she was pregnant. Her father made an almost Victorian bargain with me, that if I married his daughter and promised never to cause her hurt or divorce her, he would see me right, his choice of words. He did, and was extremely generous, finally leaving me a large legacy in his will. Gerald was also a man of influence and was instrumental in getting me placed with a national paper.'

'How extraordinary!' Hetty exclaimed, adding, 'as you say, almost Victorian.'

Rawlings finished his cigarette and threw it away. 'I suppose it must sound like that, but in an odd way it worked. I liked Gillian. She was a placid, jolly sort of girl and I thought only interested in horses, but it turned out that she'd desperately wanted a baby and after Hugo was born, she was quite content to give me total freedom. I became a war correspondent soon after this and was away for long periods of time.' He paused. 'During which I did have a long-term relationship with a brilliant photographer. At one point I told Gillian about Mia and suggested she might want a divorce, asking her if there was someone else in her life.'

'There was?'

Rawlings gave a brief smile. 'There was. It was the reason

she became quite hysterical about the idea of a divorce. She owned up to being a lesbian and in a relationship with a woman who I actually knew quite well.'

'Had you ever suspected this?'

'No I hadn't, but looking back I realise I'd probably have soon known if I'd spent more time with her. She told me divorce was out of the question and threatened me with losing my inheritance. I didn't mind about the money, but I could see that for her, our marriage was a good way for her to hide her true sexuality. She was old fashioned and the idea of "coming out" would have appalled her. It also terrified her that Hugo might have found out. A little unfairly he blamed me for what he thought was the abandonment of his mother. But the status quo remained, and things went on as they were until her death from cancer, which was both sudden and quick. I was with her at the end. I'm pleased to say we remained friends throughout our marriage. I can't remember a cross word or argument between us, which can't be said of many marriages. The one casualty in all this was the relationship with my son, who I regret to say, I totally neglected.'

'He was Felix's father?'

Rawlings nodded. 'He and his wife were killed in a car crash last year, which meant I was not only landed with the role of grandfather, but also one of his two guardians. At present he is with his other guardian in Australia.'

His expression indicated he would be saying no more on this subject. The sun was going down behind the trees. Hetty shivered and stood up. 'We'd better go in. It gets chilly rather quickly once that sun disappears.' As they walked back, she added, 'It turned out well for us that Timothy took over the estate, because Bernard and I found early on we were unable to have children. Tim has a lovely wife and family so the place will be in good hands.' She said this quite cheerfully, but Rawlings was left wondering if Hetty regretted having no children. Did her dogs really make up for this?

Almost as if she read his mind, as they neared the house she said, 'Bernard would have been a hopeless father and quite honestly I don't have any motherly instincts. When Bel's little girls were young, I offered to look after them to give her a break. It was a complete nightmare and I arrived home and told Bernard that if there'd been any possibility of my giving birth, I would have had my tubes tied!'

They arrived back and Hetty declared there was only an hour before they were due to eat supper. Bernard liked his meals on time. Rawlings was shown to his room and warned that the wood floor sloped at quite an angle. There was a bathroom down the corridor, and he was also warned that the hot water took rather a long time to arrive. Having tried the shower and watched freezing brown water gushing out, he decided to give it a miss.

Supper was both delicious and entertaining. He'd forgotten Hetty's powers of cuisine, and Bernard was erudite and charming, proving far more talkative at their second meeting. He informed Rawlings he'd greatly enjoyed his book War Memoirs and inquired if there was to be a sequel.

Rawlings frowned. 'My publisher wants me to write a more detailed account of my time spent during the Siege of Sarajevo. I'm resisting this because it is not the book I want to write.'

'Which is?' Bernard leant forward.

Rawlings thought for a moment. 'I really would like to write some sort of examination of the people who suffer mental trauma as a result of modern warfare. Recently there has been progress made with PTSD in the armed forces, but nothing has been done about the suffering of doctors, nurses, ambulance men and yes, reporters, who spend years witnessing the most horrific events, quite apart from working in terrible conditions. I remember surgeons operating with guns held to their heads and cluster bombs falling around them. You learn to live with fear and somehow, you survive all this initially, but it's after returning home that the collapse and the breakdowns happen. I thank God daily I never had to report from either Rwanda or Syria. I would be in a worse state than I already am. The Syrian war is a humanitarian disaster beyond belief and Assad and Putin are most certainly guilty of war crimes.'

His voice was full of anger and Hetty gave her husband a warning glance. Bernard ignored this and asked, 'What are the main symptoms of PTSD?'

Rawlings looked a trifle apologetic. 'Well, outbursts of anger are one of them. Others include flashbacks, nightmares, insomnia, night sweats and much more. It's thought that outside the Army, one in six of those involved in the field of war suffer from it. Many are reluctant to come forward, or admit to it, but instead turn to alcohol, drugs, or gambling. Marriages break up and children get neglected. It's the cause of terrible suffering and misery, sometimes ending in suicide.'

Bernard looked at him with interest. 'It seems it is a book that should be written. Will you do it?'

Rawlings shrugged and said gloomily, 'I doubt it. Publishers are only interested in topics that will sell. But maybe one day I'll get around to it.'

The conversation became more general after this. At

one point, Bernard turned to Hetty and said, 'Don't forget I have Martin coming over tomorrow morning. He's apparently interested in that old mulberry tree in the orchard. He noticed it on his last visit and wants to make a further study.' He explained to Rawlings: 'The man is a local farmer, but his main interest is dendrology, hence the excitement over our tree.'

Hetty looked concerned. 'Do you want to give him lunch darling? I'll be driving Rawlings to York for his midday train.'

Rawlings was immediately apologetic and offered to get a taxi, to which Bernard gave a roar of laughter and said that was completely out of the question, indeed an impossibility. No taxi drivers would venture out as far as this. He assured Hetty a cold collation would be quite sufficient.

Once they'd finished the meal Rawlings presented Bernard with a bottle of malt. He seemed genuinely delighted, insisting on opening it at once. They both had a small glass and then having drained the last drop, he kissed the top of his wife's head and departed for bed. Rawlings also stood up to leave, but Hetty stopped him. 'Unless you're exhausted, I need to talk to you about Bel.' With reluctance he sat down again. Bel wasn't a subject he really wished to discuss. He shifted uneasily in his chair and said grimly, 'I suppose you heard about the minor fracas from Max.'

'Yes, but don't worry about that. We all completely understood. Bel has made similar declarations in the past, mainly for dramatic effect. What is more worrying right now is the increase in her drinking.' She sighed. 'Bernard puts it all down to attention-seeking, but I know it's more complicated than that. I know one shouldn't blame everything on one's parents, but in this case, I think many of Bel's problems stem from her treatment as a child. Our parents were far from ideal. Father was charming to everyone,' she paused, 'except to his immediate family. With his children to be honest, he was demanding, controlling, even cruel. Both boys especially suffered from his treatment of them. Mother was a mercurial, neurotic creature, sometimes bordering on the hysterical. She was beautiful but frail both physically and mentally and looking back on it totally unfit to be a mother. Their marriage was certainly not made in heaven. I can only suppose Father fell for her looks and she for his charm. It would have been hard for him to have found a more unsatisfactory clergyman's wife. Bel, both pretty and precocious was the one Mother adored and pampered, that is until Rupert arrived. The three of us were close in age. Rupert was born when Bel was five but from that moment on, Mother devoted all her attention to her youngest son and poor Bel was completely ignored. It was a terrible shock and hard for her to understand this rejection. It was at that time she became known as a "difficult child". I don't think she ever really recovered and any affection she'd originally had for Mother turned to hatred.'

She paused and Rawlings asked, 'So what happened to her when she became older?'

'Bel was clever. She could have gone to university, but for some reason was against this however much she wanted to get away. Luckily, she somehow managed to get into a good art college. She was never a dedicated art student. For her it was just a means of leaving home.' Hetty shrugged. 'Unfortunately, she was totally unprepared for London life and soon fell in with a bad lot. It was the usual story – the parties, the drugs, rock and roll. The next thing we knew she was pregnant, having had an affair with one of her college tutors. I was despatched to sort things out. This man Roger was a dreadful man and totally unsuitable for her to be with. My parents unfortunately took the moral high ground, and using their rather high-powered family connections they insisted, with many veiled threats, that Roger do the right thing and marry her.' She sighed. 'It was completely the wrong decision for Bel, and I tried to tell them that, but they wouldn't listen. So, the marriage went ahead, and Poppy arrived a few months later, and soon after that Esther. Two babies in two years and Bel was then only twenty one...' Her voice trailed away.

'I presume it was a disaster?'

'Yes, and terrible for us to stand by and watch.' Her voice was scornful. 'Roger behaved badly from the start. He had plenty of affairs and of course there were drugs as well. But even worse than that, he was an abusive and controlling bully. At first it was only mental abuse, but when it turned physical, she and the girls were in danger and it became obvious even to Bel that she had to end it. By this time Mother had died. She'd always had a weak heart and after Rupert's departure she just faded away. Father was too wrapped up in his own miseries to worry about Bel, so Max and I were once again despatched to sort it out. This time it was mainly down to Max because I was in Yorkshire looking after Father. It took ten difficult years of struggle and hardship for Bel to turn her life around, but she did. A lucky break came when she helped a friend who was a well-known interior decorator. Bel found she had a gift for this kind of work and in no time at all set up on her own.'

'Is that how she met Clive?'

'Yes. She was doing up his new gastro-pub.' She paused again. 'Clive isn't exactly my cup of tea, but I think he's been good for Bel. He gave a stable home to the two girls who rather miraculously survived all this and are now doing well. She also has the two boys. On the surface it all looks great; beautiful home, plenty of money, four lovely children, wonderful holidays etc., but just lately the old cracks are beginning to show.'

'The drinking?'

Hetty nodded. 'That, and generally unpredictable behaviour.' She looked at him. 'While you were in Scotland, we had a family meeting. Bel agreed to go into rehab for a month. I think the only reason for this is the fact she has a major assignment coming up and doesn't want to mess it up.'

Rawlings felt selfishly relieved at this news. By the time she returned from rehab he would have left for Australia. All the same, he was perturbed by Hetty's description of their family life and of Bel's ordeals, both as a child and in her first marriage.

*

The return drive proved less of a nightmare. Just as well because Rawlings had not slept well. The bed had felt lumpy and he'd been cold. Also, he couldn't get the story of the Winterton childhood and in particular Bel's suffering, out of his head. Consequently, he didn't feel much like talking, which didn't matter in the least because Hetty kept up her chatter the entire way. At one point she said, 'I do envy you the reunion with your sister and am so relieved to hear you say that the years just rolled away. I long for Rupert's return and hope it will be just the same with us.'

Rawlings felt prompted to ask a question. 'What was the reason for Rupert leaving home?'

A long account followed but the gist was once again the tyrannical father. Rupert had been sent down from Oxford after only two terms and refused to contemplate a return. After a ferocious row and hysterics from their mother, he left the house vowing never to return. Hetty made some excuses for her father, saying he was a brilliant man who had been overlooked for preferment and this had turned him bitter and resentful. It was also pretty clear, reading between the lines, that his marriage to a febrile, fragile and demanding woman, had been a mistake, but Rawlings couldn't help feeling there was something horribly hypocritical in the way he'd presented such a caring image to his parishioners, yet was a cruel tyrant inside his own household. To him it was also odd that Hetty had looked after her father until he died and maintained a kind of loyalty to the end. Was she blind to his faults? Didn't she realise the damage he'd inflicted? Rawlings decided to find out more from Max. For some strange reason, the Winterton family held a fascination for him.

Chapter 9

Return to London

His week away had been an interesting one but also exhausting, so Rawlings was happy to be back. It was an added pleasure to relax in his now finished flat. Bel had done an excellent job and carried out his every instruction. All that was left for him to do was unpack the boxes in store and make the place feel his own, a task he was childishly excited about. It was all such a new experience for him. So far there had been silence from upstairs and he presumed Max must be away, which was a slight relief. Much as he loved them, he felt he'd had enough of the Winterton family just for the moment.

After putting down the last Afghan rug he declared the place finished and lying back on the comfortably large sofa he studied the room with satisfaction. Bel had chided him for his lack of pictures, but the truth was he didn't have any. As he informed all who asked, it was difficult to collect works of art in war zones. In any case one wall was entirely covered in books, another was taken up with the windows leading out into the garden. The only possible picture space was above the fireplace and he was determined to keep this blank and uncluttered. His one decorative piece was an Art Nouveau bust of a woman, which he'd bought in a moment of extravagance at an antiques fair on one of his rare trips to England. It was a thing of beauty and gave him pleasure. It now resided on a pedestal in the corner behind the long elm table. Unlike Hetty's kitchen table, this one was devoid of ornament or clutter of any kind. It was such an elegant piece of furniture he was content to leave it unadorned. The only clutter in the room was on his desk, by the window. He glanced at the papers and letters waiting for his attention and made a mental note to ring the office and find out how poor Jolyon was doing. He fervently hoped he was on the road to recovery because he really hadn't warmed to the fierce and ungiving Sheila.

The doorbell sounded and Rawlings frowned. His food delivery had arrived yesterday and there was nobody else who knew he was in residence. Grudgingly he climbed off the sofa and padded over to the door. A beaming Max stood in front of him clutching a bottle of champagne. Walking past Rawlings, he put the champagne on the table, and then walked round the room making his inspection. Rawlings waited for the verdict.

'Bel was right. It is minimalist, but altogether splendid. In fact, I can find no fault. Are you pleased?' He threw himself beside Rawlings on the sofa.

'Yes, I am. Bel has done a great job.' He paused. 'How is she by the way? Hetty said she'd gone into rehab.'

Max nodded. 'For a month. At huge expense. She took some persuading but finally agreed much to everyone's relief. I was so bloody exhausted by the whole thing that I took myself off to see my lady and get rehab of my own, only got back this morning. I'm dying to know how you found Hetty and Bernard? Aren't they a priceless pair?'

'They are charming and yes, mildly eccentric. I enjoyed my short stay…'

Max broke in, 'For all their eccentricity it's the two of them that always sort out our family problems. Bernard is especially wise.' He looked at Rawlings. 'How about a pre-housewarming drink?'

'Pre?' Rawlings queried.

'Well yes. You have that large dining table and Bel told me you asked for eight of everything, so the very least you can do is throw a supper party.'

Rawlings flinched at this suggestion but obediently went into the kitchen where there were indeed eight champagne glasses. He took two back into the room. Max informed him that the bottle was cold and without more ado they were sitting back on the sofa sipping the bubbly.

Rawlings frowned. 'The one thing I need in this room is somewhere to put drinks.'

'We can put our glasses down on this elegant coffee table.'

'No, I mean bottles and glasses for when I entertain. I don't want to keep going to the kitchen.'

Max chuckled. 'Bel told me she'd put in a hidden shelf that pulls down in the middle of the bookshelves, absolutely made for your drinks table.' Leaping to his feet he went over to a panel in the bookcase which Rawlings hadn't noticed. Max pulled on a small brass button and a shelf came down, firmly held by strong brass hinges.

'That woman is a genius,' Rawlings murmured.

Max sat down again. 'It's why she earns the big bucks.'

Rawlings replenished their glasses and put the bottle on his newly acquired drinks table. Max gave him a quizzical look. 'Were you aware there's to be a Royal wedding this weekend?'

'You mean Harry and Meghan?' Rawlings shrugged.

'Rather difficult to avoid, but I can't say it has affected me greatly.'

'Well you have an invitation from Clive. He's invited people over to watch it on his mega screen and then have a lunch.' He could see Rawlings hesitate. 'Don't worry, Bel won't be around, and Clive really does want to meet you.'

'Then it would be churlish of me to refuse.'

Max looked pleased, but later that night Rawlings felt he might have made a mistake.

*

The day of the wedding turned out fine, almost hot. They went in Max's car – to celebrate him getting back his licence – and arrived at a large, detached house in an elegant square of similar white stucco houses. Rawlings imagined they would certainly need big bucks to own this kind of property.

'One of Chiswick's most elegant squares,' Max informed him. 'Clive was lucky enough to pick it up before the big property boom. It's worth millions now.'

They walked up the steps and rang the front doorbell. It was immediately opened by a small, almost naked child, who turned and ran away leaving them to make their own way in. They followed the noise into a large living room which was packed with people. Rawlings recognised Clive at once. He made his way towards them, casually dressed in beige chinos, loafers, and a white linen shirt. Rawlings was determined not to make any more snap judgements but couldn't help noting that Clive's casual clothes were definitely designer, and certainly not cheap.

'Good to meet you at last.' He shook Rawlings by the

hand. 'I didn't hear you arrive.'

Rawlings thought he could detect traces of Essex in his voice, despite the exaggerated disguise.

'The door was opened by Koshi,' Max said and turning to Rawlings explained, 'Koshi is Poppy's son. She's married to a Syrian doctor.'

'Let me introduce you to some of the gang,' Clive said. 'Most of them are in the television room next door and you can meet them later. I think the wedding kicks off in about half an hour.'

He moved with ease across the room making the introductions. A smooth operator Rawlings decided. He was first introduced to Poppy, a languid replica of Bel, who looked at him curiously and forced him to wonder what her mother had said about him. The other daughter, Esther, was quite different; small, bespectacled, with a concentrated expression. She looked as if she felt uncomfortable with this social scene. She also showed complete indifference to being introduced to Rawlings.

A gangly youth burst into the room. 'Dad, can someone please come in and control Koshi? He's throwing cushions about and being a fucking menace.'

Rawlings was mildly shocked by the swearing, but nobody else seemed to notice.

Poppy moved across the room. 'Sorry Zach' she said, adding crossly, 'where the hell is his father? I thought he was minding him.' She made a quick exit and Clive laughed, while handing drinks to Max and Rawlings. 'Poor Zach. My youngest doesn't appreciate being put in charge of an over-excited small boy.'

Rawlings moved over to the window and looked out

over the extensive garden. With some amusement he noticed Poppy dragging her small son towards a man, obviously her husband, who was having a quiet smoke. They proceeded to have words. She then left the boy with him and walked swiftly back into the house. The husband threw his cigarette away and led Koshi down to a bench where they both sat. Rawlings felt some sympathy. If the man was Syrian, he probably had no interest in an English Royal wedding.

These observations were distracted by Clive calling for everyone's attention and instructing them to make their way into the television room. With some reluctance Rawlings followed the others, making sure he stood at the back. The screen was of cinema proportions, so he had a perfect view. With some indifference he watched the proceedings begin and then, greatly to his surprise he found himself profoundly moved as the bride walking on her own made her way up the aisle, to the beautiful sound of a soprano singing a Handel aria. While others in the room chatted about Meghan's dress, he closed his eyes and allowed the music to sweep over him. On the service went, and his interest was held until the fire and brimstone American bishop launched into battle. Rawlings found he couldn't stomach this and quietly left everyone to it, making his way into the garden. There was no sign of Poppy's husband or Koshi. He rather presumed they'd gone out somewhere, so he made his way to the bench and sat in the sun. After a few moments Max joined him.

Rawlings smiled. 'Was the fiery preacher too much for you as well?'

Max nodded. 'Five minutes would have been enough, but after ten I couldn't stand it. Someone should stop him. He's likely to go on for hours. The Queen and Prince Philip are looking furious.' He looked at Rawlings. 'Are you going to cope with the lunch?'

'Of course,' and then remarked, 'Clive is younger than I expected.'

This drew a smile from Max. 'He's one of those infuriating men who never gets old. Like Cary Grant. Come to think of it, you're a bit like that. Clive's the same age as Bel. They both had their fiftieth birthdays a couple of years back and that was some bash I can tell you. It took me weeks to recover.' He paused. 'I have little in common with the man, his conversation is full of hedge-funds and offshore accounts. His friends are the same. Clive is that common phenomenon, the self-made man, starting with nothing and now a millionaire. I suspect some of his methods might be devious, but I have to admit, he's been a good husband for Bel, in spite of all her problems. And loyal, I think.' Rawlings wondered if this rather ambiguous statement meant he hadn't had affairs, but he let Max continue. 'He's also been great with the two girls, who were messed up at the time Bel met him. He's a conscientious father to the boys as well, you know the sort, always there for rugger matches and that sort of thing.' He pulled out a cigarette and lit it. 'Of course, having all that money must have helped. Did you notice the pictures? All original and worth a fortune. Clive fancies himself as a collector. Not sure he actually likes any of them.'

Rawlings was silent, but privately thought Clive appeared a fish out of water among the mild eccentrics that made up the Winterton clan. The unworldly Hetty had said as much. He imagined their politics differed as well. Clive, he felt sure, would be an ardent Brexiteer.

As they drove home later in the day, he felt some relief that he wasn't put through the third degree that he'd been rather dreading. The conversation at lunch was mostly taken up with the post-mortem of the wedding to which he didn't feel he had a great deal to contribute. Clive remained throughout a charming and generous host, but Rawlings couldn't help observing family tensions, particularly between Esther and her stepfather. When he questioned Max about this, he was given a vague reply saying it was Esther's way to scowl at everyone, adding as if by way of an excuse, 'She's incredibly bright. A true academic, but outside her books she seems to find the world a problem. Bel is the only person she really relates to,' here he gave a chuckle, 'unlike Poppy. Thank God it's been better since her marriage to Clive, but before that the rows between the two of them would be deafening. A pity you didn't meet Essam Heffez, Poppy's husband. He's a charming chap and a clever surgeon or so I'm told. ENT. Useful if any of us gets ill. Essam has been a steadying influence on the volatile Poppy.'

Rawlings reflected that in the last two weeks he'd seen more of marriage and families than he'd experienced in his entire life. He thought grimly that his next family encounter would be the Australian lot and wondered how that would turn out. Naturally, he wanted Felix to be happy and settled, but the recent Skypes hadn't given him great confidence.

An hour after reaching home he had a message from Sheila, giving him her home number and telling him to ring her urgently. This sounded ominous so he called straight away. She thanked him for getting back quickly and then briefly and unemotionally told him that Jolyon was suffering from pancreatic cancer, had gone downhill fast and was now in a critical condition. Apparently, he needed to see Rawlings and she suggested he should make it a priority. This was a shock. How had the deterioration happened so quickly, and why had that bloody woman not told him sooner? He rang the Sister in the hospital and an arrangement was made to see Jolyon the following day.

Chapter 10

A Hospital Visit

Jolyon unsurprisingly, was not in one of the larger London NHS hospitals, but a secluded and private nursing home in St John's Wood. Rawlings met with the Sister who informed him that Jolyon was expecting him and that this was one of his better days, although he shouldn't stay long. Rawlings had been dreading this encounter. He had a loathing of hospitals and disliked being with sick people, but nothing prepared him for the sight that met him on entering the room. A small and shrunken man not recognisable as Jolyon, lay propped up on the pillows, his eyes hollowed, his skin parchment in colour, the many tubes coming out of him wired up to machines on the wall which gave out unnerving bleeping sounds. Rawlings had a sudden vision of Gollum from The Lord of the Rings.

He sat down in the chair beside the bed and said quietly, 'My dear fellow I had no idea things were so bad. You should have told me sooner.'

Jolyon gave a bleak smile. 'No point in worrying you. In any case, Sheila said you were away.'

'Are you in pain?'

A weak shake of the head. 'They keep me well doped up with morphine.' He raised a frail hand and wiped his lips with his finger. Rawlings waited for him to go on. The voice was thin, and words came out in a series of gasps as if each syllable were an effort. 'I need to talk to you about the next book. Have you thought any more about it?'

Rawlings shifted uneasily in his chair. The man was dying. He really didn't want to deliver bad news. He began slowly, 'As I explained when I last saw you, it is not the book I wanted to write,' he hesitated then added, 'but it's undeniably a good offer and I could probably find a compromise that would suit us both.'

Jolyon turned his gaze on him. 'Didn't you have a love affair in Sarajevo?'

Rawlings frowned. 'Well I had one that started there. It lasted until Mia was killed in the same explosion that I was in. I escaped merely with a blown-up leg. I'm not sure I'd want to use her as the focus of the book. It's all too personal.' He thought for a moment searching for inspiration. 'What about Surviving the Sarajevo Siege? In that way I could cover all angles.'

'That would do.' Jolyon closed his eyes only to immediately open them again. 'Ever thought of writing a novel Rawlings?'

This produced a harsh laugh. 'Never! I'm certain I could never be a novelist. It's hard enough writing facts. The thought of writing from imagination and inventing characters would utterly daunt me. Besides, I have no great love for my fellow man so why should I want to write about them?' Jolyon smiled at this. Rawlings hesitated and then decided to mention the subject. 'There is a book I do want to write,' he checked that Jolyon was listening, 'it's about the effect of PTSD on those involved in war zones. Maybe if I am co-operative about the Sarajevo book, they might allow me to do this?'

'Very likely,' Jolyon murmured, adding 'be a good fellow

and try to work with Sheila. I assure you I'm leaving you in good hands.'

Rawlings felt at a loss, Jolyon was tiring fast. 'I'm going to miss you Jolyon' he said, adding with a smile, 'especially all those dinners at the Garrick.'

The frail man gave a sigh. 'Me too. What fun times they were. No regrets. I've had a great life and met many wonderful people. You included my dear. I have such hopes for you Rawlings,' and he added somewhat enigmatically, 'you seem to have turned a corner…'

His voice drifted away. Rawlings felt he should leave, but then again, he wasn't sure. The man appeared to have fallen asleep, but he might wake up again and expect him to be there. He sat for a long time just watching him, but when there was no movement, he finally decided he should leave, kissed him on the forehead and walked quietly from the room.

It was one of those wet, windy days and the rain was falling heavily. By the time he reached the carpark Rawlings was drenched. He turned on the ignition and then almost at once he switched it off again and dropped his head in his hands. The sight of the dying man had left him in shock. He thought of those dinners at the Garrick Club with Jolyon in his element holding court, talking loudly in his high squeaky voice, always wearing a bright waistcoat and elegant cravat, waving at all and sundry as they passed by. He was one of those gregarious men who knew everyone, always ebullient and full of life. And now? A lifeless skeleton. He could only have been in his fifties. Far too young to have fallen into that last scene of all, sans eyes, sans teeth, sans everything.

Rawlings began to shiver, started up the engine and

turned the heaters full on. The windows soon steamed up and there was the unmistakeable smell of wet wool. Forced to drive slowly because of limited visibility, he made his way towards Marble Arch and then on sudden impulse he turned the car towards the Frontline Club. He hadn't been there in a long while. A quiet drink was what he needed now before returning home. Mid-afternoon was always a good time when it wasn't too busy, but today as he made his way up the stairs to the member's bar, to his surprise he could hear a great deal of noise coming from the room. On entering he immediately noticed a group of people at a table on the far side, some of whom he recognised. Max was among them and from quick observation he could see he was already drunk. Rawlings hesitated wondering whether to make a quick exit, but it was too late. Max had seen him and called him over. Reluctantly he joined them.

'Hey Rawlings, good of you to join us. Didn't know you'd heard.'

'Heard?'

'About Dan.'

Rawlings was bewildered. 'What about Dan? I haven't heard anything.'

Someone he vaguely recognised as a reporter called Phil cut in, 'He committed suicide, yesterday. Walked into the sea. Beth said he left his clothes in a neat pile on the beach.'

Another person asked, 'Did he leave a note?'

Phil nodded grimly. 'Apparently it just said he was sorry, he'd had enough.'

Rawlings felt numb with shock. It was as if all his emotions were used up and he could feel no more. Dan Kowalski had been with him during the Sarajevo Siege. They were about the same age and he remembered him as a tough little guy, bearded, with a piratical look. He'd had a great talent for languages which proved useful at the time. One night they'd got talking and Dan told him that his father was Polish, his mother English and his life had been divided between the two countries, until by the time he went to university he'd decided to settle in England. Rawlings remembered Dan being frustrated at being stuck in Sarajevo because he'd just got engaged to a girl in Cornwall and was hoping to make a home down there. After the siege ended Rawlings lost touch with him but read some of Dan's coverage from Rwanda and Somalia. Tough places to be reporting from. They must have taken their toll.

'The real tragedy is,' someone said, cutting across his thoughts, 'Dan was taking a sabbatical. He'd been diagnosed with PTSD and Beth insisted he took time out in order to recover. I hadn't seen him for about three months and presumed he was now back in Cornwall.'

Difficult to let go and be alone with the nightmares Rawlings thought. Those first months could be hell.

'He'd been covering ISIS. The last report I read was about a bombed-out hospital in Aleppo. There were terrible descriptions of the kids...'

Max stood up swaying. 'More drinks anyone?'

Rawlings quickly joined him. 'Let me help,' he said. He accompanied Max to the bar, which was just as well as Max had difficulty remembering the order. Once the drinks were sorted, Rawlings said 'I'm not staying Max, I need to get back. I only came in for a quick drink.' He gave him a searching look. 'Did you come by car?' Max gave a bleary nod. Rawlings spoke urgently. 'Do not drive back.

You don't want to lose your license again. You've only just got it back. Stay the night here or get an Uber. But do not drive. Promise me Max?' Rawlings was given another bleary nod. He carried the drinks over to the table then made his excuses, adding, 'I'm really sorry about Dan. It's terrible news. He was a good man. Max will let me know if there is to be some sort of party for him.'

And with that he made a quick exit.

He drove back slowly, trying to put his mind into neutral. Switching on the radio, he hoped the music would distract him no matter what was playing, just so long as he didn't have to think. He'd nearly reached home when quite suddenly a piano piece caught his attention, not just because of its beauty, but because it was the piece of Schumann that Mia had played after the terrible day when they had visited the bombed-out Sarajevo orphanage. It was also the moment he had fallen so deeply in love with her. But it wasn't Mia that now caused the tears to run down his cheeks. It was a vision that haunted him, of the naked, bearded man, with despair in his heart, walking into the cold grey waters of the Atlantic Ocean, desperate to seek oblivion from man's inhumanity to man.

Chapter 11

A Supper Party

Rawlings looked out onto the road the following morning and saw with relief that Max's car wasn't there. At least he'd managed to forestall him driving home drunk. Now he had to steel himself for his next task which was to ring Sheila. He sat staring out at the garden for a while, trying desperately to work out what to say. With a sigh he reluctantly dialled her number. To his surprise she sounded less abrasive than usual. With a certain amount of reproach in his voice he said he wished he'd known earlier about Jolyon's decline. She explained it had been Jolyon's choice to keep the severity of his illness from everyone, but his deterioration had happened so rapidly even she had been shocked. Her voice was sad. 'None of us in the office can quite believe he's dying.'

Rawlings took a deep breath. 'I think you know he's keen for me to do the Sarajevo book,' he paused, 'and in the circumstances I don't think I can really refuse him.' Then he added firmly, 'However, I did explain to Jolyon there was another book that I was keen to write,' again he paused waiting for a reaction but none came so he persevered, 'this would be about PTSD suffered by those caught up in war zones; not the armed forces which everyone already knows about, but others, like the correspondents, reporters, doctors and ambulance drivers. There are thousands of sufferers and nobody ever hears about them.' Sheila still made no comment so he finished with a note of defiance, 'Jolyon thought that some sort of deal could be made with the publishers.'

He now waited for her reaction. There was a long silence and he wondered if he'd been cut off, but then she spoke slowly as if she were thinking it out. 'That might be a possibility and I would certainly do my best to try and make it work. It would be helpful if you could send me your ideas and outline for the Sarajevo book first, before I approach them about the other book.'

Rawlings felt encouraged. 'Yes, I will certainly do that but at the end of this week I'm due to fly out to Australia to see my grandson and will be gone nearly three weeks. I can work on ideas while I am away and send something to you on my return if that's all right?'

Sheila seemed to accept this, saying she looked forward to it. He was just thankful that he'd bought himself a little more time. Before ringing off he said, 'If anything should happen to Jolyon while I'm away, will you let me know? I'm afraid I won't be able to get back for...'

Sheila cut in quickly. 'That's no problem. Jolyon has been very practical about this. He only wants a small funeral with immediate family. But he has given instructions for a party to be held later, as a celebration of his life.' Rawlings smiled. Knowing Jolyon, this would certainly be some party.

Just after finishing this call he heard Max's car draw up outside and went out to meet him, inviting him in for a coffee.

'You look all in,' he said as Max slumped onto the sofa. 'Was it a late night?'

Max nodded, seeming unable to speak. Rawlings sat down

opposite him. 'I'm sorry about leaving so abruptly yesterday. I'd just returned from the hospital, visiting my agent who is dying. It was all very upsetting, so I was in no way prepared for the news of Dan as well.'

Max drained his cup and Rawlings poured him another. 'I don't really remember much about the evening,' he admitted with a bleak smile. 'Someone must have found me a room.'

He cut a sad figure, rather like a deflated Mr Toad.

Rawlings felt concern. 'Did you know Dan well?'

Max nodded. 'Yes, he'd become a good friend, although not from work.' He was silent and Rawlings waited for further explanation, unsure if he was capable of it. Max finally made an effort, each word seeming to cause him pain. 'Over the last couple of summers Clive and Bel have taken a house in North Cornwall and I joined them. I met Dan and Beth then. Last time I saw them Beth was expecting a child. That is why his suicide is such a bloody shock. He seemed so happy about it…' His voice trailed away.

Rawlings removed the cup and said briskly, 'Go and get some sleep,' adding as an afterthought, 'if I were you, I'd drink plenty of water first.'

Max started to leave. At the door he turned. 'Bernard and Hetty are coming to stay tomorrow for the rest of the week. I know they'd like to see you.'

Rawlings gave a frown. 'I leave for Australia in four days,' and then on sudden impulse said, 'why don't you bring them down here for supper, before I leave?'

Max gave a feeble nod and made his uncertain way up the steps to the house.

*

Hetty walked round the flat, giving squeaks of delight. Finally, she sat down. 'Lovely, lovely, lovely!' she declared. 'I love it all, except perhaps the absence of pictures.'

Bernard gave a chuckle. 'You could let Clive lend you one from his collection. I'm sure he wouldn't notice its absence.'

'Really darling,' Hetty sounded cross, 'what an absurd idea. Clive gathers art works for financial reasons. Rawlings would be quite different.'

Rawlings sighed, yet again explaining it had been difficult to collect pictures when working abroad. 'In any case one wall is full of books, there's not much space left for works of art.'

Bernard murmured, 'I think the Sydney Smith quote is apt, "no furniture so charming as books."'

This produced a smile from Rawlings. 'I believe the end of that quotation is, "even if you never open them or read a single word."'

Bernard peered at him over the top of his half glasses. 'I can't believe that's true of you.'

'Some books have been more read than others,' Rawlings told him. 'I have certain favourites I dip into frequently. I think you'd find my tastes a little eclectic. Having never had a university education I rely on friends to make recommendations.' He paused. 'Books were a rare luxury during the Sarajevo Siege, we just shared whatever we had. It's how I came to know about Sydney Smith. I was given a collection of his writings. Apart from him, there are a few other books I frequently read.'

Bernard showed interest. 'Such as?'

Rawlings thought for a moment. 'Well the war poets for a start, particularly Edmund Blunden. Most of my reading is non-fiction. I'm not good with novels, except on long journeys.'

Max had been sitting silently through this exchange. His usually florid complexion was pale, and Rawlings presumed he was still recovering from the evening at the Frontline Club. Bernard was about to continue their conversation when Max suddenly stood up and declared he had forgotten to bring a bottle of wine with him. Before Rawlings could protest that there was no need, Max had left.

Hetty looked after her departing brother with concern. 'What on earth is the matter with Max? He's not himself at all.'

Rawlings explained about Dan's death and how it had involved a long session in the Frontline Club, adding that Max probably still had a touch of alcohol poisoning.

This drew a sharp comment from Hetty. 'I hope to God we're not going to have two alcoholics in the family, Bel is quite enough. She's the reason we've been summoned south again. Apparently, she now wants to discharge herself early, stating she needs no further treatment and of course, I'm the one who is being despatched to persuade her to stay. It's going to be a difficult task to say the least. She will certainly be at her most obstinate.' Rawlings was selfishly relieved he'd be safely in Australia if Bel did decide to return home. Hetty was now shaking her head. 'I think it's more than that with Max. I noticed his left-hand shaking…'

Bernard intervened. 'That could be the effect of the alcohol Hetty. Taken in excess it does lead to the shakes I believe.' He turned to Rawlings. 'I am sorry about this man Dan, was he a friend of yours as well?'

Rawlings nodded. 'I met him years ago, but I didn't know him as well as Max. I believe he saw quite a lot of Dan and his wife in Cornwall, when he stayed in Clive and Bel's summer house down there.'

Hetty looked alarmed. 'That means Bel will be affected by this man's death as well. I hope to God nobody has told her.'

Any further discussion was stalled by Max's return and the conversation after that became more general. At one point, Bernard turned to Rawlings and said, 'You're a classical music fellow, aren't you?'

Rawlings smiled. 'I love listening to it but I'm no expert and I never learned an instrument. My tastes are really for anything written before 1830. After that I become a little more selective.'

'Do you listen to Elgar?'

Rawlings nodded. 'Some. Why do you ask?'

'Hetty came across this fascinating article the other day about the Enigma Variations. You explain darling.'

Hetty smiled. 'I'm no music expert either but the Enigma Variations have always fascinated me. There are so many theories about what tune Elgar used. In this article the expert, I can't remember his name, has come up with what he says is the definitive answer,' she paused dramatically, 'which is Men of Harlech. The explanation is very complicated, but to an outsider it seems quite plausible. I have listened to the Variations again and I can see what he means, without noticing the rogue E flat, or any other of the details.'

Bernard sounded quite cross. 'These music academics are most tiresome, they over-complicate things. Far better just to listen to the music.'

Hetty gave him a reproachful look. 'At the time you said that even an outsider like you would find the article interesting.'

Her husband smiled. 'Anything for a quiet life darling.'

She laughed. 'You're an old rogue. You know perfectly

well you were as fascinated by finding out the source of the Enigma as I was. And if I may say so, you brought the subject up.'

Rawlings observed this exchange with interest. As a couple they seemed eminently suited and content with each other's company. There was often banter, but no real hostility and it was obvious there was deep affection. Maybe some relationships could work, but only if you found the right person and gave each other enough space. Space was important. That had never been possible with Mia because they worked together, and he was further convinced that had she not died, their relationship would certainly have floundered.

His musings were interrupted by a question from Bernard inquiring whereabouts he was going in Australia. He told them about the Barossa Valley and the winery which was owned by Felix's uncle. Bernard nodded, telling him he had visited that area once and assured Rawlings he would like it.

Max remained silent. Hetty turned to him and said, 'Have you seen Elsa lately Max?'

He gave a start, as if he had been elsewhere. 'Only briefly,' he finally said adding gruffly, 'it didn't seem tactful to stay long. Her husband has vascular dementia and is deteriorating fast. Until this year Elsa always had the freedom to spend as much time away from him as she wanted. We did manage to have our annual holiday in January but since then she hasn't been able to leave him. Her days seem to be spent in finding carers. Not easy where they live…' He broke off and then stood up. 'Apologies but I'm going to leave you. I have some work to do before the morning. Thank you for the supper Rawlings. I'm sure I'll see you before you leave.' He started to go and then addressed Hetty: 'I'll leave the front door on the latch. Just put the lock down when you come in.'

After he'd gone Hetty shook her head. 'Something's definitely not right.'

'This Elsa,' Rawlings said, 'I vaguely knew Max had a woman hidden away but nothing really about her.'

This drew a sigh from Hetty. 'Max's sex life has always been something of a mystery. For a long time, we all thought he was asexual.'

Bernard chuckled. 'I think my love that would mean he was without sexual organs.'

Hetty said a trifle crossly, 'Don't be so pedantic Bernard. You know perfectly well what I mean.' She turned back to Rawlings. 'When he was young, Max really didn't seem to be interested in sex, male or female. Then quite suddenly he produces the exotic Elsa, a Hungarian, beautiful and a successful sculptress.' She turned to Bernard. 'Am I allowed to use that term for a female sculptor?'

'I'm glad you did,' he replied with feeling. 'I am continually irritated by this new affectation of referring to thespians of both sexes as actors. What is wrong with using the perfectly good word actress? I like to know the gender of the person that is being referred to.'

Hetty nodded in agreement and then continued. 'We were all in shock when Max introduced us to Elsa and further surprised to learn she was his mistress. This must have been more than twenty years ago. She was already married by then, to her Bart who was apparently much older than her. One got the definite feeling she'd had to marry in order to get her British passport. According to Max they live in a draughty and decrepit castle in the wilds of Northumbria, but at least it has the vast space in which Elsa can have her studio. She never seems to have any difficulty in escaping to see Max, particularly when having exhibitions. You may have heard of her Rawlings, Elsa Kovács?'

He shook his head. This new insight into Max's life was as unexpected as it was fascinating. 'How did he meet her?'

'At one of her exhibitions. It all happened with almost indecent haste after that and took us totally by surprise. The old Bart doesn't seem to mind about Max and it all appears to be very amicable. I get the impression he's just relieved that Elsa is kept happy. He evidently enjoys Max's company and never complains when they go off on their travels together. There are no children or relations and I gather when the old boy dies the line ends with him.' She frowned. 'I suppose now he's so ill, he's making more demands on Elsa's time. I do hope her relationship with Max hasn't started to unravel, although it might account for his unhappy state.'

Bernard looked concerned. 'You worry too much darling. Rawlings is probably right. Max is recovering from his friend's death along with a rather hefty dose of alcohol.' He patted her hand. 'You have quite enough to worry about already with Bel.'

*

Two days later Rawlings was on the plane bound for Australia. He only saw Max once before his departure, still looking subdued but there was no sign that Rawlings could see of the shaking hand that Hetty had noticed. Bernard was right. She was over-worrying. He was sure all would be back to normal by the time he returned.

Chapter 12

Arrival in Australia

Rawlings was not in the best of states as his plane touched down at Adelaide airport. During the first part of the journey he'd had the misfortune to sit next to a large middle-aged woman who declared herself terrified of flying. When the captain turned the seatbelt sign on because of turbulence she became almost hysterical and Rawlings spent a good deal of time trying to calm her down. In the end he resorted to Bloody Marys and she finally drifted off in an alcoholic haze. After Dubai he had hoped to sleep but his leg became painful and he found it hard to drift off so spent the time working on some ideas for the Sarajevo book, without much success. Consequently, as he stood up to get his luggage from the overhead locker, he felt tired, grumpy and disorientated. Glancing at his watch he saw that it was nearly nine o'clock at night. This might mean Felix would not be there to meet him. Going through immigration took an interminable time but at last he emerged and caught sight of Felix at once. The boy rushed over hugging him so forcefully it almost took his breath away. He ruffled the boy's hair and laughed. 'I do believe you've grown taller in the last six months Felix.'

The stocky man standing beside him, he presumed to be Brad, shook his hand. 'Welcome to Australia, good to see you.

Felix has been bloody excited about this visit I can tell you.'

He took the luggage trolley from Rawlings. 'The wagon isn't far.'

'How's your leg EG?' Felix asked anxiously as Brad strode on ahead.

'Better than it was when you saw me last. Isn't this a bit late for you? I didn't expect to see you until the morning.'

Felix grinned. 'I insisted on coming. I have to leave for school early, so I wouldn't have seen you until the afternoon.'

They reached Brad's station wagon, put in the luggage and Felix was despatched to return the trolley. As they started the journey back Brad said, 'We've put you in the bungalow, to give you a bit of peace from the noisy kids. We built it for my mother after my father died. It's near the house but quite self-contained. When mother passed, we decided to keep it for guests and during the picking months it's useful for the overflow of workers.'

'When are the picking months?' Rawlings inquired.

Brad laughed. 'Don't worry mate you've missed them, so we won't be putting you to work. It was February and March. We also have picking in July and August and then in October into November. I'll take you over to the winery for a good look round as soon as you're over the jetlag.'

Rawlings rather wished Brad didn't call him mate. He gave an inward sigh. The man was very Australian with an extremely ripe accent. It was reassuring that Felix still sounded English.

'How far are you from Adelaide?'

'About seventy five kilometres. At this time of night, it shouldn't take long,' he gave a laugh, 'that is unless we meet a booze bus.'

'Booze bus?'

'The police vehicle used to pick up drunks or catch drunk drivers.'

There was no sign of a booze bus and the journey did indeed pass quickly. Felix fired endless questions at him but apart from telling him everyone was well and sent love, Rawlings told him he would give him all the news when he returned from school.

They reached a signpost marked Angaston.

'This is our main town, we're only a few minutes away now,' Brad told him. 'The boy's school is about ten minutes by car but takes a bit longer on the bus.'

They turned into a long drive and arrived at the house where they were greeted by a large barking dog.

'See your grandfather indoors Felix. I'm going to take the luggage up to the bungalow.'

'I expect Sarah's in the kitchen,' Felix said.

She was and greeted him warmly. He sat down at the kitchen table as she said, 'I know this has been exciting for you Felix, but you'd better go to bed now. You do have school in the morning.' Felix look disappointed and she laughed. 'It's the last day of the week tomorrow, then you can see your grandfather the whole weekend.'

The boy nodded and started to go. 'It's really good you're here EG.'

Rawlings smiled. 'I look forward to catching up on all the news tomorrow.'

The boy reluctantly took his leave and minutes later Brad returned.

'Ella sleeping OK?' His wife nodded and he turned to Rawlings. 'I expect you'd like a cold one, or maybe a glass of wine?'

Rawlings presumed the former was beer, so he accepted a glass of wine. Sarah also offered him biscuits and cheese, but by now he was rather beyond food. As soon as was politely possible, he made his excuses and Brad led him the short distance to the bungalow. It had everything he needed, and he was thankful not to be sleeping in the middle of the house. This was a place where he could talk to Felix on his own and find out how he really was. At first glance the boy looked well, but Rawlings had noticed a wariness in the eyes that had not been there before. The other main change was in Sarah. This was more striking. Gone was the jolly, healthy woman he had first met. Now she looked thin, drained, and there were strands of grey in her hair that he didn't remember her having. No doubt the reasons would emerge. He just hoped that she wasn't ill, or that having Felix was one child too many.

He woke the next morning having slept long and deeply. After a shower and shave, he made his way down to the main house and into the kitchen. He guessed the boys were long gone, but Brad was still there. Sarah was feeding the baby Ella who was in a highchair.

'Glad you could join us this early,' Brad greeted him with mildly annoying heartiness. 'We hoped we'd get a chance to have a quick word with you before I had to leave for work.'

Rawlings sat at the table and a mug of coffee was poured for him. Was it early? He had lost all sense of time and left his watch beside the bed. In the daylight he could see that Brad and Sarah were looking tense. Rawlings wondered nervously what was coming. They both seemed reluctant to speak.

'Is there a worry with Felix?' he asked. Quick reassurance was given on this both shaking their heads vehemently. It was Brad who finally spoke.

'The thing is our situation has changed a bit and we wanted to put you in the picture,' he paused and then seemed to plunge in on an almost prepared speech. 'In early January, little Ella here was diagnosed with a heart defect...'

'Coarctation of the aorta,' Sarah intervened.

Brad gave a rueful grin. 'I can never remember all the medical terms. Maybe you explain Sarah. You'll be better at it than I am.'

She nodded. 'Ella has a narrowing of the aorta, which means she has less blood flow to the rest of her body. We noticed various symptoms over Christmas and into the New Year. She had a slight blue tinge to her skin and kept becoming drowsy, kind of unresponsive. I was especially worried because she was a premature baby, so I took her to our doctor here. He immediately sent her to a children's heart specialist in Adelaide...' Her voice trailed away, and Brad took over.

'The upshot is that Ella needs a heart operation. It has a complicated name, but as I understand it the poor little mite will have a balloon inserted into the aorta to stretch and widen the valve. We're hoping this will right the problem. The operation will be done in August. Sarah will take her to Adelaide and stay with her in the hospital.'

Sarah stood up and went to take Ella out of her highchair. 'I'm going to put her down for a rest. I won't be long.'

Brad watched his wife depart. 'It's been a shock to us both as you can imagine, but a bloody great strain on Sarah. She doesn't really like leaving the baby for long and is up and down all night checking on her.'

Rawlings was also shocked by the news. 'My dear man I'm so sorry. I feel we have added an extra strain on your family by landing Felix on you...'

'Oh no mate, don't get me wrong,' Brad was quick to reassure him. 'We love having the boy here. He's a great lad and already part of the family.' Here he gave an abrupt laugh. 'Between you and me it's been good for Shane who's always been a bit of a bludger. No, the reason we are telling you is because our plans have had to change and that involves Felix.' He looked directly at Rawlings. 'I know he was due to spend the summer with you, but we were wondering if this could be postponed until nearer Christmas?' Rawlings felt his heart sink, but let Brad continue. 'The fact is, Sarah will be away for the whole of August, so I've booked a place to take the boys. It is owned by a friend of mine who runs a holiday camp with loads of activities, and they do these planned wild escapes. It will be a great experience and I know Felix will love it.' He gave Rawlings a chance to say something but as he didn't he explained further, 'Quite honestly it would be a logistical problem for us, what with Sarah in Adelaide and me at the camp, to get Felix packed up and taken to the airport. In fact, it would be an impossibility. It seemed the best solution all round to take him with us.'

He looked at Rawlings who asked, 'Does Felix know about this?'

Brad looked a little awkward. 'I'm afraid we had to tell him the plan when we broke the news about Ella to the boys. But I told him to talk it over with you when you arrived.'

Sarah came back into the room and Brad stood up. 'I have to go.' He gave his wife a peck on the cheek and then turned to Rawlings. 'I thought you might like to see the winery next week, one day when the boys are at school.'

'I look forward to it.' Rawlings said.

After he'd gone, he sat with Sarah for a while. Without doubt she was exhausted.

'Do you have anyone to help you?' He felt concerned.

She gave a weary smile. 'Yes, I have two women who come in. But I'm the only one who can deal with Ella.' Looking at him she said, 'I know this isn't quite what we planned but you must believe me we love having Felix with us. He's really settled in here and is doing well at school.' She gave a little laugh. 'Poor Shane is way behind him. Felix is now in the class above him,' and then added almost defensively, 'Shane has always preferred sport to school-work, his great passion is rugby…'

'I'd like to go over and see the school,' Rawlings cut in. 'Would it be possible to make an appointment with his teacher for next week?'

Sarah nodded. 'I'll do that. You'll like her. She's recently come out from England and gets on well with Felix. You can either take my car if I'm not using it, or there's the bus or taxi.' She looked at him. 'I was wondering if you'd like to take my car today. Angaston is a neat place to explore.'

This suggestion suited Rawlings. He needed time on his own to digest this latest news before meeting up with Felix.

Angaston was only a short distance from the house and Sarah was right, it was a 'neat' town. Easy to understand its popularity with the tourists, surrounded as it was by wineries. He parked in Murray Street which appeared to be the main street and set about exploring. Walking past the many food shops with their displays of local produce, he found a small bookshop and purchased a tourist guide of the area. At this point his leg, having not yet recovered from the long flight, forced him to find a café to sit down. There was a chill in the air, but he bravely decided to stay outside, ordered a bowl of home-made soup and started to read about the place. Angaston, he read, was considered an English town, the first settlers being Cornish miners. It apparently differed from other towns in the Barossa Valley which were German in origin, their first settlers being Lutherans. Rawlings gave an inward chuckle. They all sounded bloody Australian wherever they came from, and then chided himself for being prejudiced about the accent. It was an accent that had always jarred on him since the time a reporter from Sydney was with them in Iraq and had been thoroughly loud and obnoxious.

He read on. The area around Angaston had originally been occupied by Aborigines but they were wiped out by disease and attacks from white surveyors. He sighed. 'Twas ever thus, the curse of the white man.' Having read enough he closed the book. It was not exactly warm, and he was beginning to regret he'd elected to sit outside. It must be their autumn, if they had seasons at all, which meant they would now be moving towards winter. Felix could have avoided this had he come back to England. His anger mounted. Of course he understood the reasons and naturally was distressed to hear about the baby, but even so it was a bloody awful blow. He dreaded telling Isobel. And how had Felix reacted when told? This idea of a camp had probably been put to him in a way which meant he didn't feel he had a choice. It was imperative he found out what the boy really thought. Also, why he had that wary, shut-in expression. What was really going on inside that head? Instinctively he felt something was not right. In fact, he was sure of it.

Back in the bungalow, Rawlings decided on a short rest before Felix was due back from school. He set his alarm for fear of falling into another deep sleep, then at the appointed time, walked slowly down the path to the main house to intercept him on his return. After a while he caught sight of the three boys as they made their way towards him. Felix was slightly in front. Suddenly the thickset boy who he presumed to be Shane, gave Felix a great shove so that he almost fell. Felix gave no reaction to this, regained his balance and walked steadily on. Shane looked up and saw that Rawlings was watching him and quickly looked away. A moment later Felix caught sight of his grandfather and his face lit up.

'Hello EG. Were you coming to meet us?'

Rawlings nodded and turned to the other two boys. 'You must be Shane, and you're Davey?' Davey nodded but Shane looked sulky. 'I'm pleased to meet you both.'

Davey looked as if he were going to say something but Shane cut in rudely, 'We'd better go in for tea. Mum hates it when we're late.'

Rawlings addressed Felix as they started to move off. 'Why don't you come to the bungalow after tea and we can have a proper catch up?'

Felix nodded and followed the two other boys into the house. Rawlings left them to it, returned to his room and waited for Felix to arrive.

An hour later he did.

'It's so good to see you again Felix,' he said as the boy sat down opposite him. 'We've all missed you. Everyone sent love.'

This prompted a flood of questions which Rawlings fielded as best he could. He informed Felix about Marnie's transformation into a successful businesswoman and the boy looked astonished. 'Do you mean she doesn't wear all those baggy clothes anymore?'

Rawlings laughed. 'Apparently not. According to Isobel she looks very smart and wears a suit these days.'

'You haven't seen her?'

'No, by the time I left hospital she'd gone to the States where she will be for some time.'

There was a moment's silence while Felix took all this in. Then he gave his grandfather a shrewd look. 'Do you miss her?'

Rawlings felt uneasy. He certainly did not want to go into the acrimonious way his relationship with Marnie had ended. In any case long explanations weren't necessary now Marnie had returned the boat to him. He said lightly, 'I certainly miss those suppers, especially on the evenings when it was my turn to cook and you found me all those great recipes.'

Felix said sadly, 'I miss it too. I miss everybody,' and he added, 'and Juno. Is she still a puppy or has she grown?'

'She is certainly larger than when you last saw her but still behaves like a mad little pup. I think Isobel finds her quite a handful. Luckily Maria and Paul help out now they're living in the boathouse.'

Felix said wistfully, 'I would have liked a dog of my own. The two dogs here aren't much fun. Bongo is old and hardly moves and the dachshund Monty was their grandmother's dog. He's too fat and he smells and yaps all the time.'

This made Rawlings laugh. 'I am sure Sarah would let you have a dog when Bongo departs. She said as much to me.'

Felix shook his head. 'I don't think so. She's always complaining about the dogs getting under her feet. We're told to take them for walks, but they're both too old and lazy and refuse to move.'

Rawlings decided to change the subject and told him about the flat in London and all his new friends. Felix particularly liked the sound of Hetty with her border collies.

'We've been invited to stay in Yorkshire so you can see her dogs then.' Not wishing to tackle the subject of the return to England just yet he quickly went on to describe the Scottish visit.

'You seem to have been travelling a lot.' Felix said.

Rawlings chuckled. 'Yes, I have. You could say I am your peripatetic grandfather.'

'Peri... what?'

'Peripatetic. It means travelling from place to place. And I have more travelling to do when I leave here. I need to go back to Sarajevo.'

'Why?'

'Because my next book is about the time I stayed there during their civil war and I need to do some research into how the place has changed.'

Felix was about to ask another question when his mobile rang. He answered it with a monosyllabic 'OK' and then said to Rawlings, 'I have to go back and to tell you supper will be in an hour.'

Rawlings smiled. 'We'll have lots of time to talk Felix. I am here for another eight days.'

The boy looked mutinous. 'I'm at school during the week, and the weekends are very organised with things...'

'What sort of things?'

'Well, tomorrow we go to the Club for the Saturday Barbie. There are lots of activities; swimming, clock golf, tennis, organised races, and I'm expected to join in. There'll be no time to talk.'

'Sunday then.'

Felix said almost angrily, 'Sunday is worse.' He made a

face. 'We have church in the morning, then Sunday lunch and in the afternoon, we have to do our homework.'

Rawlings said soothingly, 'Don't worry Felix. I'll make sure we have plenty of time together.'

*

The Saturday at the Club gave Rawlings time to observe the community into which Felix had been thrust. It was not one that filled him with unadulterated pleasure. The day had already started badly with an argument between Brad and Sarah. Brad wanted them all to go together, but Sarah insisted on coming on later with the baby. After that they all had to wait for Davey who took a long time to make an appearance.

'Come along Possum,' Brad tried to keep his irritation in check. 'What's the hold-up?'

'Sorry Dad,' Davey was out of breath. 'Shane wanted me to get all his kit.'

'Don't be such a drongo Davey. In future Shane can deal with his own bloody kit. Is that clear?'

At last after a good deal of pushing and shoving, they were all in. Brad yanked at the gears and they drove off at speed. The atmosphere was strained to put it mildly, and Shane was snapped at for being too rowdy in the back. Miraculously, as soon as they arrived Brad's mood underwent a marked change. It was evident from all the greetings that he was a popular man. As someone explained to Rawlings, the Tamar Winery was one of the best and oldest in the area and the Penrose family had always been great benefactors to the community.

Felix was whisked away to play in some tennis tournament.

He'd gone reluctantly, protesting that he'd only been playing a short while and was not good enough to take part. Brad had slapped him on the back and said, 'You're already playing a lot better than Shane,' and turning to his son he added, 'you'd better buck your ideas up mate.'

Rawlings caught Shane's angry scowl, gave an inward sigh and thought yet again, they fuck you up your mum and dad...

'How are things in Pommie land?' A florid man handed him a can of beer. 'Are you going to survive this Brexit thing?'

Rawlings tried to keep the irritation out of his voice and told him he thought Brexit would be an utter disaster, but that the negotiations would drag on for some time yet. As soon as was politely possible he extricated himself from the adult gathering by the bar and made his way over to the tennis courts.

Felix caught sight of Rawlings and ran over to join him.

'I won my first game which was a bit of a fluke. I'm now up against one of the best players who's two years older than me,' he gave a grin, 'so this shouldn't last long.'

It didn't, although Felix did win two games in the set. Rawlings was impressed and told him so. They wandered back together towards the bar and barbie. It was all very loud, some of the men already tanked up. Choosing to sit some distance away, Felix organised food for them both. 'Would you like a beer?' Rawlings shook his head, wondering if he needed to tackle the plate of charred objects placed in front of him or could tactfully leave it somewhere. The sun today was more in evidence and the warm afternoon wore pleasantly on. Felix was full of chatter, explaining who people were and the activities they were expected to take part in.

Sarah arrived with Ella in a pushchair, but the baby was grizzling and as she joined Rawlings, he again observed her look of exhaustion.

'Ella's been like this all night. I never quite know if it's just teething or something more serious. I didn't panic so much with the first two but...' Her voice trailed away.

'Shall I take her for a walk Sarah?' Felix took the pushchair from her. 'It sometimes settles her to be wheeled around.'

Sarah gave him a look of relief and gratitude. 'Would you Felix? You are an angel. That's a great idea.' She flopped into a chair beside Rawlings. 'He's really wonderful with Ella,' she said. 'Nobody else in the family is nearly as good as he is, and he seems to genuinely love her.'

Rawlings smiled. 'I think Felix would have liked a younger sibling. He told me your sister had a baby who died. He was rather vague, and I didn't like to question him. Did you know about that?'

Sarah shook her head. 'As far as I knew Suzy was always adamant about not having any more children after Felix. But if she did have a terrible experience, it would make sense.' She gave a deep sigh. 'Children are lovely as long as they are well and happy. But when they're not...' She looked at him. 'This illness with Ella has thrown all our lives out of kilter. I can't remember the last time Brad and I shared a full night together...' Her voice trailed away but she was saved from saying anything else on the subject by the return of Felix. He parked the pushchair beside her.

'Ella has nodded off Sarah. I think she should sleep for a bit now.' He turned to Rawlings. 'I have to go and play clock golf, it's a competition. Do you want to come and watch?'

Sarah smiled at him. 'You go. I might try and get a nap.'

The day at the Club went on for longer than Rawlings would have liked, but he did make a few more interesting observations. These were mainly the behaviour of Shane. It was becoming evident that the boy resented Felix and took every chance he possibly could, to annoy or thwart him. During the game when he thought nobody was looking, he gave Felix's golf ball a kick, making it difficult for him to make a winning shot. Once again Felix gave no reaction, but Rawlings stared at Shane in a way that made it clear he had seen this. To his surprise, so had his father. As they walked back to the car at the end of the day, he heard Brad reprimanding the boy.

'I'm always pleased when you win Shane, but not when I see you cheating. I saw you move your ball and Felix's, several times. It wasn't a fair win. Nobody likes a cheat, so don't ever let me see you doing this again.'

Rawlings sighed. Brad was right to reprimand the boy, but not in front of everyone. It was painfully obvious that the boy longed for his father's approbation, not his disapproval.

He decided not to go to church with them the following morning, assuring a reluctant Felix he would join them for Sunday lunch. This was the first time he was to see the whole family together and it turned out to be an eye-opener in many ways.

The conversation started with the subject of the Church choir and Rawlings expressed his surprise that Felix hadn't joined it.

'He was adamantly against it weren't you mate?' Brad said quickly, 'even though Sarah told me he had a great voice and sang a solo at his last school concert.' He gave his bark of a laugh. 'In any case, it has to be better than Shane's. He has a voice like a foghorn and sings completely out of tune.'

Shane scowled and looked mutinous. Rawlings gave an inward curse for Brad's stupidity in yet again comparing his son unfavourably with his cousin. He said lightly, 'I've not seen where you sleep yet, Felix. I believe you share a room with Shane?'

Glances were exchanged. 'Not anymore,' Sarah explained. 'We thought it best if Felix had a room of his own.'

Davey piped up, 'It was after Shane put a snake in Felix's bed. He had awful nightmares and kept waking us up with his screaming…'

'Shut up Davey. It was only a grass snake and quite harmless.' Shane gave his brother a kick under the table.

Sarah said quickly, 'It was a stupid thing to do, a boy's prank that went wrong. You were really sorry for upsetting Felix weren't you Shane?' Her son gave her a sulky nod. 'And you don't mind being with your brother, do you Davey?'

'Yes, I do,' he said emphatically, 'Shane snores.'

'Don't be so ridiculous Davey.' This from Brad. 'And get on with your lunch.'

He then turned to Rawlings and suggested a trip to the winery the following day, which he accepted with relief. He was beginning to feel he was treading on eggshells.

The rest of the meal proceeded without further disruption and after they'd finished Felix took Rawlings up to his room. There were five bedrooms upstairs, but Felix explained that the spare room was being used for when Sarah had to be with Ella, which was most of the time now. There wasn't room in Ella's small nursery for Sarah to have a bed, so the cot had been moved into the spare room. Rawlings wondered yet again if this separation was putting an added strain on their marriage. Brad didn't look the sort of man who would like the removal of his conjugal rights. It also meant that with the complication of Ella's illness, the three boys couldn't have separate rooms.

Felix's room wasn't large, but it did have a good view over the garden and swimming pool. As with the rest of the house, the décor was old fashioned but cheerful. Rawlings was pleased to see that Felix had a desk on which he had room for his laptop. He was also touched to see that the framed drawing of him that Marnie had done was propped up amongst the other items on his desk. On his bedside table were a couple of books, the album of photographs from his birthday party taken by Maria and Paul, and his present of The Wind in the Willows.

Felix dived under the bed. 'I want to give you something EG, to take back to England with you.' He pulled out the small case that Isobel had given him. Taking a key from the drawer in his bedside table he carefully unlocked it. Rawlings frowned, disturbed by the fact that the boy felt he had to keep his belongings locked up. While Felix was rummaging in the bag, he idly opened The Wind in the Willows to remind himself what his inscription had been. It wasn't visible. Over whatever he had written was scrawled in large letters: A BABY BOOK FOR A BABY BOY. Rawlings quickly shut the book just as Felix emerged with the pair of binoculars Isobel had given him.

'Can you take these back with you EG? They belonged to Isobel's husband Peter and I wouldn't want anything to happen to them. Besides,' he added with a shrug, 'there's not much to see here. I'd rather keep them for when I get home and can use them on the boat.'

Rawlings, feeling both shocked and emotional tried to keep

his voice calm. 'Of course Felix. I think that's very sensible. Is there anything else you want me to take back with me?'

Felix hesitated. Maybe he was thinking about returning the books, but after a moment he shook his head. 'No, I think that's all. I can bring any other stuff back with me next time I come.'

Rawlings sat on the bed. 'About coming back Felix,' he paused wondering the best way to tackle the subject. 'Brad told me about the change of plans for the summer. You can tell me honestly. Are you really all right with this?'

Felix sat beside him and didn't speak for a while. Then he sighed. 'I think it's best if I stay. I want to do what's good for Ella, even though I miss you and Isobel and everyone.' Then he added fiercely, 'But nothing will stop me coming home at Christmas.'

He kept using the word 'home' and it went deep into the heart of Rawlings. The boy obviously hadn't made this place home, that was becoming all too evident. He was enduring it only because he had been sent here. Sadly, he regarded it like another boarding school and that definitely wasn't what had been intended. It was a situation that urgently needed to be re-thought. Right now, he assured Felix he would be returning for Christmas, even if he had to come and fetch him himself. The boy looked greatly relieved at this.

Rawlings then gave his grandson a hug, picked up the binoculars and left the room.

Chapter 13

More of the Australian Experience

The following day Rawlings joined Brad for the promised trip to the Tamar Winery. With names like 'Tamar' and 'Penrose' it all sounded very Cornish and it soon became apparent that Brad was extremely proud of his Cornish roots. After two hours of walking round and inspecting every inch of the place, Rawlings felt he knew everything he'd ever need to know about the process of wine making. He listened attentively as it was explained to him that the soil was old which gave it depth and although this meant the old vines bore less fruit, they had more taste. The Tamar was only a small winery, but their Shiraz was widely acclaimed and had won many prizes.

'It was my great-grandfather who really built up the business and that has continued through the male line ever since.'

Rawlings wondered if Shane would carry on the tradition. Somehow, he thought not. Davey seemed by far the brighter of the two boys.

'How does the actual process work?'

Brad seemed pleased with his interest and took great trouble to explain. 'There are basically five stages: harvesting, crushing and pressing, fermentation, ageing, and bottling. Each stage requires a special skill. Once the grapes are picked quick action is needed to keep in the flavour.' Here he gave a chuckle. 'Believe me, there are plenty of hazards that can be made with the fermentation.'

'Such as?'

'It's a careful balance of flavours; sugar, acid and a little yeast, and a process that has to be learned and perfected. The temperature must be exactly right. If you add too much sugar you can bloody ruin it. So can improper yeast methods, and it's imperative distilled water is always used.'

They walked on past a line of barrels.

'How long does it take for the wine to mature?'

'Two years minimum.'

The tour finally ended, and they arrived back at the entrance with its shop, tasting area and café. Brad told him proudly, 'It isn't only the wines that people come for. Nowadays wineries are big business with their food shops and cafes. Tourists want the whole experience. Before Ella was born, Sarah was responsible for the food shop and running the café, but she just can't do that anymore. We've put in a manager who's doing a great job but I think she misses the work.'

'Do you get bush fires in this area?' Rawlings asked.

'We're luckier here than some parts of the country but there was a bad one in the Barossa Valley in 2014. We luckily escaped the worst, but terrible damage was done to the Hutton Vale Winery. All their vines were destroyed. Too bloody close for comfort I can tell you.' He turned to Rawlings. 'I have to go to the office for a while. If you'd like to have a wander, I can meet you in the café in about an hour.'

Rawlings, welcoming a break on his own, began his wander. He sampled some of the Tamar's wines and chose two bottles to take back to England. After a short perambulation around the shop he made for the café where he ordered a glass of red and waited for Brad's return. He liked the man. He was simple, straightforward, with an obvious passion for his job, but it didn't take a genius to see he was under enormous pressure both with his work and now the extra stress at home. Rawlings sighed. This was going to make it more difficult for him to have the discussion about Shane, a subject which definitely needed to be tackled before his departure, especially as Felix however reluctantly had accepted the decision to remain in Australia for the summer. The holiday at the camp might be all right but after that? He didn't envisage the situation with Shane improving. In all probability it would get worse, especially if Brad continued to heap praise on Felix rather than on his son. Would it be possible to say something to Brad about this without hurting his feelings?

He ordered another wine. The more he pondered this dilemma, the more Rawlings was convinced that the wrong decision had been made last year. The major upheaval forced on Felix hadn't worked. The boy had not settled, and he certainly wasn't happy. He was just getting through it in the best way he could, in the same way he'd done with everything else in his short life. Rawlings knocked back the wine. It broke his heart that the boy's endurance was being tested once again. The more he considered the situation, the more his agitation grew. It was going to require a great deal of tact to make sure nobody felt they had failed. He didn't wish that on Brad, Sarah, or for that matter Felix. It was a labyrinth of complex emotions he'd have to find his way through and difficult to see a way out. But no matter what, he had to fight for his boy.

Bloody hell. Who could have seen this coming?

*

Two days later Rawlings borrowed Sarah's car and drove to Nuriootpa to meet Felix's teacher Mrs Lawley after school. He'd arranged for Felix to wait for him, with the promise to go out for a meal afterwards.

Nuriootpa was only 6 kilometres from Angaston. The drive was a pleasant one and didn't take long. This part of the country was entirely devoted to winemaking and on either side of the road the vines stretched as far as the eye could see. Personally he preferred a little more variety in the landscape, but it was certainly impressive in its way. Nuriootpa turned out to be a larger town than Angaston but again it had the wide central street with well-preserved, low buildings of mellow brick. Managing to park near the school, he walked up the drive, just as the pupils of both sexes swarmed out of the building in their dark blue uniforms with turquoise badges. It looked like a replica of any English school. Sarah had told him proudly it was the best educational establishment in the area and they'd been lucky to get Felix a place.

Today he had chosen to make use of a walking stick. Just lately his leg had been giving him sharp pains, which he hoped was due to the fact he'd been walking rather more than usual.

Felix ran forward to meet him and then, noticing the walking stick inquired anxiously if he was in pain. Rawlings smiled and assured him he was not, explaining his leg was just a bit tired, nothing more. 'I'll take you to Mrs Lawley and then wait for you outside,' the boy said. 'Do you think we could have a pizza? There is a really good pizza place quite near.'

Rawlings laughed. 'I'm sure that will be possible.' It

seemed pizzas, like McDonald's, were to be found in every corner of the world.

Mrs Lawley turned out to be pretty with a friendly face, probably in her early thirties and reassuringly English. She greeted him warmly and led him to a room where they sat near a window looking out over the playing fields.

'Do you find many differences between the education here and back in the UK?' Rawlings asked.

She shook her head. 'Not really although there are some, not so much in the curriculum, but in the way the school year runs. There are four terms here, not three, and they run between nine and eleven weeks, starting in late January and finishing at the beginning of December. Felix is in Key Stage Three. Those are the classes in the Secondary School that run from eleven to fourteen years of age. Initially he started in the lowest class, but it was soon decided to move him up a class, even though that makes him the youngest. I don't think Felix is twelve until August, is that correct?' Rawlings nodded and she added, 'He is naturally a bright boy, but I think he was also well educated in England?'

'Before his parents were killed in the car accident, he was at a private prep school, which between you and me he didn't much enjoy. I removed him and before coming over here he went to a new academy where he'd settled in well.'

She smiled. 'I taught in an academy before I came out here. When they are good, they are excellent, but some sadly are not. The process still needs ironing out.'

Rawlings was intrigued. 'What made you come out to Australia?'

'My husband's a doctor and was offered a good job here and that was that. I actually love this part of the country and this school is a good one.' She paused. 'I can assure you Felix is getting an excellent education. Even though he's moved up a class there's been no problem with his academic work except perhaps the sciences which don't seem to interest him, but he is fine with most of the other subjects and excels in English.'

'Has he settled down all right, being in a class where the pupils are older than he is?'

'So far that hasn't been a problem either, or none that we can see. He's a mature, self-contained boy, old for his age...' she looked at Rawlings. 'Maybe that's due to all he's been through.' She hesitated. 'There is another reason it was thought he would be better in another class.' Rawlings guessed what was coming but let her continue. 'There seems to be a certain amount of friction between Felix and his cousin Shane. Shane has always been a bit of a troublemaker. He likes to think of himself as something of a leader, which can manifest itself in bullying and this has often led to him being reprimanded. I'm afraid he rather rounded on Felix as the "Pommie" intruder. As you can imagine, quite a fuss was made of Felix in the beginning, arriving as he did in his circumstances. Shane resented this and trouble ensued. It was thought it was best to nip the problem in the bud before it developed into a major issue, especially as we decided Felix was academically up to the work in the higher class. All seems well now and there should be no more problems.'

Not here, Rawlings thought grimly, but there certainly would be at home. As she showed Rawlings out, she said 'Did you know Felix was good at art? The art teacher is really impressed with his drawing ability.'

Rawlings made a mental note to inform Marnie of this

when he next saw her. Her encouragement had obviously paid off.

They walked to the pizza place and found a table. Felix looked the happiest he'd been since Rawlings had arrived.

'I liked your school,' Rawlings said as they sat down.

Felix nodded. 'I do too, especially now I'm in Mrs Lawley's class.' The pizzas arrived and Felix dived in. Rawlings refrained from telling him not to talk with his mouth full and the boy went on, 'The school has a motto, Per Aspera Ad Astra,' and he tactfully translated this for his grandfather's benefit, 'Through Adversity to the Stars.'

How apt thought Rawlings, it really did fit Felix's present situation, but he merely said 'Nuriootpa is quite a strange name.'

'It's Aboriginal,' Felix explained, 'their word for a meeting place. Nuriootpa is one of the largest towns in the area and ours is the main school. I think it's bigger than St Bede's.'

'Do you have a special friend?'

Felix thought about this. 'I like most of the people in my class, but there is one girl called Clare who is very funny and makes me laugh. I suppose my best friend is Marshall. He and I do most things together.'

Rawlings was suddenly aware of the limitations of this friendship. In normal circumstances, Felix would invite him over to his house, as he had done with Sunil Patel his friend from last year, but in the present situation this just wasn't possible.

'Felix,' he said slowly, 'I want you to promise me, that if you ever feel you want to return to England, you'll let me know and you will be brought back.' He added lamely, 'All we ever wanted was for you to be happy. If you're not, then you must tell me. Do you promise?'

His grandson looked at him with a strange expression but said nothing. Was it anger, contempt? With sudden realisation he saw that what Felix was really expressing was mistrust. He blamed his grandfather for the wrong decision that had been made, and in that moment, Rawlings saw he had lost the trust of this boy he so loved. It left him with a mixture of guilt, regret and sadness.

*

The last few days of his visit seemed to fly by. One afternoon he had an interesting conversation with Davey, a boy he increasingly warmed to. Davey was not only intelligent, he was also observant. It was admirable how he remained the diplomat, never allowing himself to be drawn into confrontation or arguments particularly with his elder brother. His voice was deep and gruff for one so young, which gave him an air of unexpected gravity.

They were sitting outside by the pool waiting for the other two boys to appear when Davey suddenly said, 'Felix says you were blown up by a bomb in Afghanistan, but Shane says he's telling lies.'

Rawlings gave a thin smile. 'Well I can assure you Felix is not telling lies. I was indeed blown up just as he told you, which is why I walk with a limp and sometimes a stick.'

Davey looked at him with increased interest. 'Were you in the Army?'

'No, I was a war correspondent, which means I wrote about the wars for a newspaper in England.'

There was a moment of silence as Davey pondered this. 'What do you do now?'

'Now I write books about my war experiences.' Then wanting to change the subject Rawlings said, 'You play the clarinet very well.'

Davey grinned. 'I wanted to play the drums but Dad said it would be too noisy.'

'Why did Felix give up the saxophone? He seemed really keen on that back in England.'

The boy shifted uneasily in his seat. 'One day he couldn't find his sax and turned up late for his lesson without it, so the teacher said he needn't bother to come back.'

Rawlings was shocked by this. It was unlike Felix to lose his instrument. He always took such care of his things. 'Did he find his saxophone?' he asked.

Davey looked even more uncomfortable. 'Shane had hidden it. By the time he told Felix where it was it was too late, and anyway it was all dented and ruined.'

Rawlings felt another wave of anger, but also increasingly helpless at finding a solution to a situation which was fast resembling Lord of the Flies. Felix could have coped with a bully in the school, but right here where he lived? His forbearance wouldn't hold out for ever. At some point soon Rawlings felt sure this control of his would snap and a major confrontation would ensue. It was a miracle he'd lasted this long.

There was one further example of Shane's bullying which Rawlings was to witness. It happened on the penultimate day. The weather had turned unusually warm and Shane and Davey had decided on a swim when they returned from school. Felix had declined because he'd arranged to meet Rawlings. He stood by the edge of the pool waiting for his grandfather to arrive. Shane climbed out of the pool and looked as if he was preparing to dive, when suddenly he ran towards Felix and pushed him in, then danced around laughing in triumph as a spluttering Felix hauled himself out. Rawlings was nearing the pool and saw the entire incident. He also saw Sarah arrive, and she was understandably annoyed.

'Really Felix! How could you? I am now going to have to dry and iron your uniform before the morning. It's too bad of you.'

Felix, head down, said nothing as he followed Sarah back into the house. Rawlings abandoned his good intentions of not interfering. He strode over to the pool and said sternly, 'Shane I saw you deliberately push Felix into the pool. If you don't tell your mother what happened I will.'

Shane who was still laughing became quickly subdued as he saw the anger in Rawlings' face. Reluctantly he climbed out of the pool, dried himself off and walked towards the house. Rawlings followed a short distance behind.

On entering the kitchen Shane blurted out, 'It wasn't Felix's fault mum. I pushed him in. It was just a joke.'

Sarah looked at him and then caught sight of Rawlings and his expression confirmed Shane's admission. Her tone was patient, almost indulgent which annoyed Rawlings. The boy needed a severe reprimand. To add salt to the wound she said, 'Well it's good that you owned up to it…'

What? That wasn't the case. Shane had only admitted to it because he'd been seen. Rawlings felt exasperated. Sarah went on, 'But you should know better. It was a stupid thing to do. I don't need the extra work at the moment. Go and get changed and then stay in your room doing your homework until I call you down for supper.'

Shane left the room in a sulk, as Felix passed him with a neat pile of wet school uniform.

'Shall I put these in the drier Sarah?'

She took the clothes from him. 'I owe you an apology Felix. Shane tells me he pushed you in, so it wasn't your fault. I'm sorry I shouted at you. Don't worry I'll deal with your uniform. Go and spend time with your grandfather. I'll call you when supper's ready.'

As they walked back together towards the bungalow Rawlings asked why he hadn't spoken out about being pushed in. Felix shrugged and said bleakly, 'What's the point? It would only have made things worse and it happens all the time.' He looked at Rawlings. 'I'm really surprised Shane owned up. He never does usually.'

Rawlings remained silent but vowed to broach the Shane situation with Brad and Sarah as a matter of urgency. They had to be warned and told to keep an eye out for it. It was the very least he could do for his boy.

That evening after the children had gone to bed, Rawlings sat on the porch with Brad and Sarah. The atmosphere was mellow, the evening mild and he had a glass of excellent Tamar wine in his hand. It had to be a good moment to tackle the Shane problem.

He began by thanking Brad and Sarah for their great generosity to him during his stay, adding how good it was to see Felix so fit and healthy. Here he hesitated, not sure how to continue. Brad chipped in saying again how much they enjoyed having Felix living with them.

Rawlings took the plunge. 'I do have one concern which I felt I must discuss with you before I leave…' he paused, trying to think of the most tactful way to put it.

'Go ahead mate,' Brad said cheerfully. 'Tell us anything that's worrying you. We only want what's best for the boy.'

Rawlings chose his words carefully. 'I have noticed a good deal of tension between Shane and Felix, and a series of incidents have come to my attention. Although Felix has never complained, I have been watching carefully and to be frank with you, I think Shane's actions are really upsetting him.'

There was silence for a moment. Husband and wife exchanged glances. It was Sarah who spoke first. 'You mustn't worry about telling us this. To be honest, we have had a few problems with Shane in the past couple of years. We did think having Felix here would be good for him. For the first few weeks everything was fine and there was no problem. I think Shane then noticed Felix getting praised a lot, and he resented it...'

Brad interrupted. 'To be fair, Shane's had a difficult time of it. A lot of his behaviour problems started when my mother passed away two years ago. The boy adored her and her passing upset him terribly.'

Rawlings asked himself yet again, what was wrong with the word 'death'? All this reference to 'passing' annoyed him. Passing where? Passing by?

The sound of Sarah snapping at Brad restored his attention.

'Quite frankly Brad I blame your mother for most of Shane's problems. She spoiled him rotten.'

A look of annoyance crossed her husband's face. 'That's bloody unfair of you Sarah and you know it. You were happy enough to let her look after the boys while you ran the shop and cafe.' He drained his beer and stumped off to get another can.

Sarah sighed. 'Brad is right, I did leave the boys with Ivy a good deal of the time, but only because she demanded their company. The worst part of it was, she gave all her attention to Shane and hardly noticed Davey at all. I know it upsets Brad when I mention her spoiling Shane, but quite honestly his mother was an absolute nightmare.' Her voice became angry. 'I would have preferred to get in a child minder, at least then I could have kept some control. With Ivy I had none. She fed the children totally unsuitable food and gave them endless sweets and chocolates. When I tried to exert some discipline, she would openly contradict me. Every time I heard her say "they're only young once" I felt like strangling her. Quite honestly her death was a huge relief…' She broke off giving Rawlings a rueful smile. 'Sorry for the rant. That must sound terrible. I could never say any of this to Brad. He adored his mother, and she could do no wrong.' She gave a sigh. 'But the upshot is we now have to accept there is a major worry with Shane. The school have reported his bullying behaviour several times. To be honest I hadn't noticed it with Felix. I know there have been one or two incidents, but I just thought they were childish pranks.'

'There have been many far more serious ones,' Rawlings said, 'It's just that Felix never tells you.'

Brad returned and there was a moment's awkward silence. Rawlings felt a pang of guilt at causing this touchy subject to be rekindled.

'I apologise for mentioning this problem. It's just that I've heard about incidents when Felix has been unjustly punished and having witnessed a few myself I felt I had…' he broke off finishing lamely, 'it's difficult being so far away from the boy and I worry. He tells me little in the few Skype conversations we have, and he's not the sort of boy to tell tales…'

Brad was quick to reassure him. 'Honestly don't worry, we

147

do understand, and you were right to raise it. We'll definitely keep an eye on Shane's behaviour from now on. I'll split them up in the summer camp and make sure he shares with Davey.'

Sarah added, 'I think part of the problem is that maybe we've praised Felix a great deal, trying to make him feel welcome here. Maybe we should make sure we praise our boys as well.'

Brad looked as if he was going to say something in answer to this, but then thought better of it. Maybe he didn't feel his boys merited such praise. Whatever it was, the conversation drifted to other things and Rawlings went back to the bungalow soon after to do his packing. His great hope was that he'd done enough. But Shane was a sly boy. He only did these things when he thought nobody was watching him.

*

The journey to the airport was a difficult one for both Felix and Rawlings. Brad chatted cheerfully but this was more of an aggravation than a comfort. Felix sat pale and silent while Rawlings answered Brad in monosyllables. At one point, Brad addressed Felix directly.

'I've been giving Felix lessons in Australian haven't I mate? Tell your grandfather some of the words you've learned.'

Felix made an effort and recited, 'cobber, tucker, lappy, mozzies, drongo…'

'Drongo?' Rawlings queried.

Brad laughed. 'It's the Australian for making a fool of yourself, like "don't be a drongo" when you've done something stupid.' He added, 'Good on you Felix. We'll make an Australian of you yet.'

Felix gave a wan smile and Rawlings winced at the very idea. He decided to change the subject and told Brad how much he'd enjoyed the wines during his stay. This kept the conversation going for quite a while, almost until they reached the airport.

'Don't come in Brad,' he said as they pulled up at the departures entrance, 'park outside. That will be fine. I'm extremely grateful to you for driving me here.'

Rawlings was anxious to avoid any long goodbyes. Felix, his face set, was looking tense, but as always holding himself together.

While Brad was getting out the luggage, Rawlings looked directly at Felix, held his gaze and said firmly, 'Remember, you only have to tell me if you want to come back and it will be done.'

Felix nodded, then flung his arms around Rawlings almost knocking him off balance. Rawlings held on to the clinging boy for a moment, then let him go, ruffling his hair.

'Have a great holiday Felix and be sure to tell me all about it. I will see you very soon.'

Felix seemed unable to speak.

Brad shook his hand. 'It's been great having you here. You must come and see us again.'

Rawlings thanked him for the last time and then without waiting for them to get back in the car, he walked as quickly as he could into the crowded airport, avoiding the temptation to look back.

Chapter 14

The Return

'I tell you Isobel I felt like a bloody murderer, leaving him at the airport like that.' Rawlings was walking up and down Isobel's living room in a state of extreme agitation.

Isobel watched him for a few moments and then said firmly, 'Rawlings for goodness sake sit down. I can't take anything in while you're pacing about like a caged lion.' Rawlings obeyed as he always did with Isobel, throwing himself into an armchair opposite her. Once seated she said, 'Now start at the beginning and tell me about the entire visit. And please do try and speak calmly.'

She listened intently as he described his stay in detail, taking particular care to relate all the Shane incidents. At times the emotion almost overcame him, but he managed to get through it and then sat back waiting for Isobel to comment.

She looked grave and took her time. 'I understand your anxiety. I feel it too. That poor boy has been through so much and now for him to have this problem with his cousin is just terrible, and a quite unexpected and difficult situation to deal with.'

'Precisely!' Rawlings almost shouted, 'It's impossible to deal with. There was no action I could take. I felt completely impotent and meanwhile Felix is a prey to that monstrous child…'

'I think we must keep cool heads in this and try and think calmly about the best course of action,' Isobel said with a trace of irritation. Rawlings sat silent while Isobel seemed lost in thought for a while. She then spoke slowly, 'As I understand it, Felix will be spending his holiday at this camp and you've been assured Shane will be put in a separate group?' Rawlings nodded. 'Well that is some relief. At least he'll have a period of respite. The next hurdle will be in September when their lives return to normal and the boys go back to school. Until that time, there is little we can do except be sure to keep in touch. After that we will just have to rely on Felix to keep us informed.'

'But he won't!' Rawlings shouted in exasperation. 'It's as if he's shut down all his feelings. He's just determined to cope with the situation on his own and I don't see why he bloody well has to. The worst part of it is, he doesn't trust me anymore.' He stood up about to pace up and down again, but on receiving a sharp look from Isobel he returned to his seat. 'I partly blame my stupid solicitor who made the decision without knowing Felix at all. He had absolutely no idea how happy and settled Felix was with us here. For him, if it looked good on paper, he felt he had done his duty. I should have followed my instincts and insisted the boy stay in England.'

'Don't be ridiculous Rawlings.' Isobel spoke sharply. 'Nobody could have foreseen this situation. At the time, it seemed to all of us it was the best solution for the boy to live in a family with cousins of his own age. We all agreed to it, however reluctantly. Don't forget Sarah is one of his guardians and had every right to want to bring up her sister's child.' Her voice softened. 'If I know Felix, and I think I do, he won't endure this situation forever. Either things improve and

Shane's parents really do keep an eye on their boy's behaviour, or Shane does something that goes too far and Felix will lose his admirable self-control.'

'And then what?'

Isobel smiled. 'Then I think Felix will let us know. If he wants to return here it must be made clear that he can, and I for one will be overjoyed to see him.' She sighed. 'It does seem a long time until December. I also worry about those poor parents. It must be the most terrible strain on them having a baby who is so ill.'

'Which is exactly why I suggested that Felix must be an added burden they could do without and therefore should come back with me,' Rawlings growled. 'But they wouldn't hear of it and said they loved having the boy with them. Meanwhile God knows what damage is being done.'

Isobel sighed. 'We have to be patient. The next move must come from Felix. This probably means we'll be waiting until December to find out what he really wants to do.' She looked at Rawlings who was sitting hunched in gloom and said briskly, 'What will you be doing with August now that Felix won't be with us.'

He thought for a moment and then said grumpily, 'There's this new book I have to write. I might come down and spend some time on the boat while I get it started, if that's alright with you?'

'Of course, it's your boat, and I am always delighted to see you, even when you are growling at me. What's the subject of your book?'

Rawlings sounded unenthusiastic. 'They want an account of my time spent during the Sarajevo Siege. I didn't want to write the bloody thing but feel obliged to do so, because it was the last wish of my late agent. Jolyon died while I was in Australia. The news of his death wasn't a shock, I knew he hadn't long to live when I saw him in hospital just before I left, but now I would feel guilty if I didn't fulfil his last wish.' He looked at Isobel. 'I think this means I must make a short trip to Sarajevo to refresh my memory.'

As he drove back to London, Rawlings thought he'd rarely in his life felt so unsettled. Isobel's calmness for once hadn't helped. If he were honest, this feeling of confusion had been with him ever since his arrival home. Apart from the worry over Felix, a number of other things were nagging away at him. For a start, there was the letter from Sheila with the news of Jolyon's death. He'd known it was coming but it was still upsetting. Her brief missive indicated it had been a peaceful end and that his partner had been with him. Partner? He knew nothing about a partner. It had never seemed quite appropriate to inquire about Jolyon's private life. Now he found it hard to imagine him having time for a relationship, his public life had appeared so all-consuming. Maybe it was a relief that Jolyon had someone with him at the end. The man had been so gregarious it would have been wrong for him to die lonely and abandoned. He, on the other hand, would be perfectly happy to have nobody around at his deathbed. There was not a single person he felt close enough to, except Felix, and he certainly wouldn't want to put his grandson through such a harrowing ordeal. Nor Isobel either, who would probably express a wish to be with him. He'd have to insist on being alone. Also, no religious funeral. They would just have to be satisfied with a party after his demise. This produced a chuckle. Jolyon's do would be a very grand affair, no doubt with all the great and good invited. He sighed. It was definitely not an event he looked forward to, even if he did feel obliged to attend.

He swerved to avoid a suicidal fox that ran out in front of him. Thank God he would soon turn off this country road and onto the motorway. He needed to put his foot down and get back to London as quickly as possible.

His thoughts turned to Max. He couldn't put his finger on it but Hetty was right, something was definitely wrong with the man. When he'd dropped in for coffee after getting back, Max had somehow seemed strange and distant. Was it his imagination or had his voice sounded slurred? Surely, he wasn't drunk? It had been too early in the morning for that. He fervently hoped that Max wasn't going to be added to his list of worries. Fond as he was of the man, he had too many other problems of his own to deal with. It might be a case of enlisting Hetty's help.

He started making a mental list of the most urgent tasks ahead of him. A Skype to Felix should be organised as soon as possible just to let the boy know he was back safely, with a reminder that he needed to keep in touch. A letter of condolence must go to Sheila, always a difficult one to write. And what about Jolyon's partner? A letter should go to him too. He must remember to ask for a name and address. Leading on from that, he somehow had to set down an outline for his Sarajevo book, a task he had completely neglected while away. Maybe he could put that off until after he had re-visited the place which would give him extra time. He also needed to write to his sister and explain that Felix wouldn't be staying with them in the summer as originally planned. Last, but certainly not least, a visit had to be arranged to see his gloomy solicitor. There was a need for Graham to understand the Felix situation. At the same time, he could organise the documents that made Isobel an extra guardian for the boy.

On reaching home he found a note from Max pinned to his door, asking him to supper the following night. With some relief, he sent a reply saying he would be delighted and then looked out a bottle of the Barossa wine to take with him.

He arrived at the appointed time and found Max in mellow mood in contrast to that first morning and chided himself for over-reacting. Handing over the bottle of wine he said, 'This tasted delicious in Australia but I'm not sure it travels well.'

Max handed him a glass of bubbly. 'I'm delighted to try it. I've heard good reports of the Barossa wines. We'll have it with supper which is one of Hetty's beef stews. Bless her heart, she left me with a freezer full of food last time she was in London.' They sat down. 'Now, tell me all about your Australian visit.'

By the time he had related an account of his stay they'd moved over to the supper table. Max put the wine in a decanter and on tasting it gave his approval. There was a lull in proceedings as they ate and drank, and then suddenly Max put down his knife and fork with a clatter and said, 'I have some news for you.' Rawlings looked at him expectantly as he announced rather dramatically, 'I have quit my job. I have retired.'

'Good heavens!' Rawlings was startled. 'That seems rather sudden. Was there a reason? Did you have a row with your editor?' It crossed his mind that Max might have been let go. He had been a little lax with his duties of late.

Max smiled. 'I wasn't fired if that's what you're thinking, although quite frankly, I think they were relieved. I won't be surprised if I'm not replaced. My TV column can be easily covered in the daily listings and recommendations. No, there were two reasons for me to pack it in, the first being I have now reached retirement age, so my pension remains intact...' he gave a shrug, 'quite honestly Rawlings, I was tired of the job anyway and never want to watch another television programme in the line of duty. For far too long, my time has been ridiculously taken up with the most appalling trash.'

'And the second reason?' Rawlings inquired.

Here there was a long pause until Max finally said, 'I've been diagnosed with the early onset of Parkinson's.'

This was even more of a shock. Rawlings felt as if he had been hit in the solar plexus. Max, ill? He always seemed so fit, so full of life.

'Are you sure?' It was a ridiculous question, but he wanted to be certain Max wasn't just being dramatic.

'Of course, I'm sure.' Max said irritably. 'Hetty dragged me to a specialist the day after you left. She'd put me through one of her interrogations and I had to admit I'd had symptoms for a few months. My GP suspected Parkinson's and gave me small doses of the drug Levodopa. When this brought about an immediate improvement, his initial diagnosis seemed proved right and the specialist confirmed it.'

That would seem conclusive, so Rawlings said, 'I know nothing about Parkinson's. What are the symptoms?'

Max shrugged. 'General stiffness in the limbs, particularly in the right part of my body. Slight slurring of speech apparently, so that people might assume I was drunk.' He gave a short laugh, 'Added to which, my hand tends to shake on that same side...'

Rawlings remembered that Hetty had noticed this, and

her first thought had been that he was drinking too much.

'Max, this is awful news. It's truly damnable it should have happened.' He hesitated. 'What's the outlook?'

Max smiled at him across the table. He seemed more relaxed now he'd unburdened himself. 'You mean am I likely to make an early exit? Apparently not. I could last another thirty years.' That seemed over-optimistic given that he was sixty-five. 'But my life will gradually become more uncomfortable as the symptoms start to worsen. Meanwhile, instructions have been given. I'm to have regular check-ups, eat small meals, and take exercise. To this end I'm going to take up gardening. Mac can still take care of the lawn. Ours is a garden that only has lawn and shrubs, so I thought of investing in some colour.' He chuckled. 'My life is now taken up with rose and plant catalogues. It will all be new for me. I'd welcome any advice.'

Rawlings shook his head. 'I know zilch about gardening, but I could always learn.'

Max gave a laugh. 'Don't worry. Bel and Hetty are dying to get involved.' He looked at Rawlings. 'There is something I would like you to help me with…' he paused. 'It's to do with this exercise thing. I'm thinking of getting a dog. It will force me to go out if I am obliged to take it for walks. In any case, I'll enjoy the company.' He laughed again. 'Hetty offered me one of her border collies, but they're working dogs and a little too active for my needs. I was wondering if you'd like to come to Battersea Dog's Home with me.'

Rawlings thought sadly of Felix. How he would have loved to have been involved with choosing a dog. 'Of course, Max. Just let me know when you want to make the visit.' It was good he was thinking so positively about this bombshell.

Rawlings was certain he wouldn't have been so sanguine about it.

Once downstairs, Rawlings put through a call to Hetty. Forestalling her enquiries about his visit to Australia he cut straight to the chase.

'Max has told me about his Parkinson's. I must say, it's a bit of a shock.'

Hetty found it hard to keep the triumph out of her voice. 'I said there was something wrong, but nobody took any notice. Poor darling. He took it hard at first but cheered up when they said he only had mild symptoms. Of course, it's only the start of the beastly thing. From what I know about it, there are several ways it could progress. The one thing that worries Max most is having to pee more in the night.' She chuckled. 'I told him that happens to all of us as we get older.' A long pause. 'I feel more worried about the sexual problems that may ensue, erectile dysfunction and that sort of thing. It's very bad timing just as Elsa's old Bart has finally popped his clogs. Max was looking forward to seeing a good deal more of her.' She paused again. 'Have you met the lady?' Before Rawlings could reply she went on, 'She's high maintenance and very demanding, if you know what I mean.' He heard her give a great sigh. 'We'll just have to see how it works out.'

'Do you think Elsa will come down and live with Max?'

'No, not permanently. I gather right now she's in the process of selling the old house. She calls it a castle but it's actually just a large baronial monstrosity.' Rawlings smiled as Hetty in full flow, continued. 'From what my brother tells me, she'll keep on her studio and still spend a certain amount of time in Northumberland. But Max will be seeing more of her now the husband is no more, which is why…'

Rawlings did not relish hearing any more about Max's sex life, so quickly changed the subject. 'We've arranged to go to Battersea Dog's Home to find him a dog.'

Hetty sounded enthusiastic. 'Such a good idea, it will force Max to take exercise. Very sensibly he turned down the offer of one of mine. They need too much exercise for him to cope with. It's good you're going with the poor fellow. You can see that he gets one that isn't too big. Aged about seven or eight would be best. Don't forget to send me a picture.'

They chatted for a while more and then, quite abruptly she ended the call, telling him she would be down to see Max soon and would catch up on his Australian news then.

Rawlings sat in his desk chair looking out onto the garden, a garden which was soon to have the addition of urns and a dog. Hetty had asked if he was feeling 'dumfungled' after all his travels. It was a good choice of word. She must have noticed tiredness in his voice, but it wasn't the exhaustion that was bothering him. It was a kind of bewilderment at the tide of events that now seemed to be sweeping over him. This should have been the year to calmly tie up loose ends and move on with the rest of his life. But now, all around him was turmoil and he was beginning to feel like Job. What fresh disaster was to assail him next? Didn't he have enough to contend with? Felix was unsettled and unhappy, his poor agent had suffered a terrible illness and died, and now he was obliged to write a book he didn't want to, and worse still, neglect the book he did. On top of everything else there was this latest bombshell from Max.

He got up to pour himself a brandy and as he sat down, another thought struck him. Maybe the reason for this restlessness was not having a woman in his life. There was a definite gap. But where was this woman? Ruefully he thought that he had only himself to blame, having walked out on Marnie and turned down the advances of Bel. So that would appear to be that for the foreseeable future. Single and celibate he must remain. It was certainly true he'd never sought sex merely for the sake of it and wasn't about to start. But it didn't stop him from missing it.

Enough! This was all Hetty's fault for mentioning Max's sex life. In any case, there were a few busy weeks ahead of him which would no doubt keep him fully occupied, and his thoughts chaste.

Chapter 15

Finding Max a Dog

A few days later they set out for Battersea Dog's Home. If Rawlings had thought that the selection of a suitable dog would be a long and tortuous process, he needn't have worried. Within minutes Max arrived at a cage and declared that the occupant inside was the one for him. 'I shall re-name him Bolly, after my favourite champagne.'

Rawlings scratched his head. It was rather difficult to understand the immediate impact of this mutt on Max, for he really was a mutt. They could equally have re-named him Scruffy. This canine was of medium size, a definite mixture of breeds, with a shaggy brown coat. Quite frankly he more resembled a hearth rug than a dog. But there was no doubting the immediate rapport between Max and his new companion. Rawlings studied the dog more closely and was forced to admit he had a very endearing face, like a well-worn and greatly loved teddy bear. He also had a long, fluffy tail that would not stop wagging. A lot of damage could be done with that tail, especially with objects on the low coffee table.

They were informed that Bolly was about six years old and had come to the Home when his owner was too ill to look after him. Thankfully, he was obedient and enormously affectionate. On the downside, he was lazy and disliked exercise, so they were encouraged to take him for a good daily walk. Max declared Bolly perfect and talked to the animal the whole way. Rawlings couldn't help wondering whether Elsa would welcome this latest addition to Max's life. She sounded more of a Borzoi person to him.

At Max's request he rang to give the news to Hetty, who was delighted and immediately questioned him on the breed. Rawlings answered that he hadn't a clue but could make further inquiries. Hetty dismissed this. 'Battersea Dog's Home would have told you if he was a pedigree dog. No problem. Mongrels are often highly intelligent...' there was a pause, 'from your description Bolly doesn't sound the intelligent sort, but it might be better for Max if he's a placid fellow.' She continued in this vein for some time, giving a great many instructions about the care of the dog and eventually ringing off, saying she would see them in a week's time.

Max explained the visit. 'Hetty and Bernard are coming down next week just after Elsa arrives. She'll be here for a few days and of course you must meet her. I'm giving a supper party for the whole family.'

Having accepted the invitation Rawlings retreated to his flat leaving Max and Bolly to continue their bonding.

Over the next two days, he accomplished some of the items on his list. However, the Skype call to Felix was highly unsatisfactory. The boy had shut down again and his inquiries were met with replies that were limited and glum. The only time he brightened up was when Rawlings described the acquisition of Bolly, but even this ended on a sad note.

'I wish I could see him.'

'You will, in December. He won't change. He's six years old and done all the growing he needs to do.'

There was a long pause and then Felix said, 'My term ends in November. I could come home then.'

Rawlings said smoothly 'Of course, let me have the dates and I'll arrange things with Sarah.'

After this, the call swiftly terminated. Rawlings sat for a while ruminating on the Felix problem. He might not be able to Skype him for a while. By the time he was back from Sarajevo the boy would be away at holiday camp. It meant he would miss his birthday as well, which was in the middle of August. He stood up and kicked a chair. The whole situation was damnable. His irritation and anger prompted him to make an appointment with Graham. It was somehow even more important now that Isobel became a guardian.

He glanced out of the window and saw Bolly mooching around the garden. He pottered to find a spot in the sun and lay down facing the river. The endless water traffic seemed to hold a fascination for him. Rawlings forced himself back to finishing his remaining tasks before his departure for Sarajevo. His call to Sheila turned out to be another irritating conversation. She seemed aggrieved he hadn't already written a treatment of the Sarajevo book which she could present to the publishers. Rawlings disliked pressure of any kind, particularly over a book he didn't even want to write. He explained with as much patience as he could muster, that he needed to return to Sarajevo first, to refresh his memory and do some research. She grudgingly agreed to this. Before he rang off, he found out the name of Jolyon's partner, which was Brian Felton. Sheila told him he'd had a successful career as a set designer in the theatre, before giving it all up to live with Jolyon and they had been together for over thirty years. A letter of condolence would have to be sent, but that was enough for one day.

He wandered into the garden and joined Bolly to sit in the sun. The dog didn't stir, just wagged his tail to acknowledge he knew someone had arrived. There was a murmur of bees and in the distance, there was the sound of a lawn being mowed. Apart from the rumble of the occasional train going over the bridge, it was hard to believe he was in the middle of a large metropolis. But even the calmness of this scene couldn't stop him being irritated by Sheila with her persistent demands. Jolyon had never bullied him in this way. Sarajevo would only postpone things for a couple of weeks, then he really would have to tackle the bloody book. Suddenly a brainwave struck him. He would write to Mia's family. Mia had been with him the entire Siege, in fact she had arrived before him and she had kept a journal of that time. There were also the brilliant photographs she'd taken. It was an archive far more interesting than the articles he'd written. Those only brought back the personal memories he'd tried so hard to blot out. Mia's notes would not only be fascinating but give better insight into the ordeal they had shared, but this raised a problem. Would the family let him have access? It was definitely worth a try and would give him a chance to prevaricate with Sheila a little longer.

Max wandered down the garden holding a red leather lead which he attached to Bolly's collar of a similar colour. He dragged the unwilling dog over to where Rawlings was sitting.

He smiled. 'You have to face it, Max. That dog definitely doesn't like exercise. He's far happier staring at the river, which seems to hold some sort of fascination for him. It seems a pity to disturb the poor animal.'

Max sighed. 'I know but Elsa arrives this afternoon, so he

has to have his walk now. I also have the urgent task of trying to teach him some house etiquette. Last night he leapt on my bed in the middle of the night.'

'I can't imagine that will be popular,' Rawlings murmured with a raise of his eyebrows.

'It won't. This morning I organised his basket in my study. There is a low window seat where he can still watch the garden and river. I'll just have to make sure the door's shut.'

Rawlings smiled. 'At least you don't have the problem of him barking. I actually think he's well behaved for a mutt from a dog's home. That's a very regal collar and lead for a scruffy mongrel.'

Max laughed. 'You forget he's of the royal house of Bollinger.' He started to pull the unwilling animal up the garden. 'When we return from his walk, he's in for a shock, with a bath and good brush. After that he'll be most offended if you call him scruffy!'

*

Two days later, Rawlings set about preparing himself for a first meeting with the formidable Elsa. In her honour he took unusual care. As he shaved, he regarded himself in the shaving mirror and noted that although he still had a good head of hair, there were definite signs of greying, particularly at the temples. Suppose he grew a beard? Would that be entirely grey? It might be interesting to find out. He splashed on some Armani cologne, a present from Isobel, and donned a navy linen shirt, also from Isobel. The blessed Isobel, what would he do without her? Deciding against a jacket as it was a warm evening, he grabbed his last bottle of

Barossa wine and made his way upstairs.

The family were already gathered, although there was no sign yet of Elsa. Hetty gave him one of her hugs that almost winded him. Bernard acknowledged him with a friendly nod. Clive shook his hand. Bel kissed him on both cheeks and clung on to him for a bit too long. Annoyed, he could see that Clive was observing them.

'You're looking very tanned Rawlings,' Hetty said. 'Was it hot in Australia?'

'No, it was their autumn so not a great deal of sun. This tan is all English, spending too much time being lazy in the garden.'

Max handed him a drink. 'Elsa's in the kitchen. She'll be with us soon.' And then, as Bolly wandered by, he said, 'Have you noticed the difference in my dog's appearance?'

Rawlings was indeed surprised. He looked quite sleek with a brushed and shiny coat. 'What a transformation. He's almost Cruft's standard.'

A general discussion followed about the ancestry of the dog, everyone having different ideas about what breeds had been involved in his mongrel appearance. This gave Rawlings time to observe the family, which for some strange reason he now felt almost a part of. Although the three siblings were of the same parentage, there were major differences between them. This was amply illustrated by the way they dressed. Max shuffled about in baggy, ill-fitting clothes that appeared to have been bought for someone else. Bel, in stark contrast, was in a navy trouser suit of immaculate cut, along with a white blouse with navy stitching. All very designer. She'd had her hair trimmed short and now she was languidly draped in a chair which gave her an air of chic sophistication. (Her

166

husband was also smartly attired in pressed chinos and a blue check shirt, but somehow, he only managed to look ordinary.) Not for the first time Rawlings wondered what the fourth sibling was like, but it seemed unlikely Rupert would emerge from his Amazon retreat any time soon. He gave an inward smile and glanced towards Hetty who was petting the dog. She wore a shapeless, flowery frock straight out of the fifties, the sort of thing he vaguely remembered his mother wearing and in marked contrast to her sophisticated sister. (Bernard, slightly removed from the proceedings, was in the same old tweeds he'd seen him in the last time they'd met.)

His musings were interrupted by the entrance of Elsa. She was petite, something he hadn't expected, and wearing a tight low top, white trousers also tight, with a large gold belt to emphasise her small waist, and an oversized man's brightly coloured shirt worn open. Her blonde hair was piled tightly on top of her head and her only adornment was a large ethnic bangle. She was not beautiful like Bel, but striking and sexy in an aggressive way. Her voice, with a noticeably heavy mid-European accent, was addressing him.

'You must be Rawlings. At last we meet darling. Max has told me such a great deal about you. But he didn't tell me you were so handsome.'

Bel drawled, 'Don't tell him that, he'll get a swelled head.'

Rawlings ignoring Bel said with a smile, 'And I'm pleased to meet you too. I'd heard many rumours of your existence but didn't quite believe it until now.'

Max poured the champagne emptying the last drop into Hetty's glass and said, 'That's the last of the bubbly brought kindly by Clive. After this we move onto wine.'

Bolly waddled over and sat at Rawlings' feet. Elsa smiled at him, 'That dog seems to like you darling. I usually dislike dogs but this one seems friendly and thank God he's well behaved. My late husband St John had a couple of wolfhounds, but I disliked them intensely.'

'Where are they now?' Hetty asked anxiously.

'They went off to some old dog's home,' Elsa said vaguely and before Hetty could question her further she turned her attention back to Rawlings. 'Are you a lover of dogs Rawlings?'

'Yes, I am, but I've never owned one. It was never possible in my line of work as I was always abroad. My grandson is longing to have a dog of his own.'

'Then why do you not buy him one?' Elsa spoke reproachfully. 'Isn't that what grandfathers are meant to do?'

Rawlings smiled. 'I would, but at present he's living in Australia.'

Her grand inquisition continued with Rawlings patiently fielding her questions.

'What made you become a war correspondent?'

He sighed. 'Almost by mistake. I started as a journalist and then an opportunity came up and that seemed to be that, rather like William Boot in Scoop.' This reference went over her head. He added dryly, 'There never seemed to be a shortage of conflicts for me to cover.' From the corner of the room he saw Bernard give him an amused smile.

Elsa wasn't giving up. 'That must be a most dangerous and depressing career.'

'Both at times. But it could also be rewarding. An acclaimed war correspondent stated he was advised to write about the small voices, the people who couldn't write about themselves. I think that is what I always tried to do and what kept me going.'

She wasn't listening to the answers, just kept firing the questions. 'And you are now retired darling?'

'Yes, I was forced to do so after being caught in an explosion in Afghanistan.' He added, 'However, it seems I can't quite get away from it. I wrote a book last year which was a collection of my war experiences, and now reluctantly I am to embark on an account of the Sarajevo Siege. I'm actually going to Sarajevo next week to refresh my memory of the place.' Then not wishing to answer any more questions about himself, he turned the tables and inquired of Elsa 'What made you become a sculptress?'

Her answer was rather abrupt. 'My father was famous Polish sculptor. I learned from him. After he died, I just carried on.' She stood up, 'I must see to the food. It should be ready very soon.'

Rawlings turned to Bel, who had been wearing a bored expression throughout the Elsa exchange. 'How is the new job? Are you enjoying it?'

She answered sharply, 'Of course. You of all people should know I enjoy what I do.'

Clive cut in tactfully, 'Bel is so busy with it I never seem to see her.'

Thankfully, Bolly caused a minor diversion at this moment, making plain he wanted to be let out into the garden. 'He just scratches on the French window to let me know,' Max said proudly.

Rawlings glanced across at Bel, who flashed him an angry look in return. He sighed. Hell hath no fury like a woman scorned. It seemed to be true in her case, although he hadn't seen her for months. Why was she still bearing a grudge? It wasn't as if they'd even had an affair. All he had done was turn down her offer. But in spite of Bel's hostility, he was enjoying the evening and no longer felt an outsider at these family gatherings. A mutual acceptance had taken place. Sometimes he joined in the chatter, sometimes preferring just to watch the verbal sparring between them. He noticed Clive rarely joined in unless a direct question was put to him. Bernard preferred to have one to one conversations of more erudite content, rather than enter the bullring of general chatter.

Over supper the conversation turned to more topical matters. Comments were made about the Thailand cave rescue of the boys. Hetty became quite emotional over the bravery shown by the British divers. Rawlings agreed, admitting he had a great fear of being trapped underground, or in any enclosed space.

'I'm sure that's very Freudian.' Bel remarked almost rudely.

Rawlings smiled, unruffled. 'Quite possibly. Or maybe because I witnessed so many people in the war zones trapped in their bombed houses which were often burning.'

Bel looked as if she were about to reply and then thought better of it.

Inevitably the discussion then moved on to Brexit and recent cabinet upheavals. There were a lot of angry comments, particularly the general fear of a 'no deal'. Rawlings glanced across at Clive, who was keeping noticeably quiet. Was he a Brexiteer? Difficult to admit it in this staunchly Remainer family. The only contribution Rawlings made to the conversation was a mild remark about how much he disliked Boris Johnson. This was heavily snubbed by Bel, but in the general melee her comment was lost on most of the company, although Hetty shot him a look of sympathy. Elsa talked at some length about her new exhibition and then after supper Max moved over to the piano. He and Elsa sat side by side, Max taking requests. Rawlings moved to sit with Bernard and Hetty on the sofa. Bernard inquired how the Sarajevo book was going and Hetty asked him about Australia. The evening was brought to an abrupt end by Bel, who said she had to be at work early the next day. In the general goodbyes, Hetty whispered in Rawlings' ear, 'Sorry about Bel. She's been in a foul mood all day.'

The following morning, while he was in the process of doing the last of his Sarajevo packing, he was interrupted by his mobile ringing. Reluctantly he answered it.

'Hello?'

'It's Bel.' A pause. 'I've been told by my sister that I was rude to you last night and that an apology is due.'

It didn't sound as if she meant it, there was still a good deal of anger in her voice, but he said smoothly, 'Your apology is accepted.' Another long pause and then he added, 'I also apologise if I said anything to upset you.'

She snapped back, 'You didn't. I just couldn't stand the way you were basking in Elsa's adulation. It was nauseating to watch. But I suppose when Elsa comes to comparing you sexually with poor Max, it's hardly surprising...'

Rawlings, now angry, cut in. 'Stop right there, Bel. This is not a conversation I want to have and as I am in the middle of packing for Sarajevo, I am now going to end it.'

He rang off and chucked his mobile on the sofa in irritation. Damn the woman. She's becoming unhinged. He vaguely wondered if there was an underlying cause for her venom. She hadn't appeared to be knocking back the alcohol. Maybe the marriage was in trouble. He slammed his case shut, making a mental note to keep well away from the complicated labyrinth that made up Bel's emotional life and vowed he would certainly avoid her company on his return.

Chapter 16

Revisiting the Past

As the plane began its descent, Rawlings stared down at Sarajevo sprawling beneath him, while his heart began to pound. The palpitations continued as they bumped down the runway and the plane came to an abrupt halt. Why on earth had even he considered making this journey? What good could it do, apart from stirring up memories he'd much rather forget? It was a decision he was fast regretting.

From the instant they entered the terminal building, it became apparent to Rawlings that the place had undergone a radical change. Gone were the grim and menacing looks of the Serbian soldiers in their grey uniforms with their guns at the ready. Instead, friendly faces were to be seen all around him. The ever-cheerful taxi driver chatted to him in a verbal stream throughout the entire journey to his hotel, unaware of the emotional state of his passenger. Instinctively Rawlings was twitching, on the lookout for the large potholes that had once littered the road. Automatically he listened out for sniper fire, prepared to duck if they came under attack. But of course, the drive was swift and smooth, quickly reaching the city. The Holiday Inn, where he and all the other journalists had stayed during the Siege, still looked as if it had been built from Lego and still had the distinctive canary yellow walls, although now several shades brighter. It had obviously undergone complete repairs and restoration and now looked like a new building. Gone were the written messages with the warnings of 'RUN'. Gone too were the great holes in the walls from the incoming shells. Sarajevo was no longer battered and war-torn. The driver informed him proudly the hotel had reopened in 2016 under a new name, Hotel Holiday. Rawlings nodded his appreciation but felt relieved he hadn't chosen it as a place to stay. There were too many disturbing memories just waiting to surface and it was unlikely he would even feel up to visiting the bar for a drink. Instead he had booked into the more exotic Isa Begov Hamam Hotel nearby. He knew it as a fascinating old building in the Bosnian Ottoman style, restored from the ruins of old Turkish baths which were apparently still in use. It was an extravagance, but one he felt he deserved for his bravery in returning to the bloody place.

Once checked in, a porter showed him to his room which was luxuriously decorated, again in the Ottoman style. Flinging open the shutters, Rawlings noted with satisfaction that he not only had a view of the city centre but the old town as well. He looked over to the familiar spots and glanced down at the bustling crowds below. How extraordinary to see so many people out on the streets. He fully expected sniper fire or an incoming shell to send them scattering for their lives. Closing the shutters with a bang he began to unpack and had almost finished when he noticed to his annoyance that he'd failed to pack his shaving things. The oversight must have occurred after Bel's call, when he'd slammed his case shut in a fury. Damn the woman! There was nothing for it. He'd just have to grow a beard.

It was now late afternoon, but the sun was still burning

down. The taxi driver had informed him they were in the middle of a heatwave. Rawlings changed his shirt and decided on a stroll before supper.

Stepping out into the street, all the sounds and smells of a busy, modern city assailed him. Pedestrians thronged the pavements and there was heavy traffic, in what he presumed was their rush hour. He kept walking until he reached the road they'd named 'Sniper's Alley', a place where so many lives had been lost. The 'Welcome to Hell' sign was missing, but it didn't stop the memories flooding back. He thought of the risks they'd all taken when out in the streets, moving fast, dodging and diving into doorways to avoid the bullets. It was hard to believe only twenty-four years had passed since this place had been a living hell, where they had lived like starving animals, trapped in cages and in constant danger.

Feeling tired and a little shaken he stopped at a café, ordered a brandy and decided it would be a good idea to make some sort of itinerary. Pulling out a notebook he wrote down a vague schedule. It occurred to him it might be useful to hire a car for one of the days. Then he could drive out to the site of the orphanage, which was now a burial ground. He and Mia had sent money to help with the rebuilding of the new one which was nearby. Interesting to see what it had become. He made a note that Luka also needed to be contacted. The mobile number he'd been given was at the hospital, so he presumed Luka was now a doctor. It was twenty-five years since they'd pulled him out, barely alive, from under the pile of dead bodies, the sole surviving orphan in that terrible massacre. The images from that day had never left him, nor indeed many of the other horrific events that followed. Knocking back his brandy he inwardly cursed Jolyon for pushing him into this. There were going to be four days for him to get through. Impossible not to re-live the experiences, however much he might try to leave them buried. He ordered another brandy, then turned back to the page in his notes where he'd jotted down some statistics in anticipation of his return. It made grim reading. The Siege had cost 11,500 lives including 1,500 children, with 56,000 wounded. He angrily thought these bare statistics gave no idea of what had really gone on, what suffering the people had endured with all the unbearable loss and pain. If he were to write this bloody book, he was going to have to go over every detail of the three years that he and Mia, along with many others, had endured. He finished his brandy as the line came into his head: it was the best of times, it was the worst of times. How true that was. The best, for the comradeship and the countless acts of bravery, generosity and kindness. The worst, for the atrocities, the deprivations, the pain and endless suffering.

After a night where he slept surprisingly well, Rawlings prepared to spend his first full day just walking around visiting old haunts. He had a leisurely breakfast and then set out. It was only a short walk to the Holiday Inn, which was right beside the famous intersection by the Mosque. So many people had been killed at this spot while desperately trying to get across the road. He remembered the darting figures like so many ants, running for their lives, trying to dodge the sniper's bullets. But the odds were heavily against them. He'd tried to dissuade Mia from going there but she'd insisted, telling him she was shielded by the large tomb monument, but in truth it offered her little protection from the incoming fire while she took her pictures. She would often return to the hotel with tales of the brave people who had rushed out into the road to rescue those lying injured.

Rawlings stared for a long time at the entrance of the Holiday Inn and gave an involuntary shudder. There were so many who'd been shot on that doorstep pinned down by gunfire, desperately trying to get inside. It was the reason he and Mia had never used it, or the side entrance for that matter, but always made sure they dodged the bullets by running round to the back. In one major attack the lobby had been completely destroyed. The exterior walls were hit countless times by incoming shells and were so pitted with holes that one side of the building became both unsafe and unusable. On another occasion the Reuters area on the top floor suffered so many hits it had to be evacuated. The bar and long room at the back remained throughout the Siege the safest place to be. It was where Mia had played the piano the night after they rescued Luka, and the moment he had fallen in love with her. He glanced towards the second floor and could see the window where he and Mia had shared a room. From there they would nightly watch the pyrotechnics behind the Parliament building opposite them…

Rawlings looked away and forced himself to move on. This was proving more difficult than he'd anticipated. The streets which were so familiar to him were now strangely different. He still expected to see the signs of 'Pazite Snajper' – 'Beware Sniper' – which had been on every corner. Forcing himself to walk slowly and not run in panic dodging into alleyways, he almost instinctively made his way towards the Merkale market, past the cafes and the street games of men playing chess. This normality should have been comforting, but somehow it wasn't. It just seemed odd and out of place.

Finally reaching the market he paused. This had been the site of the worst massacre of the Siege, where sixty eight people had been killed while waiting in line to buy bread. Hundreds of others were injured. It immediately reminded him of the countless visits he and Mia made to the only two hospitals used in the Siege. What an endless nightmare it had seemed at the time. Both hospitals were continually under attack, while the brave doctors and nurses continued working under horrific conditions. Overwhelmed with casualties they were short of everything they needed to give proper medical attention and completely exhausted by the shear impossibility of their task. It was the children Rawlings remembered the most, so many now orphaned, sitting on trolleys with terrible injuries, their eyes staring out in horror, most too shocked and traumatised even to cry. The children's wards were full of those who were amputees, without even the painkillers or drugs to stop the infections. In spite of the best endeavours of the doctors, the mortality rate was tragically high. The image of one little girl always remained with him. She sat like a broken rag doll with her injuries, but most shocking of all was that this child had her brother's brains splattered all over one shoulder. Rawlings was told that apart from her brother, she had lost both parents, her sister and grandmother. Only an infirm grandfather was left to look after her. The doctor informed them with tears in his eyes that it was unlikely the little girl would survive the night as they were unable to deal with the complexity of her injuries. The tragedy was overwhelming, and yet scenes like it were all too common and too many for him to cover in a book.

Rawlings removed his sunglasses and wiped away his own tears, firmly telling himself this would not do. It was only his second day and he had three more to go. The midday sun was now beating down. There was an urgent need to find some shade. Putting his sunglasses back on, he moved away from the market and walked towards Baščaršija, the old bazaar and cultural centre. Everywhere he looked another incident sprang to mind. Finding he could bear no more, he decided to retrace his steps back past Sniper Alley and the Holiday Inn. Then, instead of returning to the hotel he crossed the Latin Bridge and entered Veliki Park. It was cooler here and finding some shade under a tree he sat looking out on the Sarajevo memorial to the children killed during the Siege. It was always the children who suffered the most he thought savagely, thinking of the thousands suffering and dying even now in Yemen and Syria. How many little broken bodies had he himself witnessed during those three years? It was heartbreaking. These were the images that remained with him in his nightmares. Now, as he looked out on the peaceful scene before him; children happily playing, vendors selling popcorn, lovers lying in the grass, the bicycles and the four-wheel carriages, he wondered if anyone still remembered what they had suffered in those terrible years. Their recovery seemed complete. Surely there must be some scars? He closed his eyes…

An hour later he woke with a start and at once felt a sharp pang of hunger. He decided to walk to the famous Tito café and have something to restore his blood sugar. Ordering ćevapi which he remembered as a Bosnian kebab, he accompanied it with Bosnian pitta bread and washed it all down with several glasses of local red wine. Feeling greatly restored he decided the last trip of the day should be to the Vrbanja bridge, the scene of the Sarajevo 'Romeo and Juliet' story. It was the tragic event which had succeeded in at last bringing the horror of the Siege to the attention of the world. A picture of the dead couple clinging together had been published in almost every newspaper and there was immediate shock and revulsion. In the great scheme of things, it wasn't the most horrific of the many massacres and atrocities of the war, but it represented the opposite sides of the ethnic and religious divide which had been the original cause of the fierce conflict. Admira was a Bosnian Moslem, her boyfriend Boško was a Serb. They were a young couple with a great future ahead of them. Before the Siege their mixed backgrounds would have been no problem; Christians, Jews, Moslems, Bosnians and Serbs had all lived peacefully together in Sarajevo. When this was no longer the case, the lovers decided to leave family and friends and make their escape to freedom. So, they set out. But halfway across the bridge, a sniper shot killed Boško, who died instantly. Admira was hit seconds later. She managed to crawl over to Boško, embraced him and then joined him in death. Their bodies were left on the bridge for several days, nobody brave enough to rescue them. It was the Serbs who finally removed them in the end.

Rawlings stared at the flowers that marked the scene. He knew there was also a huge heart-shaped memorial to the lovers in the cemetery, but he'd deliberately made the decision not to visit this. The miles of tomb stones bore witness to the terrible loss of life and he needed no reminders. The cemetery had also been the scene of many other horrific events. He closed his eyes trying to shut out the memory of one of the worst, when two small children burying their mother became victims themselves, the ruthless snipers turning their fire on the funeral party killing and maiming many of the grieving relatives.

He could bear no more. Turning away he walked slowly back to the hotel. This whole day had convinced Rawlings he should not be writing this book. What could he possibly add to what others had already written about the Siege? There were countless eye-witness accounts already, some by journalists who like him, had experienced first-hand life in Siege conditions. There was nothing more he could possibly add except private and personal memories, which he would not want exposed to the general public. Besides, the Bosnian War was now firmly in the past, there were plenty of other recent conflicts to be written about. He sighed. It was going to be hellishly difficult to explain this to Sheila, but his mind was made up and he would tell her firmly his decision to move straight on to his chosen topic, that of those returning from war zones suffering from PTSD.

Meanwhile, he had two more days to get through and judging by today they were not going to be easy.

Chapter 17

An Important Visit

On the penultimate night of his stay he set out to meet Luka and his wife, at their apartment near the hospital where he worked. Luka had insisted he join them for supper. Earlier, having taken a shower, he abandoned his attempts at a beard and had a shave. Growing it was going to take too long and meanwhile he just looked appallingly scruffy. No way to appear before Luka's wife. So, he had purchased a temporary razor.

Ablutions done, he decided to walk as it was such a beautiful balmy evening. His leg was not in a good state and he took it slowly but still managed to arrive on time. Taking the lift to the top floor he rang the doorbell feeling decidedly apprehensive. He hadn't seen Luka for over twenty years. Would he even recognise him? Luka had then been an under-nourished small boy, a miracle survivor of a massacre. Hard to imagine what scars that must have left. Rawlings felt a sudden stab of guilt for having lost touch with Luka after Mia's death. It was unforgiveable, especially as Mia had looked on the boy almost as a son. Luka's response to his call had first been one of surprise and then of obvious delight. Inevitably, he'd inquired if Mia was with him. Rawlings shocked by the question had automatically answered no. Only then did it occur to him that Luca hadn't heard she had died.

A short stocky man flung open the door. He had a mop of untidy hair and the only thing about him that Rawlings recognised from the past were his very dark eyes. Those were the same as the eyes of the child who'd stared at him, after they had pulled him out from under the pile of bodies.

'Rawlings! This is wonderful. Come in. Come in.'

He followed Luka into a large living room with windows that gave views over the city.

Rawlings peered out. 'That is a magnificent sight. What a wonderful place to live.'

Luka smiled. 'It is, and of course very convenient for the hospital. But the twins are now eighteen months and need more space and a garden. So in a few weeks we are moving to a house in the suburbs.'

'Your English is extremely good,' Rawlings commented.

Luka indicated he should sit. 'That was the Professor. He insisted I learned the language and I am glad he did. I went to medical school in London for a while.'

Rawlings was at once apologetic. 'I am so sorry I didn't keep in touch. The fact is…'

He was just about to explain about the explosion in Afghanistan and Mia's death, when the door opened, and a woman entered with a baby on each hip.

'This is my wife Berina, and these are our twins Mia and Davud,' Luka proudly made the introductions adding, 'my wife has no English, but I will translate for her over the meal.'

His wife was pretty, on the plump side, and definitely had that Slav, mid-European appearance. She beamed at him, nodded and then obviously under instruction, left the room. Luka explained, 'She will put the children to bed and see to supper'.

'They are lovely children.'

Luka walked over to a side-table. 'Can I give you a glass of our local wine?'

When once more seated Rawlings said, 'Luka I owe you are great apology. I only realised when I spoke to you that you hadn't heard about Mia.'

He went on to explain about them both being blown up with Mia being killed instantly, and the months he had to spend in hospital suffering terrible injuries. There was a long silence.

'When did this happen?' Luka finally asked.

'In 2010. I was lucky not to lose my leg. The five years that followed were spent having operations and also trying to recover from the death of Mia…'

Luka sounded emotional, 'It was Christmas 2009 when I had my last letter from Mia. She told me then she was in Afghanistan…' He broke off. They sipped their wine in silence. At last he said. 'I was never sure if you were married.'

'No, but I was with Mia for seventeen years until her death and loved her deeply. This place is where we met. Coming back to Sarajevo has brought back many memories, not just of Mia but of our three years living in the Holiday Inn during the Siege. It has not been an easy experience.'

Luka looked at him searchingly. 'Why return now?'

Rawlings explained about the book he'd been asked to write about his experience of the Siege, but how he felt disinclined to do so now. It was all just too personal. He then changed the subject. 'I hope you don't mind me asking. Do you remember anything of your life before we removed you from the orphanage?'

Luka shook his head. 'I remember nothing before my life

with the Professor and his family. Merciful amnesia I think you could call it. After the Siege was over, the Professor and his wife Amina adopted me. I became Luka Kovač and I acquired two sisters as well, Sara who was older and Sofia who was younger. There were no records of my existence, everything had been destroyed. They didn't even know my age. After the Siege, a dentist worked out that I must have been about nine when you and Mia saved my life. Such bravery was shown to me by so many, you included…' his voice trailed away.

Rawlings asked, 'Did you name your daughter after Mia? She would have been pleased by that.'

Luka gave a rueful smile. 'I couldn't suggest Rawlings for the boy. It would not have been very acceptable here or understood. We named him Davud, which was the Professor's name.'

'Is the Professor still alive?'

'No, he died two years ago from a heart condition, but I really think he was just worn out. He had shown such bravery during the Siege keeping us all alive. After it was over, he worked tirelessly to restore the university where he was Professor of English Studies. Shakespeare and Byron were his two great loves.'

Rawlings smiled. 'Good choices.' Then looking at Luka he said, 'He must have been pleased you studied medicine. What is your speciality?'

'I started in general practice, but all too soon became aware of the mental state of many of my patients.' He paused before saying, 'sixty percent of those who survived the Siege are now suffering from PTSD.'

Rawlings nodded. 'I suffer from it myself…'

Luka interrupted him. 'I thought that was probably

the case. You have been through too many conflicts to have emerged unscathed. As you will know, it can cause terrible problems and is the reason I am now a psychotherapist.'

Berina came back into the room with news that supper was ready, and they repaired to the dining room. The whole apartment was well appointed and there was an air of prosperity in their lifestyle. Doctors were obviously well paid.

Over the supper, which he was told was jahnija, a traditional dish of meat and vegetables, the conversation roamed over many topics, Luka sometimes translating and at other times not bothering. Rawlings told him about his son and daughter-in-law being killed in a car crash and how he had become the guardian of his grandson, who now lived in Australia with his aunt's family. Luka inquired about Rawlings' wife and he briefly explained she had died from cancer. Rawlings asked how he had met Berina. This produced a smile as Luka told him she had been one of his first PTSD patients. They had now been married five years. He also explained that his wife had suffered badly from her experiences during the Siege. Her entire family were shot in front of her and she was left with many wounds, both mental and physical. He added with some pride that she was now over the worst and that having the twins had helped her enormously. Rawlings looked across at Berina and she smiled back at him. He indicated that the food was delicious, and she nodded happily.

'I went to visit your old orphanage yesterday,' he told Luka, 'it's now a smart new building, well run and the children look cared for and happy.' Luka nodded but said he had never visited it. Rawlings didn't mention he'd also visited the old site of the orphanage, which had been completely demolished and was now just a cemetery with rows of nameless tombstones. It had been profoundly moving, but he had the feeling Luka had no wish to return to that part of his life.

'Tell me what you remember from the Siege,' Luka said.

Rawlings agreed to a second helping and thought about what he recalled most.

'In the Holiday Inn we had the same deprivations as everyone else. I found what I missed the most was hot water and coffee. The loss of electricity made our jobs a whole lot more difficult and it was one long battle to get our stories out. Perhaps most of all, I remember the cold. That first winter in the Siege I experienced conditions I'd not gone through before and thought I'd never be warm again. The freezing weather just added to the hardship and suffering of the entire population. I remember them as desperate times. People were chopping up furniture to use for firewood. Mia and I visited an old people's home out in the suburbs, where most of the inmates had just curled up and died in their beds from the cold and hunger. It was truly shocking. And then there were the queues, queues for everything. There was the food queue, a water queue, a bread queue, even a queue to buy wood, and always the danger of being fired on by the snipers. Of course, some supplies were brought in through the famous tunnel...'

'Which has now become a tourist attraction,' Luka said scornfully.

Rawlings gave a sympathetic nod. 'I agree it is odd, but without that tunnel many more would have died from starvation, although many of the supplies coming through went straight onto the black market. Inevitable I suppose.'

Berina cleared the plates away. Luka said proudly, 'She has made for you a jabukovča. It is her speciality, a filo pastry filled with apples. I hope you will like it.'

Rawlings asked Luka to thank her for all the trouble she had taken with such a wonderful meal. Luka did so and she once again beamed and nodded. She said something to him and then left the room. He explained, 'She is going to leave the coffee for us in the kitchen. I am afraid she retires early to bed. The twins keep her busy during the day and she gets tired.'

They finished eating and went back into the main room. Luka fetched in the coffee and poured more wine. 'It is interesting for me to hear about the Siege. I remember little, except for the continual noise of the shells. The Professor and his wife never talked about it once it was over. Those years became a taboo subject.'

'I can understand that,' Rawlings said. 'The people and the city wanted to recover and move on. I do find the change in the place quite remarkable.'

Luka sighed. 'In many ways yes. The libraries, the schools, churches, offices, university, hospitals, all these have been rebuilt. And the cafés and restaurants have opened. We also have concerts and theatre. It is all very civilised. But the scars remain, and I know they always will. We will never return to the liberal, multi-ethnic city that once we were.'

Rawlings nodded. 'Janine di Giovanni, another journalist who lived through the Siege, said that the fate of Bosnia was decided on the Dayton, US air base and this killed its spirit. She felt strongly the peace was an unsatisfactory compromise.'

'That is probably true,' Luka said and there was sadness in his voice. 'I would love to have lived in the pre-war Sarajevo.'

They were both lost in contemplation and then Rawlings said, 'Did anyone ever tell you about the 'Cellist of Sarajevo'? I heard him play once. It was a melancholy sound but very moving. He played for twenty two nights, sitting in the ruins of a bombed-out building, after witnessing the massacre of twenty two people in the market while they'd waited in the bread queue. He played at funerals too. It's a miracle the snipers didn't get him.'

'It is one of the two stories from those years that is told many times over.' Luka gave a shrug. 'The Cellist, and then the "Romeo and Juliet" deaths.'

'I remember both incidents,' Rawlings said, 'they were the two stories at the time that caught the imagination of the West and prompted the UN to finally do something. Just two pictures. It was always galling that we reporters risked our lives daily to tell the world the atrocities that were happening, but when our reporting became too grim our work was quickly censored back home. A great deal of what I wrote was deemed too upsetting and edited out. And yes, we became angry and disheartened. We were in constant danger just getting in and out of the hotel dodging the snipers, and then we were accused of sensational reporting unsuitable for the readers back home. One reporter, Martin Bell, was accused of "bleeding into his typewriter".' He gave a harsh laugh. 'I wrote a memoir last year, an account of my life as a war correspondent. I didn't allow anything to be edited out of that.'

'I should like to read it,' Luka said. 'Is it available here?'

'I'm not sure, but I will gladly send you a copy. It certainly gives a more accurate account of our experiences than it was possible to give at the time. I know the editors were supposedly doing their job, but they had no conception of the risks we ran in order to report our stories, in most cases accurately and without hyperbole or exaggeration, certainly in mine. We were given no protection or equipment of any kind. A month before I arrived Mia was hit in the shoulder, not a major wound but she needed surgery to remove the shrapnel, and this had to be done without anaesthetic.' He gave an abrupt laugh. 'Mia was something of a legend and incredibly brave…' Breaking off, he was silent for a moment before returning to the subject. 'Those two incidents you mentioned were by no means the ones that left the greatest impression.'

Luke leaned forward. 'Which were?'

Rawlings drained his wine and Luka filled up his glass. 'There were so many, but I think what I remember most were the visits to the two hospitals. Those will always remain with me and are certainly the most vivid. One day a shell landed on the building just behind our hotel. There were many, apart from those killed, who were terribly injured, and we helped ferry them to the nearest hospital. It was just one of many trips we made, and the sight that met us became horribly familiar: exhausted doctors in filthy scrubs, trolleys pushed into hallways because there was no more space in the wards, and the injured and dying who continued to pour through the doors. Over everything there hung the terrible smell of antiseptic, vomit and blood. Mia and I wore scarves over our mouths to stop us from gagging. We watched as surgeons amputated limbs with little or no anaesthetic and removed shrapnel from screaming children. There was no heat or water. The generator would only run for a few hours and then they had to operate by candlelight, without even enough water to wash their hands. And there were shortages of everything, impossible to imagine now.' He paused. 'It's the children that haunt me the most, lying on their cots with terrible injuries, waiting for amputations, or just waiting to die, without anything to ease their pain because there was never enough morphine. Most of them too shocked even to cry. And all the time the mortar attacks on the hospital would continue...' Rawlings stopped abruptly and gave a harsh laugh. 'At least in Afghanistan I had superb treatment for my injuries. The Army doctors saved my life, and astonishingly my leg as well.'

Luka had been watching him closely during this tirade. 'Does the leg still give you pain?'

'I had the final operation earlier this year. It's certainly better than it was. They can do no more. I have to use a stick if I am walking far...' Rawlings broke off and looked at his watch. 'My dear fellow, I'm so sorry. I'd no idea it was this late.'

Luka walked with him to the door. 'What are your plans now?'

'I leave here tomorrow and then later in the month I plan to go to the States to visit Mia's family.' Here Rawlings gave a sigh. 'I also need to let my publishers know my decision about writing the book on the Siege.'

He thanked Luka for the wonderful evening and promised to keep in touch.

Then something surprising happened. Luka took Rawlings in his arms and said gently but firmly, 'I think you should write that book my friend. It is something you need to do to find some sort of closure. Who knows, you may even find it cathartic.'

Chapter 18

Return to England

'I tell you Isobel, it was as if our roles had been reversed and that I was the younger man and he the older imparting his great words of wisdom. Ever since then I have been left wondering, could he be right? Should I take his advice and write the blasted book?'

Rawlings was once again walking up and down Isobel's living room in a state of agitation. He abruptly stopped and looked at her, then gave a great guffaw of laughter. 'I know, you want me to stop pacing about and sit down.'

Isobel said mildly, 'It would help me to concentrate on what you are saying.' He obediently sat on the chair opposite her and she gave an approving nod before adding, 'Your Luka seems to be a very impressive young man. You say he's a doctor?'

'Yes, specialising in psychotherapy and I am led to believe, greatly in demand. Apparently, there are still many who are suffering PTSD from the effects of the Siege.'

Isobel looked at him and said sharply. 'Did you tell him you were a sufferer?'

Rawlings chuckled. 'I did, but it wasn't necessary. He could tell.'

Isobel was frowning. She was obviously in a disapproving mood which made him thankful he'd decided against growing a beard. A tramp-like appearance would certainly not have endeared him further. After a long pause Isobel asked, 'Are you going to take his advice and write the book?'

Rawlings said grumpily, 'I feel I am being nobbled from all sides. Half of me thinks I should write the bloody thing because I owe it to Jolyon. And maybe Luka is right. It would be cathartic. But the other half of me wants to run away from it as far as possible.'

Isobel looked at him curiously. 'And which half will win?'

He shrugged. 'I don't know, maybe a visit to Mia's family in Vermont might concentrate the mind and help me make a decision. I'll look at her archive material from the Siege. There must be hundreds of images she took, and I do know she also kept a journal. I go at the end of the month and after that, a decision will have to be made...' He broke off and looked at Isobel. 'Do you know what date it was yesterday?'

She nodded. 'August eighteenth. Felix's birthday. I sent him an email but not sure he received it. I couldn't Skype him while he was away at camp.'

Rawlings sounded angry. 'I emailed both him and Brad. I can't bear for him to think I forgot. He leaves camp in a couple of weeks, so I will definitely put in a Skype before I leave for the States.'

Isobel examined him searchingly. She could tell something wasn't right with the man and it wasn't just the worry over Felix, but before she could question him further he burst out, 'I cannot understand why this year has been so damned difficult. I've been beset by crises and problems at every turn. I stupidly thought, once my operation was over, I could tie up some loose ends and then get on with the next phase of my life, but how wrong could I be.'

Isobel wondered what he was expecting from the next phase of his life, but she spoke soothingly, 'I think you'll find there have been some positives. You have your flat sorted and you enjoyed a pleasant reunion with your sister.'

He said grudgingly, 'I suppose you're right. One thing I have learned this year is the complexity of family life. I had no idea it was such an emotional labyrinth. Thank God I never went through it. The slightest incident and woof, everything goes off kilter!' He looked at Isobel. 'To be honest, I'm rather dubious about meeting Mia's family. According to her, they were a right bunch of neurotics. She didn't have a good word to say about any of them.'

Isobel smiled. 'Talking of families, how is your friend Max?'

Rawlings exploded. 'That's another thing. Out of the blue he informs me he's been diagnosed with Parkinson's. I had no idea. It was a shock I can tell you. Max doesn't appear too perturbed about it right now, probably because he has his mistress staying with him.' He added gloomily, 'Not that I can see she'll be much help. She's extremely high maintenance and I wouldn't be surprised if she didn't abandon him for a younger, fitter model soon. That would really throw him.'

Isobel looked reprovingly at him. 'Parkinson's can affect people in different ways, but those who have it nearly always suffer from depression. You should look out for that.'

Rawlings nodded. 'Max is in the early stages, so he doesn't appear to be suffering greatly yet.' He gave a chuckle. 'The doctor insists he take exercise, so we went to Battersea Dogs Home and found him a dog. Actually, not so much a dog as a walking hearth rug.'

This made Isobel laugh. 'Dogs can be very therapeutic,'

she said and looked affectionately across at Juno who was sprawled out by the window catching the afternoon sun.

After his departure, Isobel sat in the garden and pondered over the problem of Rawlings. From their first meeting there had always been a strange bond between them. It was not a physical one, although she could well understand why women fell for him, he was an extremely attractive man. No, he was more like a troublesome younger brother, in constant need of help and advice. She loved him deeply in her own way and understood him too. It was obvious he was in a restless and uncertain state. Probably in need of sex. She instantly reproved herself for thinking sex was the answer to all problems. Even so, one solution for his present disposition could well be some sort of stable relationship. Marnie hadn't worked out and another Marnie seemed highly unlikely at present. Again, she chided herself. The priority right now for both herself and Rawlings must be Felix. It was a worrying situation and from what she could tell, there was no immediate solution.

On arriving back at the flat, Rawlings decided to book his flights to Boston. He again read the letter from Kaye, Mia's mother. The tone was resigned rather than welcoming, and surprisingly cold and formal, considering he had lived with her daughter for seventeen years.

Dear Mr Rawlings,

I understand from your letter that you wish to examine my daughter Mia's archive for the purpose of doing research for a book you are writing, about the Siege of Sarajevo.

The family has agreed to this request providing you only make copies, and nothing is removed from this house.

Our circumstances have changed, and we no longer live in

Boston. *My husband passed away two years after Mia, having never recovered from the news of his daughter's death. We have now moved up to the family home in Bellows Falls, Vermont. My daughter still has an apartment in Boston and can drive you up here. She comes here every weekend so it will be no problem for her. You can stay in the house while doing your research.*

Please let Sorcha know the time of your arrival in Boston, so she can meet you at the airport. I attach her email address.

I believe you once met my younger daughter in New York, so will be able to recognise her.

Yours sincerely,

Kaye O'Keefe.

Rawlings put the letter down and sighed. To use the old cliché, reading between the lines two things became clear. Firstly, Kaye blamed him for the death of her daughter which consequently meant she disliked him already, and leading on from there, she somehow associated the death of her husband with Mia's death and therefore, in some bizarre way this was his fault as well, which meant his visit was going to be extremely unpleasant. He sighed again. There was no turning back now. He had initiated the visit, so he had only himself to blame; well, apart from Jolyon, Sheila and the publishing company, for pushing him into writing the bloody book in the first place. The dragon woman Sheila had been distinctly unimpressed when he told her he needed to do more research.

He rang the airline, booked his tickets and sent an email of the arrival time to Sorcha. It would be interesting to see her again. He had indeed met Sorcha in New York. She'd arrived one evening at their apartment just after the Millennium, completely out of it, high on some substance if not several.

It had taken Mia two days to sort her out, explaining her sister had always been unstable and now unfortunately she had fallen into the wrong crowd resulting in her drink and drug problems. According to Mia, she appeared to live in one long Bacchanalian orgy and could never hold a job down for long. That was nearly twenty years ago. It was to be hoped she had changed since then.

The next day Rawlings set off for his favourite bookshop in Chelsea and ordered a copy of his own book to send to Luka. He also bought two leather-bound copies of the original Winnie the Pooh books with the E H Shepherd illustrations, to be sent along with his book as a present for the twins. Luka could do the translations for them and they would surely enjoy the pictures. Pleased with his purchases, he went on to have an extravagant spend in Harrods Food Hall, buying provisions for the supper he was due to give for Max and Elsa the following evening. It was an invitation he'd issued rather reluctantly more for Max's sake than for hers. For some reason he couldn't quite fathom, he'd taken an instant dislike to the woman.

She arrived looking even more exotic than before, wearing a long dress that appeared to have been made entirely out of Hermes scarves which clung very closely to her figure revealing a deep cleavage. There's no mistaking she's a mammal he thought grimly.

'Do you mind if I bring Bolly in?' Max asked. 'We can let him out in the garden. It's just as long as he knows where I am.' Those were the last words he was to speak for some time. Rawlings assured him it was fine and opened the patio doors. Bolly immediately pottered out to his favourite spot where he sat and watched the river.

'Honestly Max, you and that dog.' Elsa said crossly. 'You pay far more attention to that wretched animal than you ever do to me.'

Max sat down without any reaction to this. Rawlings noted he looked pale and drained and felt a stab of anxiety. Maybe having Elsa with him wasn't the best idea at this particular juncture.

'I just adore this room darling,' Elsa enthused, turning all her attention upon Rawlings. 'It is minimal I agree, and yet so full of character, such a relief after the terrible clutter upstairs.' She gave Max a pointed look.

'I've never had the opportunity to collect clutter,' Rawlings said. 'My life until now has been spent abroad. The few objects you see in this room have been very recent acquisitions, apart from the books.'

She batted her eyelashes at him. 'You should buy one of my sculptures darling, they would look perfect in here.' He didn't take up this offer but instead handed her a plate of what he would have termed as a 'starter'.

'Pâté de foie gras!' she almost screamed, 'how absolutely divine. Why don't we ever have something like this Max?'

Before the poor man could answer Rawlings said with as much patience as he could muster, 'I don't suppose Max has had time to visit Harrods Food Hall lately. I only did yesterday because I happened to be in the area.' He was tempted to add, 'Give the man a break you stupid woman, he's not well', but refrained from doing so and went on, 'I lazily purchased the whole meal there, leaving me to do as little as possible.' He then deliberately turned away from her. 'It seems I'm off on my travels again Max. I go to the States in a few days. I'll be gone for at least a week.'

Max nodded but said nothing. Elsa was immediately interested. 'Whereabouts in the States are you going?'

'Vermont.'

'How wonderful for you darling,' she enthused. 'I hear it is one of the very nicest states. A man from Vermont bought one of my sculptures. He lived in Montpelier I remember. Are you going to be near there? I could give you his name and you could look him up.'

The evening progressed in similar vein, Max silent, Elsa flirty, voluble and over-vivacious. She occasionally addressed Max with seemingly innocuous remarks, but they always carried a hint of acid undertone.

They reached the coffee stage when Max suddenly spoke. 'Elsa is returning to Northumberland at the end of next week.' This was said flatly without any trace of emotion.

Elsa gave a tinkly laugh, 'I have been neglecting my work for far too long. I have so much to do before my exhibition in November. I will of course be returning to London for that.'

Three months thought Rawlings. He didn't really see the relationship surviving that long. It was on the skids and Max wasn't fighting for it. There was a character in one of the Anthony Powell books who rather resembled him. Powell described this character as not being interested in either sex, more in love with himself. It wasn't entirely true that Max was in love with himself, but he did have a definite tendency to be self-absorbed, along with a marked disinterest in sex. That wouldn't have pleased Elsa. Why on earth had he attached himself to a woman with voracious sexual appetites which he couldn't possibly hope to satisfy? Why indeed had she become attached to him? It was a paradox. They had been together, on and off, for many years. There had to be something that kept them together. Maybe it had been different in the beginning. Max could be extremely charming, especially when let loose playing the piano, but there had been little of that lately. He now seemed disinclined to socialise at all except with the family. Elsa would miss those party nights and without the social life Max obviously held little allure for her. Even so, he could tell that Elsa's imminent departure was depressing him.

The following morning, he put through a call to Hetty.

'I know I'm probably worrying you unnecessarily, but in view of Max's illness Elsa's departure has made me anxious especially as I'm going to the States in a week myself, so I won't be around.'

'That woman is an utter and completely selfish bitch,' Hetty exploded down the line, 'with her gushing and theatrical way of calling everyone darling. I wouldn't be surprised if this departure doesn't spell the end of their relationship. She doesn't have one sympathetic bone in her body. Poor Max. He had difficulty holding on to her when he was fully fit, he doesn't stand a chance now he's ill, not with Parkinson's anyway. Believe me she'll be off to find a younger model. Bernard agrees with me. We discussed it last time we were down. The writing was on the wall then. Don't worry. We'll keep an eye on the poor old boy. Personally, I think he's better off without her. At least he's got Bolly to stop him from being lonely and that's a far healthier relationship!' There was a short pause and then she said, 'Have you heard the news about Bel and Clive?'

Rawlings felt his heart sink. 'No, I haven't. I've only just returned from Sarajevo. What's happened? Is it bad?'

'We're not sure. It was obvious they weren't getting on, nothing dramatic just permanent bickering, which was rather tiresome. And then last week Clive announced he would be taking up a six-month contract in Dubai, opening a new restaurant. Why it should take that long I simply can't imagine, but he leaves at the end of September.'

Change and decay in all around I see… the line sprang unbidden into his head. Rawlings tried to sound positive. 'Absence might be good for both of them' he said, 'makes the heart grow fonder and all that.' Hetty gave a snort, which indicated she did not agree and told him he was beginning to sound like Bertie Wooster. The call finished abruptly rather to his relief, when one of her dogs started barking.

Rawlings opened his laptop. An email had arrived from Sorcha saying she would be delighted to see him again and would certainly give him a lift to Bellows Falls. Her only request was that they should leave early on the Friday morning as the weekend traffic out of Boston tended to build up later in the day and could make the journey twice as long. This was no problem. He had already booked into a Boston hotel on Thursday evening because his flight arrived late. It meant they could leave at 10 a.m. the next day, and he emailed Sorcha with this information.

His final task before leaving for the States was to Skype Felix. The boy's return from camp had been a week before, but since then there had been a notable silence. Rawlings greatly disliked Skype as a means of communication, but right now it was the only way to keep in touch with the boy. At the appointed hour he clicked on. There he was looking fit and healthy, but Rawlings immediately noticed the same wariness in his expression and the conversation that followed was stilted and difficult. In some desperation Rawlings found himself being over cheerful.

'How was the Camp, Felix? Did you enjoy yourself?'

'It was all right.'

'You're looking well.' Long pause. 'Brad said you won a prize. What was that for?'

Felix gave a shrug and then with a hint of a smile he said, 'A survival test.'

The irony was not lost on Rawlings. 'Well done for that.' Another pause. 'I gather Ella is still in hospital. Is Sarah with her?'

'Yes. They come back next weekend I think.'

'That must be difficult for Brad. Does he have any help?'

'We have a girl called Melanie who looks after us during the day.' He suddenly added, 'She makes good cakes.'

There seemed no comment he could make to this. 'I know you'll be glad to see Ella again.'

'Yes.'

Rawlings desperately hunted for inspiration. 'Felix I was sorry to miss your birthday. I just couldn't Skype when you were in the Camp.'

'That's OK. I got your email. And Isobel's.'

'Did you have a party in the Camp?'

'No. Not really. Everyone sang Happy Birthday, and I had some cards. Brad and Sarah gave me a cricket bat.'

'What a great present.' Pause. 'When you get back, you will have our presents and we will have a late party for you. It could be a joint party for both you and Isobel. She was seventy in June, so it will be a special celebration.'

Felix gave him a long look, not hostile exactly, but his reply was unenthusiastic. 'By the time I get back it will be Christmas, not much point in having a birthday party then.'

Rawlings was careful not to argue. 'I'm sure we can manage a special day for the two of you…'

Felix interrupted. 'EG I think Melanie is calling me. I'd better go.'

'All right. Talk again soon.' He was about to send love, but Felix clicked off and was gone.

Rawlings sat staring at the blank screen, trying to work out what the hell he was to make of that call. It had been his intention to reassure the boy and tell him he was there to be contacted, if life out there became unbearable. But he couldn't because the call had ended so abruptly. Maybe that particular message would be better put in an email. He had to say something, instinct convinced him all was far from well. Felix had shut down and he was helpless to do anything, stuck on the other side of the world.

Dear God! He'd made a terrible mess of this.

Chapter 19

Arrival in America

He recognised her instantly. She was lolling against the reception desk, but on seeing him she languidly straightened up giving a striking resemblance to Lauren Bacall's first meeting with Humphrey Bogart in To Have and to Have Not.

He hailed her across the lobby. 'Sorcha!'

She moved at speed towards him and after a brief hug told him to move it, as an over-officious doorman was moaning about leaving her car outside.

'I told them you were an invalid so please exaggerate your limp.'

He did as he was told, the doorman even helping him into the car. In minutes they were off moving at speed through the Boston traffic. Sorcha drove fast and Rawlings reflected this was going to be a rather different drive from the one he'd taken with Hetty through the wilds of Yorkshire. It struck him that Sorcha was like Mia, with that same air of sophisticated confidence. He inquired how long the journey would take.

'Just over two hours at this time of day. We've just taken Route 2 out of Boston. We'll then move on to Route 140 through Winchendon. You'll know it when we get there. It was the site of an old toy factory and there's a fucking great rocking-horse at the intersection. After that, it's Route 12 through Keene New Hampshire, and then north to cross the river into Bellows Falls.'

Rawlings was a little startled by the swearing. It somehow didn't fit in with the Boston drawl. Had she done it for his benefit? He studied her profile. Again, it was similar to Mia's, although she wore her fair hair long whereas Mia had hers cut short.

'I'm uneasy about staying in your mother's house,' he told her. 'Her letter wasn't exactly welcoming. I could easily have stayed in a hotel.'

Sorcha gave a laugh that was almost a bark. 'You're right in expecting a chilly reception. Mother is hostile to everyone me included, so take no notice. I should also warn you she blames you quite unfairly for stopping Mia visiting them when she was back in New York.'

Rawlings frowned. 'That is absolutely untrue. I urged Mia to visit her parents, especially when I had to return to England. To my knowledge she only went to Boston once and that was after our return from Sarajevo. I was always puzzled by this, but she never gave any explanation.' He hesitated. 'Mia didn't have a high opinion of your parents, or of family life. Was there a reason for this?'

Sorcha gave another of her barks. 'Several. Even if you only stay a few days, you'll begin to understand why.'

There was a break in the conversation while Sorcha manoeuvred her way around an enormously long truck. Everything is bigger in America he reminded himself.

'Even so,' he persisted, 'I could easily have stayed in a hotel.'

'Good God no,' Sorcha said, adding with a degree of sarcasm, 'Mother would never allow that. She wouldn't want to miss the chance to show off her great house, along with her gracious lifestyle.'

Rawlings felt some surprise. 'Is it a grand house? Mia never mentioned it, or indeed anything about her background. I do know your father had served in a MASH unit during the Korean War…'

Sorcha cut in, 'Well, that was probably the root of his trouble. He returned from Korea in what I imagine was in a bad way, mentally. I can assure you he bore absolutely no resemblance to Hawkeye Pierce in the TV series. More like the pompous Boston one, I can't remember his name.'

'Charles Winchester III.'

'Bloody hell, how do you know that?'

'MASH is one of the few TV series I really like. I still watch it.'

Sorcha said drily, 'Better not mention that. Mother and Father hated it and forbade us to see it. Of course, we did. I was madly in love with Alan Alda.'

'Why on earth was it forbidden? I thought it was one of the most popular American series ever.'

'Not for them. And you're in for a few greater shocks than that.' She gave him a quick look. 'Poor Rawlings. Don't worry I'll be there to protect you!'

He smiled. 'It sounds as if I'll need it.' They had reached the intersection with the rocking-horse and now moved onto Route 12. 'Suppose you give me a little background information before we reach the house? I'd like to be prepared.'

Sorcha sighed. 'You asked for it. OK, one potted history of the O'Keefe family coming right up.' She paused and then dived in. 'Father returned from Korea, damaged, but still working as a doctor. He fell in love with a beautiful dancer,' she flashed him a grin, 'ballet, not pole, who was ten years younger, and from one of the old "money" families. Big snobs. There followed objections from her parents, but in spite of this they were married in 1960. Mia was born in 1961, my brother Brendan was born two years later. I was an afterthought and arrived in 1968.'

'That makes you about fifty. You certainly don't look it.'

'Thank you. I'm actually forty nine for a few months more. My birthday is in November.' She gave him a strange look. 'The same age as Mia when she died.' She returned to concentrating on her driving. 'How old are you?'

'I'm about to be sixty seven. I was ten years older than Mia.'

She nodded and then said, 'All this arithmetic is giving me a headache. I'll press on with the O'Keefe background or I won't get it finished before we reach the house. Brendan, my pompous and extremely boring brother, is the only one of the siblings to follow his parent's wishes and become a doctor. He has a vacuous wife Kelly, who has an annoying laugh but nothing much else to distinguish her, and they have two very obese sons. They usually pile over for Sunday lunch.'

'You don't seem to have a very high opinion of your brother.'

'I dislike every single member of my family, except Mia, and she's dead.' Rawlings winced at this bald statement but let her continue. 'The fact that I was an after-thought meant I was considered a mistake from the moment I made my appearance. I was not necessary, and my parents made that fairly clear. Father doted on Mia and Mother on Brendan. I was an unnecessary addition to the family and an unwelcome distraction, especially as I was generally known as a "difficult child". I am pleased to say I continued to cause trouble even when I emerged from the chrysalis into the butterfly of adulthood.'

'Very poetic,' commented Rawlings and she laughed.

'We had a strict Roman Catholic upbringing with no expense spared on our education, and any accomplishment that was shown was immediately nurtured. Mia was an exceptional musician, which made Father dote on her even more. She had the best teachers, a beautiful Steinway Grand Piano of her own and finally went off to the Berklee College of Music.' She paused. 'And soon after that, the balloon went up.'

'It did?' Rawlings was fascinated. 'What sort of balloon?'

Sorcha slowed down and stopped the car. 'We've made good time. We're just above Bellows Falls now. I want to finish the family saga before we arrive. It's only fair you should know what to expect.'

'I think you're right,' Rawlings remarked drily, 'I always like to know what I'm up against. Carry on.'

She nodded. 'That "balloon" was a bombshell Mia dropped into the arena one weekend when we were all gathered in the Bellow Falls house. Her shock announcement was that she had given up her music studies and was studying photography instead, which was now to be her chosen career. You can imagine the horror and consternation. There was little action my parents could take, apart from yell and scream. Mia had become financially independent on her twenty first birthday. We were each left a generous settlement by our grandparents. It was the one good thing that came out of our early life. It made absolutely no difference if the parents threatened to withdraw financial support. In any case Mia's mind was made up and you know how strong-willed she was.' He nodded. She swivelled round to face him. 'I will never forget that night. Looking back, it was like watching a scene from some movie melodrama. Everyone except me had a violent reaction. Mother immediately had full blown hysterics. Brendan, the creep, angrily remonstrated with Mia for betraying her parent's trust. Father stood up and demanded that Mia follow him to his study. You could hear the raised voices echo through the house. She was in there for hours. I never knew what was said but later that evening she came to my room, declared she was returning to Boston and would not be coming back. I was desperately upset. She was the one person who made my life bearable, but she was adamant. To give her some credit, she did keep in touch with me when I went to the Massachusetts College of Art and Design…' she gave a grin, 'where I failed dismally and quickly went off the rails, but that's another story. Soon after her departure, word came back to us that she was leaving for Sarajevo to be a war photographer. That was the last proverbial straw that broke the camel's back. Father hated wars with a passion. Korea had left him an angry man, so this fury at her decision was kind of understandable. What was more puzzling was his anger at her taking an interest in photography. He had been a keen amateur photographer himself and when Mia was in her teens, was always whisking her off to be photographed. They would spend hours closeted away. I never saw the results. I suppose Mia saw them. But the fact is, it was Father that had encouraged her in that direction, giving her all the most expensive photographic equipment, but only he'd thought, for a hobby. He'd always envisaged his daughter would be a concert pianist, it was almost an obsession with him, and that night in one go all his hopes went up in smoke. Her beautiful Steinway piano was locked away and never played again.'

'Good God! What happened after that?' Rawlings was both shocked and fascinated. It did explain something about Mia's enigmatic character, also how she had afforded the apartment in New York, along with her lavish lifestyle.

Sorcha shrugged. 'It was pretty awful. Mother became even colder and more brittle if that were possible, and as far as I know, Father never spoke to Mia again. The one time she returned after Sarajevo he shut himself away in his study and had all his meals sent in, so he wouldn't have to confront her. She didn't stay long.'

'Didn't your Mother try to mediate?'

Sorcha gave another of her barks. 'Good God no! She doted on Father and never disagreed with him about anything.' She turned the engine on. 'OK honey, prepare yourself.'

Rawlings had further questions but knew he was running out of time. 'How is it that your family is so wealthy?'

Sorcha said carelessly, 'Mother's great grandfather was one of the founders of the paper mills in Bellows Falls. He sold out in the thirties leaving behind him a huge fortune and the family house, where we are now headed. It's a nineteenth century colonial monstrosity in my opinion, situated in the very exclusive Westminster Terrace, on the NRHP.'

'I have no idea what the NRHP is.'

'The National Register of Historic Places.' She looked at him curiously, 'Are you wealthy Rawlings? I know little about you.'

He shrugged. 'I have enough to live on, but I've no interest in making money or becoming rich. I'm afraid I am from quite the wrong side of the tracks, which no doubt your mother will quickly surmise.'

That bark of a laugh again. 'She sure will. She's the most appalling snob.'

They were climbing a steep hill and then into what he presumed was the Terrace. Sorcha turned into a drive at speed and brought the car to a halt with a squeal of the brakes.

A plump woman dressed entirely in black came down the steps of the house.

'Hello Mimms,' Sorcha said and then with an airy gesture, 'This is a friend of Mia's. His name is Rawlings and he's staying with us for the weekend.' She turned back to him. 'Mimms has looked after the family for years. We'd be lost without her.'

Mimms looked at Sorcha with a frown and a shake of the head. 'You know your mother doesn't like you driving up to the house so fast. It makes a mess of the driveway and that upsets her.' She turned to Rawlings. 'I am pleased to meet you sir. Mrs O'Keefe is waiting for you in the sun lounge.'

With that, the unsmiling Mimms took his suitcase from Sorcha and went ahead of them into the house. Rawlings retrieving his walking stick took a moment to look at the building before him. It was indeed palatial, white, with many colonial features and a true American grandeur. It rather resembled a giant-sized wedding cake. His feelings of unease increased.

'Come on Rawlings.' Sorcha called from the top of the steps. 'We'll meet Mother first, then she can retire. She won't be seen again until this evening. Once you've said hello, I can show you around. We always have buffet lunches except on Sunday, so everyone can eat when they want to. Then we all meet up in the evening. Cocktails at seven, dinner at eight.'

It sounded like something out of Noel Coward.

While she was telling him this, they were passing endless rooms and moving towards what he supposed was the back of

211

the house. Finally they arrived at what he would have called a conservatory but it was rather grander than that, a large room with gothic windows from ceiling to floor, potted palms in huge urns and elegant rattan furniture with dark green linen and white cushions. The whole room faced onto long sloping lawns with a massive cedar tree which added to the grandeur of the landscape. Situated by the middle window was a rattan chaise longue and on this, Sorcha's mother was lying, wearing an eye shade, which she removed as they entered and slowly stood to greet them. His first impression was of a small and frail woman. His second impression was that she was expensively dressed wearing a cream blouse with matching crepe trousers and a narrow belt at her waist. Her hair was coiffured and blonde and her face, no doubt with a few face lifts, was immaculately made up. She moved towards him and held out a manicured hand. Her expression was not friendly. The hand he took was veined and skeletal, with brilliant red varnish on the nails and heavy rings on the fingers. Rawlings didn't dare shake it for fear he might do damage, so just gave it a light touch. He seemed to tower over her.

'I trust you had a good journey.' Her voice with its Boston drawl was flat and without enthusiasm.

Before he could reply Sorcha said, 'Yes thank you Mother, we made good time.'

Kaye O'Keefe turned her attention to her daughter. 'Really Sorcha, why are you wearing those dreadful jeans? Surely you could have made some effort. I know you only do it to annoy me, but I trust you will be changing before dinner.' As Sorcha didn't react, she continued, 'Please show Mr Rawlings to his room and then see he has everything he needs for his research.' Her attention returned to him. 'My daughter's archive is in the small library. I have had the boxes laid out on the main table for you. All the copying equipment is in your father's office Sorcha. Please see that you don't leave a mess. Brendan will be working in there on Sunday.' With that she returned to the chaise longue and replaced the eye shade. 'I shall see you both at seven.'

Having been dismissed he followed Sorcha up a grand central staircase, down another long corridor and into what he presumed was a guest bedroom. The jetlag was beginning to kick in and he was too tired to be over-impressed, just noting that the room was of large proportions and the décor lavish, but most definitely not to his taste. His suitcase had been placed on a long chest at the foot of the bed. Sorcha kicked open a door which revealed an ornate bathroom complete with gold taps.

She gave him a grin. 'Well you survived the first meeting with Mother. I guess you'd like to unpack and freshen up. I'll come back in an hour and take you to lunch. After that, I can show you where Mia's stuff is.'

Rawlings thanked her and she left.

Two hours later, he was sitting at a long table with boxes piled high on it. Three walls of the room were taken up with books, and it set him wondering what on earth the larger library must be like, if this was referred to as the small one. Dragging his attention back to the task, his first action was to divide the files with the photos from the ones with her notebooks and letters. It was a relief, and something of a surprise, that he had been given such total access to Mia's archive.

Taking a deep breath, he plunged into the top file. It was filled with notebooks of differing sizes, all marked with the relevant name and date. How odd he thought, to be seeing the familiar handwriting again after all these years. Mia had never written letters, only sending him the occasional note which he hadn't bothered to keep. Indeed, she'd always mocked him for being a wordsmith, maintaining she disliked putting pen to paper. As far as he knew she only made these notes as a background guide for her photographs. He picked out the one marked 'Sarajevo – 1992–1995'. A preliminary glance revealed there was more to these notes than mere reference points, these were her private thoughts on all that was happening. It was a long narrative on paper, concise and outspoken, but sticking to facts rather than emotions. Or was it? Certainly, at the start it was. For instance, an entry on November 1992 read:

…I have been here six months without damage and today a bloody sniper got me in the shoulder. This caused a good deal of excitement in the camp, rather ghoulish really. Bic our resident medic removed it without anaesthetic for the simple reason he didn't have any! Bloody awful. They poured a great deal of Scotch down my throat. I don't know which was worse, the pain from the wound or the fucking hangover. Luckily no real damage done and I can still use the camera…

Rawlings read on and came to the day of his arrival. Here her tone suddenly changed.

February 7th 1993. Today a new reporter joined us. Not a TV man but a scribbler, writes for one of the main British papers under the name E G Rawlings. Apparently, he likes to be known as Rawlings. I've read a couple of his reports and they're sort of impressive, unemotional and factual. I made a short study of him from a distance. He's good looking in a rugged sort of way, tall, with dark hair and bushy eyebrows which mask his expression – difficult to know what he's thinking. Under those eyebrows are rather startling blue eyes. I only noticed those when he came over to the bar for a drink. Otherwise he retreats and sits by himself. I've made a few inquiries about him. Gather he's a loner but after a few drinks can be good company. He also has a reputation as something of a Don Juan. The few females here immediately gathered around him flirting away, but he appeared to take no notice. I have not approached him! But I like the fact that he hasn't hit on me, as some of the other pesky journalists around here have done…

February 12th Well, well, well! Rawlings has asked me to join him as his photographer. He told me his usual guy had to stay behind in England, so he's a photographer short. I'm interested but told him I would think it over. Don't want him taking my decision for granted. He seems quite arrogant, with that British air of superiority…

Rawlings smiled at this. He well remembered her making him wait. He read on.

February 19th. Today Rawlings and I started working together. So far, it's OK. I like the way he works. He says little and is almost taciturn – which I don't mind. We seem to agree about the angles we wish to take…

March 4th. This morning we were pinned down under sniper fire for about two hours. Rawlings was concerned for my safety. I told him to shut up and that we were equals. He reproved me for not wearing a jacket, but I explained it's too bloody bulky and stops the freedom of movement I need. Anyway, he doesn't wear one...

Rawlings recalled that argument. Mia appeared to have no fear. It was the same in Iraq and in Afghanistan. She was indeed brave, but as with her great heroine Marie Colvin she took unnecessary risks. He skimmed through the next pages, until he came to the orphanage incident.

...I'm almost too exhausted to write, but yesterday was the most traumatic day to date and needs to be recorded. Rawlings and I received news that an orphanage had been hit in the suburbs, resulting in many casualties. To reach it would mean a dangerous journey. Nobody else wanted to touch this assignment but we both decided we should go. We got into the old Jeep and moved at speed out of the underground carpark. Luckily, R is a good driver. The snipers immediately spotted us, so it wasn't a pleasant journey – a great deal of ducking and diving! We arrived to find the most horrific sight I have yet seen, and I have seen plenty. The building must have received several direct hits and only the skeleton of it remained. Bodies and bits of bodies were everywhere. It was carnage. There was a blackboard still upright with a child's brains splashed on it. I think I counted about twenty children and a few adults – some you couldn't tell. It was then that we found him. One small child under a pile of bodies, but he was still alive. I suppose he must have been about ten but he was so thin, limp and like a rag doll. We dragged him out and I asked him his name. He whispered 'Luka'. I gave him a piece of chocolate. He didn't eat it! Just clutched on to it and kept staring at me with his huge eyes. The child was in shock

and I told R we had to get him away from there. But where? I then thought of my friend Professor Kovač who was no longer at the University but at his house trying to look after his wife and two little girls. The snipers were out in full force and I am surprised we even made it to Davud's house. He let us in and bless him, immediately understood the situation. His wife Amina took Luka away into another room. We told them we would give them as many provisions as we could, and he agreed to keep Luka. It was such a relief. I don't know what we'd have done if he hadn't. R and I left and drove back to the hotel. We met Martin B who asked me why I was covered in blood, so we told him and then went to our separate rooms to clean up. Trying to get blood out of my shirt with cold water proved an almost impossible task, the stain seems destined to remain, as a reminder.

Later that evening and in a bad way, I found myself drawn to the piano in one corner of the bar. I hadn't played for ages – hardly surprising! – but tonight somehow, I needed to find release in something beautiful. It never occurred to me that anyone would listen. There was the usual noise and laughter around the bar. I started to play Schumann's Liebeslied. It wasn't until I finished that I realised the room had gone silent. Then everyone clapped. Thankfully they quickly fell to talking again so I was saved further embarrassment, and then I saw R. He was sitting by himself at his usual far table. I went over and to my horror saw that tears were pouring down his face. I understood – the combination of the terrible events of the day and the beauty of the music had been too much for him. I took his hands in mine – and then it happened. I suppose you could call it 'a moment', a 'coup de foudre'. Whatever it was, I knew something had definitely changed in our relationship. Yes, sex came into it – but it was more than that. Didn't ever think this would happen to me. It's still too recent, but something makes me sure R will now be part of my life. He has only just left my bed!

Rawlings snapped the notebook shut, stood up and walked to the window. A peaceful scene lay before him, with the immaculate lawn and beautiful cedar tree. A scene as far removed from Sarajevo as it was possible to be. But even here, that day at the orphanage was always present in his mind. If he closed his eyes he could recall it in detail, still hearing the noise of snipers and shells, contrasting grotesquely with the stillness of the dead bodies that were strewn across the ruins. He needed no notebooks to remind him. And yet... It was curious, now he thought about it, Mia had left something out of her account. Was this deliberate? He distinctly remembered that after leaving Luka with the Professor, he had driven to the safest place he could find, stopped the Jeep and let her sob her heart out. Later they both admitted it was the one time they had broken down during the entire Sarajevo Siege. There were many other terrible incidents they witnessed, not least the visits to the hospitals, but somehow that awful scene at the orphanage was the one that had affected them the most.

He waited for his heart rate to calm down, then moved back to the table. The New York notebooks were thinner, as were the ones written in Iraq and Afghanistan. He decided not to read those today, but have copies made of everything.

He called Sorcha on his mobile. 'Hi, I need help to find the copier without getting lost!'

She laughed. 'I'll be with you in a minute.'

He collected up all the notebooks and waited for Sorcha to arrive.

'I hope you have plenty of paper supplies. I've decided

to copy all the notebooks, so I can read them at my leisure. I honestly had no idea Mia kept such detailed accounts.'

'What about the photographs?'

'I haven't started on them yet. I was going to leave that until the morning.' He paused for a moment deep in thought. 'The problem is, if I am to use any of them in my book, I can't use prints, I will need actual photographic copies.'

Sorcha considered this. 'I have a friend who's a photographer and I'll give him a call. We could go into Bellows Falls in the morning, leave the photos with him, have lunch at the Grafton Inn, and then pick up the photos in the afternoon. You'll like the Inn, it's very quaint, as you Brits would say, and it has a good bar.'

Rawlings smiled. 'Sounds like an ideal plan. It's a relief you have a solution.'

'No problem.' Sorcha gave a sudden sigh. 'Probably best if we don't tell Mother we're removing the photos from the house. I'll just tell her I'm going to show you round Bellows Falls.' Rawlings understood at once and nodded his agreement.

It took them over an hour to finish the copying, Sorcha clipping each section together. At one point he asked, 'Have you ever read any of these?'

She shook her head. 'After Mia died everything was packed away. I didn't even know where her stuff had been stored.'

Rawlings wondered if she might be tempted to read them now and wasn't sure how he felt about that. There was a great deal in them that was private, and he wouldn't want shared. But she showed no inclination to do so and he hoped after he left, they'd just be packed away again.

'What will happen to Mia's archive after your mother's death?'

Sorcha seemed surprised by this. 'Do you know I've never even thought about it. I suppose it will be up to Brendan, he'll be in charge of everything,' and she added 'not that he's ever shown the slightest interest in Mia's work.'

Rawlings frowned. 'Her photographs are a valuable archive. She was an outstanding photographer. I'd always understood she was going to publish the pictures she took of the Siege in a book. After we left Sarajevo, we were apart for about two months when I went back to England. She told me she would return to see her family in Boston, and there she would have time to put the book together.'

Sorcha shook her head. 'She only stayed a few days. The atmosphere was terrible, but I do remember thinking she didn't look well…'

'Hardly surprising.' Rawlings tried to keep the sarcastic tone out of his voice as he explained, 'We'd been through three years of hell, in constant danger, with little sleep and a diet made up of watery soups, mainly dandelion as I remember.'

'God how awful, I'd never have survived it.' Sorcha turned off the copier, gathered the notebooks and handed Rawlings his pile of copies. 'After Mia escaped the Boston house, she came up here and I joined her. Mimms fussed over her and supervised her diet and after a few weeks she looked back to normal. Those weeks with her were some of the happiest in my life. But it came to an end when she bought the apartment in New York.'

Rawlings nodded. 'That selfishly worked out well for me. I'd been sent to New York by my paper. I think my editor thought I needed a break from war reporting. I probably looked in much the same state as Mia after Sarajevo and we were both suffering from PTSD.'

Sorcha looked at her watch. 'Bloody hell! Nearly time for cocktails. It's a sin to be late. Put the notebooks back in the boxes. We just have time to shower and get changed. If I wear these jeans to dinner my life won't be worth living.'

'I hope my blazer will be smart enough.'

Sorcha laughed. 'Of course – very English gentleman.'

The cocktail hour was evidently something of a ritual. They entered the large drawing room, where Kaye O'Keefe was once more draped elegantly on one of the many sofas in yet another flowing garment, this time he guessed it was silk, in a rather beautiful shade of pale blue. She glanced at Sorcha and remarked, 'I am relieved to see you have changed dear.'

Sorcha now clad in a dress and linen jacket made no comment but greeted a rather elderly man in a dark suit, obviously the butler, coming towards them.

'Dawkins this is Rawlings, who was a friend of Mia's'.

Rawlings winced a little as being described yet again as a 'friend'. Sorcha knew he had lived with the woman for seventeen years.

Dawkins gave a little bow and said gravely, 'I'm pleased to meet you sir. May I get you something to drink?'

Rawlings was wondering whether to ask for a Scotch when Sorcha intervened. 'Dawkins makes a mean Vodka Martini. I'm sure Rawlings would like one of those and I'll join him.'

They were indeed mean and exceedingly strong. After the second one Rawlings felt up to anything, even the ordeal of the dinner ahead.

Once seated at the long dining table, the conversation was stilted. and an air of disapproval remained throughout the meal. Surprisingly the food did not match the grand surroundings, in fact it was rather tasteless and bland. Maybe

Kaye was on a diet? He wondered who the cook was. He imagined not Mimms, who seemed to be a sort of factotum in charge of running the house. At least Dawkins was on hand with an excellent claret...

'I trust you had a successful afternoon.' Kaye was addressing him. It was clear she wasn't in the least bit interested but merely asking out of politeness.

'Thank you, yes. I think we accomplished a great deal and Sorcha was most helpful. I am really grateful to you for allowing me access to the archive.'

Kaye, who had only pecked at her food, wiped each side of her mouth delicately with her napkin before replacing it on the plate to indicate she had finished. Her voice was sarcastic in tone. 'Do you really think anyone will want to read another book about war Mr Rawlings?'

'I honestly don't know, but my publishers seem to think they will.' He looked at her. 'The Sarajevo Siege was thirty years ago, almost history. There is an interest in such events.'

Kaye persisted. 'What sort of books do you like to read Mr Rawlings?'

Rawlings smiled. 'I like poetry. The War Poets are my particular favourites.'

He didn't say this to be provocative, but Sorcha quickly intervened. 'I'm going to show Rawlings round Bellows Falls tomorrow Mother. I thought I'd take him to the Inn for lunch.'

Kaye pursed her lips and said sharply, 'Then you will please let Mimms know you won't be needing the buffet.'

Sorcha nodded. 'Of course.'

Kaye turned back to Rawlings. 'My son Brendan will be joining us on Sunday. We always have a family lunch that day. Usually his wife Kelly and my two grandsons Liam and

Lorcan come with him, but not this weekend.' She turned to Sorcha. 'Kelly's sister has just had a baby girl, such lovely news, a little cousin for the boys. Can you remember the name of that layette shop in Boston? They have the most beautiful baby clothes.' Sorcha shook her head and Kaye flashed her a look of irritation. 'Oh well, I'm sure Mimms will know. I will get her to put in an order and have something sent. It would be expected for you sent a note of congratulations Sorcha.'

Sorcha sat silent and scowling.

'How old are your grandsons?' Rawlings inquired and Kaye became minutely more animated.

'Liam has just had a fifteenth birthday. Lorcan is twelve. They are such sweet boys. I so look forward to seeing them each week.'

Sorcha's scowl increased.

Rawlings said, 'My grandson Felix is twelve.'

Kaye looked greatly surprised that Rawlings should have something as normal as a grandchild and searched around for something to say, finally asking, 'Is your wife still alive?'

'No sadly she died young, of cancer.'

There was a long silence as Kaye took this in. 'What made you become a war correspondent, Mr Rawlings?'

It was said with such distaste that she might just as well have said, 'What made you become a murderer?'

Rawlings gave an inward sigh and patiently explained. 'I began my career as a journalist in London. When my editor offered me an assignment as a correspondent in the First Gulf War I accepted.' He paused. 'I retired eight years ago when I was injured, in the same explosion that killed Mia.'

There was another long silence. Then Kaye stood up. 'It has been a long day. If you'll excuse me, I'm going to retire.

Sorcha you will take Mr Rawlings to the lounge for coffee.

I shall see you both tomorrow night.'

Rawlings rose to his feet as she left the room and then collapsed back into his chair. Sorcha roared with laughter. 'You're being so brave. Only two more meals to get through! I'll drive you back to Boston after Sunday lunch.' She gave one of her barks. 'At least you won't have to face Kelly and the boys. That's a real bonus.'

Chapter 20

A Day of Revelations

Rawlings rose early the next morning and made his way back to the small library determined to sort through the photos before Sorcha arrived to collect him for breakfast. There were several large boxes all clearly marked. He lifted out the one marked 'Sarajevo' and opened it up. The photographs were not in chronological order, but he quickly noted there was some remarkable footage. A shudder went through him. The pictures were horribly graphic. Without looking too closely he quickly put aside about fifty of them, hoping this wouldn't be too many for Sorcha's photographic contact. At the bottom of the box in a separate envelope there were a couple of pictures of Luka, one on his own and one of him standing beside the Professor. There was also a picture he had never seen before of himself and Mia, that someone else must have taken. How young they looked and yes happy, even in those dire conditions. He added these to the pile.

Turning to the other boxes, he discarded 9/11 – because Mia had done her own book of those – Iraq too, because they were of no interest, and Afghanistan because he just couldn't face it. The final one was marked 1976–1977. This was the earliest when she must have been fifteen or sixteen. Out of idle curiosity he opened the box, totally unprepared for what he saw next. He reeled back in shock. Picture after picture revealed a naked Mia in erotic, even pornographic poses. Gingerly he fingered his way through them. They were all the same, Mia naked but in different positions. His hand ran over the contours of the body he knew so well, and yet here it was horribly different. He felt revolted. This was a violation of a young girl's innocence. Patrick O'Keefe had clearly been a pervert. Did Mia realise her innocence was being exploited in this way? He studied her expression trying to read what lay behind the eyes. At first glance she appeared relaxed, sometimes even smiling, but on looking more closely there was something else. Was it anger, fear, or maybe resignation? Had she gone along with these photographic sessions merely for a quiet life? Was it her way of coping with the tyrannical father? It was obvious the man had been obsessed with his beautiful, nubile daughter, but this was evidence of something else, deeply unhealthy. Rawlings now questioned himself. Was he just being a prude? He stared at the pictures again. No, he didn't think so. Naked photographs had never shocked him before, many he'd admired, but these were somehow different. Another thought struck him. Had things gone farther? Had her father been physically abusive as well? He prayed not, but in any case, putting Mia through hours of posing in this way, at such a vulnerable age, must have affected her.

He snapped the box closed and put it firmly at the bottom of the pile, leaving only the Sarajevo one opened. He thought grimly that it was no wonder Patrick O'Keefe had reacted so violently when Mia defied him. He'd lost control. The man was a monster. Did Kaye know about these sessions and the pictures that were being taken of her child? Probably not. This was a private obsession, not one to be shared with a wife. He thought grimly that at least Sorcha hadn't suffered the same treatment. She had been damaged in other ways, the victim of rejection and neglect. They fuck you up your mum and dad…

It crossed his mind that Mia had deliberately given up music to get right away from him. She'd known just how her father would react, so it was a calculated act. Rawlings felt he was beginning to understand how her secret past had affected her in adult life. It had left her feeling worthless and might explain why she'd been so careless of her safety taking unnecessary risks, often when he'd begged her not to.

Sorcha came into the room, slamming the door behind her, causing him to jump like a guilty person caught in some terrible act.

'Good morning,' she said cheerfully and then peered at him more closely. 'Good God Rawlings you're looking pale, are you OK?'

He gave her what he hoped was a reassuring smile. 'Yes fine. My leg has been giving me gyp that's all. It does occasionally. Don't worry, it won't last long and nothing a strong cup of coffee won't put right.' He picked up the chosen photographs. 'I hope these won't be too many for your chap to do.'

An hour later they set off for Bellows Falls.

Doug the photographer, was both understanding and helpful. He gave a whistle as he examined the pictures. 'Wow! These are extraordinary. I've seen Mia's book of the 9/11 photographs, but these are even better. Why did she never publish them?'

Rawlings hesitated. 'I'm not entirely sure. I believe it was her original intention to do so, but those years spent in the Siege were pretty traumatic, maybe she just wanted to forget it.'

'You were with her?' Doug asked and Rawlings nodded.

'And now you're writing a book about it and want to use these photos.' He nodded again. 'Good,' Doug said emphatically. 'These pictures need to be seen.' Turning to Sorcha he said, 'Give me four hours. I should have them ready by then.'

They left him to it and made their way back to what Sorcha referred to as the interesting bit.

'This is a fairly typical Vermont town,' she told Rawlings, 'but it does have some historic importance, partly because of the paper mills and partly because of the railway line down to New York. It also has a bridge across the Connecticut River which links Vermont to New Hampshire.'

'Some of this architecture looks eighteenth century,' Rawlings observed.

'Well yes. It was originally a fishing village for nomadic Abenaki tribes. Then your lot, the English colonists, showed up around 1750 and took over.'

Rawlings smiled. 'My apologies.'

Sorcha laughed. 'No apologies needed. It gave my family a reason to be total snobs, the equivalent of coming over on the Mayflower.'

They reached an imposing building which boasted the name of Windham Antique Center. Rawlings wanted to look round so they spent a happy half hour perusing the very crammed floors. Among all the fascinating objects he found a pewter inkwell he liked, an old wooden bowl with interesting carvings, and a jug decorated with roses he thought might be suitable as a present for Isobel.

'Big spender!' Sorcha declared with a laugh. 'I'm sure going to be popular for bringing you in.'

After this, they visited the Village Square Bookshop and then a couple of craft shops. Sorcha looked at her watch.

'Time for lunch,' she declared. 'We have a short drive to the Grafton Inn. It's about five minutes away.'

Rawlings was relieved to be in the car. His leg had become alarmingly painful. They parked outside a white clapperboard house with a swinging sign which read, 'The old Tavern at Grafton 1801'. Sorcha seemed well known in this place, as indeed she had been all morning. Rawlings smiled. The family were obviously local royalty. She waved her hand airily, 'I'd thought of taking you to the Phelps Barn Pub across the yard, but it's an American version of a pub and probably not to your taste. Instead we'll have a drink in the Pine Room Bar first because I insist you try the Vermont craft beers, and then we'll go on to the Old Tavern Restaurant for lunch.'

The transformation in her was extraordinary. Back at the house she had been sulky and withdrawn. Here she was animated and chatted in an almost continuous flow throughout the meal. This suited Rawlings who was finding it hard to get the naked images of Mia out of his mind.

'Doug was hopelessly in love with Mia,' Sorcha told him. 'Poor man. He only declared himself after she returned from Sarajevo but by that time there was you.' She looked at him curiously. 'Did Mia ever make you jealous?'

He was startled by the question. It was something that had never occurred to him. When they were together they were inseparable, but when apart? He just presumed she was waiting for him to get back to her. 'I don't think' he said slowly, 'either of us strayed if that's what you mean, so jealousy didn't come into it.' He paused. 'What about your parents? Did either of them have affairs?'

'I presume not. They always appeared to be the devoted couple and their outward appearance mattered to them. They were devout Catholics as well. Mother certainly would never have strayed as you put it. She doted on Father. Socially, their lives revolved round this tight knit community and had a monotonous routine. They'd all meet regularly at the Country Club, on the golf course, or at ghastly cocktail parties and dinners. This way of life took place in Bellows Falls at the weekend. In Boston, my father would work long hours at the hospital, so they didn't go out socially during the week.'

'How did your mother occupy herself when your father was working?'

Sorcha said scornfully, 'Most of her time was spent on her appearance, long hours in the beauty salons, or out shopping for expensive clothes. My father insisted she always looked like something off a fashion page. If he ever criticised her, she would be devastated. Looking back, I think he could be cruel. She seemed nervous of him. He was very controlling and probably bullied her in private.'

Rawlings learned a good deal more over the next two hours. Sorcha told him how after Mia's departure she'd gone off the rails and fallen in with the wrong crowd at the Art College in Boston where she'd been despatched. The last straw came when she fell pregnant and paid to have an abortion. Somehow her father found out. Of course, being a devout Catholic, he hit the roof. She was despatched to one clinic after another, for drink or drugs or both. Being financially independent she finally checked herself out and followed Mia to New York. She gave one of her laughing barks, 'Which was when I met you. I think I was in a pretty bad way then.'

By this time they were having coffee. 'You've turned your life around now.' Rawlings observed.

Sorcha shrugged. 'Sort of. It was after Mia's death. I felt I somehow owed it to her. I stood by her grave after the God-awful funeral and I made a pact with her, that I would now make something of my life, as she had done. I came back to Boston and started working with recovering drug addicts and that's where I still am. I've been clean for eight years now. I have a good life, plenty of friends…'

'Anyone special?' Rawlings asked.

'Not really. There have been one or two relationships but nothing permanent. I'm not one for domestic life. My parents put me off that for good.'

Mia too, Rawlings thought. There had been more to her horror of marriage than just the Roman Catholic excuse. Sorcha's revelations had confirmed it.

Sorcha gave a sudden gasp. 'Oh God Rawlings. You probably wanted to visit Mia's grave. I'm so sorry. I should have thought of it.'

He shook his head. 'Don't worry. I don't need a visit to her grave to remember her. It wouldn't have any meaning for me.' He had been privately wondering what they had put in the coffin. Mia's body had been blown to bits. There was a long pause, then he looked at her curiously. 'Why did you say the funeral was so terrible, apart from it being a sad occasion? I always thought the Irish had wonderful wakes.'

Sorcha said angrily. 'Not this one. It was terrible because it had fuck all to do with Mia. None of her friends were there, not even Doug was invited, although I'd suggested it. I was told it was a private family affair. But they treated it like a social event, with their smart Country Club friends included. Mia would have loathed it. And the bloody hideous tombstone in the family plot. She would have hated that too. There were some great obituaries in the local press and one or two in the Nationals. I don't think my parents even read them. Father had a series of mini strokes soon after the funeral until a major one finished him off two years later. He was basically an invalid and pretty gaga. Mother fussed around him and relied more and more on Brendan.'

Rawlings said sadly, 'After the explosion I was in hospital and then recovery for six months before finally returning to England. I missed it all. I wrote a letter to your parents but never had a reply.'

'I told them about you,' Sorcha said. 'They just didn't want to know. Brendan saw that the New York apartment was sold and all Mia's things packed up and brought here. She hadn't left a Will, so it's all gone back into the family pot. I wanted one or two things of Mia's which I'm sure she would have been happy for me to have, but they wouldn't allow it. I'll never forgive them for that. It was petty and cruel…' She broke off, unable to say more.

Rawlings was curious. 'Why do you come here every weekend? It's not as if you get on with your mother.'

She shrugged. 'I suppose I like the place. I have friends here and it's good to get out of Boston every now and then. I don't come up every weekend. I did this time because of you.'

'And I am extremely grateful. To show my thanks, will you please let me pay for lunch?'

But she wouldn't hear of it. Nor would Doug take payment for the photographs, just said it had been a privilege to do them. Rawlings in return promised to send him a copy of the book when it was published.

Dinner that night was a replica of the previous one. If anything, Kaye O'Keefe was even sharper and more critical. During several put-downs, Rawlings found himself admiring

Sorcha's self-control in not defending herself. Her best weapon had become silence.

After Kaye again retired early, Rawlings remarked her mother looked frail.

Sorcha nodded. 'She is. According to Brendan she has a weak heart, owing to a bout of rheumatic fever when she was a child.' Sorcha sounded almost cheerful. 'She's refused all surgery. I suppose she might have undergone an operation if Father had still been around. Now she has little to live for. My brother, the doctor, tells me she probably only has about six months left.'

'What will happen to all this when she dies?'

Sorcha laughed. 'Brendan, his wife and the horrors will move in. My dear brother can't wait.'

Rawlings was quite surprised when he finally met Brendan the next day. Physically he was totally unlike his sisters. He was short of stature, portly and balding. Rawlings disliked him on sight. His attitude was of a man exceedingly pleased with himself and he strutted about like a mini Napoleon while Kaye looked on adoringly. In dismissive tones she introduced Rawlings, yet again as a friend of Mia's. Brendan shook his hand saying he was pleased to meet him but made no further inquiries.

'I gather Kelly's sister has had a baby.' Sorcha said.

Brendan looked annoyed. 'Yes. I told Kelly a visit to her sister could wait. I'm really sorry, Mother. She should have been here. I'll make sure she brings the boys to see you next weekend.'

He's a controlling bully like his father, Rawlings thought.

Throughout the meal, which was as bland and tasteless as the others, Brendan and Kaye talked business affairs, leaving Sorcha and Rawlings to chat quietly the other end of the table. Rawlings wondered whether he should mention to Brendan that he would be using Mia's photographs, and then decided not to. That bridge could be crossed when the book was ready.

As soon as lunch was over, Brendan left to go to the study to sort through some papers.

'I'll need you to sign some documents Sorcha,' he told her as he made for the door.

'Is it urgent?' she asked. 'Rawlings and I are leaving for Boston. If it's OK with you, I'll sign them next time I am down. Then you'll have time to explain to me what they're about.'

Kaye looked annoyed, but Brendan told her that was fine by him, the documents could certainly wait, adding that they probably wouldn't be ready for her today anyway.

Rawlings left to collect his case and then returned to say goodbye to Kaye. She was back on the chaise longue, just as she had been when he arrived.

'Thank you for making Mia's archive available to me. I am most grateful.' And with that he was about to leave, but Kaye said in icy tones, 'I want you to know Mr Rawlings, Mia's father and I hold you entirely responsible for her death.'

Rawlings felt a mounting anger and spoke with controlled coldness. 'Then you would be entirely wrong. It was Mia's decision alone to go to Afghanistan, I tried to dissuade her from what I knew would be a dangerous assignment. But your daughter was a free and independent person.' He paused. 'I don't think you realise just how important her work was to her. I lived with Mia for seventeen years and I know that was always her priority.'

Kaye pursed her lips. 'You lived with her in sin, Mr Rawlings.'

Making a great effort to control himself he said, 'Neither of us saw it like that Mrs O'Keefe. Mia and I loved each other deeply, a love that never wavered until the day she was tragically killed. Your daughter was without doubt the bravest person I ever met. She was also a brilliant photographer and has left behind her an outstanding legacy. You and your husband should have been proud of her.'

With that Parthian shot he turned and left the room.

The drive back to Boston was a pleasant relief after the oppressive atmosphere of the Bellows Falls house. Sorcha started to question him about his life in England, so he described his London flat and the houseboat. She also asked about Felix and he gave a brief account of how he'd become guardian to the boy, and then Felix's departure to Australia.

As they reached Boston she said, 'Why don't you come up and have a last drink in my apartment before going to your hotel?'

Rawlings hesitated. He was tired and longed for some time on his own, but in fairness Sorcha had been kind and helpful so slightly reluctantly he agreed.

She parked outside a smart apartment block and a doorman held open the door as he greeted her. They went up to the eighth floor, the top button, and Sorcha unlocked the door into an airy, open-plan space, with views over Boston and the Common.

'What a great room,' he said and moved to the window. 'Terrific view.'

'I like it.' She waved an arm. 'The bathroom is through there. I'll fix us a drink. What would you like?'

'A small Scotch would be great.'

The bathroom, like the main room, had walls that

were covered in works of art. As he returned to join her he remarked, 'This place is like a picture gallery. You have a great, if somewhat esoteric, collection.' He walked round the room stopping in front of three large unframed oil paintings, abstract, with brilliant splashes of colour. Paul Klee on speed.

'Who did these?' he asked.

She shrugged. 'They were done by an artist called Uri Jackson, a man I happened to live with for eight years, the longest relationship I ever had. He left quite suddenly, owing me a great deal of money. He was one of those men destined to be a borrower. I, unfortunately, appear destined to be a lender. However, he did leave me these examples of his work I suppose in lieu of payment, to salve his conscience if indeed he has one. Quite recently he had an exhibition and I am told it was successful. Apparently, at last he is becoming sought after. Which means for the first time in his life he will make some money of his own instead of borrowing from everyone else.' She joined Rawlings by one of the paintings. 'I'm not sure I actually like them. If he does become famous I'll sell them and buy something else.'

'No sentimental value then?'

Sorcha gave one of her barks. 'Good God no.' She handed him his drink and with some relief he sat down. His leg was starting to give him permanent pain. Taking a swig of whisky which he hoped would be medicinal, he remarked that he particularly liked the series of pen and wash drawings of Boston that were in her bathroom.

'Those are mine,' she said carelessly. 'I was commissioned to do the series years ago for a tourist magazine. They're of places on the Common that Mia and I would visit as children – Frog Pond, the Bandstand, the swan boats and various other spots.'

'Why didn't you continue with your art as a career? You obviously have a great talent for it'.

Another shrug. 'I fell into my wicked ways with drugs and booze and was out of it for years. By the time I'd cleaned up my act it was too late to go back to any sort of career. In any case after Mia died my life took another direction.'

Rawlings smiled. 'It sounds like that poem by Robert Frost, "The Road not Taken". Do you know it?'

She shook her head. 'I'm not really into poetry. Tell me about it.'

'It starts, "Two roads diverged in a yellow wood, and sorry I could not travel both…" He broke off. 'I can't remember it all, but I do know it ended… "I took the one less travelled by. And that has made all the difference". Robert Frost was a Massachusetts poet. You should read him, he's good.'

'I will. Poetry has rather passed me by. I am not as erudite as you.' She suddenly gave her barking laugh. 'I loved it when you told Mother your favourite reading was the War Poets. Her face! For once words failed her. I think she found you impossible to deal with.'

Rawlings thought of their last encounter and said drily, 'Quite probably.'

They talked on. It was early evening and a beautiful light fell on the room. Rawlings by now was on his third whisky, the pain in his leg had receded and he was feeling relaxed and mellow. It was therefore a shock when Sorcha gave him a long, intense look and said, 'Rawlings, would you take me to bed?' The question came out of the blue and almost winded him. She followed this with another shock. 'You must have known I was leading up to this?'

He put down his glass and said firmly, 'The answer to

both your questions is a most definite no. No, I won't got to bed with you and no, I didn't know you were leading up to this. I just thought we were having a pleasant wind-down from the weekend.'

She took this in and then said sulkily, 'You just think I won't be as good in bed as Mia.'

His reaction this time was one of irritation and he snapped, 'Don't be so childish Sorcha. It has absolutely nothing to do with Mia. My reasons are quite simple. I have only known you a few days and I don't do sex to order. In the short time we have known each other I have felt nothing more for you than affectionate friendship…' He broke off. How pompous was that? Oh God, he was handling this badly. There was a long silence. Then he glanced over towards her. She looked like a small child who had been told she couldn't have an ice-cream. Poor little rich girl. He finished rather lamely, 'I'm sorry Sorcha. But that's how it is.'

She uncurled herself from her hunched position. 'Please don't apologise. I misjudged the moment and shouldn't have asked.' With a sigh she added, 'I think I always wanted you, since the time of meeting you in New York. You seemed so perfect; good looking, the strong silent type, and you were kind. And of course, it was something else that Mia had that I didn't, a successful relationship.' Looking at him he could see there were tears in her eyes. 'I got a raw deal from the Gods when I was born. Mia was good at everything and made a success of her life, and she also had you. I was just a mess.'

Rawlings felt at a loss and after three whiskies his mind was a little befuddled. Even so, he managed to say firmly, 'You have to stop thinking like that. Stop comparing yourself to Mia. You are a beautiful and intelligent woman in your own right. And you have great talent, just take another look at those drawings in the bathroom. In my opinion they're far better than...' he waved a hand around the room '...all this. I know you and Mia had a raw deal from your parents, but you had other advantages. You were both gifted and you had financial stability, not to mention great looks. That is far more than most people have. And now, you are doing a worthwhile job. So, you have absolutely no reason for this self-pity. You are still young and there is every possibility that you could have a relationship in the future, if that is what you want.' He gave a smile. 'There! Brotherly lecture over.'

She didn't say anything for a while, then looked at him curiously. 'What about you Rawlings? Will you ever get over Mia and have another relationship?'

He gave a sigh. 'Who knows? If I met the right woman I might. But that hasn't happened and I'm not seriously looking. For the moment I'm just concentrating on being a good grandfather to Felix.' He stood up. 'Time for me to depart I think.' Crossing over he kissed the top of her head. 'You are a lovely person Sorcha never forget that. And great company. I've really enjoyed our time together. My parting advice? Make more of your life in Boston and make less visits to Bellows Falls.'

Picking up his case he crossed to the door. She hadn't moved but gave him a bleak smile. He said gently, 'Thank you for everything Sorcha. Take care of yourself.'

As he let himself out, he added 'And read that Robert Frost poem.'

Chapter 21

An Indian Summer

Rawlings had been back five days and done little apart from making a few necessary telephone calls. One of these was to his doctor. The pain in his leg was now so acute not even large doses of Scotch were helping. The great man summoned him to his clinic and tests were done. It was nothing serious he was told, but he was severely reprimanded. The leg had been thoroughly over-used since major surgery in February. What on earth had he been doing? Rawlings guiltily reeled off the list of his travels: Scotland, Yorkshire, Australia, Bosnia and the States. The doctor had a reproachful expression. He told his patient firmly that the travelling had to stop. He was to take it easy if he didn't want to incur a major problem, which would result in a far more drastic solution. Rawlings thought crossly that his pain was a major problem, but maybe amputation was being suggested? It had been made quite clear after the operation that no further mending surgery was possible. The ultimatum had been delivered. The doctor offered him stronger pain killers, which he refused saying they played havoc with his digestive system, but he meekly promised to rest and keep his leg up whenever possible. Which is why he was now lying in the garden with his leg propped up on a cushion on a newly acquired steamer chair, enjoying the September sun.

Mia's notebooks had remained unopened since his return, but today they had accompanied him outside and put on the table as a gentle reminder that he needed to begin work on his book soon. An alarmingly giant bumblebee the size of a small squirrel buzzed lazily round him and then made his way down towards the river. These bumblebees seemed to have no sense of direction. One had continually bombarded him yesterday when he was sitting at his desk making calls. Maybe they were affected by drowsiness brought on at this time of year. Easy to see why. A heavy scent from some sort of jasmine pervaded the garden and it was even having a soporific effect on him making it difficult not to doze off. He gazed about him. Some of the roses were still in bloom and were pleasingly beautiful. Surely a new addition to the garden? He hadn't noticed them before. Thankfully, the weather was positively mild, the autumn chills not having yet arrived. It was all surprisingly peaceful. A wave of contentment swept over him, or maybe it was just calm after the storm. His stay with the O'Keefe's had been unsettling and since returning his sleep patterns were most erratic. The old nightmares returned along with some new ones, with distressing images which left him shaken long after he'd woken up. All very disturbing. He hadn't even been up to see Max, preferring to lie low until he'd returned to something nearer normal. Today at last, that normality was returning. He'd had a goodish night and the pain in his leg had thankfully eased. Even so, as he stared at the Mia papers he wondered if it wasn't just too soon to tackle them. Chiding himself for his Hamlet-like behaviour, he knew the task could not be put off much longer. The telephone call to Sheila, informing her he was making a start on the Sarajevo book, meant he had now crossed the Rubicon. To his annoyance, she'd received this news rather ungraciously, making it plain that the patience of both her and the publishers was wearing thin. This didn't improve his opinion of her. He gave a sigh. It wasn't healthy to have bad relations with one's agent. Maybe he should take her out to lunch and turn on the charm.

Bolly wandered down the garden wagging his tail as he passed Rawlings as if in recognition of his presence. A few minutes later he was followed by Max.

'Hello stranger,' he said, 'I noted you were back.' He brought a chair up to sit beside Rawlings. 'I see you have your leg up. Is there a problem?'

Rawlings smiled. 'I just overdid it in the States. Nothing that resting it for a few days won't cure. How have you been?'

'Busy. This new gardener chappie is a splendid fellow and over the last two weeks we've done a major campaign on the garden. He's done some amazing work. Did you notice?'

Rawlings nodded. 'I was just sitting here admiring it, particularly the roses. I would like to contribute…'

'I wouldn't hear of it,' Max said firmly, then as an afterthought, 'but you could pay him to help you with your patio. Those large antique pots you bought, at great expense as I remember, are still sitting empty.'

This produced a sigh from Rawlings. 'I know nothing about gardening. I will gladly pay for some help. What's his name?'

'Sam.'

They sat for a while in silence, until Max said, 'You missed a terrible party while you were gadding about in the States.'

'I was hardly gadding,' Rawlings protested. 'What party was that?'

'Clive's leaving do. He's left for Dubai until Christmas at least. No loss I can assure you. I've always disliked the man intensely…' Rawlings was surprised at this, having never heard Max express such strong feelings about him before. Max went on, 'He has opinions about everything, won't let anyone disagree with him, and he's an arrogant bugger. Voted for Brexit you know. He's one of those men who knows everything but understands nothing.' He spat out the last word and then lowered his tone in a conspiratorial way. 'I think there is definitely something shady about this Dubai business and Hetty agrees with me.' Rawlings wondered if there was something specific that Clive had done to upset Max but refrained from asking. Maybe Hetty could enlighten him.

Max stood up. 'I'm off to take Bolly for his morning constitutional. He's becoming very lazy.' As if to prove the point it took several calls to get the dog to move. 'Come upstairs for a drink tomorrow. Then you can tell me about your latest travels.' He fastened a lead on the reluctant Bolly and dragged him up the garden. 'By the way, Mrs Bunce told me to tell you she can't get the coffee stain out of your bedspread.'

Rawlings smiled. The redoubtable Mrs B always had some complaint and tut-tutted her voluble way around his flat once a week. But she was efficient and worth the grumbles. His linen shirts were now ironed to perfection.

A large cloud moved across the sun bringing a sudden chill to the air. He looked up. More clouds were gathering on the horizon. Time to move indoors. Picking up the unread papers he limped inside and sat down at his desk. Almost immediately his mobile started its piercing ring. It was Isobel.

'How was your trip?'

'Interesting, but my leg objected to all the travelling, so I'm taking it easy.'

She sounded concerned. 'Have you seen a doctor?'

'I have actually. The pain was enough to worry me. He was reassuring, just annoyed because I'd done too much and endangered his handiwork. Don't worry Isobel. I promised the good doctor I'd take it easy, with no more travelling for the rest of the year.'

'I'm glad to hear it.' She paused. 'Would you be able to manage a visit here on Sunday? I think it's your birthday.'

How on earth had she remembered that.

'I'd be delighted. On one condition, that there's no fuss and certainly no presents.'

She laughed and rang off.

His thoughts returned to Max. It was a relief to note his improved appearance and demeanour. At that last dinner just before he'd left for Vermont, Max had appeared to be suffering from a deep depression which at the time he'd put down to Elsa's imminent departure. Today he seemed fully recovered, indeed positively cheerful, with no mention of Elsa at all.

This observation was confirmed the following evening. Max no longer had that beaten look, and for some reason that Rawlings couldn't quite fathom, he appeared to be a different man. Maybe it was a relief that Elsa had finally gone, and this thought gave him an inward chuckle.

'How was the trip?' Max asked the moment they sat down. Rawlings hesitated before answering. There wasn't a great deal he wanted to impart about that visit, except to say it had been interesting and useful, and had now provided him with enough material to start his book. This statement produced a curious glance from Max. 'I thought you were trying to wriggle out of that one?'

Rawlings sighed. 'I would have liked to, but feel I owe

it to various people to write the bloody thing, so I can't give up on it. I've managed to come up with a compromise. Mia's photographs will make up the bulk of the book and I will confine myself to writing the commentary, a task which shouldn't over-tax me. I can probably get it done by the end of the year provided there are no further interruptions.'

'No more travelling?'

Rawlings laughed. 'Absolutely not. My doctor has forbidden it if I want to keep my leg. From now on, it's the static life for me.'

Max re-filled his glass. 'I've noticed you're not smoking as well.'

'You're right. That is something of a feat, quite proud of myself. I'd already cut down before I went to Australia. It was made plain their house was a non-smoking area. Then there was all the flying when I couldn't smoke anyway and it was certainly not allowed in Vermont, so I gradually stopped altogether. I am trying to stay off it, but the temptation is sometimes hard, especially when I'm around smokers.'

Max nodded. 'I remember finding that the hardest part. But I've been off the fags for so long now I don't even yearn for it in the way I did.'

Rawlings gave him a long look. 'Tell me about this party. Why did Clive cause you such annoyance? I thought you quite liked him. You and Hettie always told me he'd been a good husband for Bel.' Annoyance seemed rather a euphemism after Max's strong feelings expressed in the garden. Anger would have been nearer the mark.

There then followed an extraordinary tirade from the usually passive Max. He explained that he and Hetty had recently learned things from Bel that had greatly alarmed them. Clive had apparently been controlling her for years. They'd all been fooled. Publicly he appeared the calm and patient husband, pitied for having to deal with a neurotic and alcoholic wife. But in private, the situation was completely different. Bel had been bullied and mocked, until she lost all self-esteem.

Rawlings was struck by the parallel to the O'Keefe's marriage, but kept these thoughts to himself. In any case, there was no stopping Max now. His account continued. Things apparently came to a head at Clive's farewell party. They were all meant to be heading to the restaurant, but Bel was on the sofa looking plainly unwell and saying she really didn't think she could make it. Clive became angry and accused her of having had too much to drink. He then callously left, taking the children with him. Bel assured them she hadn't touched a drop of alcohol all day. Hetty decided to stay with her, but he had gone to the restaurant because it was Elsa's last night. She was due to return to Northumberland the following day. An hour later Hetty rang from A & E to say Bel was suffering from kidney stones and in terrible pain. Clive showed absolutely no sympathy and just carried on with his party. The place was packed with his cronies. Max added that he'd found the whole evening deeply upsetting.

Rawlings felt shocked. 'Was Bel all right?'

'Yes. She returned from hospital the next day. Hetty reported she wasn't fully recovered but at least the pain had gone. Clive left for Dubai that evening.' There was a long pause. 'What did you make of Clive?'

Rawlings felt uneasy. 'I can't say I took to him particularly. But in all fairness, Bel wasn't behaving particularly well at the time…'

Max growled. 'She was unhappy. We know that now. It made her alcoholic situation worse. None of us realised it was Clive who was really the cause. It all poured out when Hetty sat with Bel in the hospital. Hetty later told me that Clive had been having affairs and Bel indicated they were mainly with men.'

Somehow this didn't greatly surprise Rawlings. Clive had married late. Bel was a beautiful and successful woman. A trophy wife. Wasn't that the expression? From the first Rawlings had felt there was something slightly camp about the man. The pale blue chinos and matching loafers were a bit of a giveaway.

Max went on. 'Bel is also worried that Clive is mixed up in something dubious, if not criminal. She thinks it's why he's leaving the country for a while.'

'You mean money laundering?'

Max shrugged. 'I've no idea, but I wouldn't put anything past him.'

Rawlings smiled encouragingly. 'Well at least Bel now has a breather. Maybe we should have her over for a dinner here. I'd be happy to organise it…'

'That's a great idea.' Max gave his approval at once. 'I'll find out when Hetty and Bernard are down again.'

Rawlings pondered over this latest news as he drove to Isobel's the following Sunday.

What he couldn't understand was why Bel became involved with this type of man. Wasn't this the second time this had happened to her? Did these men tempt her by giving her some sort of stability, only to turn into monsters? Bel was a needy character and probably difficult to live with. Even so, mental bullying was unforgivable. The unseen crime, as Max had so rightly noted. They'd all been fooled. The alarm bells suddenly rang in his head. Bel would be even more needy now. That could be dangerous, and he made a mental note to keep his distance, fervently hoping she'd moved on from their very brief encounter earlier in the year. He sighed. What a year. First Bel, then Sorcha. What was it with these women? Thank God for Isobel.

'Happy birthday darling!' she called up the garden. He was rather startled by the endearment. It seemed unusually theatrical for her. She walked towards him. 'We're having such a wonderful burst of September sun, I thought we'd have drinks outside.'

Rawlings once again admired her elegance, even now in her gardening clothes. Today she sported a wonderful straw hat which just added to the overall effect. She kissed him on both cheeks and sat down, but then immediately stood up to fetch him a stool for his leg. He gave her a grateful smile. 'You're very good to me Isobel. I can't think why.'

Isobel smiled at him. 'It's a relief you're not pacing up and down as you usually do.'

'Now that I've reached the great age of sixty seven my pacing days are over,' Rawlings assured her.

'Well, I've reached the great age of seventy, without ever having the need to pace about.' Maria appeared with a tray, wished Rawlings a happy birthday, and then disappeared back into the kitchen.

'Maria has something special arranged for your lunch. It's all a great secret.' Isobel handed the bottle to Rawlings and he obediently opened it.

'I feel extremely spoiled. Champagne as well. What extravagance. I've grown used to being offered prosecco these days, but champagne is definitely nicer.'

They sipped in silence and then Isobel asked how the trip had been. He gave her a brief outline, leaving out details of the naked photographs and Sorcha's advances.

'You have enough material for the book now?'

Rawlings nodded. 'Yes,' and he sighed. 'I have no excuses left. The book must be done. But the task has been made easier with Mia's photographs. They're a brilliant addition.'

Isobel re-filled his glass. 'I am glad we have the excuse of your birthday. What could be lovelier than sitting in the sun sipping champagne? Peter never enjoyed the bubbly as much as I did. Too many Embassy parties.'

Rawlings felt sadness at the thought of Peter. He'd died too young and it was obvious how much Isobel missed him. He said thoughtfully, 'Peter was more of a claret man as I remember.'

Isobel smiled her agreement and they fell silent again until Isobel said, 'You know we really deserved this Indian summer. July and August were a complete write-off, except for a couple of days which were just about bearable.'

Rawlings looked irritated. 'I don't know why the English always expect August to be hot. My memories of summer holidays were of continual rain and wind. I remember we used to do a day trip to Southend, and I have never felt such cold. There is nothing more miserable than an English beach resort in freezing weather.'

Isobel thought for a moment. 'We were lucky with Felix's birthday last year. It was a lovely day as I remember.'

Rawlings nodded. 'He Skyped me last night to wish me happy birthday which was a great surprise. Clever of him to remember.'

'That was me,' Isobel said. 'I reminded him last weekend.'

'Good of you. How did you find him?'

Isobel frowned. 'I am trying not to worry but the boy doesn't look happy. He said very little. Perhaps it made him homesick thinking of your last birthday. Stupid of me to mention it really. But as our calls have gone on throughout the year he has said less and less.'

Rawlings frowned. 'I agree. It worries me too and I find the calls an increasing strain...' He broke off and then burst out, 'I'm blowed if I know what to do for the best.'

'I don't think there is much we can do, until Felix himself says something.'

The conversation regarding Felix continued over lunch. Isobel remained adamant that Rawlings shouldn't interfere. But he wasn't so sure. The Skype call of the previous evening had him so concerned that at the end he'd re-iterated once more that Felix was to let him know at once if something was wrong. The boy just gave an abrupt nod and clicked off.

Maybe it was time to ring Sarah.

Isobel said soothingly, 'It's not long till the boy returns. He's due back here soon. We can sort things out properly then.'

Rawlings let the subject go, although it was horrible to think that Felix might have to suffer for at least another two months. He alone knew what misery the monster Shane was capable of inflicting on the boy.

As he was leaving Isobel said, 'Wait, I have a birthday present for you.' She went outside and came back with a large package. 'I think you said you had a patio, so I've bought you a rose which is suitable for a pot or container. It's called "Tranquillity". Something I thought very apt for you, at this time in your life.'

Rawlings took the package from her and feeling emotional he kissed her on the cheek. 'You're a wicked woman Isobel. I thought I told you no presents. But I'm delighted to have it and it's the perfect present. I am about to discuss with Sam our gardener what to do with the patio.'

Isobel looked relieved. 'I'm delighted to hear you have a gardener. The rose comes from David Austen and has full instructions inside for planting.' She regarded him thoughtfully. 'You might consider taking up gardening, Rawlings. It's a rewarding pastime and good for the soul.'

The next day another package arrived, with a US postmark. Puzzled, he opened it to find it was from Sorcha and contained one of the colourwashes he'd so admired.

With it was a brief message:

Rawlings, I hope you will enjoy this picture. It is of the bandstand on Boston Common, which was Mia's favourite spot. It might go some way to mitigate my behaviour on your last day.

I still think Mia was lucky to share so many years with you.

Sorcha

He stared at the picture. Yes, he did love it and tomorrow he would search for a suitable frame. It was far too small for his main room, but it could be a solitary picture in his bedroom. It might even encourage him to find more artwork. Gardening and a picture collection? His life was certainly changing.

*

September moved seamlessly into October and was mainly uneventful. There had been a dinner party for Bel, when Bernard and Hetty were down staying with Max in London. It had been a pleasant, family evening with Max almost returned to his old self. Bel was quiet and subdued and certainly not as waspish as usual. After she left early pleading pressure of work, Hetty assured him that Bel was fine, just concentrating on her career and the children.

Suddenly everything appeared to be on a calm and even keel again. Even his leg was feeling better. So, it was something of a shock when towards the end of the month a completely unexpected event threw his life into complete turmoil yet again.

Chapter 22

The Cry for Help

It was the call he had been expecting, ever since his return from Australia, but when it eventually arrived, it came as something of a shock. He was just returning to the house after watering his new roses on the patio, when there was the unmistakeable sound of a Skype call coming in on his laptop. Quickly opening it up, there staring at him was Felix. Rawlings had nothing in his diary to alert him to this, so he knew at once that something was terribly wrong. Even with the vast distance between them one glance at the boy showed that he was not only tense but in great distress. With a thudding heart, Rawlings made an effort to sound natural and calm.

'Hello Felix, this is unexpected. How are you?'

Felix wasn't going to give in to social chat and shouted 'EG, I have to come home!'

Home? Wasn't Australia meant to be his new home? Rawlings said cautiously, 'But you will do Felix. It's only a few weeks now. Isobel and I are counting the days…'

There was no time for more. The boy looked near to tears.

'I want to come home NOW.' He yelled the last word.

'Felix, what's happened? Can you tell me?'

The boy shook his head and seemed incapable of saying

more until he looked directly at Rawlings and said with unexpected vehemence, 'You and Isobel promised me I could come home if I wasn't happy in Australia. Well I'm not happy. If you won't help me come back I'll make my own arrangements, I have money, enough for an airline ticket…'

Rawlings became alarmed. 'Felix, Felix! Stop! If you are serious about this, of course you must return. Isobel and I don't break our promises. I'll talk to Sarah and after that make all the arrangements for you to come back to us. But you must give me a little time to organise this. Will you trust me?' The boy nodded. Rawlings added, 'We both love you Felix. You know that. The last thing either of us ever wanted was for you to be unhappy.'

The boy nodded again. Then, unable to speak further he clicked off.

Rawlings stared at the blank screen, trying to make sense of what had just occurred. It had to be something momentous to make him go into meltdown. In the twelve eventful years of the boy's life, Felix had withstood the many slings and arrows that had been thrown at him, dealing with each one of them with amazing dignity, acceptance and fortitude. So what catastrophic event had now happened to break him? It had to be Shane. That boy was nothing if not a recidivist. How stupid of him to expect the blasted child to reform when the presence of Felix continued to be a target for his bullying. The thought that now haunted him was that his grandson had undergone some terrible trauma which had broken him. He finally could take no more and had given up. Knowing Felix as he did, he realised the boy would somehow feel he had failed. This must never be allowed to happen. If anything, he needed to be praised for having bravely stuck it for so long. Come to that, nor should Brad and Sarah be blamed. Their intentions had been good. Nobody could possibly have foreseen the problem of Shane.

Rawlings looked at his watch and jerked himself out of his inactivity. It was just 11 am. That meant it must have been about nine in the evening for Felix when he'd rung. It was probably too late to talk to Sarah now, so he sent her an email saying it was urgent that she Skyped him as soon as possible. Rawlings knew he had to be fully prepared for her call. It must be made clear however much she and Brad objected, that the experiment of Felix staying with them had failed and the boy should be returned to England as soon as possible. He paused in thought. Maybe 'experiment' wasn't the right word. He needed to make some precise notes before her call.

His next task was to ring Isobel. She took an unusually long time to answer, so by the time she did, he poured out all that had happened scarcely drawing breath.

Isobel finally interrupted. 'Darling boy, please stop for a moment. Are you pacing about? You seem out of breath. I suggest you sit down and tell me what has happened slowly and calmly.'

Rawlings did as he was told, sat at his desk and went through the Skype call with her in detail. When he'd finished, she gave an audible sigh, 'I had a feeling something like this would happen. Well now that it has, your way is clear to bringing the boy back. I have to say, it's welcome news. When are you talking to Sarah?'

'Tomorrow morning, I hope.'

There was a pause, then Isobel said, 'It will be awkward for her. She is likely to feel she has failed both Felix and her sister. On the other hand, it could also be something of a relief for the poor woman. You told me the baby needs careful nursing and isn't yet out of the woods. Isn't that what you said?'

'Yes. Felix told me Ella may need another operation.'

'That must be terribly worrying for the parents, added to which they have this child Shane who has problems as well.'

Rawlings growled, 'I think there is every indication the boy has a serious personality disorder.'

Isobel sighed. 'There seems to be a label for everything these days. It may be the simple fact that Felix has rather outshone his cousin and Shane has been made to feel inferior in the eyes of his parents, especially his father. I'm afraid it's a case of the green-eyed monster.'

'You're probably right.' He smiled. 'You usually are Isobel, but I still think the parents are partly to blame, particularly Brad. In his efforts to make Felix happy, he over-praised him and neglected his boy. Even so, and I'm sorry to say this about any child, Shane is a nasty piece of work and urgently needs sorting out. Perhaps they'll have time to do that now, with Felix gone.'

'Whatever happens next I do urge you to try and be tactful Rawlings.' Then Isobel returned to practical mode. 'So, will you go out to fetch him back?'

'I've been wondering about that and on balance I think not. It would only add to the difficulty of the situation and make things even more awkward for everybody. Felix is old enough now to travel on his own.'

Isobel sounded worried. 'Are you sure? It's a long journey and he's only just twelve.'

Rawlings was quick to reassure her. 'I know, but the airlines are good with unaccompanied children. He'll be well looked after. I promise you someone will stay with him the whole way until he's delivered back to me.' He laughed. 'He'll wear a label to make sure he doesn't get lost, like Paddington Bear.'

Isobel still sounded worried, 'If you are absolutely sure…' Rawlings said firmly, 'I am. I will know more after the call tomorrow. There's going be a great deal to plan Isobel; where he's to live, school…'

She cut across him. 'Ring me when you've spoken to Sarah. Then we can talk things through.' There was a pause. 'It really is wonderful news Rawlings. Our boy is coming home, and now it will be for good.'

After she'd rung off Rawlings sat pondering the situation. Yes, it was indeed wonderful he was coming home. But how much damage had been done? How much trust had been lost? Felix had not wanted to go to Australia. The grown-ups had insisted. And now it had gone terribly wrong. Would he ever forgive his grandfather for this lost year?

An email came in from Sarah, saying she would ring him 10 a.m. his time the following day. Rawlings had a sleepless night, trying to anticipate what she would say and how he should react. Whatever happened, he must not let the boy down again. Felix had to come back. One comfort was that Isobel would be a guardian as well and give him support. Graham would be instructed over all the new developments. No discussion or prevarication from the gloomy man would be tolerated. It was all settled. The boy was coming back.

Sarah was on time. Rawlings noticed at once she was looking visibly upset, but instead of being sorry for her he felt a mounting anger. Sarah had been so confident that his life with her family would be best for Felix. The boy had been dragged halfway across the world and away from the people he had grown to love here. As for his damned solicitor, he had merely looked on it as the logical thing to do. Logical! Graham didn't even know the boy or had been witness to how happy and settled Felix had been with his life here. The result of their adult deliberations was that his grandson had been put through some sort of hell.

Sarah started in. 'Rawlings, I'm terribly sorry this has happened. Brad and I want you to know…' She broke off.

He wasn't going to make it easy for her and said gruffly, 'I need to know exactly what went wrong Sarah. It must have been something serious to make Felix so adamant about coming back, but that is what he is, and there will be no moving him. So please tell me. What was it that made him so upset?'

'I'm afraid it was something Shane did…'

No surprise there, he thought.

And then the whole story poured out. She and Brad truly hadn't known, but there had been several incidents when Felix had been punished for things that Shane had either organised or done. These included hiding his things and causing him to be late for school, or for lessons. There was a long list and Rawlings patiently listened. He didn't interrupt but knew that Felix had endured this sort of behaviour for many months, so it had to be something else that caused him finally to go into meltdown. At last, after the long pre-amble she reached it.

'Felix had been putting together a major project since the start of the term. He did most of it in his own time spending each evening in his room working late. Finally, when it was finished, he took the work to show his teacher…'

Rawlings interrupted. 'Did you see this project?'

Sarah shook her head. 'No, but his teacher told me about

it. She couldn't praise it highly enough. It was an account of his last summer in England with a description of the houseboat and the river birds, especially his pet goose Harrison. It was all beautifully illustrated. He really is a talented little artist. Mrs Lawley was so impressed with the work she showed it to the Head, and they agreed that Felix should read it in assembly the following week. I know Felix was reluctant to do this, but of course felt he had to. His reading was so well received the work was put on display for the day for everyone to look at the illustrations. As you can imagine, a huge amount of praise was heaped on Felix…' she paused, 'I know this made him uneasy. He's always been very modest about his achievements, but Brad was particularly impressed, saying how proud he was of him…' she paused again. 'I should have seen the effect all this was having on Shane, but I have been so taken up with Ella…'

Rawlings was determined not to show sympathy. 'What did Shane do?' He almost shouted the question.

Sarah looked distressed. 'I only know what Mrs Lawley reported to me, when we had to go and collect Felix from the school.'

Rawlings was now alarmed. 'Was he hurt?'

Sarah quickly reassured him. 'No. Not physically. But he had gone into this very strange state. He was white as a sheet and seemed unable to speak. It was frightening. We brought him back to the house, but since then he hasn't spoken to anyone, except to say he wanted to return to England.'

Rawlings almost shouted in his exasperation. 'What happened?'

Sarah talked quickly now, as if she couldn't get over this bit fast enough.

'It was a moment of wickedness and I can tell you Shane has been severely punished. It seems that he and a couple of his friends removed Felix's project from his locker in the morning and left it soaking in a basin full of water. By the time Felix discovered this at the end of the school day the work was completely ruined...'

Rawlings gasped in shock. 'Was there no way it could be dried out and saved?'

Sarah shook her head. 'No, it had completely disintegrated, all the ink had run off. The drawings too were ruined. When Felix found it, he just screamed. He was completely hysterical. The teachers finally managed to calm him and took him to the Head's office where he sat until we collected him, the remains of the wet manuscript on his lap. Mrs Lawley was in tears. As we left, Felix just threw what was left of the project on the floor. It's all so dreadful. Davey told us he had been going to give the project to you, as your birthday present Rawlings. I'm so sorry, so terribly sorry. I know I've let Felix down, and you, and my dead sister...' The tears started to flow.

Rawlings sat for a moment staring at her, stunned by what he'd heard. The news that Felix had been going to give the project to him brought tears to his eyes as well. He tried to think sensibly. For the sake of the boy they had to be practical now.

'Sarah, we have to work out what to do next...'

She said quickly, 'Don't worry. Shane is going to be severely punished for what he did.'

What he did? How would they ever know what damage had been done. In the great scheme of things, one boy's bullying action might not seem that important. To Felix, it might well turn out to be. Because of this, Rawlings spoke more sternly than perhaps he should have done.

'I'm afraid I am not remotely interested in how you deal with Shane. That is your problem. My one concern is Felix, and how to get him back to England.' She looked shocked, but then nodded. Rawlings went on, 'He can't possibly stay on with you now, for his and all your sakes. I think we must make immediate arrangements for him to travel back here as soon as it can be arranged. I will make all the arrangements and I would be grateful if you could get him ready your end. It's probably easiest if you speak to the school and let them know he won't be returning. I will write to them once he's back here. Please keep Felix in your house until he leaves.' She nodded again and Rawlings noted how devasted she looked. His tone relented. 'None of us could have seen this happening Sarah. It is just one of those extraordinary twists in life that comes out of the blue.' He paused. 'A time of quiet stability is what will be best for Felix. I will talk to Isobel. As I told you, she is now a guardian as well and will be helpful in making decisions about his future, especially when it comes to returning him to the same school.' He paused. 'Of course, you will always be consulted…'

Sarah interrupted, sounding surprisingly firm, 'I think it best if I just remain his aunt now and relinquish my role as guardian.' She added sadly, 'I know Felix won't want to return here, not until he's much older anyway.'

Rawlings said more gently, 'We should leave all major decisions like that until after the boy has adjusted to being back here.' Pausing, he added, 'Maybe this is for the best Sarah. You've had so much to deal with this year with Ella being so ill. This will give you time to concentrate on your own family.'

She looked at him with exhausted eyes. 'You may be right. Let me know when you have the travel arrangements sorted.' She clicked off, obviously unable to say more.

Rawlings sat with a thousand thoughts whirling around his mind. Then, trying to think clearly, he picked up the telephone to update Isobel. It took him a while to give her a full account of the call and when he finished there was a long silence. Finally, she spoke in a series of gasps. 'Oh Rawlings, that poor, poor boy. When you think of what he has had to go through in his short life. It's dreadful, and so upsetting.' It was an emotional response he hadn't expected. Isobel was usually self-contained and calm. In view of this, Rawlings decided not to express his worries about the effect all this would have on Felix in the future. Maybe he should discuss it with his PTSD specialist. After all, he deals with childhood trauma as well.

Isobel was speaking again. 'What happens now? I presume they've agreed to let the boy return to us?'

'They had no choice in the matter,' Rawlings snapped. He paused. 'To be fair, I think Sarah understood that. Poor woman. She's obviously distressed by what has happened and also feels guilty, although it's hardly her fault she has this monster child.'

Isobel said quietly, 'It sounds to me as if Shane needs their full attention. This whole affair will have affected him as well.'

'Let's hope it changes him for the better,' he replied tersely. Rawlings really didn't want to spend time discussing Shane. 'I think the best thing for me to do now is to ring the airlines and book a flight, making the arrangements for him to travel alone. After that there will be more for us to discuss.' He hesitated. 'Could I invite myself down for yet another Sunday lunch, Isobel?'

She of course agreed and then rang off. Rawlings sat back thinking. His first and most important task was to put the boy's mind at rest, so he sent Felix an email assuring him he would be returning to England as soon as could be managed and that he was now going to book the flight. Once he knew the date, he would let Felix have details of all the travel arrangements. Rawlings then went out into the garden and sat down, exhausted and drained. The weather had turned autumnal and the river looked cold and grey. He gave a shiver. These latest developments had come as a shock. Of course he was delighted the boy was coming back, but like a pebble thrown into the water the ripple effect had spread far and wide. It wasn't going to be easy. Apart from anything else, his own circumstances had changed. He no longer lived on the boat. Did this mean Felix should live with him here in London? On thinking this over, he rejected the idea. It was vital the boy's life should continue as before. No more upheavals. In any case, he was certain Isobel would want Felix back in her house. Therefore, the obvious solution was for him to go down to the boat every weekend and see Felix then. During the week, the boy would be in school, always presuming they could get him back into St Bede's Academy. As for the holidays? They could go travelling together, visit Stella in Scotland, spend time in Europe. He was no longer working, his time was now his own, he was free to travel when and where he wanted. This idea excited him. There were many places he would like to visit, particularly in Italy. Venice in April. What could be lovelier than that? It would be extra special for them to experience it for the first time together…

His plans were brought to a halt by a sudden heavy shower. He hadn't even noticed and was in danger of getting soaked. Limping back into the house, he set about the task of booking the flight. After an hour, and to his great satisfaction, he'd managed to get everything arranged. Felix would be back in England by November seventh.

This only left them ten days in which to get everything organised for his return.

Chapter 23

Plans for the Return

Isobel sighed. 'You're pacing about again Rawlings. It can't be doing your leg any good. And if we're to get anything sorted, we need to talk things through calmly.'

Rawlings came to a stop in front of her. 'It helps me think if I walk up and down.'

'Well it doesn't help me. Nor will it help Marnie when she arrives.'

'Marnie? Is she coming? I thought she was in the States,' he said adding sarcastically, 'being businesswoman of the year.'

'She's just returned, I think for about three months and I thought it would add a little to the continuity angle for Felix if she were around.' Isobel stopped talking and gave him a stern look. Rawlings obediently sat down. 'I merely told her he was returning, none of the circumstances. But she was excited at the thought of seeing him again. Marnie was very fond of him you know.' She gave him a reassuring smile. 'There really will be no problem. She is completely over any attachment to you.'

He said wryly, 'Thank you for that Isobel…' and was saved from saying more by a ring at the doorbell.

A moment later the new edition of Marnie entered the room, smartly clad in a straight red skirt with a fitted jacket and hair neatly groomed. Rawlings remembered her previous look – no make-up, red locks in an unruly mess and her bulky shape disguised in brightly coloured and billowing kaftans. The change was complete. An alarming image came to him. Supposing Isobel also went through a metamorphosis. Instead of the elegance he had grown to love and admire, he might arrive down one day to find her in hippy dresses and flowing scarves. These imaginings were thankfully stopped short by the Marnie apparition moving towards him. She embraced him warmly and exclaimed 'Rawlings! How well you look.'

'You too,' and he added with a smile, 'I am finding it hard to get used to the new you.'

'Only outwardly. I'm the same person underneath.'

Somehow, he very much doubted this but made no comment.

They all sat down as Isobel handed them a glass of wine.

Marnie looked at Rawlings. 'With all that is going on, do you still have time to be as agitated by politics as ever?'

'To give you an honest answer, yes I do. Agitated and deeply upset by the state of the nation. We seem to be charging towards a disastrous Brexit, however hard some of us fight against it, and without a statesman in sight. However, perhaps I'm not as vocal about it as I used to be.' He smiled disarmingly at her. 'There's nobody to rant at these days.'

Isobel said dryly, 'Don't believe that Marnie. Rawlings still has many other things, apart from politics, that cause him agitation. He has worn a path in my carpet with his pacing up and down.'

Rawlings said a trifle crossly, 'Well you know better than anyone, that the top of my list of worries has always been Felix.'

'It's great news he's coming back,' Marnie said. 'I was thrilled when Isobel told me.'

Rawlings frowned. 'We have no idea the state he's going to be in when he gets here. That boy has been through some sort of hell.'

Marnie looked puzzled but Isobel cut in quickly addressing Rawlings: 'I think we should cross that bridge when Felix gets here darling.' That endearment again. Rawlings noticed Marnie give them both a quick look, but Isobel seemed unaware of this as she continued, 'The boy may settle in fine once he's back and recover far quicker than you think.'

Isobel was usually right, but on this occasion Rawlings was not so sure, but as there were more pressing matters to be considered he didn't argue.

'One of my main concerns is the change in my situation since he left. I am no longer living on the boat.'

There was a moment while they all considered this. Isobel spoke first. 'I don't see why this should make a huge difference. I feel it's important we keep the continuity going as far as possible, so it would be best if Felix came back to his old room in this house. As Marnie has returned the boat to you Rawlings, you can come down at the weekends.' She smiled. 'It could actually work out well. Felix won't have the distraction of you and the boat in the evenings when he is meant to be doing his homework, and you can have him all to yourself at the weekend.'

It was what he had already anticipated would happen, but Rawlings felt a little miffed at Isobel presuming this would be the plan without any prior discussion with him.

Marnie, noticing his look of annoyance, tactfully changed the subject. 'Are you working on anything new at the moment Rawlings?'

His work! He hadn't even given it a thought. Everything

had been shelved from the moment Felix demanded his return. Up till then good progress had been made, but the book was by no means finished. He'd intended to have it done before Felix's return for Christmas. Now he would somehow have to try and rush it through. He turned to Marnie. 'I'm putting together a book about the Siege of Sarajevo, using Mia's notebooks and photographs.'

Isobel flashed him a look of concern. 'Will Felix's return hamper you in finishing it?'

What an extraordinary woman she was. Always straight to the point.

With a sigh he admitted, 'Inevitably I fear it will, but I'll still try and get it done by the end of the year. After that I intend to have a break from writing, no matter what my agent says.'

Maria arrived and summoned them into lunch.

At some point during the meal, Rawlings broached the topic of Felix's schooling. They had all taken it for granted he would return to St Bede's, but was this going to be possible?

Isobel gave a smile. 'Do you know, I almost gave up being a governor after Felix left. But for some reason I decided to give it another year and thank goodness I did. It will give me more clout with the Headmaster. I don't think there should be a problem.' She turned to Rawlings. 'You still want him to go to the Academy?'

'I think so. Continuity as you say will be all important. And he seemed happy there.' He paused for a moment. 'Mind you, Felix was happy at the school in Australia. He had a charming teacher who told me how well he was doing. It was one of the better aspects of his life there.'

Isobel was frowning. 'With all this upheaval, the boy

will be missing half a term. If they do accept him back at St Bede's, it might be good to have some schoolwork sent over, so he doesn't fall behind. I could organise a tutor.'

Rawlings considered this. 'I'm not sure. It might be good for Felix to have a break, settle in here and start again next term. He's a bright boy. I'm sure he'll soon catch up.'

'He'll be needing new uniform,' Marnie added. 'He's bound to have grown, and some winter clothes as well. I'd be happy to take him shopping if you'd like me too.'

The plans went on. It struck Rawlings that Felix's return was affecting all three of them. It was so apparent how much they'd all missed him, especially Isobel. She suddenly looked younger and happier, excited at the prospect that the boy was coming back and this time for good.

At some point in the lunch Marnie told them she had bumped into Lydia, who was now married.

'Is that to the woman she used to go on all those academic cruises with?' Isobel inquired and Marnie nodded, adding that Lydia was keen to see Felix as well.

Rawlings inwardly smiled at the remembrance of her. He'd written the woman off as a crusty old lesbian when they'd first met, but had greatly warmed to her later on, especially over her kindness to Felix. Although Lydia no longer lived in the house with Isobel, he was glad they hadn't lost touch. What a strange collection of women he'd surrounded himself with.

After lunch was over, Isobel left them, explaining she'd promised to visit a friend who'd been taken ill. Marnie and Rawlings walked down to inspect the boat together.

'I haven't been in it for months, not since you returned it to me,' Rawlings admitted.

They pushed the door open and were met with a musty

smell. Opening all the windows they sat down on the old sofa.

Marnie looked around. 'I took my few bits of furniture away with me when I left. I hardly made any changes and only used the boat on a couple of occasions. Then my new job arrived. There is still your desk and the round table by the window, but it could do with a couple more chairs and some brightening up. I'd be happy to do that for you.'

Rawlings welcomed this offer. 'That would be a great help. I'm not sure I'll manage to get down again before Felix arrives. Maybe Maria can give it a bit of a spring-clean. I'll also ask Paul to give it an overhaul. Luckily, he had a similar boat to this in Poland.'

Marnie smiled. 'I remember. You were hopeless. He was always having to sort you out when things went wrong.' She hesitated and then rather sheepishly added, 'I haven't been in the bedroom since…' Her voice trailed away.

Rawlings gave a roar of laughter. 'I thought at the very least you'd have been entertaining a long line of lovers.'

'Oh really! How ridiculous you are.'

Rawlings looked at her. 'Talking of lovers, do you have anyone special, or is all your time taken up with work?'

Marnie smiled. 'There was a possible someone a few months back, but it didn't work out, too difficult with the Atlantic between us. Besides, I really am busy with my work.'

'And you enjoy it?'

'I love it. It's the best thing that ever happened to me.' She looked at him curiously. 'What about you? Is there anyone?' He shook his head and she said tentatively, 'I thought maybe you and Isobel…'

Rawlings looked at her in astonishment. 'What on earth gave you that idea?'

Marnie hesitated, now feeling embarrassed. 'It was when she called you darling. I just thought...'

Rawlings laughed. 'Well you thought wrong. I am very fond of her, but Isobel looks on me as an annoying younger brother, nothing more than that I can assure you. The one she really loves is Felix.'

They were silent for a moment, then Marnie asked why Felix had suffered so much in Australia. Rawlings told her the whole saga of Shane's persecution, finishing with the meltdown moment. She looked shocked. 'I've always been puzzled why some children turn out to be such bullies. It's almost as if they were born that way.'

Rawlings shrugged. 'It's usually the ones with low self-esteem. They assert themselves by controlling others. If not checked they become a Hitler, Stalin, or one of the other long line of cruel dictators that have inflicted suffering on mankind.'

'Don't tell me you have this child Shane down as a potential dictator.'

Rawlings replied crossly, 'Of course not. I was only talking about extremes. But Shane has already managed to inflict a good deal of damage in his short life and unless he is dealt with properly...' He paused. 'I think, unhappily for him, it was the perfect storm of events. For years he'd been utterly spoiled by a doting grandmother and then she suddenly died leaving the boy bereft. This loss was made worse because it coincided with the arrival of his baby sister, who naturally took up a great deal of his parent's attention. Just as he was re-asserting his position in the family, this cousin arrives to live with them, who outshines him in almost everything and who his own father continually praises. So, he takes his revenge by making Felix's life hell.' He gave a mirthless laugh. 'Even Shane's appearance was against him, definitely on the obese side with a look that was unpleasantly shifty.' Looking at his watch he said, 'I must be getting back Marnie. I've a hundred things to do. Feel free to buy anything you think the boat needs and let me know the damage.'

They closed the windows and started walking back up the garden.

'Do you remember telling me about the "turning points" in your life,' Marnie suddenly said, 'those events that had made you change direction?'

'I remember how relentless you were in forcing me to tell you my entire life story.'

She ignored this and persisted, 'Have you had another "turning point" since we parted?'

'I think the arrival of Felix in my life was enough of a turning point to last me a lifetime. I don't expect another.' He paused. 'But what I was trying to explain to you, is that you never know when these events will happen, just as with Felix. They arrive out of the blue.'

She nodded. 'Exactly. I had my "turning point" at the beginning of this year, after you dumped me. The job fell into my lap and it's changed my life.' He felt 'dumped' was a bit harsh, but let it go. As she climbed into her car, no longer the clapped-out Citroen but now something smart and racy, she said, 'What will you be doing this New Year's Eve?'

Startled he exclaimed, 'Good God woman. I have absolutely no idea.' He raised his eyebrows. 'Were you suggesting a repeat performance?'

She laughed. 'Certainly not! I just wondered where you'd be.'

'Again, I have no idea. My life from hereon in depends on Felix.'

Marnie gave a nod and drove off at speed, leaving Rawlings feeling puzzled. Any physical desire he'd once felt for her had gone. Their one night of passion had been a moment of madness. But sitting with her on the boat he remembered how much he'd enjoyed her company. Marnie was one of the few people he liked to be with, so it was good they could now be friends. But in that case, why the reminder of New Year's Eve?

It was probably nothing and he put it quickly from his mind.

*

The following few days kept Rawlings fully occupied. Felix had been told to Skype if he was worried about anything. But as he didn't, he presumed the boy was satisfied with all the arrangements. When he talked to Sarah, she told him Felix had no qualms about travelling alone and that Brad wouldn't leave the boy until someone from the airline came to collect him. It didn't stop Rawlings feeling anxious and he wondered yet again if he'd made the right decision. The flight was indeed a long one and there were two stops as well. He'd been assured that someone would be with Felix all the time. Even so, it was going to be an anxious time.

He put a call through to Graham, which left him thoroughly irritated. The bloody man kept raising objections and endlessly queried Rawlings about his actions.

'You and Lady Mallinson aren't in the first flush of youth you know. Wouldn't it be sensible to keep the younger guardian as well?'

Rawlings tried to keep his temper in check, saying dryly, 'I think one of us will live long enough to see Felix reach twenty-one when he will come into his inheritance. In any case, this was entirely Sarah's decision and she will be confirming it in writing.'

Graham muttered something to the effect that people didn't usually throw guardianships around like confetti. Rawlings presumed he disliked the extra paperwork, or maybe he felt partially responsible for making the wrong decision over Felix. For God's sake! The man was well paid and had no justification for being so bloody-minded. He was obviously anal and loathed changes. Graham also seemed to presume that his title of 'family' solicitor gave him the right to interfere, instead of merely taking instruction. His annoyance increased. The 'family' in question were his late wife's and really had nothing to do with him. It was time for him to consider finding another solicitor. Isobel could help him with that.

A letter arrived from Hetty asking him to stay, so he called her to explain Felix's sudden return made this impossible. She was volubly excited by his news, saying she couldn't wait to meet the boy. The call was prolonged with the latest news of Bel and Max's welfare. Rawlings dearly loved this family, but sometimes the endless complications of their lives could become tiresome.

The next task was to ring Stella and tell her about Felix. This call thankfully was of shorter duration than Hetty's, his sister being a woman of few words. She was delighted to hear of the boy's return, and he promised to arrange a visit early in the new year.

An appointment with his doctor was postponed, assuring

274

the good man he was well rested and the pain in his leg greatly improved. This wasn't strictly true, but he really didn't have time for a visit right now. It would use up a whole day, what with x-rays and all the other palaver involved. If it became necessary, he would make an appointment once Felix had settled back in.

To his great relief, Isobel informed him the headmaster would be delighted to welcome Felix back to St Bede's the following term. He'd also suggested the boy should join them on the school skiing trip after Christmas, pointing out it would be a good way for Felix to meet up with his fellow pupils again before term began. Rawlings reflected that Felix's social diary was filling up. It was important they didn't rush things. A period of calm was what was needed now.

With some satisfaction he noted almost everything was now crossed off his list. But one item stuck out. His bloody book. Since returning from Boston, he'd only skimmed through Mia's Sarajevo account, matching her dates to the pictures he'd chosen. It was now necessary to make a better study of the notebook, making sure he'd missed nothing. Therefore, with some reluctance he put aside an evening to reading her notes in their entirety. Pouring himself a large glass of wine, he picked up the papers Sorcha had printed off for him, sat on the sofa and started to read. Progressing well, he'd almost reached the end of the Sarajevo notebook, when one page caught his attention...

November 17th. Had a tricky evening with R tonight. Somehow we got on to the topic I most dislike – marriage. It's always been a relief that R's married, although occasionally we've been on dangerous territory when he's mentioned asking his wife for a divorce. I've firmly declined this suggestion each time, making the excuse that I am a Roman Catholic so marriage with a divorced man definitely not allowed! It's a damned useful excuse. Little does R know I am totally lapsed and have NO use for religion. R claims he is an agnostic and keeps an open mind. I'd never tell him this, but I'm a confirmed atheist. I also can never tell him the real reason why I won't marry. He wouldn't understand. But I know only too well what marriage involves and what torture children are put through. I will never put myself, or a child of mine through that. Luckily, I don't seem to have any maternal instincts whatsoever...

Rawlings poured himself another drink. His hand was shaking, and he felt a rising anger. This revelation was a shock. No, it wasn't only shock, it was the feeling of betrayal. All those years he'd been living with a lie. Obvious now why she hadn't agreed to marry him even after Gillian died, something that both puzzled and hurt him at the time. The more he learned about Mia, the more he realised he hadn't known her at all. Had he been wrong about her from the outset? Was their relationship founded merely on lust rather than any kind of love? Had he been with her all those years, merely to suit her sexual needs? It was hard to believe.

Reluctantly he went back to the notes, determined now to finish them. There was little more of personal interest in the Sarajevo notebook and with some relief he moved on to the New York journal. This was not nearly as detailed. It started with a cryptic account of her brief visit to Boston in 1995.

...Went back to stay with parents for a week. It was the anticipated disaster and I soon gave up and left for Bellows Falls

with Sorcha. Poor kid, she's really been through it. I'm also pretty wrecked myself after three years in the S. Siege. We are the walking wounded. Two sad wrecks, results of the O'Keefe upbringing...

Again, he could feel her bitterness. She moved on to her return to New York, where there were long accounts of their social life; the people they'd met, the events they went to see. It was an interesting fact that he was hardly mentioned here, except for an irritated note when he'd returned to England to be with Gillian when she was dying of cancer. He remembered how her callous objection to this had surprised him at the time.

He reached the page where Sorcha had suddenly turned up.

...Tonight Sorcha arrived at the apartment completely out of it, high on drugs and booze. I think R was shocked by the state of her but as always tactful and made no comment. Thankful for that. I'd mentioned to him that Sorcha was a wild child, but now anyone can see she's a complete mess. Will she ever recover? I rather doubt it, but I'll have to get her into rehab again. This time the damned parents will not be told or get involved. They are responsible for this. God! No wonder I don't want marriage or children. I do love R – but if he ever insisted on it, it would be the end for us.

Rawlings put the notebook down. The under-linings in her writing showed her anger, but at least there was some comfort in that she admitted she loved him, even if it was love on her terms only. Why on earth hadn't she confided in him, told him about her terrible childhood, made him understand? The reason he felt her betrayal so deeply was because she had continually lied to him, kept him hanging on, knowing full well he hoped they would eventually marry and settle down, all the time knowing full well she never would.

The wine was almost finished, and it was past midnight, but he forced himself to get to the end.

Her accounts of 9/11 were vividly written, but this was all familiar territory. She'd used it as the commentary to her published book of photographs. They were astonishing pictures. He remembered that day so clearly. How terrified he'd been about her rushing down into the middle of it, with so much potential danger still in the situation. She made a brief reference to this…

…Poor R. His 60th birthday party totally ruined by the terrorists. But it's been an extraordinary day for me. I don't think I've ever had a better opportunity for taking pictures. I was right in the middle of it – as it happened. It was all terrifying and dreadful – like some horror movie – but I witnessed many incidents that only I was close enough to get to. Thank God R didn't try and stop me. I know he was worried for my safety but we both know the risks we have to take in our work, and he accepts this…

He skimmed through the rest of the New York years. There was nothing further of personal interest. Reaching for the final notebook, Afghanistan, it immediately became more revealing, almost from the first entry:

…I know R didn't want me to join him here. I can't help feeling in some way he has changed a lot since Iraq. I wasn't with him for that, the actual war was over so quickly. The interesting part for me would have been the awful mess left behind, but then

R came out here and I decided to follow him. Afghanistan is a country that has always held a fascination for me. Of course, I'm aware of the dangers. For some reason R has suddenly become over-protective and this is starting to be bloody irritating. I'm his partner, not his WIFE!

I can also see that his PTSD is getting worse. He has nightmares almost every night. I know I'm not the person to get him through this. He needs special counselling. I feel he is near the edge.

Apart from his deteriorating state – I have reached the conclusion, that at some point soon I will have to tell him we should go our separate ways. What I always dreaded in our relationship has happened. We now want different things from our lives and I don't really see a future for the two of us together. It's not a matter of feelings, it's a matter of priorities. However much I might love him – and I do – certainly there has been no other man in my life – my priority is my work and always will be. Recently he has started to get in the way of this...

Another entry followed along the same lines:

...There have been many casualties and deaths recently. Today, Bic, another reporter out here with us, had to have several pieces of shrapnel removed from his leg after a nearby explosion. He nearly died. R has become even more agitated about me being here. He's driving me mad. The fire has gone out of him. We'll have to have it out soon. I know he's only hanging on here until he can retire next year. He's not the hungry reporter he used to be, his PTSD is awful to see and I know he's suffering – BUT he has to understand ME. I will never retire. I will carry on working until I am no longer able to. Or until I get killed like Marie Colvin...

Rawlings drained his wine and sat lost in thought. She'd been right about him wanting to finish with war reporting, right too about his PTSD, but how stupidly mistaken he'd been to think she would ever settle down with him. Now he knew for certain. Again, the under-linings indicated how strongly she'd felt. There were only a few pages left, much of it in the same vein, until he came to the very last entry:

...A good evening. Unexpectedly happy and relaxed. R almost back to his old self. He and I discussed plans to visit the orphanage once this tour is over. I'd like us both to do that, whatever happens to us afterwards. It will be great to catch up with Luka. Good God, he must be in his twenties now. Makes me feel quite old. I'm going to be 50 next year. Life begins at 50? I do hope so...

The next day she was killed.

He took the empty wine bottle out to the kitchen and chucked it in the bin. Returning, he scooped up the papers and put them away in the bottom drawer of his desk. There was no need to read them ever again. Once the book was published and the notes were no longer needed for checking the odd reference, he would dispose of them. That period of his life was over. He and Mia had been inseparable for so long. With her death their love affair ended. He'd grieved deeply for Mia, grieving for what he thought was their lost life together that had been cut so tragically short. Now he knew that the future he had imagined for them was mere fantasy. It would never have happened.

He sat back on the sofa and the minutes ticked by as he tried to make sense of Mia's revelations. It was strange, odd even, that although his immediate reaction had been one of anger at her deception, he realised this was now being replaced by a kind of relief. It was some comfort that she had loved him in her fashion, right up until she was killed. It had lasted seventeen years, but he now knew for certain their relationship would have ended after Afghanistan. Mia, knowing he would retire, intended to go on alone, undaunted by the fact it was likely she would be killed in some other conflict like her heroine Marie Colvin. He realised it was pretty likely she had a death wish, thinking her life worthless, and this made her totally careless of her safety. At last too late he understood her. Poor, sad Mia had been so damaged by her childhood, nothing would have changed her, least of all him. But on the positive side he was now released. He could put his life with Mia behind him, no longer needing to mourn. Their relationship had been wonderful and terrible at the same time, but the revelations in her notebooks now set him free to concentrate solely on the future. A great weight had been lifted from him. Slowly he stood up and walked to the bedroom, exhausted but calm.

Drifting off to sleep, he made a silent vow that the happiness of Felix would be all that mattered to him now, to the exclusion of everything else.

Chapter 24

The Return

Rawlings waited nervously at Arrivals. The flight had landed some time ago and the luggage was in the hall. He now desperately searched for Felix among the milling crowds. So many people were pouring in but so far, no small boy. He started to worry. It seemed a long time since he'd noticed anyone from Felix's flight coming through. His heart was pounding. Ridiculous thoughts went through his head. Suppose something had happened to the boy. He could have been taken ill… The line had thinned out now and only the stragglers were left. Should he go to enquiries? While he dithered, at last he caught sight of him walking beside an air hostess who was wheeling a trolley with his luggage. Felix had his head down, so Rawlings waved at the hostess hoping to catch her attention. To his relief she saw him, said something to Felix who immediately looked up. On seeing Rawlings, he ran over and threw his arms around him, almost sending him of balance. He ruffled the boy's hair and waited for the hostess to catch up.

'You must be Felix's grandfather?' She spoke with a heavy Australian accent.

He smiled. 'I am. Thank you for taking such good care of him.'

'It's been a pleasure really. Sorry we took so long coming through. I had to wait until everyone else was off the flight.' She handed the trolley to Rawlings. 'Well, goodbye Felix. Have a lovely time with Grandpa.'

Rawlings winced slightly at this. Grandpa implied something rather alien to him. Felix thanked her politely and she left. The two of them started walking towards the carpark.

'How was the flight?' he asked.

'Good,' was the only reply given and nothing more was said while Rawlings put the luggage in the boot and returned the trolley. Felix strapped himself into the front seat. As Rawlings started the engine, he gave the boy a sideways glance. He was looking straight ahead, his expression tense and his hands clenched by his side. It was puzzling. He'd thought the boy would at least show some relief at being back, if not excitement and joy. With a sinking heart he remembered the time he'd collected Felix from his prep school, after breaking the news to him that his parents had been killed in a car crash. There was the same look of tension, the same clenched hands. It had taken time then for Felix to settle in. But he had. Before he left for Australia, he was both settled and happy. God damn it. Now they would have to begin this process all over again. Or worse still, there could be permanent damage.

'Isobel can't wait to see you,' Rawlings told him. 'She's so excited to have you back.'

A nod was all he received in acknowledgement.

'I expect Maria has made you a splendid tea. Are you hungry?'

A shake of the head. Rawlings sighed. That was a pity. Poor Maria's efforts might go to waste. He tried again.

'You'll be pleased to see Juno again.'

At last a response: 'I don't suppose she'll remember me.'

'I'm sure she will.'

The boy gave a shrug, as if to say it wasn't worth arguing about.

After this Rawlings gave up, and they drove on in silence. Reaching the house, he could see Isobel with Juno waiting for them on the doorstep. Felix got out of the car and as he had done with Rawlings, ran to Isobel and gave her a hug.

'Dear, dear boy. Welcome home.' She looked very emotional, but Felix didn't notice this because he had turned his attention to Juno. The dog was leaping up and down in excitement and licking Felix's face.

'You see?' Rawlings said. 'She does remember you.'

'Why don't you go into the kitchen Felix.' Isobel smiled at him. 'I know Maria has made your favourite chocolate cake.' The boy nodded and went in.

As soon as he was out of earshot she said, 'I can see from your face that all is not entirely well. Let's leave him with Maria and go into the living room.'

Rawlings for once didn't pace up and down. Suddenly overwhelmed by emotion he collapsed into a chair. 'It's not good Isobel. The boy hardly said a word. I tried talking to him, but he wouldn't respond. It's almost as if he's still in shock. Or maybe he's punishing us...'

Isobel sounded tetchy. 'Don't be so melodramatic Rawlings. It is far more likely he's exhausted from the long flight. And maybe he's nervous about another change of scene.'

Rawlings shook his head. 'I fear it's more than that. I know that look of his. It's like the time after his parents were killed. It took time for him to trust us then but now I'm not so sure. I think real damage has been done.'

She regarded him gravely. 'Well if you're right, we are going to have to use all our patience and tact with him. Did you bring up the subject of Australia?'

'No, I didn't.' He sighed. 'That particular boil will have to be lanced at some point, but I must choose the moment carefully.'

Isobel considered this and nodded. 'Felix might like to see the boat again. Why don't you go on down and I'll send him to join you when he's finished his tea? He could take Juno with him as well.' She added with a smile, 'At least he responded to the dog.'

Rawlings wearily stood up. 'Good idea. It might give me a chance to explain to him about spending my weekdays in London. I think I'll go back tonight Isobel. This will give you three days on your own with Felix and a chance to settle him in.'

He left the house and walked slowly down to the boat. The nights were drawing in. Looking at his watch he noted it wasn't yet five, but it was already dusk. There was no fog, the sky unusually clear for November. The moon was already visible along with a few stars.

Letting himself in, he turned on the lights and was relieved to find that Paul had put on the heating. Marnie had also worked her magic, having added two more comfy chairs and a table by the riverside windows adorned with a bowl of fruit. The bookshelves were still empty, and he had the idea of letting Felix fill them up with books of his choice. Wandering through into the bedroom he noted that the bed had been made up with clean sheets and towels laid out. Guessing this was all Maria's doing, he made a mental note to send her payment. He was about to make his way to the kitchen when he heard a knock at the door. It was Felix, along with the dog.

Rawlings let him in, and he asked politely, 'Is it all right if I bring Juno in with me?'

'Of course. You must look on the boat as an extra part of the house.' The boy sat down on the sofa making no comment, while the dog settled at his feet. 'How are you doing? Are you feeling tired?' Felix shook his head. Rawlings sat down beside him and cleared his throat. 'Some things have slightly changed around here Felix.' A wary look came into the boy's eyes, so he added quickly, 'It's nothing that need worry you. It's only that I don't spend all my time on the boat now, as I used to. I think I told you, I have a flat in London.' He paused, realising he had to tread carefully. 'Isobel and I thought it best if you continued to live with her in the house.' At this Felix nodded and Rawlings feeling encouraged, continued, 'I will spend weekdays in London working in the flat, and then come down to the boat at the weekend. That's the general plan so I hope it's all right with you. Once you're back at school you'll be out of the house during most of the day and then doing homework in the evenings. You can bring friends back to be on the boat as well, as long as you tell Isobel. I can catch up with your week each Friday.'

Felix took his time to take this in, nodded again, but still said nothing.

Rawlings added, 'While you're not in school, in the holidays or half term, you might come and stay with me for a couple of days in London. There's a room for you in the flat, and plenty of things for you to see and for me take you to.'

This time there was no reaction at all not even a nod of the head, and there followed a long silence. Rawlings was struggling. He was not handling this well. Finally, in some desperation he blurted out, 'I'm truly sorry for the way things turned out in Australia Felix.' The boy turned to him with an expression that left Rawlings feeling chilled and he added rather feebly, 'None of us could have known that Shane would be such a problem.'

The boy finally spoke, and his voice was cold. 'You all knew I didn't want to leave you and go to Australia. You sent me there all the same.'

'Yes, we did,' Rawlings answered. 'We all thought, wrongly as it turned out, that it would be better for you to be with a family and children of your own age, rather than older people like Isobel and myself. We also thought, again wrongly, that your resistance to leaving here was a fear of the unknown and that once you were settled in, you'd be fine.'

Suddenly the boy yelled at him, 'But I wasn't! I wasn't fine at all. It was horrible, like a prison and there was no escape.'

Then, to his horror, Felix broke into what seemed like a primitive howl and his whole body became racked with sobs. It went on and on, as if at last he was letting out all the pain and frustration he had suffered over those long months. Rawlings watched helplessly until he finally took the boy in his arms and stroked his hair trying to calm him. After what seemed an interminable time, the crying subsided. Felix sat limp and exhausted. Rawlings stood up, passing him a handkerchief, and walking to the kitchen he fetched a glass of water. With some relief on his return he noticed the boy was looking more composed, stroking Juno who had leapt on his lap.

'Drink this. You tend to become dehydrated on long plane journeys.'

Felix did as he was told, the fight having completely gone from him. Then he handed the glass back to Rawlings, who sat down opposite him.

'I realise now we made a terribly bad decision Felix. I thought so at the time, but everyone convinced me you'd be better off with a family and it seemed selfish to keep you here for my sake.' He looked at the boy. 'For God's sake Felix why didn't you ask to come back earlier?'

Felix shrugged. 'I thought I was coming back in the summer and could have told you then, but Ella became ill and all the plans changed, and Brad booked us into the holiday camp. I didn't feel I could. I was going to stick it out until Christmas and tell you then I didn't want to go back, but after Shane…' He faltered and came to a stop.

'After Shane ruined your work you couldn't take anymore,' Rawlings finished the sentence for him.

Felix nodded and then said slowly, as if considering his words carefully, 'I understand you did what you thought was right EG, but it was wrong of you to send me so far away. It wasn't as if I could just ask you to fetch me back if things didn't go well, and it was impossible to explain things to you on Skype. In any case I was never left alone to speak to you.' He paused and Rawlings, not liking to interrupt but relieved Felix was now talking, waited for him to continue. 'It wasn't just Shane who made things impossible, although it was mainly him. There were other things as well.'

'What sort of things.'

Felix thought about it. 'I was never given any time to myself. We were always made to do everything together. And I could never bring a friend of my own back to the house because of Shane. And I wasn't the only person Shane bullied. It was Davey as well. He'd say to Davey, "slave, do this. Slave, do that". And Davey always did. I'm worried that now I've left there'll be nobody to stand up for him, although Shane is being sent away to boarding school and that might make things better.' Rawlings thought privately that Davey could fend for himself and was just biding his time. Felix went on 'Brad was really angry with Shane for what he did to me, so Shane will have to be very careful how he behaves in the future.' He thought for a moment. 'Davey's cleverer than Shane, who's really rather stupid,' adding sadly, 'I'm going to miss Ella. She was the only one I loved. She's still not well and everyone has to be very careful with her. Sarah was always blaming us if she cried when it wasn't even our fault. Everything changed in the house when Ella became ill. Sarah was always cross and often unreasonable, which she hadn't been before…'

Rawlings felt he had to defend Sarah here. 'I think it must have been a strain on her, having a baby that was so ill. She must have been constantly worried and tired.'

Felix thought about this. 'It wasn't just her who changed,' he said, 'Brad did as well. When I first arrived, he and Sarah got on well, but recently they just argued all the time.'

'They did? What about?'

Felix shrugged. 'Lots of things. I could hear them at night after we'd gone to bed. My room was next to theirs. A few nights before I left, they had this huge argument about the way the white Australians treat the Aborigines. Sarah kept saying it was disgraceful and being English she felt ashamed of it. I think the reason they had a row about this was because there had been a case in the paper about an Aboriginal boy who had been beaten to death. The news was full of it. Brad got furious with Sarah for saying this and he said it was no worse than the way the British had acted in the past with the Empire and the slave trade. It went on and on until Sarah burst into tears. That's usually how their rows ended. I didn't want to listen, but I couldn't help hearing them. They always ended up shouting at each other. I hated that.'

Rawlings listened to this with a sinking heart. It was all far worse than he'd expected. He tried to sound reasonable. 'It's a pity they argued about that particular subject because they were both right in a way. Throughout history one group of people has always been guilty of persecuting another lot. It's happened in every country in the world and sadly it still goes on. There's never been a shortage of conflicts Felix, and sadly never will be. You only have to look back through the centuries. The Romans fought the English, the Normans fought the Saxons, and so the wars rolled on over the years. And then there were the persecutions. The Americans and British indulged in the slave trade, the Germans persecuted the Jews and racist problems still abound in most countries.' He looked at Felix and sighed. 'All we can do is try and learn from the past and put things right in the future.'

Stopping himself he thought, 'What the hell am I doing giving the boy a potted history lesson?' Looking at Felix he said, 'Can you try and forgive us for sending you to Australia and put the past year behind you? I give you my solemn promise we will never send you away again.'

He waited for an answer and it was a long time in coming. Finally, Felix said, 'I'll try. But I'm not sure I can ever forget what happened to me.'

'I understand that.' Rawlings considered this and then said slowly, 'Sometimes, when terrible things happen to you, it's possible to learn from them and grow stronger.'

Felix looked very doubtful about this, so Rawlings decided on a complete change of subject. 'Marnie is excited at the prospect of seeing you again.'

The boy seemed surprised at this. 'Marnie? Is she here? I thought you said she'd gone to work in America.'

Rawlings smiled. 'She has been working in the States, but she's back in England right now until the New Year. Isobel has asked her to lunch on Sunday, so you'll see her then. Lydia too, do you remember her?'

'Yes, I do. She took me to see War Horse.'

The boy suddenly looked completely washed out. Rawlings stood up. 'I think we'd better be getting you back to the house. Isobel will be wondering where you and Juno have got to.'

As they left the boat the cold air hit them, and Felix shivered. Noticing this Rawlings added, 'I think you're going to need some new, warmer clothes. We're moving towards winter here. Marnie has offered to take you shopping if you'd like that.'

'Cool.' Felix said. It was a word he hadn't heard the boy utter for a long time and it brought a lump to his throat. Felix turned to Rawlings and asked, 'Will you be returning to London tonight EG?'

Rawlings nodded. 'If that's all right with you, I thought I'd leave you to settle in. It's only three days and then I'll be back. Isobel has a great deal planned and I expect you'll want to meet up with Sunil Patel. I'm afraid I haven't seen the Patels for a good while although Isobel has kept in touch. She goes into the newsagents often and they always wanted news of you. They know you're coming back.'

Felix suddenly seemed nervous. 'I always meant to keep in touch with Sunil but only did at the beginning. I wonder if he will be different.'

Rawlings said soothingly, 'You've been gone less than a year. I don't think you'll find he's changed that much.'

He thought back, remembering how Sunil and Felix had been inseparable. Breaking them up had been one of the issues at the time of parting that most upset the boy. It might be difficult now to pick up where they left off. He hoped not, but boys at that age changed their friendships and allegiances rapidly. He gave an inward sigh. This settling back process might not be as easy as he'd hoped.

When they reached the house, Rawlings said, 'Why don't you go straight up to your room and get ready for bed. You've had a long day. I'll be up to say goodnight before I leave for London.' The boy nodded, took Juno into the kitchen and then went upstairs to his room. Rawlings went to join Isobel in the living room, where he was pleased to note the log fire had been lit.

'You look all in,' she commented handing him a glass of wine. 'You could probably do with one drink before you go.'

He nodded gratefully and sank onto the sofa. She sat down opposite and regarded him questioningly.

'Well?'

He gave her the gist of what had happened on the boat, and then knocked back the wine.

Isobel appeared shocked. 'That poor boy. But I think a relief it all poured out.' And she added sadly, 'How could we possibly have known what would happen?'

Rawlings nodded. 'That's what I told him, but I think he'll find it hard to forgive us. Who can blame him after what he's been through? We're going to have to fight hard to regain his trust.' He put down the glass and stood up. 'I hesitate to give you advice Isobel, because you always know the right thing to do, but could I suggest we don't refer to Australia for the moment unless he does? Nor should anyone else. You might warn Marnie and Lydia. Over the next few days, the boy should be given the chance to settle back into his old life without thinking of what he's just been through. I mentioned Marnie's offer to buy him some new clothes and he seemed to welcome that idea and he was pleased to be seeing Lydia again as well. There also was a mention of him visiting Sunil, but he seemed a bit nervous about that.' He smiled at her. 'I hate the phrase, but I think it is a case of playing it by ear for the next few weeks.'

A few hours later he arrived back in the flat and found two letters waiting for him. One was from Sheila – thankfully not nagging him about progress on the book –inviting him to a celebration party for Jolyon. It was a grand invitation, embossed and gilt-edged and not the sort of 'do' he enjoyed, but he felt obliged to make an appearance for Jolyon's sake. At least it was just drinks and canapés which meant he could make an early escape. The other envelope contained an invitation from Bel for a lunch the following Sunday. To his relief, he now had a valid excuse to avoid what he imagined might be an awkward encounter. Bel without Clive was a potentially dangerous combination. He would ring her and explain about the return of Felix.

Isobel reported the next day that all was going well, so far. Felix was to go on a shopping expedition the following day with Marnie. This had become urgent, as the only warm clothes he appeared to have were the ones he'd travelled in.

Three days later, Rawlings was once more sitting on the boat with Felix now looking very smart, clad in navy corduroy trousers and a dark blue Aran sweater. Rawlings also noted new trainers, but tactfully refrained from asking the price. Instead he remarked, 'I like that sweater Felix. I think I used to have one rather like it.'

The boy smiled. 'Marnie said to tell you it was a late birthday present from her. She has the bills for everything else. I needed quite a few things as only my summer clothes were packed. I think I'd grown out of everything warm.' He shot an anxious look at Rawlings. 'I'm sorry EG, the trainers were rather expensive.'

Rawlings smiled back at him. 'Don't worry, they can be a late birthday present from me.'

He reflected that Graham would need to be tackled again about the new financial arrangements, grimly recalling how the boring man insisted everything for Felix should be paid out of the Trust, which provided an allowance for the boy. This annoyed Rawlings at the time, and he'd objected, protesting that he could easily pay for his own grandson's needs. Graham had instantly become testy, stating his suggestion would over-complicate things and make unnecessary work for him. Rawlings sighed. It was going to be even more complicated now that Isobel was a guardian as well, especially as she would be paying for most of the boy's upkeep. Graham would need to transfer the allowance from Sarah to her. He envisaged lengthy discussions as it would all have to be talked through, both with Isobel and Graham. It would necessitate a visit to the gloomy man...

'I went to see Sunil,' Felix said, cutting through his cogitations.

'Oh yes, and how did that go?'

Felix shuffled uneasily in his seat. 'I'm not sure. Mr and Mrs Patel seemed pleased to see me.' Rawlings gave him an enquiring look, and after a moment Felix added, 'Sunil talked about his girlfriend Scarlett all the time which I found a bit boring. But he did say he was pleased I was returning to the school.'

Rawlings thought for a moment. 'Didn't Scarlett have a twin sister called Sapphire?'

Felix shot him an admiring look. 'How did you remember that EG?'

Rawlings said dryly, 'They're not names you easily forget,' and he added, 'people will soon get used to having you back. Sunil was probably a bit in shock. Stupid of me. I should have warned him of your return.' He hesitated. 'The headmaster wondered whether you'd like to join them on the school skiing trip after Christmas. It's your class that's going and it might be a good opportunity to get to know everyone again before the start of term.'

This had a positive reaction. 'I'd really like that. I enjoyed the last trip we went on.' He gave his grandfather an anxious look. 'I think I will need new ski clothes.'

Rawlings smiled. 'I'm sure we can manage that.' And then asked curiously, 'How did you find Marnie?'

'Just the same,' was the reply, but after thinking about it he added, 'except she looks a bit different. She's more like a schoolteacher now.'

Rawlings found this an amusingly accurate description.

Sunday turned out cold and foggy. Rawlings felt the pain in his leg increase. Bloody arthritis setting in he thought. If it became much worse, he would have to go back to the medical man. He couldn't put it off much longer.

To his relief, the lunch was a happy and relaxed occasion. Lydia arrived seeming much the same, except that her usually stern expression had somehow softened. She expressed delight at seeing Felix again and had brought him some more Michael Morpurgo books. Felix thanked her and went on to explain, 'EG has said I can use the bookshelves on the boat for my own books. I only have a few so far, so these will be the start of my collection.'

'We all know what to give you for Christmas then,' Marnie said. 'You'll have to give us a book list.'

'I haven't even given you a birthday present yet,' Isobel said. 'Have you any idea what you'd like from me?'

They all looked expectantly at Felix, who seemed to be giving this a great deal of thought.

'Well,' he said slowly, 'what I really, really want, and it would have to be both birthday and Christmas,' he paused looking anxiously at Isobel and then declared, 'what I want most in all the world is a dog of my own.'

There was a slightly shocked silence at this request. Rawlings looked anxiously at Isobel but as always, she rose to the challenge.

'I don't see why not Felix. It might be good for Juno to have a companion.' She looked indulgently at him, 'As long as you promise it will be the same size as Juno, or smaller. Gone are the days when I could deal with a Labrador in the house.'

Felix flung his arms around Isobel. 'Thank you so much Isobel. It will be the best present ever and you can help me choose it, to make sure he's the right size.'

Isobel laughed. 'I think the dog had better be a she as well, otherwise there could be problems.' Everyone laughed, but Rawlings remained worried by this request. Later he asked Isobel if she was sure about getting another dog. She again insisted she was fine with it, saying it might make

Juno less demanding and anyway Felix would be there to help look after them. So, Rawlings decided to tackle her on another subject. He said tentatively that it would be all too easy to indulge the boy, out of a sense of guilt. It was very important Felix shouldn't become spoiled. Isobel laughed at this, assuring him it wasn't going to happen and told him not to be such an old fusser. Fusser or no, another matter was nagging away at him and would need to be tackled soon, which was the tricky subject of money and Felix's upkeep. Rawlings had always presumed Isobel to be quite comfortably off, inheriting Peter's healthy Foreign Office pension. Even so, the boy's return would mean many extra expenses for her and he disliked having to inquire into the state of her finances. He decided it might be best to tackle Graham first, and then present the allowance to Isobel as a fait accompli. He resolved to set up a meeting as soon as was possible.

Returning to London later that day he hoped they might be over the worst. There were signs that Felix was almost back to his old self. But some instinct warned him against complacency. He felt sure the boy's recovery was not yet complete. There could be further evidence emerging of the damage that had been done, and he determined to keep a watchful eye.

The following morning, he rang Graham's office and made an appointment for later that week. He also sent an email to Brad and Sarah telling them Felix was settling back well and thanking them for all they had done for the boy. After all, it wasn't their fault their son was a monster, or at any rate, not entirely.

*

'What you don't seem to understand Graham,' he was near to shouting, 'is that the boy was bloody miserable in Australia and was driven to begging us to let him return. 'No,' he corrected himself, 'it was more than that, Felix gave us an ultimatum.' Rawlings was endeavouring to keep his temper. 'Sarah has already informed you she no longer needs to be a guardian to the boy. I do not see the problem. And please don't mention again the ages of myself and Lady Mallinson. It is very unlikely one of us will expire before Felix comes of age. Lady Mallinson is like a surrogate grandmother to the boy and he's already happily settled back with her and pleased to be returning to the school we so regrettably removed him from.'

Graham put his hands together and pursed his lips, giving Rawlings a look that was plainly disapproving. He said in prim tones, 'I really do not understand your reasoning as to why Sarah cannot remain a guardian as well. It would mean Felix could go back to Australia in the future without further paperwork.

Rawlings almost leapt out of his seat at this suggestion.

'Good God man! Don't you understand that he won't? I can assure you of that fact. He went through the most terrible experience out there, and I for one feel guilty about it. We sent him, against his wishes, halfway round the world, where he had to endure months of appalling bullying from his cousin, with no way of escaping.'

Graham gave him a patronising smile. 'I think you are rather exaggerating the situation. I have two sons of my own. I know what boys can be like at that age.'

Rawlings yelled in exasperation, 'Shane is not just like any boy of Felix's age. He is a deeply disturbed child who urgently needs sorting out. I am sure your sons had someone to go to if they had problems. Felix had nobody. And it wasn't as if he could hop on a train and come back to where he was happiest. In any case, aren't you rather missing the point? Sarah has relinquished her role as guardian of her own free will. I didn't ask her to.'

Graham gave a curt nod. 'Well, I realise the illness of the child could have been a factor behind her decision. The extra worry with the baby might have exacerbated the whole situation. Felix became an added burden she didn't expect.'

Rawlings said sourly, 'I can assure you Felix was the least of her problems. Her eldest son needs a reform school.' He looked at his solicitor with dislike. The man seemed to him as obstinate and as Uriah Heep-like as ever. 'I am only here now Graham, to sort out the financial situation, not to go into a post-mortem of the recent past. The boy is residing with Lady Mallinson and will be, for the foreseeable future. This means the allowance for his upkeep needs to transfer to her.'

'Did you not think of having the boy with you in London?' Graham asked. 'There are so many more good schools for you to choose from.'

Rawlings asked himself again, why the man was being so deliberately perverse and raising unnecessary alternatives. With as much patience as he could muster, he said, 'There would be absolutely no reason to bring the boy up to London and give him further upheaval in his life. Continuity is what is needed now, and familiarity. He already has a place at St Bede's Academy, the school where Lady Mallinson is a governor, and it has an excellent record. He was happy there before, and for the moment I consider it the best place for him. Felix is only twelve. We can always make other arrangements about his education in the future if that becomes necessary. He is also happy and settled living in Isobel's house, where he has a spacious room, which is well appointed with its own bathroom.' Good God, he was sounding like an estate agent! He ploughed on. 'I would be unable to give him all this in my London flat. I'll go down to the houseboat every weekend and see him then. This all works perfectly well, and I see absolutely no reason to change any of this unless something warrants it. Felix and Lady Mallinson have a wonderful relationship.'

Graham held up his hand. 'Yes, yes,' he said testily, 'I understand all the points you are making Rawlings. However, you must also understand that as the family solicitor I administrate the Trust and I represent Sarah as well as yourself. I have to make sure, in the present circumstances she is being fairly treated and not shut out.'

Rawlings looked at him in astonishment. 'We are talking about the boy's best interest here, not a competition between Sarah and myself. And if we are talking of fairness, I didn't appreciate my grandson being whisked away to the other side of the world where I had almost no opportunity to see him. We know that particular decision has failed, so we have a duty to the boy to organise things in the best possible way for him in the future, now that he has returned.' He added firmly, 'I am only here today to sort out the financial arrangements and give you my instructions.'

Graham pursed his lips again, his long face set in an expression of annoyance. Then reluctantly he started to shuffle the documents in front of him. It took another hour to finally settle things and Rawlings left exhausted but satisfied with the outcome. On the drive home, he found he was still seething and vowed to get shot of Graham and find another solicitor to take care of his affairs, one without 'family' complications. Isobel was bound to know of one. To add to his frustration, he was now stuck in traffic. He should have travelled by tube, but his leg had been giving him such pain he'd decided against it. Now alone with his thoughts, he realised the next and rather embarrassing task was to explain to Isobel the financial arrangements that Graham had set up for Felix. Once that was done, it was his fervent wish there could be a period of calm.

The traffic at last cleared and the rest of the journey was relatively painless, apart from all the cyclists and endless traffic lights. Were they breeding? As he parked the car, a thought nagged away at him. Suppose bloody Graham was right. They'd presumed Felix would be better living with Isobel, but maybe he ought to have the boy with him in London. In staying with Isobel, Felix would be surrounded by older people and it would be all too easy for them to spoil him. It was vitally important they made the right decisions now. He sat on in the car, going through the permutations in his mind until finally he dismissed Graham's suggestion. Right now, the boy was in the best place, he was sure of it. His solicitor, soon to be ex-solicitor, had absolutely no conception of what Felix had endured over the past ten months. Even so, some ground rules should be laid down. Just because the boy had been through a bad time, didn't mean he should be indulged by the doting females that now surrounded him. Isobel had tried to reassure him on this point, but he would still keep a watchful eye. On a positive note, once term started Felix was bound to make friends of his own age and unlike in Australia, he could bring them back to the house. The teachers at the school would certainly instil discipline, so maybe there was no need to be over-strict at home. His impression of the Academy last year was of a school that adhered to stringent rules. It could make a good balance for the boy. Comforted by these conclusions, he felt he could now relax on the Felix situation, for the moment at least.

Letting himself into the flat, he decided he now needed to work on his book. If there were no further distractions he'd have five clear days to work on the blasted thing. It would be a great relief if he could hand it to Sheila before Christmas.

For three whole days he worked uninterrupted. And then the call came in from Isobel.

Chapter 25

Setbacks

'I don't want to worry you Rawlings,' she said, which meant she was going to, 'but yesterday we ran into something of a problem with Felix...'

He waited with impatience for her to continue but there was a silence from the end of the line, so he finally prompted her. 'What sort of a problem?'

'It's rather difficult to explain. But I thought... I thought it was best to...'

'For God's sake Isobel just spit it out and tell me what happened.'

So she did and explained that yesterday, Maria had gone into Felix's room to deliver some clean clothes only to find it in complete chaos with everything taken out of the drawers and swept off his desk onto the floor. Felix was going round and round the room shouting hysterically, 'He must have taken it! He must have taken it!' Maria had fetched her, and after a while she managed to calm him down.

'What was it that had been taken?' Rawlings asked, his anxiety and frustration mounting.

'It was the book you gave him. That special copy of The Wind in the Willows.'

A memory flashed across his mind. He remembered

opening the book when visiting Felix and finding Shane's large hand across the dedication: A BABY BOOK FOR A BABY BOY. Nothing would surprise him about that fiend child ever again.

Isobel went on, 'Felix was adamant he'd put it with all his things to be packed. Now he's convinced Shane must have gone into his room and taken it.'

'Tell him not to worry about the book Isobel.' Rawlings said. 'I'll replace it, although it might take me a while to find that particular copy. It was a leather-bound edition.'

'I think,' Isobel said slowly, 'that every time he finds something else missing it brings back exactly what he went through. It's why his reaction was so extreme...' She hesitated before saying, 'There's something more...' Rawlings felt his heart sink. What more could there possibly be? She added, 'I noticed there was no laptop on his desk. When I asked him about it, he became upset again. His laptop had been ruined by Shane quite recently when he'd poured orange juice over it. Felix merely told Brad and Sarah there had been an accident and they reprimanded him for being careless but did agree to let him use one of their spare ones. After Felix made his decision to return to us, Davey told his parents it was Shane who had ruined the laptop. There were more apologies, but by that time it was too late for them to replace it.'

'That boy should be locked up,' Rawlings growled. 'I'll talk to Felix about the laptop at the weekend. Of course, we'll get him another one. I feel like sending Brad and Sarah the bill.'

Isobel gave a bleak laugh. 'You can add the saxophone to it as well. That was completely ruined when Shane apparently wedged it under a rock when he hid it. The instrument was so dented it was beyond repair. Felix explained it was why he gave up the lessons. He didn't want to give you the expense of replacing it.' She paused. 'I find that so touching.'

Rawlings thought for a moment. 'This is bad, Isobel. Really bad. No child should have to experience what Felix has done in this past year. I'm worried there will be lasting damage. Do you think we should get him counselling?'

Isobel said slowly, 'My instinct says no, not yet. Let's see how we go, taking one day at a time. We can talk more tomorrow when you get down here.'

With that the conversation ended. Rawlings was left with his thoughts raging. Instinctively he wanted to drive down immediately to sort things out but couldn't because he had the celebration party for Jolyon that night, and that was a party he really did have to attend, however much he might want to wriggle out of it.

From the moment of his arrival, his worst fears were realised. The chosen venue was one of the huge hotels on Park Lane in one of their reception rooms, all white and gold with large floral displays. Rawlings could find nothing to recommend it. The ceiling was so low the noise was deafening, especially as it was packed to the gills with what appeared to be wall to wall celebrities. It took him a while to obtain a drink, the poor waiters having a difficult time pushing through the shrieking hordes. Good God! Did Jolyon really know all these people? This was going to be an ordeal of the worst kind and he suddenly longed for a cigarette. No chance of that, it was certainly a non-smoking room. In any case, to light up in this crowded area would in all probability, have resulted in setting fire to one of the guests. He looked around recognising several faces he knew, but still had no idea who amongst all these people, was Jolyon's partner. He tried asking a fellow journalist, an old acquaintance from his days at the Frontline Club.

'I haven't a clue old boy,' was the shouted reply, 'I only know his name is Brian Felton. I am reliably informed he was a set designer originally but then gave it up to be with the wife. I never met him. Jolyon kept his private life exceedingly private.'

'How did you know Jolyon?'

This produced a smile. 'I think from where most people met him, at the Garrick Club. I was introduced by a mutual friend. I really didn't know him that well, just a couple of dinners after that, but I guess that warranted me being added to the famous address book. And you?'

Rawlings was just about to reply when there was a shriek from behind him.

'My God! It has to be Rawlings!' He turned around to find the exotic figure of Fanny Markham, an actress friend of Isobel's, clad in what could only be termed as a revealing dress. Maybe a little rash for someone of her age? 'How wonderful to see you darling,' she gushed. 'It's been such an age. Last Christmas wasn't it?' Rawlings nodded, remembering only too well the disastrous Christmas lunch, where Fanny had flirted outrageously with him, causing Marnie to be overcome with jealousy. 'You're looking very theatrical,' she said. Was he? He didn't think so, having merely donned his blue velvet smoking jacket instead of wearing black. It had seemed more appropriate for Jolyon somehow, who had always been so colourfully attired. By now Fanny was in full flow, firing questions at him but never giving him time to answer. 'It's utterly divine to see you again. But what are you doing here?

Did you know Jolyon? But of course you did. And how is darling Isobel? That Christmas was such fun. Do remind me, what was the name of that other woman? Marnie wasn't it? You really must fill me in on all the news.' A waiter arrived with more champagne. Rawlings managed to down two more glasses before Fanny caught sight of someone else and to his relief rushed off to the other side of the room with a loud shriek of 'Darling!' There had been one moment during the one-sided conversation when Fanny had pointed out their host and Rawlings now made his way across the room, introducing himself to Brian. The exchange was short as the poor man was being mobbed.

The evening wore relentlessly on. Rawlings scoffed down some canapés to mop up the endless supply of champagne and dutifully did his best to have a conversation with a few more acquaintances including a brief word with Sheila, but the volume of sound was increasing and it was quite impossible to hear anything that was being said. It was therefore some relief when there was a call for silence. Two speeches followed in tribute to Jolyon; one from an actor which was amusing and witty, the other from poor Brian which was lengthy and dire. As he finally came to an end, Rawlings trusting he had done his duty by his late agent, ordered a taxi and thankfully returned to his flat.

'You look terrible,' Isobel said, as he arrived the next morning.

'I feel terrible,' he replied grumpily. 'A black coffee wouldn't go amiss.'

He swilled down two paracetamols with his coffee and explained about the party, assuring her it was the volume of noise that had done him in, rather than the copious amounts of champagne. Her expression was sceptical, but he ignored this. 'The venue was hideously vulgar which was all wrong. Jolyon was a man of taste and style. The poor man would have been appalled. It would have been far more appropriate to hold it at the Garrick, with the added advantage that there wouldn't have been space for the dreadful hordes who had been invited.'

Isobel smiled. 'We used to have Embassy parties like that, desperately tiring and one had to be charming and attentive throughout. I found them a terrible strain, but it was Peter's duty as ambassador to give them poor darling. Thankfully I only had to endure them for thirty years. I can't think how the Queen manages.'

Rawlings made no further comment but drained his coffee and asked, 'Has there been any more trouble with Felix?'

Isobel shook her head. 'No, but he's seemed a little subdued. He'll be pleased to see you.'

Rawlings sighed. 'I think it's going to take time and patience Isobel. Where is he now?'

'He's in the garden talking to old Tom, Jake's father.'

Rawlings walked slowly down the garden giving Felix a wave. 'I'm going to the boat,' he called out. 'Come and join me when you're ready.'

Once on the boat he fetched himself a glass of water, drank it in one go, then drank another. Feeling a little revived he settled into one of Marnie's chairs. Moments later Felix burst in. Out of breath he declared, 'Tom has been telling me about the snakes that can be found in England.'

It seemed an odd topic. 'Are you interested in snakes?'

Felix shook his head vigorously. 'No, I absolutely hate them. Ever since Shane put that snake in my bed, I've had nightmares about the horrible things. I had one the other night.'

This gave Rawlings an immediate worry. Nightmares at his age were not a good sign. He said slowly, 'I used to get a recurring nightmare too, about something I witnessed in the War. They do go eventually.' This wasn't strictly true. One of the aspects of his PTSD was he continually suffered from bloody awful nightmares but didn't want to add to the boy's anxiety, so he said, 'I actually made a study of snakes when I went out to the desert. It seemed a good idea to know what I was up against.' He smiled. 'I don't think you have a problem with snakes here. Adders and vipers are quite rare. You might catch sight of a grass snake, but they're quite harmless.'

Felix shivered. 'I hope I never see one again.'

Rawlings looked at him. 'Everyone has a fear of something. I hate bats. I think a fear of snakes is called ophidiophobia.' This information didn't seem to provide much comfort to Felix, so he changed the subject. 'How would you like to come up to London for a short stay next week? As we're now in December, I could drive you round to see the decorations and after that we might do a bit of Christmas shopping.'

Felix nodded. 'I'd like that.'

'Make a list of all the things you want to do.' He paused. 'I'll discuss it with Isobel, but we could go to Battersea Dog's Home and find you a dog.'

The boy leapt out of his seat. 'Could we, EG? That would be the best possible thing we could ever do. I want a dog more than anything in the world.'

Rawlings laughed. 'You must meet my friend Max who lives above me. We recently found him a dog who is called Bolly. To be honest, he's not so much a dog as a shaggy rug.' Felix laughed as Rawlings reminded him, 'Isobel doesn't want a big animal, so we must remember that when choosing.'

Later, Rawlings broke this plan to Isobel who again raised no objections, so Rawlings brought up another subject on his mind. 'When I take Felix shopping, it might be good for him to have some money of his own. I've no idea what sort of pocket money is given out to twelve-year-old boys these days, but you might make enquiries and tell me how to organise it.'

*

The London trip, rather to his surprise turned out to be highly enjoyable, and a reminder of how much he'd missed the boy's company. Rawlings thought back to when he was of similar age and recalled that he had never been allowed to leave Essex to explore London. Much later, on his occasional trips back to England he'd generally stayed with Gillian in Essex, sorting out family matters. After she died, his brief visits to London were idled away in the Frontline Club. This meant he knew little of the riches that London had to offer. It would be interesting to experience it all now through the eyes of Felix.

At the boy's instigation they made a list of the main attractions they wanted visit. These included the London Eye and the Whispering Gallery in St Paul's Cathedral, which Rawlings reflected would not be good for the vertigo he increasingly suffered from. He studied the long list and it seemed easiest when trying to satisfy as many requests as possible, to take a river cruise and hop on and off at the various places they wanted to visit.

This turned out to be an excellent solution and after the first hectic day, they returned happy but exhausted. Max asked them up for a drink and almost immediately Felix and

Bolly were rolling around the floor together.

'Are you in London for long?' Max asked. 'Felix could be extremely useful taking Bolly for his morning constitutional.'

Rawlings shook his head. 'Not this week. We're only up for a couple of days and tomorrow we are back to Battersea to find Felix a dog of his own. He's longing for one and Isobel has given her permission on condition it's small.' He gave a laugh and said ruefully, 'Battersea Dog's Home will be a positive rest cure after today. Felix insisted on us climbing up to the Whispering Gallery in St Paul's. There was a spectacular view, but it'll take me a day or two to recover.'

Felix had returned from the floor with Bolly and overheard the end of this conversation.

'You should have said EG. Is your leg all right?'

Rawlings quickly reassured him. 'It's fine. I'm glad we did it, although it was quite a climb.'

'257 steps,' Felix said. 'The guidebook said it's 30 metres above the ground. I liked the way you could walk all the way round below the dome. That was cool.'

'Why is it called "the Whispering Gallery"?' Max asked.

'You're meant to be able to whisper into the wall one side, and be heard the other side,' Felix told him. 'I'm sure it must be true, but we didn't try it.' He added, 'We were going to do the London Eye as well but EG said he'd had enough heights for one day.'

Rawlings smiled indulgently. 'Something for another time.'

Max stood up. 'Let me get you another lemonade Felix.' As he did so he called out, 'How do you like the flat?'

'It's great,' Felix replied. 'I like the way it goes into the garden and then down to the river, although the river is quite different here with buildings on each side and there are so many different boats. Some of them are huge. We went by river today and it was really busy.' He drank his lemonade and added, 'I think EG needs a few more pictures. I have one in my room but that's about all. Isobel's walls are covered in pictures.'

Rawlings smiled. 'Maybe you could help me choose a picture or two. I've never had much time for collecting paintings.'

'What are your plans for the rest of your stay?' Max asked.

Felix looked inquiringly at Rawlings, who gave this some thought. 'I've been thinking this over. If we're getting the dog tomorrow, it might be best if we returned to Isobel's to get it settled in down there, then come back to London next week. I had an idea we could combine Christmas shopping with a visit to the National Portrait Gallery. I think it's the gallery Felix might enjoy the most for his first one. I'll book a table in the gallery restaurant which has great views over London.'

Max smiled. 'Sounds like a good plan to me. You must bring the dog in to show me when you get in. Bolly and I would love to meet him.'

'It'll have to be a her,' Rawlings said with a smile. 'Isobel already has a bitch, and a dog would complicate things.'

As they were leaving Max issued an invitation: 'Hetty is coming down next week. She'd love to meet Felix and would make us supper. It'll save you bothering after your long day's excursions.'

'Who is Hetty?' Felix inquired, as they returned to the flat.

Rawlings reminded him about Hetty and how she bred border collies. 'You'll like her. She's fun,' and he added, 'a bit like Marnie.'

For the first time in a long while he slept soundly,

untroubled by nightmares. The thought came to him that maybe he should climb 257 steps more often. The physical exhaustion had knocked him out. However, he did notice a certain stiffness in the back of his legs as he gingerly moved around the room but there was no time for recovery. Felix was already up and in a state of excitement.

'How soon can we go EG?'

'When we've had breakfast. The Dog's Home won't be open yet.'

As soon as it was, they were outside the door waiting to be let in.

Finding a dog for Felix was a more difficult task than it had been for Max. All the dogs Felix liked were either too big, or not bitches. After about an hour, Felix was getting disheartened. Seeing this, one of the attendants asked if she could help. With relief Rawlings explained their dilemma. She nodded and thought for a moment.

'We have a batch of terrier pups recently in. The poor lady owner didn't even know her bitch was pregnant, so it was a bit of a shock if you know what I mean. She couldn't possibly look after the puppies, so handed them over to us. I think there were four originally, but only two are left, luckily they are both bitches.'

She led them to an outside kennel and Felix was let in. Success at last. The pup, apparently called Dido, crawled all over to him and the boy immediately declared her to be the one. Once the paperwork had been done and they had purchased the necessary equipment, they made their way home and immediately went to show her to Max.

'She has the sweetest face,' Max said approvingly, 'and terriers are always a good idea.' Rawlings smiled. 'I am reliably told the mother was a pedigree, a Glen of Imaal. The father was also terrier, but the dog of a friend and they were not really sure what sort.' He gave a laugh. 'Just the sort of friend you need who gets your prize bitch up the duff! Anyway, Dido we are assured, should remain a smallish size. The main thing is that Felix loved her at first sight.'

Dido was at present jumping at Bolly, who took absolutely no interest whatsoever.

'I like the name,' Max commented.

Rawlings smiled. 'We didn't have much choice. All the puppies had been given names beginning with D. She is young enough for us to change it, but I rather agree with you. Dido is good.'

Isobel at once declared the puppy adorable and they watched as Felix took Dido and Juno out into the garden.

'I'm beginning to feel I am living in the middle of Crufts,' Rawlings grumbled. 'I hope that is the last time I ever have to visit Battersea Dog's Home. The whole process is both exhausting and financially ruinous.'

'Don't be such an old grump.' Isobel reproved him. 'Look how happy the boy is.'

*

The following week Felix returned to London. He had done so rather reluctantly not wanting to leave the puppy behind, but Rawlings told him they would be out all day which would leave Dido shut up in the flat, so he reluctantly gave in.

'I can't believe we're in the middle of December,' Rawlings said, as they climbed out of the underground at Oxford Street.

Felix grinned. 'I don't know why you have a problem with that. It's difficult to miss all the Christmas decorations.'

Rawlings had been going to say that the year had flown by, but then stopped himself. Maybe it wasn't tactful to remind Felix of the year he'd just been through, so instead he said, 'You're right, along with the hordes of people out doing their Christmas shopping, hordes we're now going to have to fight our way through.'

After a successful morning buying presents, they walked all the way to Charing Cross Road, ending up at the National Portrait Gallery. They had lunch at the restaurant first. Rawlings was pleased to be taken to a table at the window and pointed out to Felix the spectacular views across Trafalgar Square, down Whitehall to Big Ben and the Houses of Parliament. After two glasses of wine and excellent food, Rawlings felt restored enough to tackle the pictures. 'The trick is,' he told Felix, 'to do one gallery at a time and not overdo it. I thought we might do the Tudors today and see how we go.'

They started their slow perambulation.

'People haven't changed that much to look at,' Felix observed. They had stopped in front of a portrait of Thomas Cromwell and he burst out laughing. 'This man looks just like the science master at my old prep school. We nicknamed him Grumblebones. Nobody liked him much.'

Rawlings smiled. 'Well this happens to be Thomas Cromwell, a man of great importance in the reign of Henry VIII, but both ruthless and brutal. I'll get you a book on the Tudors and you can read all about him.'

They had completed the third gallery when Rawlings declared it was enough for one day. 'Don't forget we're having supper with Max, and his sister Hetty is coming.'

They took a taxi back which proved an excellent move. Apart from the fact that Rawlings was experiencing horrible pain in his leg, Felix took delight in having the sights pointed out to him. The driver had been instructed to take the scenic route past the Houses of Parliament and Westminster Abbey. As they went along the river by the embankment, Rawlings was reminded what a beautiful city London was.

After their tiring day he would have welcomed a quiet evening, but almost immediately it was time to go upstairs.

Hetty threw her arms around Felix and crushed him in one of her hugs. 'How wonderful to meet you Felix.' Finally releasing him, the poor boy came up for air. 'Now tell me all about your new puppy.'

'She's called Dido,' Felix told her. 'I can show you a photo of her on my phone.'

Hetty studied it. 'Who did you say the mother was?'

Felix looked at Rawlings. 'Who was it EG?'

'A Glen of Amaal.'

'Really?' Hetty looked impressed. 'A good and somewhat rare breed. I think you said the father's origins were unknown except he was a terrier?' Rawlings nodded. 'I see a bit of Aberdeen in there, but Dido is an original and an absolute darling.'

Felix seemed impressed by all her knowledge. 'EG says you have border collies. I saw one of those at the Dog's Home and really liked it, but we had to get a small dog to go with Isobel's spaniel. Juno and Dido do get on very well together.'

Hetty nodded. 'Always good to have two dogs. They're far happier with a companion.' She paused, 'Juno and Dido, both classical names, one Roman and one Greek. How pleasing. You must come and see my dogs Felix. We'd love to have you to stay.'

Rawlings was thankful that over supper the conversation at last turned away from the canine species as they described all the events of the day. Felix seemed to enjoy their company, but towards the end of the meal he could see the boy was tiring.

'This has been great Max,' he said, 'but I really ought to get Felix to bed. He's had a long day.'

'I'll come down with you if that's all right,' Hetty said. 'There's some news I wanted to give you. Max already knows it.'

Once Felix had gone to bed, Rawlings looked at Hetty expectantly.

'It's Bel,' she said. 'The most awful news really. Clive wants a divorce.' This was not totally unexpected but from Hetty's expression he could see it wasn't all and waited for her to continue. 'It's been a terrible shock for Bel. You see, it's not another woman he's left her for but a man. His partner in Dubai. Clive is selling up in London and they are settling out there.'

Rawlings thought for a moment. 'How have the two boys taken it?'

'Not well. I think it's not so much that their father is leaving as finding out he's gay.'

Rawlings sighed. 'And Bel?'

'She's a mess. We're all so worried. She's back on the drink again and has become fearfully thin. It's just a relief there are no financial problems. Clive has left her well provided for. She's to have the house, as well as a lump sum from the sale of the restaurant. No, it's more a case of self-esteem and she's very bitter at having endured what she now considers a sham marriage for so long. We had her to stay last weekend and she moaned on and on about her life being a failure and disaster.

I'm afraid Bernard finally lost it. By Sunday night the poor darling had come to the end of his patience and told Bel to snap out of it!'

Rawlings said drily, 'I can't imagine that went down well.'

Hetty sighed. 'Alas no. We had the full hysterics and she threatened suicide, to which Bernard told her that those who talked about it seldom did it. He also went on to say she should count her blessings – lovely house, lovely children, plenty of money, good job. This seemed to sober her up and she merely sulked for the rest of her stay. For once I also felt impatient with Bel. She should be worrying about her boys, not herself. It's not as if she and Clive were a great love match. In fact, he was perfectly dreadful to her. Quite frankly she should be relieved he's gone. But she remains in a dreadful state which is very worrying.'

Rawlings privately thought it unlikely she would snap out of her present mood for some time. He could well imagine it and fervently hoped it would be possible to distance himself, even if he did have some sympathy for her plight.

'What did Hetty want to talk to you about?' Felix asked as they drove back to Isobel's the next day.

Rawlings sighed. The curiosity of small boys. He considered what he should answer. 'She's worried about her younger sister, Bel.'

'Why?'

'Her husband has left her.'

'Has he gone off with a younger woman? That's what usually happens.'

Rawlings was startled. 'What on earth makes you say that?'

'It happened to a few boys at my prep school. They used to find it rather amusing.'

'Good God! I'm really glad we didn't send you back to that school.'

Felix smiled. 'Who has he gone off with then?'

In for a penny in for a pound. The boy might as well know, he was pretty sure he wouldn't let the subject drop. 'The fact is, he has gone off as you put it, with another man.'

'You mean he's a pouf?'

Rawlings frowned. 'I dislike that expression but yes, it seems Clive has discovered he's gay and Bel is very unhappy about it.'

'Didn't she know he was gay when she married him?'

Rawlings said dryly, 'Obviously not. He may not have realised it himself until now. It can happen.'

There was silence for a moment and then Felix said, 'Shane called everyone he disliked poufs or poufters. He was always calling me a pouf.'

Rawlings said sharply, 'Then it was very stupid of him. By now you must realise that most of what Shane said was better ignored, or better still forgotten.' He finished the conversation by saying tersely that it was a distressing situation for everyone, particularly Bel's two boys, but happily she had a great family to help her through it.

This seemed to satisfy Felix, besides which his thoughts had now turned to seeing Dido again.

'If I have to hear one more canine conversation, I think I'll go mad!' Rawlings said as he joined Isobel standing at the window watching Felix playing with Juno and the puppy.

'Don't be so grumpy darling,' Isobel reproved him. 'Look how happy he is and even you can see that getting Dido was worth it. Felix is almost back to his old self.' Rawlings sat down, giving his leg a rub as she added, 'The puppy is so easy to look after and almost house trained, only one or two…'

Rawlings held up a weary hand. 'Spare me any further details about the puppy Isobel.'

She sat down opposite him and gave him a long look. 'Was it a tiring two days?'

'You could say that, but they were very enjoyable. We seemed to do an enormous amount. My worry was that I'd have to drag an unwilling boy around the Portrait Gallery, but he clearly enjoyed it and his comments were hilarious. Apparently, Thomas Cromwell reminded him of a master at his old school who they'd nicknamed Grumblebones'. Isobel smiled at this and privately thought it quite an appropriate name for Rawlings in his present mood but refrained from saying so. Rawlings went on, 'Strangely enough, I even enjoyed the Christmas shopping…'

'Ah,' Isobel interrupted. 'Talking of Christmas, I wanted to tell you I've invited Marnie to join us for lunch on the day, also Lydia plus her new wife.'

Rawlings gave a groan. 'How on earth am I going to explain that relationship to Felix? I've just had a long conversation about gays in the car on the way down here.' And he relayed the news about the Clive situation and Felix's reaction to it.

Isobel gave a laugh. 'It sounds to me as if Felix is fully aware of all sexual relationships. Children get to these things far earlier than you or I did. I don't think there'll be any problem explaining Lydia and Patricia.'

As usual Isobel was right. Felix cut through his rambling efforts and said casually, 'I know Lydia is a lesbian EG. You don't have to explain it to me,' and he added, 'did you know gays and lesbians can get married now?'

Rawlings was taken aback but finally managed to say, 'That's exactly what I was trying to tell you. Patricia is Lydia's wife,' and before Felix could ask him how you could tell which was the wife, he hurriedly changed the subject. 'I hope you don't mind I'm returning to London tomorrow. There's only just over a week to go until Christmas and I want to try and finish my book.'

Felix told him this was fine by him. Isobel and he had a great deal planned. Tomorrow they were going to get a tree and then would have to decorate it. Sunil had invited him over and of course he would be looking after the dogs. He intended to teach Dido some tricks.

Later that day Isobel regarded Rawlings thoughtfully. 'You're limping again? Is your leg giving you pain?'

He gave a rueful smile. 'I think I overdid it on the shopping day. We rather stupidly walked from Regent Street to Trafalgar Square. I'll be fine if I rest for a few days. Are you sure you can manage? I'll be back on Christmas Eve.'

Isobel smiled. 'No, you go. You'd only get irritated with all the Christmas preparations.'

He looked at her. 'I was worried about Felix having so little company of his own age, but I've come to realise he feels happier and more relaxed in the presence of adults for now. And can you blame the boy? However, I'm hoping the skiing holiday will ease him back into mixing with his friends again.' He laughed. 'It'll make a change for him, after being completely surrounded by women.'

Chapter 26

Moving Towards Christmas

Rawlings regarded himself thoughtfully in the shaving mirror and some lines floated into his head as he stared at his reflection, in sooth, I know not why I am so sad. He picked up the towel to finish his morning ablutions and reflected that perhaps it was not the best idea to have Shakespeare's works by his bed. Recently it had been his habit to dip into the plays when unable to sleep, but this remedy for insomnia was now proving an irritation. The Bard seemed to have a quotation for every situation and without bidding, lines would float into his head at the oddest moments. He fetched his coffee, made his way back to the desk and sat staring out at the wintry landscape. How bleak it all looked. The river was a dark, murky grey and few boats were out on the water. The garden had a winter look too. One brave and solitary rose had survived the incoming blasts. There had been gales for a week straight from the arctic. Would they bring snow? Felix would like that, but this being England, it would perversely turn mild and a white Christmas was unlikely.

With a sigh he forced his gaze back to the list on his desk. Was it a sign of age to make endless lists? Probably. This one looked depressingly long, although on second glance he found he'd done most of it. His main task the bloody book had been despatched to Sheila yesterday, with the proviso that the publishers needed to negotiate with the O'Keefe family for permission to use Mia's photographs. Good luck to them on that! He'd also given instruction that a portion of the royalties should go to the Sarajevo orphanage. Sheila could negotiate that. He smiled grimly. The blasted woman had to do something to justify the large percentage she fleeced from him.

This was the moment he longed for a cigarette. Instead he refilled his coffee and thought about the book. Strange how emotionally detached he'd felt while writing it, leaving Mia's pictures to do most of the work. Now it was finished, he wondered if anyone if anyone would buy it? His War Memoirs he was reliably informed, were going to sell better once the documentary was out. No such boost for this one. In any case, it was a different book altogether. The Siege made grim reading and the pictures were all too graphic. Because of this, he'd made a late decision to add one positive note at the end, the story of the young boy who'd survived the destruction of his orphanage, become a doctor and was hopeful for the future. Rawlings was careful not to mention Luka's name, but his story provided him with the final chapter, the one part of the whole book which had given him some satisfaction. Otherwise it was just memories he would now try hard to forget.

In sooth I know not why I am so sad. The line kept returning, nagging at him. There was no reason for it. And yet it forced him into considering what his future was to be. Felix would remain the priority of course, but that wouldn't be enough to fill his life. What else was left? He had no work and no relationship, by which he meant a woman. Maybe it was the lack of a woman that was the problem, a void he needed to fill? This brought to mind the two women who had thrown themselves at him this year, first Bel and then Sorcha. He gave a shudder and reflected he was probably better off celibate and single.

His introspection came to an abrupt halt by a loud ring on his mobile. It was Isobel. What timing that woman had!

'Everything all right?' he asked with a certain nervousness. There had to be a reason for her call. He was due back on the morrow.

'Yes, nothing really to worry about.' Isobel sounded hesitant.

'But there is something.'

'It may be nothing.' She stopped and Rawlings once again felt an impatience. Isobel always took so long to spit it out. Speaking slowly, she explained. 'I may have been ill advised, but yesterday I suggested to Felix that we put in a Skype to Australia, to wish them a happy Christmas.'

Not a good idea was his immediate thought. 'And I presume this didn't go down well?'

'No, it didn't. In fact, he screamed at me flatly refusing and ran out of the house. I didn't mention it again...' She paused. 'He's been perfectly all right since, but I just thought you might talk to him about it when you get back. After all, he was fond of Ella and Davey, and those parents must be feeling rather guilty. It could help heal the situation.'

Rawlings wasn't at all sure their healing process was up to Felix and said a trifle crossly, 'It's still far too raw for the boy Isobel.' Then feeling he'd been a bit sharp he added, 'I'll try and find a moment to talk to him about it. He may need more time.'

With that the call ended. Rawlings sighed. Isobel was such a fair-minded person. She probably felt sympathy for the parents. He didn't feel so merciful, but then Isobel hadn't experienced the situation as he had done. Instinctively he feared there was more to Felix's extreme reaction than just the Shane problem. It was more likely that Felix wanted to put the entire Australian experience behind him and have no reminders thrust upon him. He sympathised. It was rather as he felt about the Sarajevo Siege.

The next day he arrived to find Felix in an excited and voluble state, describing in detail all he had done, including decorating the extremely large tree. 'We had to get a step ladder to put the star on the top. Jake came and did it.'

Isobel seemed determined to make his first Christmas with them a memorable one.

Felix helped him unload the car and carry the many packages down to the boat.

'I'll need some help wrapping this stuff up,' he told Felix, 'and you'll have to keep control of your puppy, or we'll have nothing left to wrap.' Dido was pulling at the packages, tearing off the paper. Felix laughed and picked her up.

'She's such a clever dog EG. I've been teaching her tricks. She already sits when I tell her to.'

Rawlings smiled. It seemed a pity to break the boy's happy mood, but the elephant in the room was there and he needed to tackle it before Christmas really took off.

'Isobel tells me she suggested you Skype the family in Australia and wish them a happy Christmas.' Felix said nothing but his expression changed markedly. Rawlings persevered. 'I know you don't want to, but might it be a good thing to do? After all, it was only Shane who was horrible...'

Felix went red in the face and yelled, 'No, it wasn't. It wasn't just Shane. It was Brad and Sarah too.' Once started, the words poured out of him. 'They always took Shane's word for everything that happened. Always. And he told lies. He lied all the time. They never tried to find out the truth, ever, just punished me for things that weren't my fault. Brad and Sarah didn't have any time for me. I was just someone who made problems for them and got in the way. Not once did Sarah ask if I was all right, or if I was happy. They just presumed I would fit in with everything they did. Well I didn't. I hated it. I hated them. I hated it all!'

Rawlings was bewildered by this outburst. He really hadn't seen this coming. How had he missed this when he was out there? Sarah and Brad seemed to him to be making every effort with the boy. Had he been completely blind to the real situation?

'I'm truly sorry, Felix. Why on earth didn't you tell me all this when I visited you?'

The boy calmer now just shrugged. 'What was the point? The grown-ups decided what I was to do. I knew things wouldn't change, I just had to get on with it. And I didn't want to upset you.' Looking at Rawlings there were tears in his eyes. 'Sarah never bothered to find out what was really going on with Shane and I know she knew. Brad was away working nearly all the time and never talked to me on my own. He sometimes praised me but that just made things worse with Shane. Davey kept to himself. I had nobody to turn to, nobody…'

Rawlings cut in. 'All right Felix, say no more. I am sorry I suggested it. I promise Isobel and I won't ever ask you to contact them again.' He looked at the boy desperately wanting to say something to help him. He decided on another tack. 'You know I've been writing a book?' Felix nodded. 'Well, I've finally finished it, and now I don't want to think about the subject of that book ever again. I just want to forget it all and put it right out of my mind.'

He had Felix's attention now. 'Why?' the boy asked.

'Because it was about a bad experience I had, during a terrible conflict that happened in a place called Sarajevo. The city was under siege and dreadful things occurred that I had to witness. Now I want to forget all about it.'

'Why did you write about it then?'

Good question. Rawlings gave a rueful smile. 'Because I was asked to, but the fact is in many ways writing the book helped me to finish with the experience. I can now put it away and never think about it again. And this is maybe what you should try and do, with the time you spent in Australia.'

Felix looked bewildered. 'You want me to write a book?'

Rawlings roared with laughter, and then stopped. Maybe that wasn't such a bad suggestion.

'Not a book,' he said slowly, 'but you could write down an account of what happened. It would be a good way of getting it out of your system. It would be private. You wouldn't have to show anyone.' He paused. 'I'm not telling you to do this Felix, you can make up your own mind about that. But it might help you to put the Australia experience in the past.'

The boy considered this, then nodded.

'And please, if you ever want to tell me about anything that's worrying you in the future, you must promise me you will. I'll always be here for you.'

The boy nodded again, then suddenly threw Dido on the floor and flung himself into the arms of his grandfather.

Rawlings held on to him, letting them both have a moment of recovery. He then said briskly, 'Now Felix you and I have a great deal to do. First, I need to get some wrapping paper from the Patel's. Do you want to come with me?'

Felix picked up the puppy. 'Yes, I'll just take Dido back to the house and get a coat.' As he reached the door he added, 'I could get a notebook too, for this account you suggest I should write.'

Rawlings hoped this would end the Australian saga but that evening a Skype came in from Sarah. Luckily, it arrived while Isobel and Felix were in the house wrapping up presents. The conversation started warmly enough. Then came the moment when Sarah asked to talk to Felix.

'I'm afraid he's not here,' Rawlings told her, relieved at least he could be honest.

She frowned. 'Well when would be a good time to call back? We all want to wish him a happy Christmas.'

There was a long pause. 'That's not going to happen Sarah,' he said at last. 'Isobel and I both suggested to Felix that he should ring you, but he flatly refused. I think the whole experience is still too raw for him. He needs time.'

She looked shocked as she took this in. After a moment she said, 'If it were just me, would that make it all right? After all he is my nephew. It's only natural I should want to wish him a happy Christmas.'

Rawlings thought angrily that after all he'd learned this morning she had no bloody rights at all but making an effort to keep his voice calm he said, 'Quite honestly, I don't think your rights come into this, Sarah. When we asked Felix to make the call, he became quite hysterical. We're just beginning to get him back on an even keel. His memories of the time spent with you are angry and bitter. It's not just with Shane, but with you and Brad as well. He felt you took Shane's side. It would be stupid to push him on this. It's going to take him a good while to recover and we need to be patient. I am sorry if I sound brutal, but that's the way things are. I know we both only want what is best for the boy, so I hope you understand.'

She didn't sound as if she understood at all. Her voice was angry. 'I think you're exaggerating the situation. There is obviously nothing I can do about it right now, but I would remind you I am still his closest relative. I will certainly be speaking to Graham in the new year.'

And with that veiled threat, she removed herself from the screen.

Rawlings walked slowly over to the house where Isobel and Felix were doing their best to wrap presents while Juno and Dido pranced about sabotaging their efforts.

'I think if we're going to get this finished before supper,' Isobel said laughing, 'the dogs will have to be put in the kitchen. Can you see to that Felix?'

The boy obediently collected them up and took them out. Isobel glanced at Rawlings, noting his tense expression. 'Has something happened?'

He gave a nod. 'I've just had a most unpleasant conversation with Sarah. She'd wanted the family to wish Felix a happy Christmas, and I had to explain to her that this was not possible. She didn't take it well and said they would be discussing the situation with Graham in the new year. I propose we don't talk about this further until Felix has departed on his skiing trip, but I fear we may be in for a bumpy ride.'

*

Isobel 's efforts to make the boy's first Christmas with them a success, were happily rewarded. From the first moment he opened his stocking to the last game of mah-jong in the evening, it all passed in pleasurable blur. Felix didn't appear to mind being surrounded by women at the lunch. Throughout the day he behaved impeccably, excited but not over-excited and was seemingly delighted with every present he opened. Rawlings, looking at the chaos of wrapping paper and boxes strewn across Isobel's living room, inwardly reflected that it seemed an enormous amount of effort and expense for something that was over so quickly. But it was good to see the boy so happy.

On Boxing Day, he suggested he and Felix cook the lunch in order to give Isobel a break. Rawlings could tell she was tired although she would never have admitted it. After the meal they left her in peace and took the dogs for a walk.

'Do you know one of my best presents?' Felix asked, then without waiting for an answer he said, 'It was from Lydia and Patricia.'

'What was that? You had so many presents I can't remember.'

'It was a book about training your dog. It came with a little clicker. You make the noise every time you want the dog to do something and then you reward them with a treat when they do what you ask. I'm going to start training Dido properly when I get back from skiing.'

Rawlings smiled. Getting that damned dog had certainly been a good idea.

The following day he took Felix to the station where he joined the others departing on the trip. Felix had been nervous about meeting the boys he'd not seen for a year, but as they grouped around him he gave Rawlings a cheery wave and with some relief he left him to it and limped back to the car.

'What are your plans while Felix is away?' Isobel asked.

'Do you know, I hadn't seen much further than Christmas. What about you?'

'Well, my immediate task is to organise the boy's uniform. Marnie and I plan to spend a day shopping. We need to have it all ready for him as he only gets back the day before term starts. They've sent me the list.'

Rawlings felt concerned. 'I should be helping you with that.'

Isobel laughed. 'Nonsense darling you'd be no help at all and probably moan about the expense of it all. No, Marnie and I will enjoy the day out.' She looked at him. 'Marnie's boss is giving a party on New Year's Eve. She extended the invitation to both of us. I have politely declined. My preference for New Year's Eve is a quiet evening in watching an old movie. How about you?'

'I will be politely declining as well. Max is throwing one of his parties, and I'll probably look in on that. Difficult to avoid as he's right above me.' He smiled at her. 'I think I might leave you to recover from Christmas in peace Isobel and return to London. I have a few loose ends to tie up before we move into 2019. I'll be back to collect Felix from his trip, and then see him off to school the following day.'

As he left, he kissed her on the cheek. 'I can't thank you enough. You do know you're an angel don't you.'

*

Once back in his flat he found it difficult to settle. The loose ends he'd hoped to tie up proved nigh on impossible. Everyone was away, nothing was open except the shops with their endless sales. This would have been a good moment to end his relationship with Graham, but his office was closed until January fourth. It was the same with Sheila and this meant there would be a frustrating wait to hear how his book had been received. Upstairs Max was totally preoccupied with preparations for his party, evidently to be a lavish affair, even using caterers. Any help from him was refused so Rawlings left him to it, after suggesting he take Bolly out for a walk, an offer that was gratefully accepted.

Although the weather had turned mild, Putney Common was almost deserted. Bolly, who had to be one of the laziest dogs ever, looked aggrieved at being dragged through the woods, but Rawlings enjoyed it and delivering the mutt back, told Max he would do this every day until the party. Retreating once again downstairs he opened his laptop, and an email caught his attention. It was from Sorcha.

Hi Rawlings, I hope you enjoyed the festive season. Ours was rather blighted by Mother suffering a stroke on Christmas Eve. It was a bad one and left her unable to move or speak. Being in a frail state already, the doctors are giving depressing bulletins and the outlook is bleak. They think another stroke is likely, or her heart will give out. She may only last a few days. Nobody in the family seems greatly affected by this, her two grandsons just furious that their Christmas should have been disrupted!

I received your message about finishing the book and offer congratulations. I don't think you will have a problem over the copyright. Brendan will be far too busy winding up Mother's affairs.

I will let you know any developments. Meanwhile happy 2019, love, Sorcha.

He sent her a return message thanking her for letting him know. It was a sad fact, but Kaye O'Keefe had been a bitter woman all her life. Now it seemed her end would be unhappy too, unloved and un-mourned even by her family. For him, quite callously her imminent death was timely. Sorcha was right. It was unlikely Brendan would have time to raise objections to the use of Mia's photographs. At least it was one loose end tied. Everything else would have to wait until the beginning of January.

Chapter 27

New Year's Eve, 2018

The party upstairs was well underway and the volume of sound increasing by the minute. Reluctantly, Rawlings donned his velvet smoking jacket and made his way up the garden steps letting himself in by the back door. The wall of noise hit him as he walked into the room which was already packed. He glanced at his watch. Two hours to go until midnight, unlikely he would last that long. A waiter came round with a glass of what he presumed was prosecco and a waitress thrust a tray of canapés at him.

'At last a friendly face! Thank God you've arrived! I know absolutely nobody here, although some I do recognise from previous parties.'

He turned round to find Hetty, attired in a garment that looked as if it had come straight out of her great aunt's wardrobe, but she still managed to look endearingly magnificent. Avoiding one of her hugs in order to preserve his rib cage, he kissed her on both cheeks. 'It's very lavish. Max has certainly pushed the boat out.'

She sighed. 'It's been like this every year for as long as I can remember. Even when he was completely broke, his New Year parties went on. Weren't you here last year?'

'No, I was on my boat.' He smiled as he recalled drinking

far too much champagne which was then followed by a night of passion with Marnie.

'It's odd,' Hetty went on, 'but I feel you have been a family friend for ever, yet we've only known you a year.'

'Not odd at all,' he replied. 'I feel exactly the same way.' He looked around. 'Where's Bernard?'

Hetty laughed. 'Not here. He hates large parties, so the naughty man made the excuse he had to stay and look after Bel's boys. Ridiculous really, they've both gone off to see the fireworks and won't be back until well after midnight. Quite honestly, I would happily have stayed with him, but that would have hurt Max's feelings.' She gave a sigh. 'Besides, I do need to keep an eye on Bel…'

Rawlings glanced across the room to where Bel was surrounded by a coterie of male admirers. 'She seems to be managing to enjoy herself.' Then noting Hetty's worried expression he asked, 'How is she?'

'Not great,' Hetty sounded grim. 'I fully expect problems getting her home.'

Before he had a chance to hear more, there was a shriek from behind him, 'If it isn't the ubiquitous Rawlings! Darling we really do have to stop meeting like this.'

The ringing tones of Fanny Markham forced him to turn away from Hetty, who quickly made her escape. He gave Fanny the obligatory kiss on the cheek.

'I suppose Max must be a journalist friend of yours.'

Some instinct told him not to tell her he lived in the flat below. She was the sort of woman who could easily have landed on him uninvited. 'Max is one of my many acquaintances from the Frontline Club,' he answered her quite truthfully. 'How do you know him?'

Fanny gave a tinkling laugh. 'I met Max at a dinner party, given by one of the few theatre critics I actually liked. By that I mean the one who always gave me lovely reviews. That was years ago but since then he has always invited me to his New Year parties. I love them, such fun to meet so many old friends. Do tell me, how is Isobel? Did you have a lovely Christmas? I adored the one I spent with you both...'

Rawlings was saved from answering her by Bel who flung her arms round him, reproaching him for ignoring her. Fanny disliking any sort of competition made a quick departure. With some difficulty he disentangled himself. It was obvious that Bel, looking beautiful but dishevelled, was well on the way to being sozzled. After a rather disjointed conversation, she complained that the waiters were ignoring her, and despatched Rawlings to find her another drink. Obediently he made his way across the room only to hear his name being called. Turning, he saw one of his Frontline cronies among a group of people.

'Rawlings, you're a journalist. Tell us what you make of this argument between Meghan and the Daily Mail over publishing the letter she wrote to her ghastly father?'

Rawlings was already disgruntled with what for him had been a thoroughly irritating evening and this question proved the last straw. With barely disguised anger he said icily, 'Please don't equate the Daily Mail with serious journalism. It is a disgusting rag that prints right-wing propaganda and salacious lies merely to rake in ill gained profits. As far as publishing the letter, it's just a typical move to please their middle-England readership, appealing to the gossip-starved, blue-blooded Brexiteers, who are largely responsible for making this country the insular and mean-spirited place it has become!'

There was a shocked silence, then someone said, 'Why don't you tell us what you really think Rawlings.' This was followed by nervous laughter. He shrugged, gave them all a disarming smile and walked away in search of a waiter for Bel's drink. Having despatched this errand, it seemed to him the moment when he might quietly leave but he was stopped from doing so by Max.

'Oh, there you are Rawlings. Do me a favour. Bolly's been shut in my study all evening poor fellow. He probably needs to go out. Could you take him into the garden for a quick walk?'

It was a simple enough request. How could Rawlings have possibly known it was to precipitate him into another turning point in his life.

Letting himself into the dimly lit study with only a faint light coming from a desk lamp, he didn't see Bolly at first, only hear his wagging tail beating on the floor. Having finally located the mutt he told him firmly it was time for a walk, and for once Bolly offered no resistance. It was just as he was making his way towards the door that he caught sight of someone silhouetted on the window seat. A husky female voice said with quiet amusement, 'Were you escaping from the noise as well?'

He smiled. 'I was actually about to take my leave altogether but then Max asked me to take Bolly out, so I postponed my departure.'

There was a long silence and then, in an almost despairing way she murmured, 'I shouldn't have come. I knew it would be a mistake.'

For a moment he was at a loss. Then for some unknown reason he said, 'Look, I live downstairs. Why don't you get a breath of fresh air while we let Bolly out, then you can either brave the party again, or ring for a taxi from my flat.'

She looked at him with interest. 'You live downstairs? Then you must be Rawlings. Hetty told me about you.' Standing up she nodded, 'Yes to your offer. I'd like a look at the river.'

In the light from the desk he could make out she was painfully thin, but there was something ethereal about her. Her face was framed by fair hair cut like a pageboy. In her fitted, high-buttoned velvet jacket and trousers, she reminded him of a character from one of those paintings of sixteenth-century Venice. Realising he was staring at her, he quickly inquired if she had a coat. She shook her head and they left.

It was a cold, clear night.

'That's a waning crescent moon,' she commented, 'there won't be much light from that.' She gave a shiver, and he removed his jacket and wrapped it round her shoulders.

'The whole sky will be lit up soon with the mammoth firework display' he said, adding crisply, 'I personally won't be watching.'

'You don't like fireworks?'

'I don't like the noise they make.' He didn't want to explain that the explosive sounds were too full of painful reminders, but she seemed to understand because she said, 'Ah, yes. In that case, let's go back in before they start.'

Grateful for her tact, he suggested she let herself into his flat through the French windows while he returned Bolly. She accepted this offer without any argument and moved back across the lawn. Rawlings grabbed Bolly and hauled him up the steps and into the office with all speed. When he returned to the flat, she was sitting on the sofa, having removed his jacket, staring at the non-existent fire. He turned it on, and the flames shot up.

'I always think of the John Betjeman poem,' he said rather apologetically, 'the line, and switch on the logs in the grate. The fire is vulgar I know but the best I can do in London. We're not allowed logs or coal.'

She held out her hands towards it. 'It actually looks very real and not vulgar at all.'

There was a silence until she turned to him and said, 'I like this room, clever of you to have kept it uncluttered and all the muted colours are calming.'

The huskiness in her voice somehow added to her waif-like image. Smiling back at her Rawlings said, 'I never managed to collect possessions, due to my working abroad for so long.'

She nodded. 'Hetty told me you worked as a war correspondent, but I actually already knew that. I'd read many of your reports. You wrote well. Many didn't.' She paused as if considering whether to say something else. 'Hetty also told me you were injured in an explosion and that someone you loved was killed at the same time.'

Rawlings was startled and tried not to sound irritated. 'Hetty talks far too much.'

Instantly she looked worried. 'I'm sorry. Please don't blame Hetty. You must understand, we are almost like sisters. The Winterton family lived near us when we were children. My father was an archaeologist and he and my mother were away a great deal, so we spent much of our childhood with Max, Hetty, Bel and Rupert. They were like our extended family. I was nearer in age to Bel, but Hetty was my greatest friend. She's the one I'm in constant touch with now.'

Rawlings gave an understanding smile. 'From what I can gather, Bel has always been a difficult character...' He stopped. 'Do you know, I don't even know your name...'

'Ophelia. Ophelia Stanhope.'

'You said we. Do you have brothers or sisters, Ophelia Stanhope?'

To his alarm her eyes filled with tears and she answered in a whisper, 'Just a twin brother, Alexander. He died three months ago very suddenly, from leukaemia.'

Alexander Stanhope. The name rang a bell. Why was that? He searched his memory and then it came to him. Her brother had been a fashion designer. He vaguely recalled the obituaries, saying what a tragedy he had died so young when at the height of his powers.

She angrily wiped away a tear. 'I'm sorry. I'm finding it impossible to get over him dying. I really shouldn't have come tonight...'

He had a sudden urge to take her in his arms and let her cry it out. Instead he gave her a moment and then said gently, 'You have absolutely no need to apologise. It's taken me years to recover from Mia's death.' The silence that followed was filled with the noises of revelry from upstairs. He glanced at his watch and came to a decision. 'This may be a tactless suggestion, but there are five minutes to go until midnight. I have a bottle of champagne in the fridge.' He paused then added, 'It might do us both good to have a glass.'

She hesitated and then, with a glimmer of a smile she said, 'Why not.'

Upstairs the partygoers were counting down the chimes. He grabbed two glasses and the bottle. Popping the cork to the cries from above of 'Happy New Year', he could hear in the distance the fireworks starting. Rawlings and Ophelia made no toast but drank in silence, staring at each other.

It was she who finally broke the moment. 'I think Hetty

only told me about you because she said we had a great deal in common. You see, I'm a doctor. I worked in Médecins Sans Frontièeres,' she paused, 'and I also suffer from PTSD.'

He stared into the dark pool of her eyes uncertain what to say, overtaken by the strangest sensation that left him uncharacteristically uncertain, almost shy. Ophelia seemed disinclined to tell him more without prompting, so he finally asked, 'Where were you based?' She shrugged. 'All over. I went from place to place, wherever the need was greatest. I was in Libya for a while, then a long time in Yemen. Recently I worked on the Syrian–Turkish border…' He re-filled her glass. '…Mostly in the refugee camps, trying to stop the spread of cholera and measles.' She was now gulping her champagne. With obvious difficulty she forced herself to continue. 'In 2015 the MSF hospital in Sa'dah, Yemen was bombed by Saudi Arabia. My partner, a surgeon working in the hospital, was killed. I returned to England and for a while I worked in a London hospital. I lived with Alexander and now I wish I'd stayed, but a year later they needed me again in Syria, so out I went. I only returned to nurse my brother through his final months.'

As he listened, he could see that in many ways she was right. Her story greatly paralleled his own.

'So what now?' he finally asked. 'Will you return to MSF?'

She shook her head. 'I think not. Not for the moment anyway. I am taking time out from medicine while I wind up Alexander's affairs. He left me his house in Chelsea, so I'll stay on there for a while.' Regarding him she said gravely, 'I'm trying not to think about the future, just trying somehow to get through the present.'

They were both silent. The sounds of the party were

fading, and some guests were leaving. Ophelia looked at her watch, then gave an apologetic smile. 'It's late, I hadn't meant to stay this long, or talk so much. It must be the champagne. I'm sorry, I'm not used to it…' Her voice trailed away.

Rawlings stood up. 'Why don't I make some coffee. Then while you drink it, I'll call a taxi. How does that sound?'

She looked grateful. 'That sounds good. The champagne has gone straight to my head. I'm actually feeling quite woozy. Black coffee might be the answer. I don't want to fall over getting into the cab.'

As he walked towards the kitchen he said, 'On one condition.'

She raised her eyebrows questioningly. 'Condition?'

'Yes,' he said, 'on condition you don't disappear out of my life and that you promise to meet me again very soon.'

The grey eyes held his, but she was smiling. 'That's actually two conditions. You must know, there was no need for you to make them.'

Rawlings took his time making the coffee, trying to sort out his jumbled thoughts. He really didn't believe in fate, but something had definitely happened tonight. This woman, who for some strange reason had fallen into his life, already seemed part it. Was this another turning point? It had happened so quickly. Even so, she was in a broken, fragile state and instinctively he recognised it would need patience from him, not to rush her into anything before she was ready, however much he might want it.

Pouring the coffee into a cup, he decided to add a glass of water to the tray, then quietly returned to the room. In his short absence she had fallen into a deep sleep. He put down the tray and gave her a gentle shake. She didn't stir. He stood for a moment uncertain what to do. Her face in the glow of the firelight looked beautiful, somehow all the pain and anguish had gone. Why disturb her? It was obvious she was completely exhausted. Fetching a quilt and pillow from his bedroom, he gently lifted her feet onto the sofa. Then placing the pillow under her head, he wrapped the quilt around her. She still didn't stir. He retreated to the seat opposite. Above, he could hear Max saying his farewells to the last stragglers and vaguely wondered how Hetty was managing with Bel. It suddenly occurred to him that this was New Year's Day, the start of a new year. He hadn't even noticed its arrival. Nothing seemed to matter anymore, except this sad little soul lying asleep on the sofa opposite. Overcome with a strange emotion he whispered softly to himself,

Soft you now, the fair Ophelia. Nymph, in thy orisons be all my sins remembered.

So, Rawlings sat on watching over her, until the dawn came up on the first day of 2019.

About Jane McCulloch

Since leaving drama school Jane has pursued two careers, one as a director of theatre and opera, the other as a writer.

For her own company, the English Chamber Theatre (President, Dame Judi Dench) she wrote and directed over 30 productions which took her all over the world. Her career involved her meeting and working with some fascinating people including Margot Fonteyn, Robert Helpmann, Jackie Kennedy Onassis, Anthony Quinn, Derek Jacobi, Jessye Norman, and many others.

For 10 years she was the Artistic Director of Opera UK and apart from directing operas and concerts she wrote three English translations of librettos and an original oratorio, The People's Passion. This work was filmed for BBC 1 and is available on DVD. Jane also wrote an original children's opera, Hello Mr Darwin, a work for young children and professional singers. Jane produced two recordings which were adaptations of Peter Pan and Lamb's Tales of Shakespeare, both starring Derek Jacobi. Her carol, This Christmastide, was first performed by Jessye Norman for a TV Special, filmed in Ely Cathedral and has now become a standard Christmas favourite, especially in the USA.

Since 2013 Jane has concentrated on fiction. She is now in the process of writing The Rawlings Trilogy. The first book in the trilogy, The Strange Year of E G Rawlings, was published in 2019 and received excellent 5* reviews. The third is due to be released in 2022.

Jane has four children, ten grandchildren and is now based in Putney, London.